DEATH ON ICE

CW00551952

A BLANCHARD TWINS MYSTERY

DEATH ON ICE

R. O. THORP

faber

First published in 2025
by Faber & Faber Ltd
The Bindery
51 Hatton Garden
London EC1N 8HN

Typeset by Faber & Faber Ltd
Printed and bound in the UK by CPI Group (UK) Ltd, Croydon CR0 4YY

*This book is a work of fiction. Any references to historical events, real people,
or real places are used fictitiously. Other names, characters, places, and events
are products of the author's imagination, and any resemblance to actual events
or places or persons, living or dead, is entirely coincidental.*

A CIP record for this book
is available from the British Library

ISBN 978-0-571-38658-1

MIX
Paper | Supporting
responsible forestry
FSC® C171272

Printed and bound in the UK on FSC® certified paper in line with our continuing
commitment to ethical business practices, sustainability and the environment.
For further information see faber.co.uk/environmental-policy

2 4 6 8 10 9 7 5 3 1

For Bex, whose fault this is.
For Jane (1957–2023), whose love guides all my journeys.

DRAMATIS PERSONAE

Dr Rose Blanchard PhD, marine biologist (tropical ray behaviour), sleuth

Dr Finn Blanchard PhD, marine biologist (Arctic sea life), sleuth

Captain Anders 'Stingray' Johannsson

Alexander 'Boo' Moreland, man about town

Patrick & Gladys Moreland, barristers

Detective Inspector Thomas Heissen, harried

Detective Sergeant Titus Williams, academic and competent

Sandy & Bloom Highcastle, crystal hippie snobs

Alicia Grey & Sunila Singh, quiet luxury snobs

Aabria Scott, elderly writer

Kate Berg, private nurse

Chef Elisabeth Lindgren

Dr Ben Sixgill PhD, marine biologist (leporine adaptations)

Dr Sally Palgrave PhD, biologist (colouration changes in nature)

Dr Klaus Eder MD, marine biologist (algae)

1

The *Dauphin* slid gracefully out of the freezing Northern English port without drawing undue attention, as was its wont. The docks were deserted, but even if Michael, the young and romantically inclined port intern, had been watching, the passing vessel was perhaps not the most interesting. It was not as aggressively expensive as a millionaire's yacht, or intent on breaking records for fuselage or speed or fittings; it was sleek and clean as a seal. Only the most discerning would have noted the luxury of the curtains in the visible windows, the precise lines of the hull, or the array of top-of-the-line radar and sounding equipment on its roof. Just as the wealthiest person at a party slips through unnoticed in their perfectly tailored bespoke suit and the most discreet of jewels, it swept out of the harbour quietly, and was gone.

It was, of its kind, a remarkable vessel. It was constructed rather like an opera cake, as the Danish designer, given free rein and inclined to take as much of said rein as possible, had intended. The top layer was navigation, manned by a series of brutally competent Swedes, Greenlanders and a handful of morbid Norwegians, who were largely morbid because people kept assuming they were also Swedish. The middle was luxurious accommodation, and not the kind where a state room meant a double bed stuck in a kind of

I

plexiglass bubble and not enough room to move without bumping one's head, limb or both, as was the case on many so-called luxury liners. The *Dauphin* had space, and plenty of it; just six suites, all with their own sitting rooms and private bathrooms, and hot water that whispered out of chromium taps, with towels replaced faithfully and soap that smelled of olive oil and citrus. These swept the curves of the ship, holding it in at the waist. Below was the ship's intrigue, its mark of distinction among the pedigreed cruises of its type: two scientific laboratories, divided in half like lungs. The *Dauphin* bore its clientele into Arctic waters, and its publicity materials promised that while they dabbled on ice floes and witnessed the glories of the deep, champagne in hand, the Real Work of science was continuing below. In fact, the publicity aimed to give the guests a sense of sanctimony: that theirs was a vessel with real purpose, carrying knowledge forward. Unlike those selfish guests on other, more craven cruises, they were witnessing a journey with a greater goal. As wealthy people like nothing better than being told how humble they are, the *Dauphin* was a great success, booked out many months in advance for its winter journeys.

'I expect they'll want us to be grateful, too,' said Rose Blanchard, resentfully. 'They've paid all this packet to come along and eat *foie gras*, and they'll say they're funding us.' Rose was technically Dr Blanchard, after she'd terrified her examiners into giving her a doctorate after barely ten minutes of examination, and looked nothing whatever like a rose at all, a remark people had been making since she was very small and which had made her develop an expression that resembled a feral wolverine. She was tall and fair-eyebrowed and had an intelligent, shifting face, one that always looked on the brink of moving into something else, something new.

'They *are* funding us,' Finn said mildly. Finn was also Dr Blanchard, having helpfully been given a doctorate the year after Rose, though in his case the examination had been a three-hour-long gentle chat in which Finn gangled and murmured his way through a remarkable innovation in shark biology, looking up occasionally with an expression that unfailingly gave his examiners the urge to give him a tea-cake and a reassuring pat. Instead they gave him his Pass With Minor Corrections and went away feeling, as one generally did with Finn, a kind of ruefulness at the cruelty of the world because it was not filled with Finns.

'Yes. I suppose.' Rose looked over at Finn's unpacking, which was extremely tidy and scrupulously organised. 'What if they're awful? We have to eat with them. Some of the time. On the big special occasions, wasn't it?'

'I don't think they'll be *awful*,' said Finn. Finn never thought anybody was awful; his oversized head covered in loopy curls seemed unable to contain anything mean about another being. He also stooped slightly at the shoulders, drawing himself inward over his chest, as if to hide from bad news.

'You never think *anybody* is awful,' said Rose. Like most marine biologists on field work – she'd spent the past six months throwing harpoons at rays to tag them, and was an

3

excellent shot – she was tanned to the neck and hands and feet, and the rest of her was an odd, swimming white. In the light it created an image that she was barely a person, barely there. She was, however, very much there, and was prone to making sudden and incisive pronouncements at just the moment people had uneasily forgotten her. 'You should. You should have thought *Martin* was awful.'

'Martin wasn't. I mean. He was.' Finn made a quiet face that made him look like a put-upon sheepdog. 'He was just – going through a bad time.'

'He stole the watch I bought you for your graduation and gave it to his husband as an anniversary present,' said Rose, reasonably. 'The husband we weren't told about. He was a rotter.'

They both breathed in the tart disinfectant of the laboratory, which was happily blank and clear, untainted by any trace of Martin, who had doubled as both Finn's last laboratory supervisor and a feckless charmer who had hidden husband, home and several children until the secrecy became inconvenient. Rose, who had immediately and equally secretly made some very hard-to-trace trouble for Martin when this truth was unveiled – not an easy thing from a laptop in the Azores, but achieved nonetheless – regarded her brother gently. His face – unsettled, pale, still a little too thin – bore witness to the damage Martin had left.

'I'm sorry. I shouldn't be so flippant. Come here – you'll be all right.' She wrapped her arms around him from behind. Brother and sister stood pressed neatly to one another like

4

two folded spoons. They were on the same lines, growing muscle in the same places, fat in others; it was comforting, if contorting. The lines of twins, swimming up at them from the mirror. When they'd first been told they weren't the same person, as very small children, Rose had cried.

The *Dauphin* slipped serenely onward, through the mizzling curtain of North Sea fog. Michael the port intern should by all rights have been watching it from the dock, getting slowly soaked, wondering dreamily about its insides, its smell, the inner workings of its confoundingly quiet engines. Or perhaps he'd have been worrying, as he often did, about the manifests, and whether he had time to get a new cup of tea before the dock manager, Kevin, came down to bellow about shipping schedules like a furiously territorial goose.

Michael, however, was not on the dock. His body was turned on its side, his hand lying unfolded behind the docking-shed bales, one palm upward. His fingernails were as blue in death as violets.

2

Aboard the *Dauphin*, in quiet ignorance of anything to do with Michael or his solitary death, the Captain looked at himself in the mirror one more time.

Captain Anders Johannsson was not a man given to romanticism. He was a tall and immensely pale Swede born of professional parents in Gothenburg, who had acceded to his wishes to enter the Navy with the same quiet acceptance they applied to everything, including their car once sinking into a lake. Johannsson had flourished, but his talents unsettled his superiors. *Too suave*, they would say among themselves. *Like a concierge in a fancy hotel.* And he was suave; or at the very least he had the talent of soothing irascible and powerful people through his sheer force of personality. One never truly forgot Captain Johannsson's face as it absorbed, with astonished concern, the troubles, violences and inconveniences of your complaint; you left with the surety that it would be dealt with, that his breast was the one to be trusted to hold all these plaints and solve them immediately. A rear admiral once left a meeting in which he'd been intending to tell Johannsson off and immediately reconciled with his wife, who'd been living in another country for four years.

Captain Johannsson was also a linguist, which meant his listening abilities included Dutch, English, Norwegian,

6

Danish, German, French, Spanish, Arabic, and a good smattering of other languages including Mandarin and Pashto. He treated his underlings with unfailing and painstaking concern, which was partly why the Navy was intensely relieved when he was poached by the *Dauphin* to man its journeys. That much care for the lower scrubbers, they thought to themselves, was bound to create unrest.

Now, however, he was discomfited. He was prepared for all manner of disturbance to routine, and was perfectly capable of piloting his ship through it with minimal fuss; his crew were paid well and adored him, and were all at ease with explaining to angry persons with antique Cartier binoculars that dolphins could not be summoned on command.

There was, however, something out of place – something amiss. And it eluded his vision. He had checked everything, inspected everything, and still there was that floating feeling of out-of-kilter strangeness. A captain of his calibre sensed the running of his ship and passengers as a person works a loom or a harp; fingers on many strings, feeling their hums and vibrations in air. The port had receded into the *Dauphin*'s wake, the open sea beckoned, and yet one note, somewhere, was sour.

As befitting a man of naval background, Captain Johannsson had a rigorous organisational system for everything, including amorphous feelings of vague unease. He placed this sensation carefully in a mental envelope and filed it among his brain's notes for this voyage, hesitating between *Events* and *Miscellany* before plumping for

7

the latter. Then he adjusted the mirror to perfectly reflect the light of his cabin, and began unnecessarily adjusting his immaculately pressed uniform, straightening the epaulettes, for dinner.

3

The next morning, at the same moment when Finn Blanchard rolled over on his bunk on the *Dauphin* and exclaimed at the flinty morning light through the porthole, several degrees of latitude north, Detective Inspector Thomas Heissen put down his pen, made a face that evoked nothing so much as a screwed-up ball of paper thrown at a dustbin with great force, and said, 'Well, that's another dead end.'

'Just so,' said Detective Sergeant Titus Williams, colourlessly.

Detective Inspector Heissen leaned back in his chair and put his sizeable arms behind his head. He was the sort of man an enterprising artist of propaganda for the early-colonial Americas would have found irresistible: broad of shoulder, vast and blond-red of beard, possessed of the wide stomach and arms of a working person who hauled things for a living (logs, perhaps, or large bovines) and drank deep at night. The fact that he resembled nothing so much as a large, stocky Paul Bunyan – with, it had to be said, clear and intelligent eyes – was emphasised by the fact that he was at present wearing an extremely well-knitted Aran-patterned jumper. Titus was wearing a matching one. They had been gifted by Titus's aunt, on hearing they'd be venturing up to an Arctic port, and were absurdly and irresponsibly

9

comfortable. Heissen's cat, Biscuit, had attempted very enthusiastically to convince Heissen not to pack it, so she could spend his absence kneading it and purring with her many chins.

'Well, let's look at what we've got so far,' he said, looking around the disappointingly Biscuit-less cabin. The town, on Svalbard – the northernmost archipelago of Norwegian territory, far up in the Arctic Circle – was one of the most populous in the area, but it still only ran to about 2,500 people, several of whom had taken time out of their busy days of Being Very Cheerful About The Cold to grant the visiting officers a spare room, a tea kettle and a whiteboard. 'We can trace the smuggling ring from Dover northwards. Definite English origins, but they've been brutally careful. Sweden, or Denmark. And then – no trace. And the goods, give or take a few months, then appear out of apparent nowhere, anywhere in the world. They don't go via the conventional ports, they aren't on planes, they don't show up in customs checks or in false-bottomed bags or any of the usual or unusual stuff. Human mules don't seem to be indicated. The normal operators don't know the faintest thing about it, and are a bit indignant that they don't, because somebody has hit on an extraordinary system.' He and Titus had been working this case all over England for many painfully slow months and knew the details backwards, forwards and likely in Morse code, but he felt the pressure to get everything Absolutely Correct. The Norwegian authorities had given them gracious permission to poke around in their jurisdiction, though Tom felt caustically that they probably didn't want to expend any of *their* resources chasing English smugglers across ice floes.

'It's profitable,' said Titus briefly, 'but must take a great deal of capital to run.' Titus was one of four brothers, the others named Cato, Lysander and Aethelred. His parents, William and Myrtle, were of farming stock and clearly had Ideas about what their progeny would achieve. Lysander and Aethelred, Tom understood, had bucked all name-related aspirations entirely and started a small chutney business together. Cato, perhaps catching at the *concept* of glory more thoroughly, had a rap sheet of several ambitious yet bone-headed scams, and was currently languishing at His Majesty's Pleasure yet again. Tom had spent a secret afternoon reading Cato's case file and boggling at it; his favourite scheme on the list involved painting jerky to look like prime bacon.

The streak of nominal whimsy was an astonishing one that had not left Titus, who'd got an excellent 2:1 in foreign relations and economics and then joined the force for reasons that remained unexplained, any the worse. Persons who met Titus tended to think he was charmless and inscrutable ('a dried-up brittle stick', another detective inspector had said dismissively to Tom at a police dinner), but Tom recognised a well-organised academic mind when he saw one. He hadn't one himself; his was more like an extremely elaborate writing desk with about fourteen secret drawers and a thriving household of mice in one leg.

'And now there's murder.' Heissen looked again at the report in front of him. It had been forwarded to Svalbard by an officious somebody at the National Crime Agency who'd given his request for 'anything new and suspicious about port stuff' more grace than it probably deserved. A port intern, at a small and busy northern English port given over to the departures of small cargo vessels, large yachts and the occasional pleasure cruise, had been found under a pile of sacking a day ago. Name: Michael Keren. He'd died of blunt force trauma to the ribs, the clear mark of a well-aimed punch. His horrified co-workers had told the police on the scene that he'd come into some recent money which they couldn't explain, and about which he'd been vague, but excited. Perhaps on the verge of telling somebody. Perhaps he had.

'It may not be connected,' said Titus. 'But you think it is.'

'I don't like it. They took his phone and passport, you know, but the wallet was untouched.' The email accounts and messages on said phone had been wiped forensically clean by the time the police could get remote access to anything, and the company who had employed him was, Heissen had the distinct sense from the report's subtler edges, uneasy. The intern was clearly being paid incredibly well in cash to do something off-book, and it had come back to bite him. What had his involvement been – and why, in a very contained and elegant operation, this sudden, messy murder?

'And the lead in Svalbard turns out to be a vague hint at nothing. We know it's happening around here – somewhere – but where is it and what?'

Heissen felt dissatisfied. He wished he could have brought

along Biscuit. Biscuit had adopted him by climbing in the window of his flat one day, knocking the lid off the biscuit tin and sitting in it while purring beatifically, crushing an entire packet of digestives beneath her weight. She was Very Helpful when it came to investigations, mostly by sitting on his lap kneading him with her oversize white paws, and responding to being talked at (like most good investigators, Heissen talked to himself rampantly) with small chuckling noises. Biscuit was instead being cat-sat, and probably fed far too much, and he was here in the northern tip of the devil's frozen undergarments chasing – something.

Their chief in London had appeared enthusiastic. After months of nothing and Interpol making sniffy remarks about 'mirages' and 'so-called smuggling rings' in Zoom calls, a member of a well-known Southampton-based gang had talked – or rather, had intimated that he knew all about this mysterious new operation, and when Heissen told him flatly that he believed that as much as he believed the moon was made of a particularly fragrant piece of Époisses, sulkily said that at least he knew *something*. The something he knew was that the hand-offs occurred up in this region of the Arctic Circle, which was more than they'd known before and yet still a point of knowledge in a large sea of upsetting nothing, like a lone, sad crouton in a gigantic soup tureen.

The chief had encouraged crouton-fishing. 'It's better than nothing,' he'd said. The chief was not uniformly enthu-siastic about anything, with the possible exception of golf, a game that seemed to Heissen an extremely poor excuse to bulldoze owl habitat. Owls were incredibly talented at chasing things like field voles into holes, in Heissen's opinion, without any assistance from argyle-dressed men bearing unwieldy clubs.

So when the chief decided this was Worth It, most likely because he wanted Interpol to stop being smug and disbelieving at joint task-force brunches, Titus and Tom and their jumpers and their lack of Biscuit had fetched up here, to be frozen and learn that Norwegians apparently get more cheery the further north they go (and that they insist on boiling their coffee, which was the local standard for intense flavour, and by Titus's expression in the local police cafeteria was also a scientific nine days' wonder). And everything they touched seemed to come up resoundingly empty.

'I worry,' said Heissen, looking out the window at the blue and white and grey, and stroking his jumper contemplatively, 'that we're running after an undomesticated and vicious waterfowl.'

'A wild goose chase, sir? Millions in diamonds don't go into holes in the earth and vanish,' said Titus, matter-of-factly.

'They might,' said Heissen, grimly.

4

The first full day of the trip dawned bright and gritty in the tooth-parts if you left your mouth open enough to the wind; icy spicules were coming off the tops of waves. They were powering north on the *Dauphin*'s elegant, emissions-friendly, morbidly quiet engines.

The ship had departed in the late evening, and this was the first time Rose had had the opportunity to examine what she'd actually be working with. After breakfast in the mess below deck with the crew – mercifully, they were to be separated from the paying guests most of the time – she and Finn investigated their workstation in the laboratory, which was clearly designed by a person who had met and conversed with at least one scientist. It was clean, surrounded by accessible power sockets, and made of materials that could be easily wiped if covered in fish guts. Rose, who was used to doing her work on half a counter or the ship floor, was deeply pleased.

It was a happy morning. She and Finn spent a good amount of time doing what you *always* did on the beginning of a research boat trip, which was figure out all the ways in which your precious equipment could be damaged, bludgeoned or nicked, and plot to thwart them. (Other people had different procedures, she understood, but this was overall a superior one.) She wedged their four horribly expensive underwater cameras into a nest of foam, bubble wrap and packing tape inside a lockable drawer, while Finn hovered, thinking up new and extravagant possibilities for damage. The boxes were, they eventually decided between them, secured against giant waves, thievery, somebody falling with their full weight from most angles, floods and rats. (If there *were* rats on this sort of ship, Rose thought, they'd probably ignore standard fare in favour of obscure and costly electrical cable, so it was a perfectly fair risk assessment.)

'Shall we check on the submersible?' said Finn at last, vibrating gently with excitement. Rose could barely contain herself either.

The dives in the *Dauphin*'s little submersible vessel were what Finn, and by extension she, was there for: to lay four camera-traps to peer in on the habitats of the Greenland shark, one of the longest-lived animals in the natural kingdom. Some specimens happily floated in sub-zero waters for hundreds of years. It was an extraordinary opportunity, and the potential rewards were mighty. Good, clear results would be satisfying for Rose, but they'd launch Finn's research career with the force of a moon rocket. Cosmetic companies were devoutly following Finn's research, as were some tech billionaires in San Francisco and Hong Kong who were giving an unseemly amount of attention to the potential for immortality. If you were willing to bob in polar-grey nothingness in a deep freeze and expend perhaps one neural connection's worth of thought a week, Rose felt like telling them, living forever would be easy. The Greenland shark was notoriously elusive; any footage they managed to capture of its gentle, gigantic weight in the frozen dark, particularly how it mated or ate, would send scientists into a minor frenzy.

She would be diving with him. This was a new model of submersible with internal heating for the frigid temperatures, and one did not, in any circumstance, dive alone. Which was why one only dived with people one liked and trusted; she had once broken up a fist-fight inside a submersible, thanks to an accusation of theft about some eel data, and was intent on not doing that again.

Rose's own research was largely tropical and based on stingrays, but she knew what she was doing; of the two of them she had the far more practical resumé, and could anchor Finn's beautiful models and theorems in reality. Together they'd submitted this combined application in a horrible rush. Finn had originally proposed it to the *Dauphin* with Martin, but with Martin now dealing (Rose highly suspected) with a flood of spam calls and compromised identity claims after his various ID numbers and security details were carefully disseminated on the Dark Web, she was more than capable of filling in.

They talked over one another as they mounted the stairs. Their voices were different in timbre, but carried the same patterns, the same tricks of emphasis; a person trying to deal with the Blanchards speaking excitedly at the same time often had the sensation of getting an entire performance in stereo.

'I hope it will be what we wanted. I know they sent us the schematics, but—'

'It'll be fine, Finn; we'll do all the standard checks for camera placement, and I'm sure—'

The open decks of the *Dauphin* were, of course, wide and gorgeously polished. She and Finn passed the remains of the elaborate passenger breakfast buffet – açai bowls, burritos, sanctimonious granola, a pineapple carved somewhat confusingly into the shape of a dolphin. Everything was crowded; passengers and scientists, grouped together in the wind. There were so many new sheens and textures that Rose momentarily couldn't focus. It was like being plunged into a reef for the first time; your senses required recalibration, a new adaptation to the flickering layers of light and the roaring in your ears. She had ascended into a new world, and all she could do was gaze a little helplessly, half-expecting a seahorse to drift out from behind somebody's head.

'Snacks!' said Finn delightedly, and wandered over to the buffet. A crew member with the name tag OTSO – there were many of them present, she now realised, all starched to the point of acute angles, and with uniformly hard-parted hair – made a movement as if to dissuade him, but then, perhaps feeling Finn's palpable aura of geniality and innocence, let his hands fall back to his sides. (This was a common occurrence with Finn, who had once been allowed to look at a rare specimen of baleen jewellery in Christie's by a normally immovable Head of Sales who couldn't quite explain herself afterwards.)

Without Finn to occupy her, Rose took a second to steady herself. If she was going to survive on this reef, or at least not make horrible *faux pas*, she thought, she wanted data. Data was stable. It allowed for courses of action.

So. The person with the most bars on his jacket was, she supposed, the Captain, a bewilderingly pale man whose long face, watching the proceedings on deck under an extended forehead, looked almost blank. No: his face turned to listen to somebody talking to him, and it transformed; his attention was wholly focussed, like a series of beams had suddenly formed out of a prism onto this one point.

The person who was talking to the Captain moved slightly more into the light. Rose, observing, thought at first that this was a person with the flattest face she'd ever seen, an oval almost featureless – but then the figure angled their head slightly and the shadow of a reflected light caught it, and Rose saw with a kind of astonishment that she was wrong. The face only appeared to be flat; in fact it had deeply carved cheekbones starting very high, eyes set right back into the skull, and a line of delicate bone above the brow. The shape of the mouth was intense and precise, thin lines worked down around the nose. *What a thing to have a skull like that*, Rose thought. It was beautiful, certainly, but in the sort of way that a Madonna is beautiful: you'd want to sit and revere it and anything it said might terrify you.

Her first instinct, as with all extraordinary things, was to want to study it – but there was something in the face that made the idea of measuring its aspects, of laying hands on it and extracting data, an unreal prospect, almost uncomfortable. Rose realised she was shivering slightly. It was a cold day, and they were heading north rapidly.

The person attached to the face was wearing chef's whites, she saw. Whatever they were saying to the Captain was being said very fast. His face bore no reaction aside from rapt attention, but then, Rose thought, it likely rarely did.

The Captain made a kind of final gesture to this person, and then turned to the remainder of the deck's occupants and spoke. He had, Rose noted, a well-modulated voice, not loud but with the clarity of somebody used to holding complete attention without effort, and the collection of people quieted.

'Welcome to the *Dauphin*. We are honoured to welcome you on board one of the only vessels of its kind, one that will, as we traverse the Arctic Circle, be performing groundbreaking scientific research in various areas of marine biology.' He paused for what was, perhaps, a less than inspired amount of appreciative noises.

He mentioned with grace the scientific efforts they would be undertaking on the voyage, pointed out several stops for sightseeing and the expected journey times between them, and added that the scientists would be given the opportunity to lecture on their particular area of interest. 'We are also, on this journey, gifted with the presence of Elisabeth Lindgren, who will be in charge of the menu and whose reputation has doubtless preceded her.' This, then, was the chef with the extraordinary face. Rose hadn't heard of her, but clearly other people had; the appreciative noises this time were far more marked. The woman bowed with no sign of embarrassment, or, in fact, any emotion at all.

The Captain then talked of the adventures, the deep cold, and the unexpected nature of the holiday, emphasising that nobody could predict quite what would happen, and that it was important to obey the orders of crew members at all times. Rose detected a polite but firm emphasis on this last point. She wondered how many entitled guests had disregarded *Dauphin* staff in the past because they didn't like being told what to do. The position of Captain, she thought, was not an enviable one.

'You were given a brief safety demonstration on embarkation, but there will be a full briefing shortly, so please remain on deck. Thank you.' Then the speech ended, and the burble of conversation lifted again. Elisabeth Lindgren, she noticed, immediately turned and went indoors.

There were clumps of people between Rose and the object of her attentions, the submersible, which was nestling at the rear of the ship. Most of them, she thought, were probably passengers. And they would want to talk to her, and ask about her work, and Be Polite, and ask for her to Explain In Layman's Terms—

She had the sudden urge to put on her dry suit and throw herself over the side to bob up and down in the Arctic currents until something more sensible picked her up – a cargo vessel full of dried herring and IKEA furniture parts, for instance, or a particularly well-armed submarine. She could cope with a submarine.

Deep breath.

The primary obstacle between Rose and the submersible was a group of five. (Five – yes, she could handle five people.) Everybody was in the *Dauphin*'s bright orange all-weather jackets, made of state-of-the-art waterproofing and fleeces, and lined with a kind of silken netting Rose kept thinking was a pocket and absently poking pencils into. Finn, she'd noticed, had been doing this as well; between the two of them they'd hooked at least four writing implements and a calculator to the interiors of what must have been six-hundred-pound outerwear. The seething orange was nominally the *Dauphin*'s brand colour, but the Blanchards knew, with the certainty of people used to oceanic work, that it was brightly coloured in case somebody wandered off a dinghy or was dragged away on the ice. Orange for flares, for visibility over miles.

As Rose approached, considering her move – ask briskly for people to move aside, with an air of *important science that needs doing?* – she was, alas, observed. One of them turned and said, 'Ah! A *scientist*!' with a little cry, as if she'd uncovered a treat at a treasure hunt. No escape.

The woman drew her into the group with happy gestures. She was short, and she and her husband – they introduced themselves as Bloom and Sandy Highcastle – had the tans of St Moritz skiers and yacht-goers. Sandy, a man of slightly overdone blowsiness, was struggling with a cashmere scarf-cravat in the wind. Bloom had a high, performatively light voice that swelled and squeaked when she was over-excited. She must, Rose judged, be at least fifty, hardened into her carapace and soft balayage over decades.

Years of scientific research while cramped on tiny boats meant Rose had developed a particularly good set of antennae for personality on first grasp. Like, she thought, a lobster, or a shrimp with long whiskers, sent out across the sand to detect friend or foe or passing bit of tasty gristle. You had to be pretty clear on the strengths and shapes of others when you had to rely on them to lever you out of the water if an orca decided to nudge at your fins in a brunch-wise sort of manner.

So she looked at the Highcastles and thought, dispas-sionately, Bogus. Was Bloom the woman's original name? Possibly it was once something like Barbara. Well, let her be Bloom if she liked.

The rest of the circle was made up by a trio, two men and a woman, who looked initially like a family. She revised that initial idea immediately, though: the older man and the woman merely had that alignment of faintly similar people who've been together for a very long time. Their bones seemed to grow into the same shapes. The younger man was definitely a relation, probably of the older man, and had a way of flourishing happily without care of his coffee cup. He grinned at Rose as if they were co-conspirators. 'We're the Morelands,' he said.

'And what do *you* study? Or do science on. Or – I don't know the right words – you know.' Bloom fluttered overtly.

'I specialise in tropical rays, but I'm largely here to help my brother in his work,' said Rose, and prepared to explain what Finn did – but Bloom gave a little scream.

'Aren't they very dangerous? Rays?' she asked.

'Not hugely,' said Rose, feeling the weariness she always experienced when people asked this. 'I study manta rays, which are pretty docile. So are Greenland sharks, which are what we're in the Arctic to observe—'

'It's funny.' Bloom gave no indication that she'd absorbed this. 'We have a candle called Rays of the Sun God. I do hope people don't think it means the other kind.'

'Interestingly,' said Rose politely, 'that's where the name stingray came from – like the rays of a fan or a sunbeam, because they're so flat. So you have nothing to fear.'

'Oh, good! Darling, tell them about the candle range.' Bloom beamed at Sandy, who embarked on what could be best called a well-greased sales pitch, oriented far more towards the Morelands (who seemed, in a subtle manner, extremely expensive) than her. The Highcastles, it appeared, ran a sort of wellness empire, and in fact specialised in devastatingly expensive candles with crystals embedded in them. 'They change the energy of the room,' said Sandy, very seriously. Rose felt a mild rekindling of the urge to dive overboard.

'How fascinating,' said the female Moreland. She was tall, thin, and had a slicingly polite and impeccably British voice. 'My husband Patrick and I are barristers.' Her exceptionally clear grey eyes blinked. 'I didn't know candles could affect energy flow. *Do* explain how it might work.'

This revelation produced markedly different levels of delight in the party. The Highcastles appeared to bleach slightly, like coral in overheated water, and Rose felt a sudden buoyant delight that compelled her to stick around and watch. The subsequent discussion – the Morelands asking incisive and serious questions, the Highcastles alternating between mystic vagueness and bloody-minded repetition of half-chewed talking points – was all she might have hoped for.

'But you know water has memory,' Bloom said at last, and Sandy boomed, 'Yes, there was that Japanese study, you know—'

'Really? Where does it keep it?' asked the grinning young man, who addressed his family members as Pat and Gladdy, and whom they called, very confusingly, Boo. Boo had, Rose noticed now, very defined, darkened features, the sort that looked straight out of a 1930s film (she'd watched a tranche of them from the collection of an eccentric movie-buff professor in the Canaries one year, when internet was only available for an hour a day). He wouldn't have made much of a movie star, though; he was much more inclined to make remarkably expressive faces than smoulder at anything. He was making one at Bloom, of intently polite interest, which somehow contrived both to look innocent and make Rose want to cough-laugh into her hand.

Bloom said, 'I don't know, you know—'

Sandy laughed. 'I'll look it up for you, Boo. What kind of a name is Boo, by the way?' he said, in the kind of loud off-hand way that was clearly meant to be insulting. His skin in the scouring light of the fresh sun looked coarse and highly porous.

'When he was younger he would perpetually try to

scare people with practical jokes,' said the man named Patrick, placidly. 'He was very bad at them because he'd get over-excited and say *Boo* before he jumped out.'

Boo grinned. His eyes crinkled up at the corners. 'Never very good at keeping secrets.' He nodded at his family. 'These two were going to bring along their daughter, my niece – lovely girl, you'd like her, Bloom; she reads me my horoscope regularly – but she nabbed a good summer job at PricewaterhouseCoopers, and so they gave the berth to me last minute. So I get the seals with my older brother and Gladdy, and she gets the spreadsheets.'

'You must see a great deal of *complicated* things, as a barrister,' Bloom said to Patrick. 'So intelligent!' Rose felt vaguely revolted.

'Patrick spends most of his time telling impressionable young students about the finer points of jurisprudence, and utterly ruining their passion,' said his wife drily.

'Gladys actually dons the wig,' said Patrick. 'Terrifies the life out of judges. We've just come from London a few days ago. Time off court, thank the lord.' Which did, Rose thought, fit the choice of the *Dauphin*; the Morelands would not condescend to a cruise without some worth to it, some kind of moral heft, like watching scientists poke haplessly at seal poop. Otherwise they'd chafe. Boo, funnily enough, seemed to have no such stipulations.

'And what do you do?' said Sandy to Boo, still with a faintly offensive air.

'I'm a scientific journalist,' said Boo. 'Good at it, too. Tell me more about water with memories, please.'

Rose bit her lips.

'I have a headache,' said Bloom in a high voice. 'I think – I'm so sorry – but we'll have to postpone this delightful discussion until a little later?'

Rose took the opportunity to slip away. The younger Moreland turned his face over his shoulder at her and – ludicrously – wiggled his eyebrows.

There, at last, was the submersible – and there was *another* group of people, listening to an elderly man declaim in the wind. This, Rose realised with relief, was a different kind of crowd: it was clearly the scientific collective on board, with whom she and Finn would be subdividing the laboratories and the ship's various resources. Scientists did tend to gravitate together, finding there might be others who bore a sympathy for the rigours and damages of fieldwork, publishing woes, tenure, low salaries, impecunious lifestyles and uncooperative fish. She and Finn had been so busy with their laboratory preparations that they hadn't yet properly introduced themselves to a single one.

The man, she realised with a slight shock, was Dr Klaus Eder himself. A giant in the field of coastal algae! And not a small man personally, with a forthright beard and expensive spectacles and an assertive stomach. This ship, she had been warned, was a sort of settling ground for some near-retirement marine researchers who wished to do a little light work, eat excellent food, and look impressive to tourists.

At this particular moment the famous Dr Eder was

loudly exhibiting the prize of the journey. 'A brilliant machine,' he said happily, patting its sides as if it were a racehorse or a particularly good purebred dog. It was in fact a round submersible, named the *Mouette* of all things, around the height of a well-fed eight-year-old child, inside which two people could sit on comfortable seats in a bubble of reinforced clear plastics and be lowered into the deep. Its ballast and electronics and various clusters of elaborate machinery formed most intensely around its front, where two pincer arms dangled, rather like the front append-ages of a gigantic crab. It had cost, Dr Eder informed the company, an extraordinary sum (Rose privately estimated in the millions), and would allow them to do remote and manned dives – 'Should anybody be devoted enough!' he added, with a bluff sort of laugh to indicate that *his* devotion should remain unquestioned.

Rose, who thought she'd see Dr Eder haul his consider-ably well-padded bulk into the submersible at around the same time pigs soared across the prow, quietly made her way into the melee, introduced herself without fanfare, and began looking at the *Mouette*'s folder of safety protocols. Nobody here, she noted happily, demanded she explain anything.

'Ah, the first explorers!' Dr Eder looked at her with pleasure. She blinked at him, then smiled. Of course, he meant the schedule – she and Finn would be the first to use the *Mouette*, according to the ship's scientific program, then the other scientists could if they so chose, at a maximum of two dives per day when the *Dauphin* was stationary.

Another woman stood beside Eder, looking loosely off into the flinty distance, as if being on a ship beside a horrifically expensive floating bubble was of no interest whatsoever. 'Dr Palgrave,' Dr Eder boomed, presenting her to Rose and the others, and she nodded, absently.

Here Rose felt a sudden and surprising gap, or a void; Dr Palgrave was watching, but not really there. Her orange jacket hung on her impassively. This, Rose recognised, was not snobbery. It was a person who had segmented herself, so that her bodily form could walk and talk and do the minimum of social duties while her mind was elsewhere, working ferociously, often without pause. Rose knew many of these people, and felt for them an odd sadness. People often fell for them, thinking their distance and intensity a kind of romance, but rapidly discovered that their own presence was superfluous, and the savagery of the person's attention was destined forever for something else. Finn, she felt, would have become this person if he weren't so alive to the happiness of the world.

(He was now, she noted with pleasure as she put down the *Mouette* folder, talking to the hapless Otso about the leftover breakfast burritos and encouraging the poor man, who'd clearly been warned against this very act, to take at least one, piling them up in his victim's hapless hands.)

'D'you think they'd let me take a spin in it?' said a voice from somewhere around Rose's upper elbow. A miniature old woman, she discovered, had come to the stern to observe proceedings, swathed in more wool and complex combinations of scarves and headgear and anorak-toggles than would be deemed possible even by non-Euclidean geometry. Definitely not a scientist. The tiny circle of her face was only just visible, beaming like a baby in a snowsuit, and she was regarding the *Mouette* with frank tenderness, as if it were a nice heifer.

She was black and completely white-haired, and wore no spectacles. *She must have been utterly magnificent in her day*, thought Rose, looking at the lines of the full mouth, though now she was desiccated to this pocket form. 'Aabria Scott,' she added, thrusting out a mittened hand. Rose remembered the name: a celebrated author now in her eighties, who'd been writer-in-residence at a prominent Ivy League for decades. (Rose only knew the last bit because Finn had applied to said Ivy League for a postdoctoral appointment, and they'd both boggled at Aabria's younger, grinning face on all the college publicity materials. She appeared to be some kind of beloved campus mascot.)

'Dr Rose Blanchard. It might be a little cool for you, even with the heaters,' she said diplomatically. She was, as a rule, not fazed by the famous, even in her own discipline; one Nobel winner in biology had come away from a meeting with Rose feeling more needled than he had since he'd been an undergrad, and had frankly liked her more as a consequence.

'Nonsense. Catch Kate letting me go anywhere without fifteen layers of cashmere in this weather.' She indicated the woman behind her, who grinned. She was a small, powerful-looking person with a bland, ironic face and a nurse's watch on her lapel.

'Even if you keep pretending to lose the gloves,' the

aforementioned Kate said sardonically, fastening the mittens even more tightly to the sleeves. Rose was slightly startled to hear the affection in her voice. She looked to be without any extraneous lines or emotions whatever, but her devotion was marked on her face. A soldier watching Hannibal, or Caesar.

'Kate Berg, my nurse and my centurion,' Aabria said, with astonishing astuteness. Rose jumped slightly. 'She fights all my battles for me and forces me to enjoy myself.' Kate made a frank, pleased face. Rose doubted, privately, that this elderly specimen required any assistance at all in the enjoyment field. 'And why are you on the *Dauphin*?' she asked, politely. *Please*, she thought to herself, *don't talk to me about water having memory.*

'I encouraged her to do something edifying on a cruise,' said Kate drily, adjusting one of the trailing frills of wool on Aabria's back. 'Rather than sending me onshore to get her souvenirs while she flirted with all the pursers.'

'For some reason,' said Aabria Scott, 'Kate believes that pursers alone are not a sufficient form of intellectual stimulation. This is very rude of her. The one on the cruise to Spain a few years ago, for instance, was *extremely* bright.'

'You gave him five art history texts and quizzed him on them every night,' said Kate with a daughterly asperity. 'You should have tipped him more.' She grinned at Rose. 'I thought watching some actual scientists at work might give her some more educational entertainment.'

'We can only do our best. It may be very boring to observe most of it, but I'll try to say *Eureka* at least once,' said Rose, smiling back.

Aabria said, in the tone of somebody making a scholarly survey of deep importance, 'Now is the handsome curly one your brother?' She gestured to Finn with a hand. Around the wrists, between the mittens and the fourteen layers of material usually used to warm astronauts in space, were vast black pearls on bracelets, which somehow looked no more incongruous than anything else.

'Finn? Oh, yes. We're twins.'

'Isn't that remarkable, now. He looks a little wounded. A dose of icy air will be bracing for him, no doubt.' Rose gaped. To most observers, she knew, Finn was a perfectly standard example of the enthused scientist flapping around in his parka. The fact that this perfect stranger had detected the slight blueness under his eyes, the miniature soft pauses between sentences, seemed akin to witchcraft.

Another person emerged and stalked past them to the *Mouette* – a red-haired man with a pallid face, which against the *Dauphin*-orange parka looked rather sallow. This, she thought, might be another scientist – an assumption she confirmed as fact when he knelt down to inspect the *Mouette*'s fastenings with an expert's movements. Dr Eder looked down at him disapprovingly, and he looked up – the lines of his face, she noted, were sharp – and said something Rose couldn't hear, in a low joking tone.

Everybody seemed to seize up. Kate, who clearly had heard, made a sudden movement, and Dr Eder produced a blustering noise. Even the distant Dr Palgrave blinked and looked around enquiringly, but the red-haired man only laughed. Rose wondered about him. He was younger, and sleek-looking, with what Rose guessed was an expensive wool sweater visible under his parka, and had perhaps a slightly too large mouth, with too many teeth.

In the taut lull this exchange left, the red-haired man looked away from the *Mouette* and his gaze fastened on Finn, who was still encouraging the distribution of breakfast leftovers to anxious crew. Rose felt an intense and slightly confusing sense of revulsion. She had no time to understand or remark upon it, because it passed so quickly, but it was a reaction, she knew, that she would never truly be able to separate from him. It had coloured him for life.

Then the scientist got up and walked off to the other side of the ship to light a cigarette out of the wind. Nothing strange about him, Rose thought; simply a man with red hair smoking and squinting in the sidelong light. Just a young scientist.

'He's one of your lot, isn't he,' Aabria said, following her eyeline. 'Not, perhaps—'

'Oh, quiet,' said Kate, possibly hearing the beginnings of a comment without basis – though would Aabria Scott ever, Rose wondered, say something entirely without basis? She'd been right about Finn – and her novels were said to be incisive and strange.

The remarkable face of the chef Elisabeth Lindgren emerged onto the deck level, and looked up as if to check the weather. The wind ran over her chin and pulled several strands from her bun.

The man made what appeared to be a glancing sort of remark to the chef as she walked past. She turned to look at him full-on – Rose wished haplessly that she was a painter, and could do something with the planes and depths of Elisabeth Lindgren's skull, lit up from above like a saint's – and said nothing, but passed on. If the man was at all disturbed by the full force of that stare, he showed nothing, and went back to smoking and grinning loosely in the sun.

'Poor girl,' said the smothered head of Aabria Scott. Rose and Kate looked at her, Rose in astonishment, Kate in what was a more accustomed kind of curiosity, but nothing further was apparently forthcoming.

'She's a very celebrated chef,' said Rose, a little bewildered.

'Sympathy is not just reserved for the underachieving,' said Aabria Scott, and with that enigmatic remark progressed inside like a tiny royal weighed down by ruffs.

5

Later in the day, the man rejoicing in the name of Boo Moreland slouched up to the *Mouette*, where Rose and Finn were planning the precise route they'd track underwater, and asked a completely extraordinary question.

'Does it fly?'

Rose looked at him. Finn looked at him. Boo looked back with the baldly innocent face of a particularly stupid and charming baby. Rose wasn't fooled.

'Why,' she said with the sort of patience in her voice she usually reserved for colleagues' toddlers, or their less intelligent dogs, 'would it fly?'

'Because it's called *Mouette*. That means seagull.' Boo Moreland said this as if it were a kind of QED, which it was not.

'That *is* odd,' said Finn generously. Finn was generous to everybody; Rose had once caught him getting flummoxed by a small child's argument about why it was perfectly all right for said child to climb out an upper-floor window to launch paper planes. Finn, when removed from the argument, had explained haplessly that the child was very persuasive.

'I suppose it flies underwater,' said Rose, screwing up her face to think about it in an attempt to consider the question fairly. 'What's French for jellyfish? That's more like what it does. It sort of bobs.'

'*Méduse*,' supplied Boo helpfully. 'Do you drive these often?'

'She's very good at them.' Finn was very proud of his sister.

'If you bump them into things do sirens sound? Are there reverse alarms?' Boo was looking the *Mouette* all over, possibly for its non-existent wings.

'There are no reverse alarms,' said Rose. 'They can't really go backwards. Don't touch that, please.'

'Well, that's inconvenient. What if a shark is coming at you full speed and you need to go the other way?'

'It has a top speed of about five miles an hour, Mr Moreland. If a shark decides to come at you full speed, it'll end up with a nasty bruise on the browbone.'

'We don't tend to submerge in places where there will be fast-moving things anyway,' Finn added reassuringly. As if Boo Moreland needed to be comforted about their potentially being bulldozed by undersea traffic. 'Nowhere near orca pods or walrus colonies or anything like that. And mostly big animals stay away; it does make a lot of noise when it moves, this thing.'

'Maybe that's why it's called the *Mouette*,' said Boo cheerfully. 'Because it yells about itself at great length.'

'Who yells about themselves?' A woman in a righteous Barbour and sensible sheepskin-lined boots appeared beside them to look at the *Mouette*, which was clearly an attraction. Another scientist? Scientists did wander into places wearing fieldwork clothes. A friend's supervisor had gone to High Table at a Cambridge college once bearing the dried sludge of a day cataloguing midges in the weeds. But this woman's kit was clean and barely worn; she turned her head and the throat was white, the hair was auburn and perfectly set. She had decided Not To Dress Like A Passenger, Rose saw with amusement, and was making a display of it.

'Have you been afflicted by the Highcastles too?' Her voice was very crisp, and probably carried well in the frigid air. 'Alicia Grey,' she added, thrusting a very forceful hand into Rose's.

'Hush,' said another woman, nudging her at the elbow. Alicia turned and smiled, and touched the woman's wrist. This person was dressed, Rose was interested to note, in distinct contrast to Alicia: her things looked reassuringly and obviously expensive. The purple hat with angora trimming was designer, the gloves were fur-lined leather, the boots from the finest outdoor ice-sporting retailer. She had very long, beautiful dark hair plaited down her back.

'I'm Sunila,' the woman said now. 'I apologise for my wife's usual and astonishing lack of tact.'

'If they ask me once more to buy their candles with rose quartzes enriched with the light of the waxing moon,' said Alicia, at a lower volume, 'I'll show them how well wax floats.' Sunila made a quiet laughing noise. Whatever kind of wealth these two were, Rose noted, they were not the kind that played well with people who sold eucalyptus-scented candles. There were so many divides, she thought somewhat crossly; all these people were apparently here for the same thing, which was to watch her running around like a headless chicken while they sipped hot toddies. Surely they could all get along slightly better.

'We were discussing the little ship that sails under the sea,' said Boo grandly, gesturing at the *Mouette* and putting on a very bad French accent, in the manner of somebody who likely has a very good French accent, Rose noticed. 'The bubble that does not fly.'

'Better you than me,' said Alicia vigorously. 'I've seen some cold places in my time, but the ocean here will beat 'em all. Though this jaunt is certainly giving me a run for my money! Brrr. Give you some whisky when you come back up, tell you what. That'll kick you in the cockles.' She beamed with a big wide mouth, and her auburn hair moved away from her thick neck in the wind. There was, Rose reflected, something out of tempo about Alicia Grey, not quite real. Heartiness in women like this, she thought, so often deflected, or shifted viewers away; you looked too long at the wrong thing, to avoid seeing the right one.

Sunila, on the other hand, was very real, and carried in her expensive cocoon an air of deep, settled competence. She introduced herself as working in technology, and Rose had the distinct sense that she was secretly amused by everything she saw: the *Mouette*, Boo Moreland, the Highcastles, the Captain, Rose herself, even perhaps Aabria Scott. It was something in the brief turn of her eyes. Her quietness was not shyness, Rose thought, but the sort of silence people kept on doctoral panels, watching people sweat and stumble their way through their presentations, and terrify them-selves into knots under her gaze. Rose was totally unaffected by these people, though she secretly resented their internal mirth and often upset it in academic contexts by asking them direct questions in a loud, bland voice.

For example: 'Are you and your wife interested in science?' she said now.

Sunila looked at her in the expected manner, which was faint confusion and affront, but then smiled. It was a very charming smile, a complicit one that said *Ah, you see me, that's very good.* 'We find it difficult to reconcile our requirements for vacations,' she said in a low voice; her wife was now yell-talking at Boo about whisky and advocating for expensive ones from Japan. Boo, Rose felt pleased to note, looked slightly taken aback. 'Alicia requires physical activity, while I prefer to lounge and be pampered. We usually ski, but that's boring every year, and this offers an excellent combination of both.'

'Have you ever tried water skiing?'

'Alicia,' said Sunila, with the faintly wry expression of somebody who has married something they do not understand at all, 'attempted parasailing on our honeymoon in the Maldives. It was our first day. She broke both hands and we had to airlift her home.' She looked at the auburn-haired woman with exasperated adoration, then at Rose. 'Do *not* give her any more ideas.'

'I'll endeavour not to,' said Rose, seriously.

The Captain called them all to the mandatory safety briefing shortly afterwards, in which he explained what must happen if there were emergencies: persons overboard, any kind of shipboard fire or accident, or a person taken ill or injured. They were drilled well. Alicia Grey, Kate the nurse and the

39

Morelands all took the training in hand, paying good attention to the locations of dinghies and life buoys, and commenting to one another as they were walked from spot to spot on the deck. Sunila and the Highcastles, Rose saw, were slower, more inclined to drag their feet; they perhaps didn't like the idea of realities intruding on their shell of magnificence.

Dr Eder and Aabria Scott were too busy arguing to focus. The venerable scientist was holding up his hands and saying things like 'My dear lady' as she fastened him on a particular point – she wanted detail on the inner workings of the *Mouette*, and he was being too vague for her, possibly because (Rose had had many of these discussions with condescending old scientists) he didn't know the answer himself.

Today, the Captain explained, was a travel day, but tonight they could gather for a lecture by the first of the scientists on board, Dr Ben Sixgill, on the Arctic hare and its cultural and ecological significance. This was the repulsive redhead, who was following the safety briefing with an air of insouciance.

Bloom Highcastle raised a trembling hand at the end of the talk. 'Suppose,' she said in a terrified voice, 'something tries to get *near us on the ice*?'

Her husband made soothing sounds; he may have called her 'Pookie'. She was not to be deterred. She had been blonde and fluffy once, and fluffy and blonde she would remain, as long as it inclined people to respond to her in a manner she deemed acceptable, Rose thought. 'What if there's a polar bear – or a *leopard seal*?' She was inclining herself to squeaking hysterics.

'Leopard seals live in the *Antarctic*,' Sixgill sneered. Bloom looked at him with undisguised dislike.

'There is no cause for concern,' said the Captain, with charming seriousness. In all likelihood, Rose reflected, there was somebody on every cruise who worried to death about being devoured in the night with only Tiffany cufflinks left behind. (In fact this was quite true, and the Captain and crew had reassured several travellers that walruses did not eat humans.) 'We operate at the highest standards of safety, and the ship is equipped with several flares and tranquilliser guns, in accordance with international Arctic maritime law. We have never had cause to use them,' he added, smiling genuinely at Bloom Highcastle, who visibly relaxed as if subjected to a stream of calming water.

'Only tranquilliser guns?' asked Sandy. One of those big eco-friendly types who nurtures a deep, shameful fascination with the safari, the game hunt, the blood sport. Rose had met many men like this. The kind who took too readily to the tagging-gun for whale tours.

'Any kind of hunting is illegal here,' said Finn helpfully. 'Even spear fishing!'

'You might not want to eat the fish here, in any case,' said Elisabeth's voice. She had watched the safety briefing in silence.

'Not for all your witchcraft and *cordon bleu* skill could you make them palatable?' asked Sixgill, smiling lazily at her. Nobody, Rose realised, liked that smile, and he knew it, and appeared to be pleased about it.

'Fish in these waters contain anti-freeze proteins that

have evolved to protect them from sub-zero temperatures,' said Elisabeth, not looking at Sixgill, but addressing the company in general. 'They pose no threat to humans, but people make complaints. They do not want antifreeze, they say, in their food. And so it is not worth the trouble.' She was definitely Scandinavian, but her inflections sounded slightly Dutch. Perhaps she'd trained there, Rose thought.

'I must say I don't blame them,' said Alicia Grey, with emphasis.

'So.' Elisabeth shrugged. 'Tonight's menu will be on your pillows at six; please telephone the kitchen or the purser if there are to be changes or requirements. Thank you.' And she left.

'Oh,' said Gladys Moreland, sounding disappointed, 'I wanted to compliment her on last night's food. I've wanted to eat her work for *years*.'

'Gladdy is a gourmand,' Boo said to Rose, happily. 'Pat and I are the cheerful recipients of her enthusiasm.'

'I'll pass it on,' said the Captain, with a clear note of professional pride in his voice. 'Elisabeth is truly the jewel in the crown of the *Dauphin*, you know. She trained with René Redzepi in Denmark and spent five years in the Netherlands earning Michelin stars for restaurants all over the place.' *There's the accent*, thought Rose.

'What's she doing here?' Sixgill, being objectionable again.

'We pay better,' said the Captain, with a small smile.

Tomorrow morning, when they were anchored, the *Mouette* would go down for the first time.

42

6

When Rose looked back on the evening of the talk, she found it contained several vaguely unsettling incidents.

One was the odd atmosphere at dinner. They had eaten in the crew mess, which was to be the standard for the scientists throughout the voyage. This clearly didn't suit Dr Eder at all – he made constant noises of disapproval at being excluded from the main hall and the persons who'd paid £24,000 for the privilege of a berth. For Dr Eder, Rose thought, the privilege of Dr Eder's company at one's dinner table was cheap at the price.

Drs Sixgill and Palgrave – the not-quite-there woman, in her fifties – had eaten without complaint. The crew members, Rose noticed, all seemed to be avoiding Dr Sixgill. 'A little disagreement about paying off a bet,' Sixgill had said easily, when Eder commented on it. He had a slight American drawl. 'They know they have to play fair and they're bridling at it. They'll get over it.' Rose, who had wanted to make alliances with the crew against the rampantly confusing landscape of wealthy backbiting on board, felt faint despair at this. But she also realised that there were gulfs already, deeply entrenched: to the crew, she and the scientists were not so easily distinguished from the paying guests, for all they lived in vastly different environments. They were all just visitors, expecting a background of silent and functional seamlessness while they did what they were there to do. She was reminded strongly of her attempt to strike up a conversation with her cleaner when she was on a prestigious one-term fellowship at a residential college; he had looked at her in faint disgust at what he perceived to be condescension, and she'd wanted one of the college's on-grounds pelicans to fly through the window and swallow her head.

'You have already laid bets? We have only been on the ship two days.' Dr Eder did not seem overly impressed.

'I find my fun,' said Sixgill. Definitely, Rose had thought, not a pleasant person.

'What,' Dr Palgrave had said, in a sudden and rather flat voice to Dr Eder, 'are your thoughts on the re-evaluation of Dr Fothergill's research in the latest *Nature*?' One got the distinct impression that she had seen Dr Eder's head dimly through the many-coloured film of her own internal workings, connected it to a question that interested her, and resurfaced into her own body to ask it. It was, Rose thought, a bit like seeing a beluga whale unexpectedly shove its solid white head up through the anchor-head of a boat. She'd seen this happen, and it had made four crew members fall over backward, while the beluga looked enquiring and slightly put out that its want – fish – wasn't immediately being understood and met.

Dr Eder had met the question without any outward show that Dr Palgrave was being a beluga. Dr Fothergill, she remembered Finn mentioning, with his usual precise memory, had been Eder's mentor, a Cornish professor who'd died many years ago at some unfathomable age; Rose recalled seeing a photograph of him in black and white, unbelievably desiccated, leaning on a stick and grinning. Rose had read the *Nature* article; his seminal early work on the value of shore algae for clean air was being reappraised, because, the editors hinted, it had been far too sensible for the universities in the 1960s and they'd shipped Fothergill off to a remote beach so he'd stop talking about it.

'I knew the establishment would come to understand his value eventually,' said Eder pompously. 'Even when we met – I was twenty-three, you know, and had been paddling about being an amateur biologist in that remote Basque village for eighteen months—' (Rose sensed this was a standard part of the Eder Mythos, and that they would hear of it frequently) '—I knew then that he was a genius. A genius.'

'Why were you in a Basque village?' asked Dr Palgrave. The beluga blinked at him.

'A bad love affair, my dear lady,' said Dr Eder generously. Part of the Mythos again, Rose noted. 'One does get so upset about things in one's twenties. But I met Fothergill, and came under his wing. An extraordinary man. I did think *Nature* might have mentioned more about the contributions of his *assistants*—'

'You'd better get going if you want to get some of the upper-crust food,' said Sixgill calmly.

'Yes.' Dr Eder had returned to his sense of sulk. 'Extraordinary. They should have at least considered that the guests might *appreciate* intelligent repartee. Good day.'

And he put back his chair and left, Rose guessed in search of the Captain, to insinuate himself onto a table in the main hall.

'You should come to the talk this evening,' Sixgill had said to Palgrave then, looking almost charming. 'You're the specialist. It would be good to have your views.' Palgrave was – Rose had read it – also an expert on Arctic fauna, wasn't she? Something about mammalian responses to reducing sea-ice levels.

'I will certainly come and give my perspective,' said Palgrave seriously. *And good luck to you with that*, Rose thought to Sixgill, *and may she beluga you*. Though she caught a thread she wasn't quite sure about – the manner in which Sixgill had extended the invitation. There was a note in it Palgrave hadn't caught, one of – condescension? Threat? Or perhaps Sixgill couldn't help himself and even the most innocent of pleasantries sounded as if he was going to colour it all over with tar. Really, she thought, he seems to be relishing behaving like a bully.

He looked over at her, then. 'Are you coming? Or are you going to be off giving the journalist his first big scoop?'

Rose, having anticipated him being extremely rude, had simply said, 'I'll be there.' And Boo Moreland, she thought to herself, could ask all the very silly questions he liked of Sixgill, and see whether Arctic hares could fly.

And then there had been the talk itself, and the incidents around it. For one thing, Bloom Highcastle came alone, and her husband could be heard most distinctly in the passage beyond the lecture room, saying, 'No, thank you, my heart and soul, I'd rather eat our yak milk soap,' and exiting in what sounded like a very good interpretation of 'storming off'. Bloom had come in uncertainly and sat down, folding her gold-threaded scarf-cape (woven, Rose noticed, with some jumbled iconography from Native American and Hindu art that looked very pretty and would make a cultural expert on either specialty have a conniption) around her neck several times. Sixgill had given her an understanding smile, which did not appear to comfort her at all.

Boo Moreland had indeed come along, and sat beside Rose, and did not ask her any questions about flying lagomorphs. (Finn had stayed below – socialising wasn't his forte, and nor, to be frank, were land mammals of any kind, up to and including humans.) But the real surprise came towards the end of Sixgill's presentation, in which he was explaining his theory that Arctic hares, which famously change to pure white during the winter months, were beginning to adapt to climate change. It was, Rose thought, an interesting hypothesis – that as snow and ice cover were diminishing and the pure white of hares' winter coats were making them vulnerable to predators, they were beginning to show behavioural signs of camouflage, rolling their whiteness in dirt and mud to give them some kind of protection.

Midway through this, Dr Palgrave simply stood up and left.

Finn, when she described this later, said, 'She probably had a good thought and went to go write it down. I do that sometimes.' He did have a tendency to wander out of places – meetings, birthday parties, weddings – to doodle down a particularly good concept.

'No,' said Rose thoughtfully, flattening her pillow. Even in the bunks of the scientific sleeping quarters, things were scrupulously comfortable, and the linens were markedly clean and didn't smell of scales and soggy socks, as those on most other research boats did. 'No, it was something else. She looked as if she'd been smacked awake. Her face was – suddenly very alive, very present.'

'You always see things so clearly,' said Finn wonderingly.

'Yes,' said Rose, 'I do.'

There was a quiet moment of resettling; she could hear Finn stretching out in his bunk, looking at the ceiling.

'We're going down in the *Mouette* tomorrow!' Finn said it as if it were Christmas morning. It was, in fact, better than Christmas morning, an occasion that now carried fraught memories for both of them; years of identical pink dolls and white fluffy dresses and hard little Mary Jane shoes, which they chafed against in different ways; Rose furious at the yearly denial of newt-gathering nets or chemistry sets, and Finn dealing with a different set of evolving realisations that carried him further and further away. Rose remembered clearly the way in which she and Finn had regarded one another over goose-fat potatoes at a horribly quiet table, their last year living at home, and made slow silent winks at each other, a signal from deep childhood that meant *I'm here, we're together, I'm here*.

Finn was still talking. 'I have all the notes. I should go over all the precautions again, just to be sure—'

'Don't stay up reading them too late,' said Rose, sleepily. All these people, their threads and strangeness and fighting and secrets. None of it, she thought, clicking off her light as Finn leafed through pages below her in the bottom bunk, could truly affect them. They, at least, were safe. *I'm here. We're together. I'm here.*

7

The day dawned bright and a little uncertain on the horizon;
Bloom Highcastle swore blind she'd seen narwhals off the
port bow, but there was nothing there when everybody
rushed to look. This, Rose reflected, might be more important to her than the animals themselves: this almighty rush
to follow her lead. Sandy Highcastle, whatever had afflicted
him yesterday, looked as bluff and tan and industriously
devoted to his market expansion as before. He was spending the entirety of the post-breakfast lull attempting to
convince the Captain, who had appeared briefly to explain
the ship's mooring position, to furnish every cabin with
one of their Energy-Enriched Boutique Amethyst Bougie
Candles. The Captain, being charm himself, intimated that
he would discuss it with the ship's design team, though Rose
noted as the conversation ended that no promise of any
explicit kind had been made. Sandy seemed to have realised
this too, and looked around the room with a downcast and
slightly dogged expression. Rose, who had come up on
deck to arrange her notes on Greenland shark migration
and assess weather conditions, noticed with some surprise
that Sunila Singh was watching him too, with what could
only be described as curiosity.

Ben Sixgill was also looking a tad out of sorts. Over
breakfast in the crew mess he'd snapped vigorously at Dr

Eder, who'd made some kind of innocent query about some-body at Sixgill's alma mater, a university in the American South. (The drawl, it seemed, was not performative, but the legacy of degrees in Kansas and Tennessee.) Now he'd come over to pigeonhole Rose. She wished fleetingly that she'd stayed in the laboratories below deck.

The conversation was bizarre. Rose rapidly discov-ered, to her honest shock, that Sixgill wanted to take her place on the *Mouette* beside Finn. It turned out that he'd requested the first dive, but the scientific committee on land that ran the *Dauphin*'s laboratories had overruled him.

'But your research is entirely land-based,' she said, bewildered.

'It's not my *research*.' His redness was even more pro-nounced this morning. His freckles had a faintly bilious look between them. 'I looked at your resumé. You've only done, what, five dives? It's a million-dollar piece of equip-ment. I worked one for eight months; I've logged hundreds of hours. You might crash the thing. And then we'd all be fucked.' This was true, oddly enough; despite his specialisa-tion in land animals, Sixgill had spent a while on a research ship gliding through the upper areas of Greenland, presum-ably hopping off to actively annoy hares on the coastline. Possibly he wasn't allowed to set foot on land anymore for being too aggravating.

'I will not crash the thing, Dr Sixgill,' said Rose, with astonishment.

'Why did they even let you come along? Your stuff's all

to do with the tropics. What are you really *doing* here?' He was looking at her with an odd, furious suspicion. He was, she saw, in a deeply foul mood this morning, and she was increasingly sure it wasn't anything to do with her, or the *Mouette*, or anything else; the bright American smugness of the talk yesterday had disappeared entirely and this spinule-covered poisonous stonefish was in its place. Had he perhaps upset Dr Palgrave in some way? She hadn't appeared for breakfast in the mess after disappearing from his talk.

'She's educating me on underwater seagulls.' Boo Moreland had appeared. He sounded mirthful, but his eye-brows meant danger.

Rose was not in the mood to be rescued from one man's infantile temper by another's infantile cheeriness. 'Dr Sixgill,' she said, with the kind of acidity that had liquefied a condescending questioner at her last conference paper, 'your concerns relating to my presence on board have been noted. I wish you a pleasant rest of the morning; you may spend it on the deck watching my brother and I conduct his research, which, unlike yours, involves things that do in fact *swim*. Good morning.' And she got up and left the breakfast room.

Boo Moreland, infuriatingly, tagged along behind her, but sensibly didn't say anything, at least until she got to the *Mouette*. 'Might I suggest,' he said, with a gentle kind of brightness, 'that you don't take out your frustrations on the sea-pig, because it might crack and we'd all be very annoyed, not least me, because you'd drown.'

'This isn't a sea-pig,' said Rose, checking over the seals with angry attention. 'Sea-pigs are scotoplanes, sea cucumbers. They live in deep oceanic abysses and are highly toxic.'

'I have never heard of a scotoplane,' said Boo, 'but I'd quite like that Sixgill to go live in a deep oceanic abyss and be toxic there instead.' After a pause, he added, 'Have you ever seen one? A scotoplane.'

'No, I work with stingrays in the tropics.'

'Why?'

'What do you mean, why?'

'I want to know why you work with stingrays in the tropics.' He was doing his innocent routine again.

'Because I'm here on an Arctic ship and there are no rays in these waters, is that it?' Rose was beginning to feel mildly volcanic.

'No,' said Boo Moreland, looking vaguely injured. 'As it happens I didn't know that about rays. I don't know much about rays at all. They go flop and flip, and poke people with their tails, yes?'

'They— I have never been poked with a stingray's tail in my life.'

'Well, then, you'd know. What are you doing with them?'

'I'm tagging giant stingrays to see how they migrate,' said Rose, feeling faintly exhausted, but mysteriously no longer inclined to bite the jugular veins out of the world in general. Boo's idiotic questioning had a soothing effect.

'How do they navigate? Pigeons use the stars, don't they? Or little magnets in their nostrils, or something.'

'Pigeons have what? Listen, your brother said you were a science journalist.'

'I write about why things labelled *homo sapiens* are not in fact homosexual,' said the black-haired man nobly. 'I'm in the demystification game for the masses. I swear I once read pigeons have magnetic nostrils.'

'If I ever find a pigeon fancier who'd answer the question without throwing me out on my ear,' said Rose, 'I'll tell you. I can promise you that stingrays do not have magnetic nostrils.'

'Why not? They sound useful. I'd like one.'

'What —'

'It'd mean I didn't need GPS.'

Rose beat him over the head with a nearby diving flipper. He raised his arms over his head in protest and yelled. 'That's what you get,' said Rose furiously, with her hair all disarranged. 'I'm meant to be going into sub-zero temperatures in this oversized bath toy, and all you can talk about is why seagulls don't fly underwater and whether stingrays have piercings that point north.'

'Serves you right,' said Patrick Moreland, who was passing. 'Stop annoying the scientists, Boo. You aren't getting an interview now. Actually, give me one of those.' He picked up another of the flippers and whacked Boo around the ears, bringing out another yelp. 'That was for cheating at poker last night and pretending you didn't have a flush to let Gladdy win. It offended her sense of justice.'

'Everything offends her sense of justice,' said Boo Moreland, looking for all the world like a cartoonist had

54

drawn Man In A Fit Of Sulks. 'She's a prosecuting barrister, that's the *point*.'

'Oh, are we hitting Boo?' Said lofty barrister had now appeared and reached for a flipper.

'I'm off,' said Boo, and ran down the deck with his sister-in-law, famous ornament of the courts of England, sprinting after him.

The *Mouette* proceeded gently into the startlingly clear waters of the Arctic with a small, faintly reptilian hiss. The air began to let out of the ballast tanks, and vast curtains of bubbles slowly marked their descent; Finn, Rose had noticed with great amusement, had tied his hair back in a sort of piratical bandanna to keep it out of his eyes while he looked out of the bubble-front of the apparatus and wrote notes. The reprehensible Sixgill, she'd been thankful to see, had hung around the *Mouette* for some time before they got into it in the possible hope that she'd give in and grant him her seat instead, but had vanished when it came time to actually submerge the thing. *Bon voyage to you too*, she thought.

These were decidedly not tropical waters. Very little moved here; whereas the submersibles she'd used in the Azores and off the coast of Africa were inclined to be surrounded by teeming reef-dwelling fish, this one looked into increasing degrees of blank blue darkness. The cold was penetrating, even with the heating system well-managed and both of them rugged up neatly, like matryoshka dolls covered in five layers of squishy socks. The temperature gradient outside the submersible plummeted as the atmospheric pressure intensified. Both crab-arms held the great prize of this expedition aloft: an underwater camera, baited with squid. This was a known area of Greenland shark activity, Finn had explained to anybody who'd listen, and the video cameras he intended to place all along the *Dauphin*'s route could help gather valuable information about their feeding and movements. Unfortunately he'd said most of this while holding the dead squid, so few people listened for very long. It had come out of Elisabeth Lindgren's kitchens, and she had watched with what appeared to be interest as they hooked its legs in knots around the camera. 'It is a good treat for a shark,' she had said seriously. 'Big size. Lots of meat.'

Finn had decided this was a declaration of friendship, and beamed at her. She gave a very slight upward turn at the corners of her eyes, and returned to the kitchen.

This was also, according to a radio beacon, a place where former scientific occupants of the *Dauphin* had left their own equipment, to be picked up by the next people through. This was standard with ships on regular research routes; cameras, rigs and acoustic soundings would be gathered at decent intervals by ships passing by on their next turn. This time it was a recorder – for something Rose couldn't remember, possibly sea temperatures. It had a small red blinking beacon on it, and they drifted towards it in the dark.

'This is *amazing*,' said Finn. 'Do you know that if the water came in we'd almost immediately die?'

Rose laughed and held his hand. They floated for a second in silence, gazing at the enormity of the sea below them, and above them, and all around.

'I know it's very different from the Azores,' said Finn anxiously, after a beat. 'It's very good of you to come – I mean—'

'I know.' Rose squeezed his hand, and an infinite amount of history and love and unquestioning promises to one another went into it. *I'm here we're together I'm here.* She'd flown back with virtually no notice, half-blind with jetlag, thrown herself into rewording the *Dauphin* application and scratching Martin's name into non-existence on all the forms, gone back to the Azores and stingray monitoring while they waited for confirmation, and was just now, it seemed, breathing again. 'Besides,' she added, 'Grapefruit was being an idiot and scraped her tag off on a rock.'

Grapefruit was a rare albino wild manta ray named by another marine biologist's precocious child; vast, white-pinkish and prone to being sunburned. Rose's phone calls to Finn at ungodly hours (somehow the time zones always meant one of them was blearily woken up mid-sleep) involved many stories about this behemoth, who was simultaneously an astonishing gift to science and an unmitigated nuisance. She proved many of their theories about rays being highly socially intelligent and playful, but she tended to do that by rampant eccentricity. They'd placed a mirror in her habitat for two days, and she'd figured out it was a reflection, performed in front of it, given them enough material for eight papers, then pushed it out of its holder so it shattered, and then swum around looking, in an expressionless manta way, very pleased with herself.

'How many tags is that now?' Finn asked sympathetically. He was now named in several papers about Grapefruit as an expert contributor, because he tended to sleepily suggest helpful things when Rose called him in consternation. He'd once said, in a half-awake voice, 'Sounds like she needs acne medication,' when Grapefruit had shown up with a pattern of odd new dots on her stomach and panicked Rose's entire station. And so it had proved: she'd had a skin infection in her mucus, and was back to circling her territory terrifying fish in days.

'Four,' said Rose, in mock despair.

The radio made a sniffing noise and asked for a check-in: this was Eder, who was doing the communications on board. 'All A-OK, going for deposit and collection now,' said Rose. The flailing arms of the squid looked faintly absurd in the lights of the sub; it was as if they were leaving the sharks a beautifully wrapped birthday present. She imagined them, vast and slow, eyeing it gently, and singing a little happy song.

One crab arm collected the radio beacon, barely the size of a fist. Its red eye blinked, on and off; the scientists, she thought, would be pleased.

'Repositioning to place shark camera,' she said, using her Proper Scientist Voice, and they drifted neatly to the other side of the ship, propelling silently through the water. The camera was positioned nicely with its hat of waving tentacles – 'Like a little cheerful Medusa,' said Finn with delight.

'Second objective achieved. Camera placed. Returning to the surface,' Rose said into the radio, and Finn grinned.

They began to drift slightly – upward – rejecting water, regaining the light vacuum of air—

There was a warning whoop.

Rose jerked her head up. Finn looked wildly around, but wisely didn't touch anything; he knew better than to flail, his standard response to strange alarm noises. The whoop was penetrating: it was one of the seals, they were showing an error in the sensory array of the upper hatch, but that wasn't possible, she had checked everything four times, it must be a microscopic fault—

But there was the equivalent of hundreds of kilos of pressure on every square inch of the glass. There was no room for microscopic faults.

She hauled upward out of her seat and checked the seals with her fingers. Inch by inch. Not a single drop of water; no moisture except her own breath, her own clammy, sweaty hands. The whoop shut off, as abruptly as it had begun.

They drifted upwards. Finn reached over and pressed both of his hands to her face, and said, 'It's all right. It's all right. Breathe.'

'Yes.'

'It was just an error.'

'Yes.'

Still, when she radioed Eder asking permission to surface, she must have sounded as if she was talking from some miles away, since he asked her to repeat, twice.

Sixgill's face loomed at her when she opened the hatch

on board the *Dauphin*, and the freezing air fell all over her. 'Everything go well, then?' And he smiled.

'Here's the whisky for the brave explorers,' roared Alicia Grey, and handed Rose a warm toddy that roasted as it went down her throat. But it left her cold, colder than she'd been, and not even Finn's hands on her face could warm her.

8

Tom Heissen looked at Titus with more than his usual degree of confusion.

'Titus,' he said, 'why do you have a collection of knives.'

Heissen had had a full if fruitless day. He'd been looking at docking registrations in the harbour, asking questions of various harbourmasters of authority, and generally looking for something – anything – that might indicate a ship could slide in unnoticed, or with something slightly amiss, and hook itself to the pylons on the quays without anybody the wiser. Unfortunately, the Scandinavian authorities who manned the ports here were inclined to believe nobody *could* ever be the wiser, and Tom was forced, on the whole, to agree: they kept meticulous records, were unfailingly helpful at producing every ship manifest for the past ten years in electronic and paper form, and all their thick woollen jumpers were perfectly darned at the elbows with nice straight stitches. Their fines for anything Untoward on their ships were hefty and their susceptibility to bribes non-existent. Tom felt a little exhausted. He also felt very full, because they'd kept feeding him cardamom pastries as part of their campaign to be Helpful and so he had consumed the flour weight of a large Newfoundland.

And now Titus, who had been dispatched to make discreet enquiries around the ships themselves – particularly the ones that were in a state of dilapidation or were very large – had reappeared at the office, looking officious and sweaty, and deposited a raft of very sharp knives onto the desk. They weren't uniform; many of them, in fact, appeared to be small bits of sharpened metal attached to handles by means of twine or tape.

'Some of them,' said Titus, with his inexhaustible instinct for correctness, 'would be better described as shivs, sir.'

'Titus,' said Tom. 'Who gave you eighteen knives and ten shivs.'

'The sailors in the sailors' pub, sir.'

'Why.'

'I made enquiries, sir. They discovered I was a policeman and wanted to assist. I gather carrying knives isn't legal here, sir.'

Titus Williams was, Tom reflected, a wonder of a person. His colleagues didn't appreciate the point, because they'd never seen Titus, one hundred and fifty pounds soaking wet without boots on, politely make enquiries. The fact that Titus had entered a pub full of international sailors, all men and women who could hurl a crate easily at somebody's head, and had been given twenty-eight knives by terrified hands eager to Make Him Go Away was par for the course. He was able to produce what could only be described as a *gentle aura of horrifying threat*, though he abhorred violence personally and refused to join any kind of armed unit. Titus had, Tom reflected, been averted from his true calling as an absolute gangster by some accident of moral fate, for which everybody should be deeply grateful.

'They were,' said Titus seriously, 'very nice.'

'I'm sure they were. But they didn't know anything about this, did they.'

'No, I'm afraid not.'

They progressed down to the harbour together, leaving the knives behind on the desk to mystify the local force and likely give them a dim view of the budget for English policing. Gulls floated over the slate-grey water, and rosy-cheeked children in pom-pommed hats cycled past in mittens, laughing. How small people fuelled entirely by pickled herring and incredibly expensive imported fruit could be so cheerful remained a mystery to Tom.

'Perhaps we're looking in the wrong direction.' A sheen of light passed over Tom's face, and he squinted. A million-aire's yacht – mostly dark glass and metal and gold lettering on offensively well-polished dark wood – had just entered the harbour, and the reflection from the sun off its morbidly sleek bridge had been briefly blinding.

'A private person of wealth? More like it, sir, but—'

'They don't keep to regular routes, do they.' The itinerant rich who owned these sorts of pleasure craft, Tom knew, were notoriously flighty; they'd be here for a weekend and then off to Croatia, or Provincetown, or the South of France, or some naked mud music festival on the Cape of Good Hope. Any vast million-dollar pitcher that had come up to this well too often would have shown up in the manifests; but nobody appeared to spend irregular amounts of time getting their nipples blown to freezing beads in these winds, and why should they, if they could be in bikinis in the Aegean instead, Tom reflected.

A horrible honking, and something else came around the headland: one of those cruises that looked like a god's birthday cake, floating ominously, twenty storeys high. It bore down in great stateliness with thousands aboard, looking in curiosity at the tiny town below. The most senior harbourmaster had treated mentions of these vast bleached collections of vacationing humanity with a slight reticence, which Tom knew meant he loathed them and wanted to see them all burned.

Tom and Titus looked up at it, and then at each other.

'I shall,' said Titus, 'go to the tourist office to gather brochures of luxury cruises, sir.'

'Please don't come back with any more knives,' Tom said wearily.

'I cannot make promises,' said Titus's departing back. 'They may simply wish to give me knives.'

Rose's patience, never intensely thick at the best of times, was presently wearing very thin. She and Finn and Dr Eder had been over the *Mouette* for an hour looking for the fault in the seal and had found nothing. Dr Eder, to give him credit, refused to let Rose curse herself. 'There is nothing there,' he said. 'Not a crack, not a chip, nothing. Therefore you could not have detected a fault. Let us be logical about this. Possibly a small piece of detritus lodged in the seal as it was being closed, so small that the *Mouette* itself did not register it until at some depth. You followed the safety directives, you surfaced safely, and you achieved your objectives in retrieving the radio and placing the camera. Thus: a success.'

Finn looked as if he wanted to hug him, but Dr Eder drew himself up so that the barb of his pointed beard looked faintly like a spearhead, and Finn fell away, chastened. He resorted instead to showing Eder the feed from the video camera on the seafloor, which was showing a pleasingly clear picture of nothing in particular except some moving silt. Eder was gratifyingly fascinated; there was some undersea weed off in the distance that would be very interesting to observe long-term. 'Should we go show Palgrave?' asked Finn.

'Ah. No. Dr Palgrave has been in her laboratory all day. She is due to give her talk in some days, so perhaps . . . that is why.' Dr Eder looked a bit discomfited. Rose, remembering Palgrave's sudden exit last night, thought nerves about forthcoming talks weren't the issue.

'She left Sixgill's talk just as he was expounding his big new theory,' she said thoughtfully. 'About Arctic hares beginning to camouflage themselves with mud because of climate change.'

'His – I beg your pardon?' Eder looked at her in some astonishment.

Rose recounted the theory to the best of her memory, wondering increasingly if there was some sort of conspiracy about hares she hadn't been privy to.

This was not helped by the fact that Eder said, 'Excuse me, I must find Sixgill,' and left them. Finn looked at her with raised eyebrows. Rose shrugged.

'Did you find any sea slugs?' This was Boo Moreland again, irrepressible in his orange parka and looking none the worse for having been beaten by flippers. 'You know. Scots on planes. Those ones.'

'Deep-sea cucumbers. Listen,' said Rose, 'I need some hot tea. If you will furnish me with that, I will give you a very basic lecture on sea cucumbers, sea slugs, their meaning and importance. If you ask too many dumb questions I will pour the tea on your hands.'

'This suits me fine,' said Boo, with alacrity. 'Onward to the lounge! Oh, nice undersea view,' he added to Finn's video screen. 'I hope some sharks show up and try to eat it.'

'Thank you,' said Finn, glowing.

The lecture proceeded about as well as Rose had expected; Boo Moreland asked some stupendously silly questions about basic things like whether they would taste like normal cucumbers, but seemed, to her mild surprise, to handle theories on sea cucumbers' asexual reproduction and the evolutionary origin of their defensive capabilities – one, for instance, blows its internal organs out of its anus when threatened – without too much difficulty. Clearly some of his scientific work had seeped into his brain, possibly, she thought, through an unattended orifice while he wasn't looking.

'I am,' said Boo at one point, refilling his own teacup, 'not particularly bright about these things, but you explain them very well.'

'I feel I'm only really giving you material for more terrible puns about Scots on planes.'

'Och,' he said brightly, and drank.

Bloom and Sandy Highcastle entered then; they appeared completely reconciled, though Bloom was, Rose thought, slightly more fluttery than normal, and a little tired around the eyes. Sandy was overly solicitous and kept fetching her blankets, teas, chocolates, a magazine. They had, they said, seen dolphins – skimming off in the distance – and had tried to take pictures, but to no avail. 'I felt their spirits,' said Bloom in her high voice. Sunila Singh and Alicia Grey had actively rolled their eyes at one another, but kept it hidden entirely from the glowing Highcastles.

When Sixgill came in, Sandy Highcastle very distinctly did not look at him, but instead fussed with Bloom, who appeared to love the attention. If she was having an affair with Sixgill, thought Rose wildly, she was certainly hiding it very well – but no, Bloom gave no apparent glances to Sixgill either, under her eyelashes or otherwise. She beamed up at her big husband as he bent over her and fixed things. 'You spoil me,' she gurgled.

'Of course I do,' he said, in an embarrassingly throaty voice.

'May I have a look at the radio transmitter you got off the bottom?' Sixgill asked Rose, remembering, after a beat, to add: 'Please. I know the person who put it there – Spivet, he's at the Sorbonne – he told me all about it.'

'My brother has it,' said Rose, with minimal flourish. She wasn't prepared to spend more time on Sixgill than was strictly necessary, not after the day she'd had.

'Your brother? I wondered about him.' Sixgill's smile widened fractionally. Rose didn't like it. 'I'll go find him.'

And he disappeared off to go down below and presumably bother Finn, who would at least be too nice to notice. How, Rose thought, did one person appear to derive so much pleasure from being unpleasant? It was like he was on the stage.

'That boy,' said Dr Eder from behind her, echoing her thoughts, 'is no good.' He was looking in Sixgill's direction with the sort of disgusted sneer he probably gave substandard butler service. Whatever he'd wanted to see him about, it clearly hadn't gone well.

'Dr Eder,' said Boo Moreland with gravity, 'have you ever eaten sea cucumber?'

'Have I – yes. Yes, I have. It does not,' he said, with a gimlet eye, 'taste at all like cucumber.'

'What sort of a fool would think that.' Boo downed the rest of his tea, and proceeded over the next twenty minutes to ask Dr Eder so many absolutely outrageous questions about shallow water environments that the man looked to Rose as if to query Boo's potential need for a straitjacket. 'But if a hermit crab has a shell house, and it moves to a bigger house any time it needs, why can several hermit crabs not share a shell? Surely they can rotate and take turns eating and sleeping. I lived in a sharehouse all through my twenties. And if starfish can regrow arms when they get pulled off, why don't they just grow hundreds of arms and go around beating up their predators? And why haven't we made a glue out of what sticks limpets to rocks?' Boo had the moon-like face of the fascinated person who was unburdened by either brains or filter.

'The limpet,' said Dr Eder desperately to the last one, 'does not glue itself to anything, but uses its very strong muscular foot to create suction and hold onto rock surfaces. And now, as I am very tired of answering questions my five-year-old niece would be ashamed to ask, I leave you.' He bowed, for some reason, and left.

The Morelands had drifted in; it was coming close to dinner time, when Rose would have to go below decks and eat with the scientists. She wondered if she should reproduce some of Boo's questions for Palgrave, but decided the good doctor had likely gone through enough without worrying that Rose was concussed.

'Your brother,' she said to Patrick happily, 'has been entertaining Dr Eder with his scientific knowledge.'

Patrick took a seat and smiled at her with his long, serious face. He looked like a very good-natured borzoi. 'Well, that's good to hear. He took a First at Jesus in biology and organic chemistry before turning his much-abused grey cells to the journalist grind. I'm glad to know he's retained at least some of it.'

Boo was of that particular tint of person who carries a natural bloodied flush in their cheeks. Embarrassment, Rose thought, must typically show a little scarlet and then swiftly remove offstage, a rapid flick and disappearance on the high boards of his face. A person who moved easily, so it seemed, through shame. Now, however, he was white, and the corners of his mouth had no colour at all.

'Oy!' she said helplessly, feeling caught in a terrible dragnet.

'What, Boo?' Patrick looked disturbed. Boo mumbled something and walked a little too fast from the room.

'You've rumbled him,' Gladys murmured to her husband. 'He was having such a nice time being an idiot.'

'Oh, dear.' Patrick looked disconsolate. 'For such a bright man he does act like a lunatic.'

'Excuse me,' said Rose, who exited with as much grace as she could muster. She was, she was pretty sure, red to the tips of her hair.

Boo was hanging about fiddling with the rigging on the railing.

'It did seem like the quickest way for you to talk to me,' he said, with the air of a sheep left out in the rain all night. 'I see boyish gormlessness isn't the right technique.'

'I want neither your technique nor your gorm,' said Rose with asperity. 'You nearly annoyed Dr Eder out of his wits. And you made me look a fool in front of your family.' Why this should needle at her in particular she wasn't sure. The Morelands seemed so sensible somehow.

'Oh, they don't think you're a fool, I promise.' The sheep now looked as if it had been dragged through a bog backwards. 'I genuinely don't know a lot about stingrays. Really.'

'It will be difficult to teach you anything new as there really aren't any in the Arctic.'

'Ah. Not even one?'

'Not even casual passers-by.'

'Pity.'

'Idiot.'

He bridled. 'I take offence.'

'Go ahead and take it. I'll gift-wrap it.'

'Are you offended that I'm *not* in fact an idiot? To be clear.'

'I knew you weren't an idiot. I was wondering why you understood difficult scientific terms but appeared to struggle with easy ones. I thought perhaps you were a very poor journalist. It appears you just like to lie.'

'I concede that point, though you must admit it reveals I'm not a very accomplished liar.'

'Lack of skill is no indication of frequency of attempt.'

'You could at least be flattered that I tried.'

'You'd think less of me if I were.'

'Upsettingly, another point to you. I get a nasty view of our future.'

'You are completely impossible. Is this how you get all your scoops?'

'I am, unhappily, a highly skilled and intellectual interviewer who never gets to ask really stupid questions,' said Boo. 'I was having a very good time letting loose.'

'Do continue. Don't mind me, I have to go be a jobbing scientist on a stipend who lacks the opportunity to swan about on luxury cruises playing at dimwittery.' She turned her back and set off towards the gangway to the scientists' quarters.

'I deserved that,' said Boo behind her, faintly.

'I know you did,' she said, and left.

9

It was the third full day, one for travelling through the
choppy and increasingly opaque waters; on the fourth, the
Captain explained, they'd be anchoring once again, on the
edge of a substantial glacial ice sheet on which Scheduled
Activities (Rose had noted the Champagne Brunch on the
itinerary with some confusion) would be occurring. To
make up for the lack of entertainment during the day, there
was to be the Masked Ball that evening.

The scientists, much to their surprise, were invited to
this – though, Rose reflected, it shouldn't have come as such
a shock. The *Dauphin* explicitly promised its paying guests
the presence of all the scientists at informal daily buffets
and evening events as a 'chance to socialise' – provided, of
course, that the scientists weren't busy with science. This
loophole, Rose thought, was a very tactful way to give
unsociable researchers an out from fatuous stories about
somebody's dog's webbed feet. (She had been subjected to
this tale once at a cocktail party, by a woman whose enthusiasm was only matched by her invulnerability to Rose's
escape attempts.)

'But why are we to be masked?' Dr Palgrave asked, when
it was explained to her that she had been invited to attend.
'Is there a safety issue?'

'When I was invited to the great New Year's Ball in

Vienna,' Dr Eder said with fond importance, 'the masks were quite extraordinary. Ornamented with lace, and pearls, and the gentlemen all wore black velvet ones. It's just a charade, dear lady. A bit of glamour.'

'Did you wear your glasses over yours, or did you get a prescription mask?' asked Palgrave, with interest.

Eder made a bravado laugh and went off, presumably to drape his face in various expensive materials and smile at the mirror.

Rose and Finn had made their own masks, a little shyly; they matched, because once you get out of the strenuous efforts of your teens to show that you are *not* identical, you do come slowly back to the fact that in many ways it's easier simply to buy two of things. They were white cardboard and string, because that was all they had, but they were nicely shaped. Finn's hair sprung over the top of his like a bunch of sea anemones going after a tasty morsel. Sixgill, he said, while fastening Rose's, had taken the radio transmitter to fiddle with, but had hung around asking a bunch of questions about Finn's life and his work. 'He seemed genuinely curious,' he said. 'I think he's all right, really, Rosie, I do.'

Rose refrained from mentioning Finn's utter lack of ability to discern nefarious motives in anything, up to and including rampaging brown bears. (They'd once had a narrow scrape while camping in Yosemite because Finn refused to believe the massive bear rooting through their lunch was going to harm *them*, since he'd seen an interesting documentary about their sociability. In the end Rose had terrified it off by popping a blown-up paper bag, and made

Finn go to a lecture by the park rangers on the dangers of half-ton ursines. Finn had emerged chastened but with the nicest park ranger's number.) 'I'm glad he was nice to *you*,' she said, with spirit. Perhaps Sixgill was powerless against Finn's barrage of sweetness, or had detected Rose's rampant protectiveness and decided Finn was one arena he wasn't willing to battle in. Or he was hoping for some smooches, which thankfully would be unlikely, as Finn liked them large, bearded and able to bench-press heavy machinery.

The vast oval of the formal dining room had been cleared and filled with light, round tables were covered in linens that would have made Nefertiti weep her kohl off with envy, and everything beamed with a sense of profound and unutterable wealth, like the nacre inside a well-developed oyster. The ship had its own, branded scent, a mix of dark musky tones and a flurry of florals, which must have reminded the guests of five-star splendour, but made Rose feel as if she was about to be attacked by a furiously sweating deer in an arboretum. Each place setting was hand-filigreed in what Rose noted with slight alarm appeared to be real gold leaf (done by a pallid Norwegian crew member who was earning his way towards fine arts college).

The Highcastles saw a shape off the side in the dark which a crew member with a torch identified as a bit of partly submerged ice but Bloom insisted was a narwhal. They came in laughing and excited, Sandy with his mask half off his head, but Bloom holding hers precisely on her nose. 'Arrange it for me, darling, please,' she said, and the two of them together made the vast construction straight. It was,

Rose was told when she asked politely, an adapted sleep mask from their Exaltation Zodiac Collection, made of fine blue silk and custom-studded all over with various crystals and quartzes. They'd cut out some eye-holes, slightly too small, so Bloom's eyelash extensions poked through painfully. 'The crystals don't come with the normal mask,' Bloom hastened to add. 'You wouldn't sleep very well! They're usually suspended in the candles. But it is nice to look so *glittery*, isn't it?'

'You look like the jewel of the Nile,' said Sandy grandly.

'Wrong climate,' said Boo Moreland, coming up then, 'but certainly very grand.' He kissed Bloom's hand gallantly and she made what was meant to be an elegant gurgling noise. He was, Rose saw, wearing a mask he'd clearly made himself, which was in the shape – she gawped at him – of a seagull wearing a snorkel and diving trunks. 'What? I thought it was fetching,' he said to her innocently, and wandered off.

'He does like to look completely ridiculous,' said Gladys Moreland with fondness. She and her husband were wearing masks with little tiny cut-out paper legal wigs at each corner. They looked as if they had extraordinary eyebrows. Rose felt a wave of affection for them.

Bloom Highcastle clearly felt, in her magnificence, like a patron of the sciences, because she floated over to them and asked Finn, with a pat of her bejewelled hand on his arm, what precisely he was looking for in those murky depths – a shark, was it? She was *terrified* of sharks. And was he never *scared*?

'Oh *no*,' said Finn, with a surge of enthusiastic colour in his cheeks and lips, 'never – Greenland sharks are one of the sleeper sharks, you know. Because they're so slow and gentle it's like they're sleepwalking!'

'*Sleepy* sharks? You're studying sleepy sharks! Oh, Sandy, honey, the boy scientist studies sharks that are asleep all the time!'

'Wish *I* led that kind of life, snoring under an ice cap,' came Sandy's boom, as always tinged with a little sourness, like a twist of lemon on the edge of a cocktail glass.

Rose grinned. She was uncertain whether Bloom was genuinely misunderstanding, or else doing the thing some people did when faced with Science, which was to undercut it with silliness so as not to feel stupid. But the enormous eyelashes batted underneath the dazzling silk as Finn gently attempted to explain, and everybody in the interaction seemed wholly happy. Finn, she thought with a proprietary air, looked healthier than he had in weeks.

The food was magnificent, somehow marrying foams, smears and other faintly ridiculous elements of nouvelle cuisine with robust flavours and what Rose recognised, even in her ignorance, as a culinary *point of view*. Elisabeth Lindgren came in, unmasked, at the dessert course (choco-late beads that exploded on the tongue like ballistic seeds) to receive praise, which the by-then quite drunk guests hollered at her. She stood as if she was quite used to being brayed at by wealthy people, which, Rose reflected, she probably was. She simply stared straight ahead, with her chef's whites and her formidable face, until she judged she had stayed long enough, at which point she bowed, and left.

Beside her, Aabria Scott – her own ancient Venetian carnival mask now laid by her knee, as it was, she'd explained apologetically early in the evening, very heavy – clapped enthusiastically. Rose was glad the mask had been put to one side; it was one of those that was fully white and covered the face entirely, and looked like porcelain. Even with the benign twinkle of Aabria through the eyeholes it retained a sense of icy impersonality.

'I really feel very spoiled,' Aabria said quietly to Rose. 'What a menu. Crab cakes with basil-oil caviar! I gave Kate the night off. She doesn't like these things.'

Kate Berg had in fact hovered for a while, herself in a mask that looked in its professional indifference – it had likely been made efficiently and in a hurry – somehow cheap, or flimsy. She had offered food, tea, a fluffed pillow. Then Aabria had dismissed her – not furiously, but absently, with a wave of the hand and an instruction that she 'go take some time for yourself now' – and even below the paper mask Rose had detected the small smart on the cool face. The hand wave had reminded Kate Berg, Rose thought, that she was not daughter or niece but payrolled employee, and that her devotion was considered as much a parcel of her care as skill with a syringe or rapidity changing sheets. Aabria Scott was not unkind, and had in that moment likely thought she was doing a generous thing, giving her carer some freedom, but it was a gesture that seemed to sink under Kate's surface uncomfortably, and she'd left looking performatively carefree, pulling the mask off her head. A less loyal woman, Rose thought, would gleefully badmouth her employer to the crew at the food tables, but Kate Berg would do nothing.

'What did you mean when you said *poor girl*, about Elisabeth?' said Rose, unable to contain herself.

'Oh, that,' said Aabria. 'Women like that have such a hard time.'

'What, working women?' Rose felt a strange horror: had she stumbled into one of those unreconstructed women who would soon be telling her to breed and wear soft skirts? But Aabria shook her magnificent head and laughed at her.

'No. Intense, and sheltered. You saw her face. They so often, you see, pick the wrong people.'

'How do you know?'

'I've seen a lot of things. Women making bad decisions, mostly. I worked at a women's college for many years, teaching writing. Every mistake under the sun – I've seen it. And I haven't judged. No, I haven't.'

But you haven't forgotten either, thought Rose.

Rose mostly stayed close to Finn and the Morelands, who were resolutely not mentioning Boo's ridiculous mask. Sixgill, she noticed in the corner of her eye, was rotating through the tables, and nobody appeared to be attempting to punch him, so he must be of a sweeter temper. His own mask was hot orange, the same shade as the parkas. Dr Palgrave had not, in the end, condescended to attend, which disappointed Rose, because she'd wanted to ask her quietly about the scene with the Arctic hares, or whatever it was. But – the champagne was rising through her head, bubbles pricking at the top of her skull – what did it really matter? Patrick began telling them the remarkable case of a boy who had come to him, primed from expensive tutors and Etonian teachers and God knows what else, with all the answers to an admissions test to read Law, but when given an unexpected legal question had stopped, looked at Patrick with an astonished mulish face, and said he'd be *telling his father*.

He stopped suddenly after the punchline and said, 'What's up?'

Gladys Moreland was staring hard at a person in the corner. Rose, turning, saw Alicia Grey, who had removed her (very plain, hunter-green) mask for the moment because its strings had become tangled in Sunila's confection, a mass of sparkles and bits and what looked like a crystalline starfish. The two of them were giggling, and in the light looked suddenly quite young.

Rose looked at Gladys for the traces of subtle judgement she faintly expected, firing out from behind that aristocratic reserve like so many arrows at Hastings – *not quite our kind* – and was confused to see no such thing.

'You all right, Gladdy?' Patrick said softly, with an air not of interruption but of bringing a distant mind back into the room. His wife's expression had taken on a cast Rose took a moment to place, but then realised was intense internal concentration – as if rifling through thousands of entries in an extraordinary and well-indexed memory, until it found the one it required. Her eyes, Rose noted with unease, had the same look as a hovering bird of prey.

The features clicked back into focus. The mind had discovered what it sought, and relaxed. 'Yes,' said Gladys, mildly. 'Ms Grey has a very interesting face.' Which Rose quite agreed with: it was very broad, and the eyes very large. But Gladys Moreland was not, she thought, looking at Alicia Grey with aesthetic interest. The woman's intellect had given her something, and for the moment she was satisfied.

'Seen her up on the bench for poaching the king's deer, have you?' said Sandy Highcastle, with a bluff laugh. He, Rose thought, had met that upper-class wall before too, and being unable to scale it, reviled it.

'I can say pretty definitively,' said the barrister, with some firmness, 'that I've never seen her prosecuted for anything,' and the conversation drifted into other channels, though Rose later wondered at how she'd phrased it. Gladys Moreland was a very precise woman.

The evening was getting late. Dr Palgrave had, to Rose's mild surprise, turned up midway through the proceedings, bare-faced, but appeared just as distracted as ever. Dr Eder had attempted to lend her his mask – which was, of course, made of perfectly cut black velvet – but she said, 'Hm? Yes,' and walked off between the tables, randomly picking up a bit of leftover dessert here, a cup of half-drunk coffee there. Really, Rose thought, it was as if she barely knew where she was. She'd probably heard voices, registered that she should probably go towards them, and would have no memory of it in the morning.

She was sitting down, watching Boo Moreland try to do magic with a set of cards for several crew members and fail radically, when Ben Sixgill came over. He'd taken his mask off.

'Are you having a nice evening?' he said. He sounded much more Southern than usual. He must, she thought, also be slightly drunk.

'Perfectly pleasant, thank you. You'll be in the *Mouette* tomorrow,' she added.

'Yes. I'll have to be careful with it. It sounds like you whacked the seal pretty hard. It's all right, it happens to everybody.' His smugness was so strong it almost had a smell.

'I'm sure it does,' she said evenly. The mask fitted slightly too close to her face, which was likely why it suddenly felt very hot.

'Still, I'd ask you to come down with me for a spin if you liked. Eder's coming, but he'd give up his berth in a second. Don't think he's done his own field work for at least fifty years.'

'You should ask Finn,' said Rose, without any emotion. 'He would be more than willing, I'm sure.'

'Oh, I know. I asked Finn a lot of questions. I know a lot of things about Finn.' And Sixgill looked at her with his horrible casual smile, and she had the distinct feeling that the rest of the room was getting rather blurry.

'I know,' and his voice was too loud, far too loud, 'and you know, and so does everybody else with an ounce of sense, that it's extremely uncommon to get identical twins who *aren't of the same gender*.'

81

Rose, suddenly very sober, felt a series of reactions that were, at this point after so many years, unpleasantly familiar. The start of nausea, then a friction as bits of bone in her head began to grind against one another and anger started showering from between them. Sparks, everywhere. Burning her skull from the inside. She did not look at Finn, who was standing by the canapé table. Bending over himself, always trying to hide.

'What you mean, I think, is identical twins of the same sex.' She also had a very clear voice. 'Sex and gender being different. A thing that we all learned in first-year biology. Did you not pay attention?'

'I paid attention. I pay attention to a lot of things. I can tell, you know. Your sister thinks she's fooling people, but she didn't fool me for a second. I knew immediately.'

'I'm afraid I don't have a sister,' said Rose, with the patient voice of somebody speaking to a deaf maiden aunt.

'You can tell each other that all you like,' said Sixgill, in a tone that was, Rose knew, designed to carry, to be heard by as many people as possible in this enclosed space with its precisely tuned and clarified acoustics, 'but when she's dead her bones will show quite clearly what she is. If we got her into an X-ray machine I could show you both. It could be a double date! I know how to show girls a good time, even perverted ones—'

Rose didn't quite understand how she had hit him so hard. Sixgill's face was suddenly a shocking mess of purples and reds that seemed impossible from one punch, even strong as she was, but then she saw that Boo was beside her and had in fact likely punched at the exact same time, their knuckles colliding at the mark, which was Sixgill's nose. The organ in question no longer appeared to be extant. Sixgill collapsed with a strange noise that could be interpreted as half-gurgle, half-scream, and rolled.

Rose was, in herself, extremely calm. She was looking at a point at the far wall.

Kate Berg came over and told him to shut up. 'Sit up and put this on your nose.' She was packing gauze angrily onto the mess that was Sixgill's face. 'Now get up and come to the office and we'll bandage it.'

'Didn't do anything wrong,' said Sixgill thickly, with a kind of sulky laugh. Rose wanted to put her foot in his already-broken nose, which was at least preventing him from speaking at any length. 'And look – ruined my sunglasses.' He was, in fact, pulling bits of polarised blue glass out of his top pocket. It must, Rose thought, have been smashed when he came down hard on his side. 'Gonna talk to Captain.'

'I'm sure you will.' Alicia Grey, hearty of voice but, Rose noticed, now very red and mottled of throat, was close by, looking at him with the expression somebody of her temperament reserves for a particularly repulsive bit of deer viscera left on her heirloom carpet by dogs. 'I'm sure I will, at that. The Captain will find himself crowded with accounts.'

Sixgill was steered out of the room. Rose heard noises swim at her out of the silence: Dr Palgrave was saying in her clear, uncluttered voice, 'But that's nonsense; you can't sex a human skeleton with accuracy. Our sexual dimorphisms aren't clear. I remember once at an archaeological dig—' while Dr Eder said, 'My dear lady, my *dear* lady,' at her, or perhaps at somebody else, over and over. The guests were all very carefully avoiding looking at Finn – except for Boo. He had gone over and taken Finn's very thin shoulders and was steering him out of the room. Finn was, as usual, not saying anything; Finn very rarely said anything when these things happened. The rage that emerged and held Rose, like lava that fused into obsidian glass, was hers and hers alone.

10

The *Dauphin* moved slowly through the night, which this far north was many hours long. Full polar night was still some months off, but the periods of daylight were marked for their scarcity, and the glorious green-pink of their sunsets. The lights of the cabins flowed over the sea-ice, which was beginning to gather in greater glowing lumps as the ship carried itself quietly through the Arctic Circle, closer to the roof of the world.

Finn and Rose were in their cabin talking until very late. Boo Moreland had dropped in, some hours after midnight, and was allowed entrance without anybody commenting.

'I'll be put off at Svalbard, most likely,' Rose said. She'd been packing her things for several hours without great success, because Finn kept taking them out again. 'Then I can get a plane down to Oslo, or something, and wait for you in Paris.'

'I keep telling you, you won't be put off anywhere, and if you are they'll have to put me off too, and then there'll be a lot of annoyance with the *Dauphin* scientific committee, because scientists aren't supposed to be thrown off research vessels after being harassed, and if we go, *he* goes as well.' Finn was waving around a pair of her socks for emphasis.

'I still say the Crimson Horror is more likely to go than either of you,' said Boo Moreland, who was by this point sitting on the bottom bunk, occasionally being handed bits of Rose's things by either Finn or Rose, and holding them politely in his left palm until either twin removed them again. His right arm had been strung in a sling. 'No, it's not for sympathy, it's because I'm an idiot,' is what he'd said when they opened the cabin door. 'It turns out not bracing your wrist when you punch gets you a boxer's fracture. And I'm bloody right-handed, too.' Apparently the estimable Kate Berg had returned from mopping up Sixgill's fragmented nasal passages, noticed Boo holding his hand gingerly, and diagnosed the odd position of his knuckle-bones with sympathetic speed and a gauze-wrap.

Rose, who had braced her hand properly but still felt the sting of the impact, went down on her knees to look for her charging cables. Her own knuckles, she registered dimly, would likely be a little swollen tomorrow. 'He didn't throw the first punch,' she said, 'and you know the Captain will apply some sort of very stringent naval idea of logic to all of this. He looks the type.'

'I'll ask Gladdy,' said Boo. 'She was fuming. She asked,' he nodded at Finn conversationally, 'to pass on some recommendations for good human rights lawyers in London, if you'd like some. I've met most of them; they're all very charming and eat far too much of Gladdy's spiced apricot goose at dinner parties.'

'Gladys is so nice,' Finn said despairingly, and looked miserable. The evening, Rose saw, had shaken his faith in the unutterable goodness of humans. Even after transitioning very young and having the concomitant decades' worth of nonsense about it, including from their idiotic parents ('But we have two *girls!*' they'd wailed, as she and Finn bolted down the driveway to her waiting Toyota Yaris), Finn retained a sense of unfailing cheeriness. That was the worst part of these episodes: not that they hurt Rose, which they did, but that they made Finn question his beliefs.

She headbutted him hard on the forehead. 'Oy. I'd do it again.'

'I know,' said Finn, perking up.

'I'd say we were a good team but my smallest knuckle-bone disagrees with me,' said Boo. 'It's more crooked than Sandy Highcastle.'

'You clearly don't punch people very often,' said Rose, absently. She heard the casual note of elitism in Boo's voice about Highcastle – *not quite one of us* – and for the first time lacked the energy to yell at him about it. 'Finn, put those books back.'

'At least you didn't need bail this time,' Finn said, hurriedly putting the books in Boo's lap, where Rose couldn't reach them from the other side of the table. 'She's been up three times for public affray and – was it public nuisance? I can't remember. The charges always get dropped, because she's very persuasive.' His pointed face beamed. He looked, Rose thought, most like her when he smiled.

'Gladdy and Pat would probably help with that as well, if the Captain wants to put you in some freezing Norwegian prison for a bit. Although I've been reading about Scandinavian prisons and they do look remarkably comfortable, to be honest.' Boo poked at the books. 'You realise I can't move these, right? I am but a man with a clipped wing.'

'The thing I don't understand,' said Finn at length, when they'd given up on fighting over books and jumpers and underpants (Boo priggishly refused to touch these, even though they were clean and covered in little pictures of goldfish) and sat in unspeaking exhausted silence as a trio, 'was *why* he was so nasty. I know that people sometimes just are, Rose, and that's another thing, but – he's awful to *everybody*. It's as if he wants people to hate him. It's baffling.'

'Maybe he's working up to a lawsuit against the *Dauphin* for discrimination because nobody will talk to him,' Boo said cheerfully. 'I knew a few boys like him at prep school. Nasty, creepy little soul-suckers who noted down all your infractions against the rules and went to the master about them every fortnight. Some people never grow out of being morbid bullies.'

'Of *course* you went to prep school,' said Rose, and Boo threw a pair of her socks at her with his good hand.

Nothing to do but wait for my fate now, thought Rose. But she had meant what she'd said earlier to Finn: she'd do it again.

What there was, instead of a throwing-out of half or both of the Blanchard twins (or, Boo's fondest hope, a public Sixgill-lynching), was a printed note on *Dauphin* stationery under everybody's door in the morning. It reminded them that instances of violence or verbal harassment would not be tolerated, and that further infractions would incur severe penalties. Rose, reading it, reflected that Alicia Grey, and likely the Morelands, had done their work.

Gladys Moreland came down to find them after breakfast to confirm this impression. 'Nasty business,' she said crisply. 'I pointed out to the Captain that while we might be in another nation's waters right now, possibly Greenland or a walrus-run autocracy, the ship is registered to a British corporation and therefore follows British law. I once prosecuted a very boring case involving people misbehaving on a Brighton millionaire's yacht in decidedly non-British waters,' she added. 'To be honest, he didn't require convincing. The last thing a luxury cruise company wants is the appearance of expensive lawyers. The second-last thing is bad publicity.'

And that, Rose thought, was likely very true.

'I will write,' said Dr Eder nobly, 'to Sixgill's superiors at his university. His conduct will not be unpunished.'

'Oh,' said a colourless voice. They turned and saw Dr Palgrave in the crew mess, staring at Dr Eder. She looked as smacked awake as she had the evening of the lecture.

'Yes?' said Dr Eder, with a small question in his tone.

'I suppose – yes, you must be right.' Dr Palgrave opened and closed her mouth a few times, then turned and left. Rose looked at Finn and Boo with utter bewilderment. What was this sudden urge to protect the Crimson Horror? What, thought Rose with exasperation, had happened with those bloody hares?

'I wouldn't have figured her for a prejudiced sort,' said Gladys, squinting after her with her sharp brown eyes. 'You almost get the sense it wouldn't really occur to her.'

'She likely doesn't like being associated with scandal,' said Dr Eder soothingly. 'She hasn't tenure, you know. But these sorts of things must be dealt with.' He beetled off sniffily, probably, Rose thought, to write an email to Sixgill's supervisors that would feature Eder himself as a prominent hero, dashing in to save the day at great personal risk to himself. She'd once whacked an abusive skinhead with a shoe outside a queer bar, and then discovered, several days later, that an activist who'd been standing smoking with his back to them had gone to the press to take credit. No matter. She had the satisfying memory of the whack of sole against skull to keep her warm at night.

Sixgill himself remained completely out of sight, and the Captain, showing no signs of strain, appeared at breakfast to reassure everybody that the day's activities would continue as planned. The Champagne Brunch, he said, would occur at a later point, when they were securely moored off the ice-sheet and silvery daylight had fully established itself.

Bloom Highcastle was flipping cushions idly, looking, she explained, for her mask. It had disappeared at some point in the evening's festivities. 'Not a valuable thing,' she said with a small girl's giggle, 'but I did put so much effort into hot glue gunning! Lift up your chairs, everybody.' But the lost mask was not in evidence. Her husband, it was hinted delicately, was sleeping in with a thunderous hangover.

'Mine's missing too,' said Aabria, kindly. 'It was a very disordered night, sweetheart, we'll find them all later.' Kate Berg, showing the intense vigour of somebody who blossoms when useful, was turning the room upside down and pinioning hapless crew members as to the mask's whereabouts; having been deprived of opportunities to show her worth to Aabria last night, Rose thought, she seemed pleased to have the chance this morning, and was at this moment making herself as beadily aggravating as a blackbird to Elisabeth Lindgren, who had entered the dining room.

'A mask? No, no masks at all,' said Lindgren shortly, and Rose noted with a start that she talked to Kate Berg without any of the forbearance she reserved for guests, or indeed for the scientists. It was not a closeness, but it was not the barking Lindgren used for kitchen crew, either; and Rose recognised, as perhaps Elisabeth consciously had, that on this ship the chef and the carer were of the same floating rank, suspended by skill and utility above the sailors and swabs but only granted proximity to the elite, not acceptance. This could, in other people, have made for a friendship, but the sublime lines of Elisabeth's head paired with the round, hard-looking skull of Kate made that seem unlikely.

Rose was relieved beyond words to discover that the guests were fixated on treating Finn normally. Bloom, perhaps, fluted a little bit too often and fastened herself to Finn's awkward arm in an attempt to feel as much of an ally as possible, but ostentatious correctness was a lot easier to deal with than the alternative. 'Nice aim,' whispered Sunila to Rose, conspiratorially, as they walked out of breakfast. Rose grinned.

The Captain, she discovered to her surprise when she headed downstairs to the cabins to finally unpack her things (she'd still worried about the possibility of a Dramatic Denouement at breakfast), was arguing with Elisabeth Lindgren outside the kitchen.

'I know, I know——' He had his hands out in wide soothing waves, as one would before an agitated Komodo dragon. It wasn't working, just as it wouldn't work with a Komodo, either.

'But they must be out! There is no room! I spoke to you about this before and you said it would be dealt with.'

The Captain threw a significant look at Rose that was, Rose felt sure, meant to imply that as a guest was present, this situation must be either resolved or at the very least contained to a Less Public Arena, but Elisabeth, as befitting a true artist on a mission, took Rose's presence in another way entirely.

'If you had to do your job with a host of irrelevant pieces of detritus underfoot, Dr Blanchard, could you?'

Faced with Elisabeth Lindgren's expression, Rose decided not to truthfully remark that all jobbing scientists on boats were used to attempting complex feats of measuring and theory around and on top of rolling barrels, nets, two-ton shipping containers, the Captain's wellies, and any number of large and uncooperative-feeling live specimens. 'Not really,' she murmured, and wondered how a pimply, callow sous-chef would feel with those eyes staring down at them.

'See? Dr Blanchard is a sensible person. And in my cold storage!'

'I'll have a word,' said the Captain, who understood perfectly well when his powers were futile, and went off to commit actions that would hopefully prevent Elisabeth Lindgren from terrifying him in any more corridors.

'What's up?' asked Rose, more out of curiosity than anything else.

'Candles,' said Elisabeth Lindgren, with slightly white nostrils, 'in my cold storage. Mr Highcastle somehow argued to bring them aboard, then he said he couldn't keep them in his stateroom because there is no space. How is there enough space in my freezer? I trip over candles getting ice, I trip over candles getting liquid nitrogen, I am enormously sick of candles.'

'That sounds deeply inconvenient, yes,' said Rose helplessly. 'I'm sure the Captain will find somewhere else for them to go.'

'He had better,' said Elisabeth Lindgren, and disappeared smartly through the doors of the kitchen.

The Champagne Brunch was one thing to which the scientists were not invited, much to Dr Eder's probable chagrin. Rose watched the preparations with interest. The *Dauphin* had manoeuvred itself neatly between drifting, loose ice floes, and was now moored some hundred feet from one of the distant edges of the ice cap. The polar day was full of new, bright noises: snaps, clicks, the leisurely percussion of the huge shelf severing parts of itself and setting them floating away. Ice ricocheting against the *Dauphin*'s hull in the dark current sounded like the scrape of bird beaks against stone, while a crack far off as a significant chunk decided it was time to leave home resembled an echoing gunshot, and made several passengers jump. It was, Rose reflected, like parsing the underwater auditory landscape on her beloved reefs: parrot fish nibbling on coral, skittering crabs, the occasional looping whistle of whale song, and somewhere, faint Geiger-counter clicks as manta rays sighted a shark. Another scientist's discovery that some rays communicated danger this way had, Rose remembered, been one of the most dizzying days of her life, but she'd somehow been listening for it all along.

Another underwater radio beacon, the scientific notes on the *Dauphin*'s journeying said, was relatively close to the mooring site, and should be fetched at the *Mouette*'s nearest convenience. But that wasn't the priority at the moment; Rose leaned over the side and saw Elisabeth and her swarms of miscellaneously Scandinavian helpers haul sundry materials off a dinghy hooked to the ice, and begin to construct—

'I never,' said Boo, who as ever popped up beside her when left unattended. 'They're making a space pod.'

It certainly looked like it, Rose admitted. It was a vast geodesic dome, made of some kind of matte white material that meant it blended with soft ease into the ice without throwing glare. At its central point it must, Rose thought, have been around eight feet tall. It curved magnificently around its various pegs and guy-ropes and fastenings and looked, with its frontage open to the air, like nothing so much as a giant's solitary and imperious eyeball. Bloom Highcastle came to the front with them in pursuit, as ever, of polar animals, real or imagined, and had her binoculars to hand. As the three watched, Elisabeth and her minions began to fill this ice palace with what appeared to be a deconstructed bar and heavy, *Dauphin*-orange bottles of champagne, their gold noses all looking veritably ready to foam.

'That thing must be able to withstand polar vortexes.' Boo sounded flummoxed. 'I don't want to brunch in it, I want to go to Mars and see whether it'll protect me from Martians.'

Bloom Highcastle screamed.

She pointed, and for an instant, and in complete contravention of all her training, Rose thought she was seeing a yeti. A completely white-clad shape with a white face and huge reflective eyes was ambling around the back of the Champagne Brunch site. It removed its furry ears – and there was a shock of red hair. Rose made a disgusted noise.

'What's Sixgill doing dressing up like an albino penguin and scaring the life out of people?' Boo asked the Captain, who had popped his head out of the bridge to see what the screaming was about. Boo's tone was carefully humorous; he clearly didn't take the Captain for a fool.

'Ah,' said the Captain, a line appearing between his eyes. 'Dr Sixgill stated he would prefer to spend the day today conducting research on hares on the ice. I suggested this was indeed the best alternative.'

The white thing beneath Sixgill's sunglasses – which were, of course, the reflective yeti eyes, and had apparently been borrowed from a crew member, as they were far too big for his face– resolved itself into a white nose-bandage.

He'd covered it with a sort of white windcheater thing, to protect the rest of his face from the Arctic breezes, or potentially to spare his own blushes as much as possible. He didn't look up at the scream, and continued to prowl around doing some kind of measuring.

'Why is he all in white?' said Bloom Highcastle, now sounding rather disappointed that she hadn't discovered some kind of rare Arctic gorilla.

'He studies camouflage animals on the ice and snow, and it's coming into their winter season now,' Rose said, feeling a little sorry for her. She wanted so badly to see interesting things. 'If he wears white they're much less likely to spot him.'

'Redheads shouldn't wear all white,' said Bloom, with the air of a moral judgement – which, Rose thought, it quite possibly was, in Bloom's world – and then said, 'Oh, that's Sandy,' in response to a growl from the lower deck, and teetered off.

'Does this mean we have use of the *Mouette* today, or would Dr Eder still like to descend?' Rose asked the Captain, with her best air of deferent politeness. She, as her grandmother used to say, wasn't pushing her luck further than the Captain could throw her.

'Yes, Dr Blanchard, it does, though I'd ask that you refrain from any actions rearranging its frontal areas.' And the Captain disappeared back onto the bridge.

If that was all the telling off she was going to get, Rose thought, she was luckier than a handful of four-leafed clovers picked in a leap year.

Elisabeth Lindgren, in her bright orange *Dauphin* parka, looked up at the moving white body with, Rose thought from this distance, an absent indifference, then went back to arranging champagne flutes. Maybe Sixgill would keep to himself and not make any more sneering remarks or enemies or God knows what else until he got to solid, non-glacial land again. Somehow Rose doubted it.

There were, Tom Heissen thought, such a lot of luxury cruises around the Arctic, and all of them seemed to promise the same things: seals, and foxes, and dolphins, and the Northern Lights. Could one order seals ahead of time? Were they all coordinated by a central agency who organised their appearances in the best light for passing cameras?

Titus found him making confused noises under the mound of brochures, some of them extremely heavy, and said, 'Got something, sir.'

'What?'

'An American documentary crew. They came through a while back and told various stories,' Titus said. 'Some were slightly wild and the locals here, sir, aren't inclined to give documentary persons the time of day, but one was repeated widely and appears to have caused consternation.'

'Well?'

'There is,' said Titus, 'a hut, in a particularly unbothered area of the ice cap. Nobody appears to know why it's there.'

Tom drew himself up and a collection of new brochures slid to the floor with an expensive-sounding thwack. 'We have an unexplained hut too?'

'Constructed without permission or reason, sir. Documentarians aren't meant to leave traces, and scientists would at least have labelled the place or left explanations of what it was for.'

'Scientists can be rather lax,' Tom said.

'Sometimes, sir. It's not in the right area for any survey-ing, which is why the documentary crew found it so odd. It's very far inland and away from anything of interest. They suggested illegal poaching or some kind of oil chicanery. Surmises without basis, mostly, sir, but I had those who'd remembered the conversation mark a map for me, and the points are all within an approximate quarter-mile radius.'

The area on the map was a considerable distance away by boat, and snowmobile, and God knows what else. Tom estimated it was a few hours' travel from the edge of the glacier in any direction. It would take them away from Svalbard and whatever was to be found there – but, Tom reflected, Titus wasn't the sort to bring up an out-of-the-way lead unless it really had weight. Tom looked hard at the map, considered the fun of expensing a husky team back to London, and began to get to work. Then he paused.

'Titus. Did they also,' he asked, 'give you more knives.'

'No, sir.'

'Very good.'

'They did, however, give me a nice gun and two sets of good-quality knuckle dusters. I have,' said Titus, with the delicacy of a man who understood his superior's limits, 'left these outside. If you'll excuse me, sir.'

11

The Champagne Brunch was, from what Rose could glean afterwards, a fabulous success. Bottles were popped with gratifying foaminess, the vistas were as silvered as a well-polished christening-present spoon, and the *Dauphin*'s paying residents cavorted and took cheery photographs of their faces squinting in the diaphanous sunlight. Sandy Highcastle had apparently adopted the philosophy of hair of the polar dog when it came to his hangover, and took several *coupes* with gusto. Bloom clapped her vast, be-mittened hands at everything, and Aabria Scott, according to Boo – who related all of this to the Blanchards later – spent her time flirting adeptly with two of the tallest and most heavily moustached sailors, ultimately goading them into crossing their arms like a swing and bearing her everywhere, as if on a particularly well-muscled palanquin. Kate Berg followed behind in an apparent quest to make sure nobody fell through the ice, though Boo was sure she was actually doing it for the best possible view of sailor-buttocks.

'There was, of course, one extremely serene-looking fellow who had charge of the tranquilliser gun,' Boo added. 'We weren't told what it was, presumably so we wouldn't get overly liquid inspiration and try to fiddle with it, but I recognised the shape of the long box well enough. One hint of a rampaging walrus intent on our innocence or our blinis and he'd have whipped it out with all precision. I was a little scared of him.'

They'd all come back rowdy and happy after a few hours. Rose stood at the top of the rope ladder intent on helping the sailors take up the parts of the dome on the dinghies – she, like them, was on a stipend, though she felt sure theirs was probably healthier – but they waved her off with gentle Swedish-Norwegian-Danish smiles. Theirs was a well-oiled machine. Half of the Dome, as she'd started to capitalise it in her head, had been left on the ice, with a variety of tent pegs and ropes and the bar; the entire thing, she gathered, was a hassle to deconstruct in its entirety, so they tended to remove it in parts. Cautious enquiry had revealed that the Crimson Horror (as Rose and Finn now couldn't help calling him) had been transported back to the ship well before the brunch, and he'd now hidden himself below again. Rose hoped he reappeared chastened, or at least asked for all his meals in his room and wrote obnoxious things about Arctic hares in solitary confinement.

She looked down the ladder at the dinghy; only Elisabeth Lindgren remained, looking back at the Dome and drifting a gloved hand dreamily over the water.

'All OK?' said Rose, wondering at this small show of apparent daydreaming. Lindgren must, she thought, be a creative genius, based on the food; nobody was supposed to be able to eat sturgeon popcorn, and yet her brain had produced it. Perhaps she was taking a rare moment to think up new ideas for sustainable oyster ice creams.

'Oh, yes.' Elisabeth Lindgren looked up, fastened things neatly in place on her seat, and rose up the ladder. Her face was slightly wind-burned from the ice; little spots of pink were seared onto the top of each smooth cheekbone, like paint on stone. 'I was thinking,' she added to Rose as she landed on deck, 'of the canals. I worked beside them in the Netherlands, for a long time. This is how I would get to work often, on water in the winter.'

'It must have been beautiful,' said Rose, frantically hoping she was saying the right thing. One didn't often have seraphim voicing their internal thoughts, and she was a bit concerned Lindgren might burst into holy flames if she dropped a wrong word. She had a stray, odd thought – what would it be like to marry this woman? It felt impossible. Attraction by mere mortals felt like it would wither under her singular glare. You'd have to be a supreme egotist to even try. Rose was not, and retreated from the thought like a terrified crab.

Lindgren nodded, and in a reassuringly non-angelic voice said, 'The candles have been removed. You will be pleased to know.'

'A victory well-won,' said Rose, feeling more secure, and hoped that the Captain had found somewhere else to put the offending waxen articles that wouldn't get him into trouble with any more geniuses on board. Dr Palgrave, for instance. Though she probably wouldn't notice even if she were sleeping on them, Rose reflected. 'I hope your freezer remains clear.'

'I also,' said Lindgren, and went off to dry her gloves,

which were of course wringing wet from all the digging tent pegs out of ice.

The scientists, though not invited to the brunch itself (some pleasures were purely for the paying clientele), had been instructed not to do any journeying in the *Mouette* while the activity was ongoing, which was very sensible, Rose reflected; you hardly wanted to split the party only for one half to be attacked by a walrus and the other to sink to the bottom with a mysterious hatch-seal problem. (She had her own theories about this problem, but kept them to herself as they were likely coloured by personal events, which should not influence the perspective of a good scientist.) Instead, they were asked to stay their hands until after lunch, which was a buffet set up for one and all in the dining-hall, and which most of the brunch-takers ignored, being full of salmon blinis and caviar covered in gold leaf and 'something that looked like aubergine on toast, except it wasn't', was Boo's best assessment. He'd smuggled some of it back in his jacket pocket for the scientists, and Finn ate it with enthusiasm, despite half the bits being smashed together. Definitely not aubergine, was his own contribution.

The Captain was on hand around a single round table, as was Aabria Scott, still cackling about her adventures on the man-made arm-swings, and Kate Berg, telling her gently to stop eating so much. 'Hush,' said Aabria with spirit, 'I've the constitution of an ox. No, thank you, dear,' as a crew member attempted to provide her with a resplendently full Wedgwood coffee cup.

'Even oxen,' said Kate, looking despairingly at the plate of cakes, 'experience the wonders of indigestion,' and plopped some cruciferous vegetables on it prominently, where Aabria could ignore them.

'Probably quite brutally,' said Boo, who was eating an egg salad sandwich with one half of his face and talking out of the other half. 'They have four bits to their stomachs.'

'Dromedaries,' came an unexpected voice, 'have *three* compartments in their digestive tracts. I remember an interesting problem on a camelid farm in California in which the animals were all bleaching unexpectedly. They called me, as I had just published a paper on animal colouration change, and the local vet feared some kind of outbreak.' It was, of course, Dr Palgrave, who had appeared out of the blue as she usually did, and was randomly picking at things on the group table.

'Was it to do with their three stomachs?' Finn asked with fascination.

'It was not,' said Dr Palgrave, with two coffee cups in one hand and a bun in the other. Boo made a noise – one of the cups had been his – but the Captain, who had been the other cup-theft victim, made a very clear soothing face at him, and he subsided. 'It turned out that a staff member on the farm had seen an instance of an albino camel on the news – in a Chinese sanctuary, I believe – and thought this would be profitable for the business, so was coming in at night to dye the camels bright white. It looked for all the world like vitiligo. Why are you all laughing? Oh,' she added, drinking from one cup and then the other, 'yes, I suppose it is funny.' And she also laughed, and wandered off.

'It is,' said the Captain, with minimal apparent sarcasm, 'always a privilege to meet the scientists on this journey,' availing himself of another cup of coffee from the hovering crew member, a Dane named Niilo who had looked for an instant as if he was going to tackle Dr Palgrave to prevent her stealing more beverages.

Finn beamed at the Captain. 'You should come along to my talk tonight. It's all about sharks!' Finn had spent some time carefully putting together the PowerPoint, which featured many photographs of Greenland sharks – not the most attractive of animals, Rose conceded, though of intense scientific interest – in high technicolour, some of them decorated with clipart of little bow ties and hats.

'I will do my very best,' said the Captain, and nodded at Finn with his fiercely attentive face, and there, thought Rose, was the clearest sign of support they would receive from the ruling class on this ship.

But there was to be no talk that night.

The *Mouette* journey went, at least initially, as planned. This time Boo Moreland assisted Dr Eder in manning the radio, though Rose had to make him promise to produce only sensible comments with a series of ever more outlandish threats, and finally enlisted Patrick as a third helper, to convince him to behave.

They submerged, and the curtain of bubbles once again rose, and Rose felt a brief flinch of panic – but she, Dr Eder,

Finn and several crew members had all gone over the seals with intense concentration. Elisabeth Lindgren had even come out to the *Mouette*'s launch platform in what seemed like an attempt to help, though mostly she stood back and made serious remarks about the smoothness of the sea and the low wind rate off the ice, which was, Rose thought, probably her method of being reassuring. The fact that Elisabeth had bothered to emerge, and was still standing on the platform when the *Mouette* went beneath the waves, left her vaguely touched. Apparently the Candle Saga had united them somewhat.

This time they moved swiftly to the port side of the ship, where the other radio transmitter was bleeping, and the second Greenland shark camera would be laid. This water was sufficiently cold that the shark, a known lover of absolutely freezing conditions, would possibly drift into it out of its known haunts in far deeper waters, Finn had explained to Bloom Highcastle, who seemed a bit concerned they were going to their deaths. 'They love the cold,' he told her, happily. 'Can't get enough of it. If the water gets too hot for them they go where it's colder.'

'I know a few ski birds like that,' said Sandy Highcastle. Now that he'd sobered up post-brunch, Rose had thought, he looked coarse and unhappy again. Sunila Singh had then engaged him in an extensive discussion of good high-end ski spots, and was doing a good job of cheering him up with comparisons of Vail and Zermatt. It was a skilfully diplomatic move on her part, though it was, perhaps, also an opportunity for her to poke fun; there was an enhanced dryness in some of her responses to Sandy's enthusiasm about après-ski places with bottle service that, inevitably, he did not catch. An act could be kind and at the same time incisive. Bloom, thought Rose, looked relieved.

The greenish light underwater was smoothed, gradually, into dark blue, and then near-black. The lights on the *Mouette* spread out into the darkness, and flecks of undersea detritus passed before them.

'I wish,' said Finn suddenly, 'that he wasn't on the ship anymore.'

'I know,' said Rose.

'Everybody's being so nice, but – I just wish it.'

'We'll get you a whole collection of Greenland sharks doing extremely interesting things on camera,' said Rose. 'Four full cameras' worth! It won't make up for it, but it will make it feel worth it.' The next twenty minutes in the darkness was spent in pleasurable discussion of the silliest things Greenland sharks might do on camera, up to and including a very slowly interpreted can-can. Work was, Rose thought, always the easiest way in which to resettle Finn; the years with the ego-bloated Martin had been strained even before the man revealed himself to be an unutterable pile of refuse, but even then Finn had sent her beautifully enthusiastic emails with videos of new shark behaviour, and once Photoshopped one of his favourite ancient and ugly specimens into a photo with Grapefruit with the title 'Best Friends'. It was now on the wall of the Azores research station, to the utter confusion of new scientists.

She herself was comforted by – what? By Finn. By Finn being all right; by Finn being protected. He was one of the core anchors of all her happiness, and keeping a wall around the soft underbelly of his gentleness – like the carapace of a crab, or a lobster – was her job. Boyfriends who had not understood this had been jettisoned with the same neatness and energy one usually gave to the disposal of biological waste materials.

They were gathering the red-flashing radio beacon and depositing the shiny Greenland camera, now baited with some rotten meat, when the crackling came down.

'Ssst – can you—'

Rose and Finn exchanged looks. 'Say again, *Dauphin*?' said Rose, with some confusion. They were quite a way from the surface; was there some further request from Dr Eder to gather weeds or something? Coming up again would take them at least fifteen minutes.

'Ssst – emergency. Please surface. Come back, please. Come back. Over.'

Boo's voice was smothered by a lot of atmosphere and water, but both Rose and Finn heard the substantial panic in it. Boo's voice became deeper with worry, and it sounded frankly baritone.

'Damn it, what now?' said Rose aloud. 'Has the Crimson Horror bitten somebody?' She took hold of the radio and said, 'Copy. Returning now. Stay in contact.'

'Copy.' That was Patrick Moreland. What was happening up there?

The *Mouette* switched its engines and began the slow,

buoyant rise to the surface. They waited for more information over the radio, but nothing was forthcoming; whatever was happening, Boo had decided not to do any running commentary.

As they came up, Finn said, 'Look!'

There was a dinghy out on the left side of the *Dauphin*, round the side. They could see its underside against the sky, bobbing through the transparency of the surface. It wasn't clear what it was doing.

'Clear to return to dock, *Dauphin*?' she asked, with some anxiety.

'Yes,' said Boo crisply, through the radio. 'You'd better get up here, you two.' There was a noise behind him that sounded like the Captain murmuring.

The *Mouette* surfaced, the bubble of it breaking through like an egg out of a saucepan, and Rose restrained herself from standing up and flattening herself against the glass. It seemed to take an age for the vehicle to be raised and moored on its perch, though it couldn't have been more than a few minutes. Boo Moreland and several staff members were working with an agility she knew indicated some kind of intense strain. The dinghy behind them, she could see through the slick on the *Mouette*'s glass, was filled with more *Dauphin*-orange clad crew, apparently investigating the water.

When the top seal cracked and the cold air dunked on her head, she grabbed Finn's hand, took a hot, sour breath, and said, 'Well?' There was the distant sound of a siren.

'Sixgill's dead,' said Boo.

—

Dr Eder came over as they were still standing in the *Mouette*, both blinking at Boo and looking very at sea. He hauled them out with surprising strength and gripped them both by the necks. 'You must be strong,' he said, 'you must be very strong. Come.' Finn held onto Rose's hand very hard, as if they were children again. They were led to the front of the ship, because it was seen as inevitable that they would want to see – whatever it was.

In absolute chaos, Rose found, it was helpful to return to first principles.

For instance: there, in fact, was a body. Nobody could deny, thought Rose clinically, that there was a body. It lay on the ice, at least eighty feet from the ship, and was clearly Dr Ben Sixgill.

He was flat on his back, and bleeding, bleeding astonishingly onto the ice, and had a sharp protrusion from his chest that made it look, at least from a distance, as if he had fallen and skewered himself on a tent peg. She noted the flare of a sock – for reasons she couldn't comprehend, he was wearing only one shoe.

Thus far incontrovertible. A body. With a tent peg in it. One-shoed. So.

'What happened?' she asked nobody in particular, in the vague hope that there was a good and scientifically sound explanation. Her mouth felt oddly sour and dry. She also nudged Finn's shoulder so that he might – look away.

Boo and Dr Eder began to explain things at full speed, at the same time, and at the sort of volume one would expect from competitive yodellers. Rose had to stamp her foot dangerously close to Boo's toes before he relented and slowed down. Dr Eder was puffing, his entire body vibrating with a kind of frustrated insufficiency that he couldn't communicate all data to her at once, in a single stream of breath. She felt profoundly sympathetic.

It turned out that nobody really knew *what* had happened. The two men, they explained to her disjointedly, were watching the *Mouette*'s progress off the left side of the ship, with the Morelands, Aabria and her nurse, and Sandy Highcastle, when there was a tremendous noise.

'Astonishing,' came the voice of Sunila suddenly. 'We were playing cards on the top deck, and we heard it clear as day.' Her set wry expression was slightly lopsided at the edges, as if it had been shaken hard. Alicia was nowhere to be seen; sometimes, Rose thought, these stentorious people weren't strong of stomach.

The noise – everybody agreed on this – was loud and animalistic, like a cry of terror. Somebody had screamed. Then there had been a gigantic splash, followed by a smaller one immediately afterward.

'It came from the stern, so we ran there,' said Dr Eder, 'to the place where the *Mouette* docks, and there was nothing—'

'—except a life buoy, the one from just by the *Mouette*'s perch, bobbing along in the brine,' chipped in Boo. His light tone was belied by the absolute bloodlessness of his lips. 'So Sandy Highcastle started to yell "Man overboard!" and the crew all arrived in a hurry. And I radioed down to you. I'm sorry. I thought we could use you, or—'

Rose said she understood. If there was a living person flailing in the water, two people in a giant seaborne bubble out of contact were less than useless.

But there hadn't been a living person, not there. Only a bobbing life buoy, and the curl of the ice off round the stern of the ship.

'And then as we were all watching,' said Dr Eder, in an astonished, almost furious voice, 'what should come bobbing up there but one shoe. *A single shoe!*' The lack of sense in it clearly offended him; he wished for an explanation, which was not forthcoming, and could not even complain about it to a Person In Charge.

Rose gathered that as the *Mouette* began its laborious journey upward like a much-beladen bumblebee, people had begun to panic about who was missing. The Captain demanded a headcount, and went to find Elisabeth Lindgren, who was in the kitchens but came to help immediately. Bloom Highcastle had been found in hysterics on the stairs to the upper deck. 'She's still going,' said Sunila, with a raised eyebrow, and Rose realised now that the sound she was hearing wasn't a siren, but a high-edged female voice wailing continuously.

'Where's Dr Palgrave?' asked Finn. Rose felt a brief surge of miserable terror.

Boo and Dr Eder exchanged a glance that Rose recognised, with some surprise, as deep exasperation. 'Asleep,' said Dr Eder, 'in her bunk. Wouldn't wake up, though I did my best. An extraordinary woman!'

'He roared fit to raise the dead,' said Boo. 'I went down with him. It was a bravura performance. But she definitely wasn't overboard, so we've left her to sleep.'

The full machinery of the *Dauphin*, Rose gleaned, had been in motion by that point. Crew members had lowered dinghies; one was rowed round to the stern to look for more evidence. Another was loosed to join in, but it had barely come away from the ship when one of the crew, a Swede named Linnea who had an unusually deep voice, stood up in it (a thing no able sea-person should ever do, but nobody could blame her) and shouted. She was pointing, not at the stern but at the prow, where the ice cap spread and the cave from the Champagne Brunch still stood half-constructed, its shell pulled back like a bonnet. And there – was the body.

First principles, thought Rose. She stood gripping Finn's hand.

Things were continuing to happen around them. The Captain was at the prow too, saying to several naval officers, 'But the water is far below freezing – how strong a swimmer is he? How did he get this thing through him? This seems unbelievable. And you say all the dinghies were on the *Dauphin* when the alarm was sounded?'

'In their standard positions on the side, with all their knots,' said Niilo unhappily, 'we'll all swear to it.'

Below them the body blossomed in a terrible combination of white and red. White coat, red blood. Rose thought improbably of the York-Lancaster rose, with its overlapping petals. Fragments of ice were breaking away from the shelf all the time, and moving past the ship in small fleets, in impersonal silence. Beside it, she noticed dimly, was a white mask, porcelain and heavy-looking, with a long velvet ribbon at each ear.

She looked over at the body – forced herself to – and said, involuntarily, 'That's not a tent peg.'

'I beg your pardon?' The full force of the Captain's tremendous attention turned to her. She could tell, even from a distance. She knew what she was talking about.

'That,' she said, with her lips nearly freezing in the wind, 'is the harpoon of a spear-fishing gun.'

There was silence.

'Captain!' came a cry from on the ice.

'Yes?' Even under extremely trying circumstances, Rose saw, the Captain was completely in command of his face. He looked at Rose for a second more, then moved his impressive head over the side of the top prow. Somebody, Rose noticed distantly, had put a blanket on her; she realised it was Dr Eder, who had also given one to Finn. A kind man, she thought dispassionately, and the thought bounced around inside her head like a jellyfish.

'The body, Captain,' said Linnea, standing beside Dr Sixgill and staring over at them, having to shout over the distance. She was unable to hide the absolute confusion from her voice. 'The body's *dry*. It's bone dry.'

12

The *Dauphin*'s inhabitants naturally gathered in the dining hall, and Rose felt that this was quite natural; there was nothing like sudden bewildering violence to make people clump together like animals in protective, whirling forma-tion. She'd seen rays do this when faced with sharks, with the weakest in the centre. Who, on the *Dauphin*, was really the weakest?

Bloom Highcastle was still sobbing off in a corner. It was, apparently, her long, wailing scream people had heard; her best explanation was that the incredibly loud shout of horror as . . . *something* went overboard had horrified her. 'It sounded like it was right next to me!' she said, with Sandy patting her hair and feeding her cups of their own branded relaxation tea, which smelt strongly of eucalyptus and expensive spas. His giant tanned face looked ashen. He had, Rose reflected, possibly not seen very much blood in his pampered life.

The crew were attempting to circulate and give pas-sengers assistance, but they were also, Rose saw, in a kind of disarray that carried a note of frustration. She eventu-ally gathered, by questioning Juhani, the crew member who'd been handed four canapés by Finn that first night and clearly felt a degree of protectiveness towards him and his family, that the vast majority of the crew hadn't been present on the deck or the bridge. Juhani revealed that they'd been attending a scheduled crew meeting on bonuses and benefits in the downstairs mess, arranged by the union representatives; even the collection of highly strung-looking kitchen skivvies had been learning about their rights. Around three had been on deck to give aid if the *Mouette* ran into difficulty, and the rest had all hurried out the second 'Man overboard' had been hollered, but it was too late.

'There were no eyes on any of it,' said Juhani, sadly. His mouth turned downward at the corners in sincere misery. 'It was bad luck.'

Was it? Rose wondered.

A thorough headcount had revealed that there was, in fact, nobody missing beyond Sixgill. 'Are you sure? Are you absolutely sure?' said Alicia Grey to the purser, who was reassuring. 'Perhaps there is somebody hiding on the ship. We should search everywhere, all the cargo and cabins.' Rose, looking at her, was astonished to see that the woman was terrified. Her broad face had shrunk closer to its bones, and looked gaunt. Sunila had come inside and was standing soothing her, stroking her white wrist, but there was something else on her face – if anything, Rose would call it a lack of surprise.

Finn was beside her making a gentle noise she recognised as his whimper of distress, so faint it would have gone unheard by anybody except her. She placed her body right beside his; they were precisely the same height, their arms pressed the length of one another, their hands wound in tightly. They were, before anything else, one another's comfort.

The Captain called for order. He spoke some excellently chosen words of regret for the fate of Dr Sixgill, which Rose thought might come from a playbook on what to say if a person died on board.

(As it happened, they did. The owners of the *Dauphin* had prepared for every eventuality, and the possibility of a wealthy, dyspeptic guest giving themselves a heart attack after too much Krug, or dying of horror at the sudden appearance of an orca off the port bow, was written into the plans.)

The Captain travelled on those directives as smoothly as if on rails. The staff doctor, whose name was Alva, had been dispatched to regard the body and grant a death certificate, with Kate Berg, Dr Eder and several large crew members for assistance in another dinghy. The crew, Rose reflected, were likely to make sure there was no funny business; but both Kate and Dr Eder had brought back the same story. 'Skewered, straight through the left lung, just below the heart,' said Kate, in a low voice to Aabria. 'We won't remove the object, but I've never seen the like.'

'Bastard stole my mask,' said Aabria with some astonishment, and Rose realised with a start that she was right; that was what *was* lying beside the dead scientist. The thick Venetian porcelain was so white that it had looked absurd on the ice, almost unreal, as if it were part of a picture-book tableau.

The unfortunate Sixgill had then – departing from the

playbook somewhat – been covered with large tarps, left with an armed guard and a spare dinghy in case of animals, and a solitary dinghy had returned to the *Dauphin*. The sight off the prow was still remarkable: now there was a *Dauphin*-orange rectangle of hammered-down weather-proof plastic, with a single stoic-looking Swede and a tranquilliser gun, and a lone white lifeboat moored off the ice. There was no longer any visible blood; any passing traveller would think it was the site of some kind of harmless accident, a luxury jape gone wrong. The Swede stared into the distance, possibly contemplating why everybody ignored the fact that he was in reality Norwegian.

The Captain then said, in his clearest tones – they were so well-projected that persons on other decks anywhere on the ship would probably have heard them, along with any circulating Greenland sharks – 'There are many questions that remain to be answered. We are confident that no other person known to the *Dauphin* has gone overboard. We do not know how, without the assistance of a dinghy, Dr Sixgill arrived on the ice; we do not know how he came to have what was identified provisionally as a spear-fishing harpoon,' and he nodded with professional gratitude to Rose, 'lodged in his body; and we do not know what, or who, went overboard prior to the discovery of his body. A preliminary search has been conducted, and a tranquilliser gun has been found to be missing.' A small ripple went through the assembled people.

'Yes, very good, that's all a fine mystery, but what is going to be *done*?' asked Alicia Grey. The heartiness had returned slightly, there was colour in her cheeks, but there was a thinness in the high notes of her voice that Rose recognised as contained hysteria.

'We are now,' said the Captain with gentle courtesy – he'd clocked the note too, thought Rose, and he knew what to do about it – 'within several hours' helicopter journey of Svalbard. It was to be a later docking point, but under the circumstances it has become necessary to fetch the Norwegian police.' There was a small noise at this announcement, but Rose didn't know where it came from. Bloom Highcastle did make a weak moan, and Sandy Highcastle pulled her to him manfully, as if he were the character on the front of a romance novel. She appeared to find it comforting, at least.

'We don't have a helicopter,' said Boo Moreland, with some confusion.

'A member of the fleet, the *Undine*, possesses a helicopter and is close by. It will shortly arrive on our helipad,' said the Captain, with the air of somebody who had everything in hand. It was a deeply calming air, a bit like having a very competent nanny ready to wrap you in a warm blanket and give you hot cocoa. Of *course*, thought Rose, there was an emergency helipad for people who were too important to travel terrestrially. 'Personnel will be dispatched to fetch the police, who will hopefully return promptly. We hope that their investigation will be conclusive and that we may continue on our proposed itinerary with only a day's delay; we will remove one later planned mooring-day so that we can remain on schedule, and you can make all your return journeys.' RIP to the second Champagne Brunch, thought Rose, though she wondered if anybody would want to go into the Dome ever again after this. They'd kept it up, probably to help protect the lone Swede from the wind – and also, she realised with a shudder, to preserve the scene. The scene!

The Captain made some future assurances that the investigation would disrupt things as little as possible – not a promise he could likely make, thought Rose grimly – and that the ship would be thoroughly searched for interlopers, two things that seemed to contradict one another, but nobody appeared to notice. Then the meeting was broken up. 'God help the people who go through my cabin,' said Aabria Scott cheerfully, in what was clearly a fulsome attempt to help people feel better. 'I should hide some salacious materials in my bedsheets to give 'em a bright spot.' Kate Berg nudged her and rolled her eyes.

'If I might speak to you both,' said the Captain's voice at Rose's elbow. She looked at him with confusion, but she and Finn went dutifully to the bridge, where they were informed – much to their shock – that *they* would be going on the helicopter.

'What? Why?' Finn looked gobsmacked.

'There is,' said the Captain, 'not much precedent for it, admittedly, but I have faith that you will be able to both convince the police that this is not a joke or a mere misadventure, and also make yourselves discreet. There are, you see, a pair of English police already on Svalbard, per the Norwegian police on the radio; and this is by registration a

British ship. My crew members may not be as persuasive as two British subjects.'

'Saying that we're feeling threatened would do more than saying a big expensive ship's reputation is at risk?' said Rose.

'Quite.' The Captain did not look put out. 'You put it very well, Dr Blanchard. You will, of course, be accompanied by a *Dauphin* representative.' Juhani promptly appeared, looking smart and well-pressed and deeply worried.

'I have,' he disclosed, 'never been in a helicopter, Captain.'

'We have,' said Finn, soothingly. 'Don't worry. You don't do much. You cover your ears and don't look down.'

'Be sure to emphasise that this is serious, and that speed is of the essence, not least because there is only so long—' The Captain gestured to the ice. Rose understood. The cold was currently working to preserve the body, but there would come a point where it would have to be removed, or it would freeze.

'What are a bunch of British police officers doing up in Svalbard?' Finn wondered as they put on their warmest coats in their cabin. Helicopter travel was often quite open to the elements; Rose put on a hat, considered, then put on another.

'Likely not anything to do with us,' said Rose. 'An Interpol investigation or something. Hopefully they'll be OK to leave it alone for a few days and certify the Crimson Horror.'

'We should probably stop calling him that,' said Finn, quietly.

They were interrupted by a knock on their cabin door. It was, much to Rose's astonishment, Sunila Singh. She was alone.

'I have to tell you something,' she said without preamble.

'Me?'

'Both of you.'

'What?'

'I saw the redheaded doctor arguing with Sandy Highcastle the night before he died.' She was speaking very rapidly. 'They were on the stairs from the top to the middle deck, and Sandy was making furious gestures with his hands. They whispered something about exhalation or exhaling to one another. I don't know what that was about. Then Sixgill threw up his hands and said, "I don't know what else to tell you; I said it was off so it's off," and ran away. Sandy looked as if he could punch his own shadow.'

'Exhalation?' That rang a vague bell for Rose – not to do with breath, no, something deeper and more convoluted – but it wasn't visible to her at this moment.

'Why are you telling us?' asked Finn, anxiously.

'Because you're about to go get the police, and because you were underwater the whole time,' said Sunila, simply. 'You're the only ones that can be trusted. You see that, don't you?'

And, horribly, Rose and Finn did.

Tom Heissen was intensely frustrated. He'd spent a day organising travel to what was, on the face of it, the only lead they had – on truck and snowmobile and horse-driven carriage and God knows what else – and had been brought up short by a call from the Norwegians asking if, please, they would have time to see some English people in a helicopter who were coming in from a boat named after a French dolphin. 'What do they want?'

'The authorities here said they were unwilling to disclose it over radio communications, sir,' said Titus. And this, thought Tom, was pretty natural, if you were wealthy and something had gone radically wrong that you didn't want to share over public lines. There must be serious money involved if they were running around in helicopters.

'The *Dauphin*. What a name.'

'I researched it in the brochures. It is,' said Titus without expression, 'a luxury yacht that began its journey in England.'

'It was at the port where the murdered Michael Keren was found, wasn't it.'

'As it happens, sir, it was.'

This was, Tom thought, almost definitely a supreme time-waster, but he was intrigued. A small port, but still, five or ten ships left it every day. What had got the wind up some British toffs so badly that they popped into their flying vehicle and came to demand his attention? He steeled himself for the usual when encountering the horribly over-privileged: treating him like smudges on the bottom of their shoe while simultaneously announcing that they paid his salary as a taxpayer (not that they paid their taxes) and that therefore he was basically their Justice Butler.

There was a mild chaotic burst of noise outside the office, which sounded like three young vigorous voices talking at once. Titus exchanged a look with the Detective Inspector, stood, and opened the door.

What arrived was, needless to say, not what he had expected.

A person dressed in a sailor's uniform, with close-cropped hair and a faintly nauseated-looking face (*ah, the helicopter*, thought Tom, who was quick off the mark) appeared first, then moved aside. Two more faces emerged, bundled up to their necks in horribly orange parkas. Tom had the brief sense of intense vertigo one has when meeting identical twins. The faces were mirrors, though the woman's, he saw, was the more intensely stamped with feeling. The man was, simply, heart-strikingly lovely.

She said, in a very clear voice, 'I don't know – they said to come to you – if you—'

She stopped.

'There has,' said the very beautiful man beside her, flapping his hands haplessly, 'been a murder.'

13

Heissen and Williams were not cleared by their headquarters to depart for the ship until the next morning, but the delay had its advantages. For one, Tom had learned the very beautiful man's name, and had the privilege of observing him drinking his morning mocha while wearing a too-big pistachio-coloured woolly hat. For another, approaching the *Dauphin* in morning light via helicopter was, Tom judged, perhaps one of the best ways to see it. It felt thoroughly cinematic: the dark prow, the gilded layers of deck shining below against the jadeite green of the Arctic water, the luxe lines of white and bronze. And, looming on the ice cap nearby like a dark sun in a child's picture, the note of strangeness: a rectangle of vivid orange tarpaulins, so bright they appeared to drag in light.

'Berths starting at £24,000 for the journey, save for the scientists, who are paid a small stipend for their period aboard,' said Titus briefly in his ear, as the Blanchards disembarked ahead of them. 'Six suites with bathrooms, one reserved for the captain and family; upper dining hall and function room with extended lounge; lower mess, crew dormitories, cabins for scientists and chef, laboratories, kitchen, storage and cargo, observation lounge on upper deck, bridge, mounting for submersible.' He would, Tom was certain, later resurface with ship schematics.

The Captain was here to meet them, and fitted exactly with what Tom had expected: a naval personage with the diplomacy of somebody used to mediating extraordinary egos. He was without pomposity or excess; he simply was what he was. Time would tell whether the smoothness of his manner was covering over some kind of nick or scratch beneath the surface of the Captain's estimable reserve.

They were given the separate bedroom off the Captain's own suite for operations – it was, the Captain said, usually kept free for family of senior staff, with the unembarrassed implication that he was not encumbered by any such complications – and were made aware of the basics of the situation.

'A strange series of events, which would lead one to believe in a man overboard but in fact seemed to lead to a man done to death on ice,' said Heissen, briefly.

'That seems to be the sum of it,' said the Captain. 'If you'd like to view the body? We would prefer to make it available to you as soon as possible – the weather conditions being—'

There was no need for this Sixgill to be turned into a popsicle after the first indignity of being murdered, thought Tom, and acquiesced to being put in a white dinghy and puttered gently towards the ice. It was, he reflected, far too far to jump onto the ice from the prow. Swimming or the dinghy: the two possible options. Or somehow secreting himself there beforehand?

The ice shelf was slippery, almost blue underfoot in the light. The body, with its shock of red hair, had definitely died from the very sharp-tipped object they'd sensibly left in the wound. Identified, the Captain had said, by the female twin as a harpoon from a spear-fishing gun, though there wasn't supposed to be anything of the kind on the ship. Tom had asked briefly after the cooking staff, but had been informed of the laws of the Arctic and of the chef's stringent policy against hunting. (Something that would be far less readily accepted on a non-scientific vessel, he reflected; if this were just a pleasure cruise for the super-rich, some exception might be made to spear a little Arctic cod off the side for dinner. With scientists and an oversight committee? No. And yet that harpoon had come aboard somehow.) And yes, there was that missing tranquilliser gun, which had still not been found.

The shoe that had floated around off the rear of the ship had been positively identified as the scientist Sixgill's, though it was not possible for him to have dived off the back, swum to the ice and dried himself completely in the time between the splash and the body's discovery; in fact it would have been a mission to swim that far at all. The water, the Captain explained, was so low a temperature that death would be very rapid if anybody fell overboard. So swimming was out. But the dinghies seemed not to have moved, or at least nobody had observed them. Which, he thought, looking at the bright white body of the dinghy bobbing up and down on the darkened sea like a particularly large white cat (he was, at that moment, missing Biscuit badly), seemed unlikely. But unlikely things did happen.

He and Titus inspected the body, and turned out the

pockets. Nothing. He was very warmly and nicely dressed, and there was the matter of that weird mask, which was lined inside with some kind of felt. If he'd been out and about for some more hare-poking, he'd be attired for it, but there was no scientific equipment or in fact anything of any kind; nothing on him except for a packet of tissues in one white pocket. There was some slickness about the knees, which was very likely from where Sixgill had fallen over after being struck, but otherwise – nothing. That broken nose would certainly have to be explained, but it was band-aged and at least a day old.

The dome and its pile of abandoned tent pegs, materials and deconstructed elements were inspected too, but there had been no sign of any other instrument of doom, and the crewman who'd been left to guard the body had insisted no one had touched anything, and neither had any passing wildlife. And this, thought Tom, was probably true, as people would have been gawking at the body all day with precious little opportunity to meddle unnoticed. The ice bore far too many footprints, around the body, around the dome, and all over the place; wind and water had also done their work to smooth down the surface radically. At least, thought Tom with mild disgust, it was clear that there was one wound, and then Sixgill went over backward. But from where?

'I think,' he told the large and obedient crew members who had attended them, 'this can be safely removed back to the ship now.' He hadn't a clue what the protocol was for bodies on ships like this – put them in the cold store?

– but guessed, accurately, that they probably had one. The collection of *Dauphin* crew started to move Dr Sixgill onto a stretcher, which they decorously covered in a sheet. There was no paper clutched wildly in the hand, no mysterious clue under the body when it was moved. Just a dead man with a strange sharp stick in him, thought Tom with annoyance.

He stood with Titus looking back over the water at the *Dauphin*. A broad, white face was staring at them from the top of the prow. Its auburn hair flashed and blew in the sunlight.

'I wonder who that is,' said Tom, and with a faintly mischievous air he waved. The face disappeared immediately.

A staff member said, 'Sir. Should we clean – the scene? Would that be helpful? I ask because blood will – there's wild animals out here, sir.'

Blood from various assailants? The body hadn't any defensive wounds, but that didn't mean much. Titus said, 'I'm afraid freezing and thawing of blood samples has been shown to degrade the DNA, sir, but we can take samples for analysis in any case.'

'Yes. Do it anyway.' Tom sighed and left Titus to his work with Q-tip and sample bottles, though he probably wouldn't have much luck with chipping bits of blood off the ice. He had detected something – something withheld, something on the verge of being told – in the Captain's face as he handed Tom into the dinghy, and planned, when he got back to the vessel equivalent of the Queen of Sheba, to pump him extensively.

It didn't actually take any prompting at all. 'I would,' said the Captain, 'like to tell you something that may have no bearing whatever on this affair, but could be important nonetheless.' And he mentally removed his note from its filing-place and detailed his sense of unease at the beginning of the voyage, with the crisp delineation of detail of a man who is always procedurally sound.

Tom had been given a healthy distrust of people's Sensations Of Doom from years on the force, but knew this was not an after-the-fact piece of attention-seeking and that the Captain was, in fact, not particularly pleased at having felt it, as some people were.

'I am aware,' said Captain Johannsson, with what some people might view as mind-reading but public-facing specialists knew was merely part of their job, 'that this may seem emotionally driven and fantastical, but I can assure you it is not so.'

'I know,' said Tom, and he did. The Captain was an instrument, measuring all aspects of his domain at all times; that he had noted *something* wrong and been very disturbed by his inability to diagnose it, Tom believed implicitly.

There was some light shouting outside, which Tom ignored. 'What did you do to investigate this sensation?'

'My enquiries came to nothing. The crew are as they were. The cargo is all accounted for. All passengers appear to correspond with their identity documents,' said the Captain, with a faint gesture of worry.

Tom had a brief flash – 'Did you get this sensation in port?'

The Captain looked at him with very clear eyes. 'Yes. It began then.'

'A port intern,' said Tom, 'was found murdered several days ago.'

The Captain absorbed this information with what was clearly shock, but also – Tom noted it without judgement – a kind of quiet reaffirmed faith in his own instincts. 'There were, I remember, only the dockworkers handling the mooring ropes to see us off – usually there's an administrative person with a clipboard as well. Not necessary, but usual. It was the one point of change in the entire experience, and yet – it seemed quite innocuous. They do change personnel schedules, you see. And yet.'

'Quite.'

'This would be why you are up in Svalbard, then.'

'It was relevant to another investigation,' said Tom smoothly, with the quiet professional implication that he could discuss nothing else. As he'd assumed, the Captain read this with the clarity other people reserved for newsprint.

'Yes, of course. Well. We are at your disposal.' The Captain had now come onto familiar ground, which was to represent the ship against forces of chaos and upset.

'The body will be kept on board until it's released to the victim's family?'

'That's the usual procedure, yes. It will go into a storage locker that is unheated. We carry body bags. The door of the locker will be locked.' There was, at this point, a substantively escalated yelling explosion in the corridor, shared between what sounded like four crew members at once, all in separate but identically unhappy-sounding Scandinavian languages.

The Captain put his head out the door and said, 'It's what? You must be— During the night? Well, this is most catastrophic. Detective Inspector, I am afraid I have bad news for you.'

'Are the victim's papers all stolen or burned?' asked Tom, with interest.

The Captain looked at him as if he'd suddenly appeared in the sky bearing a thousand burning eyes and barking BE NOT AFRAID.

'The window's open,' said Tom, relenting. 'I heard some yelling on the bottom decks about papers and a cabin a few minutes ago, and thought it was probably a good guess.'

'You are,' said the Captain, in apparent relief at not being visited by somebody of supernatural omniscience, 'unfortunately correct. Please.' And gestured with his huge freckled hands for them to go together.

Sixgill's cabin had, it seemed, been guarded during the daytime but not overnight, for which Tom couldn't blame anybody; they were not police or investigators, and there was a corpse lying drastically close to the ship, which they had at least managed to preserve valiantly. A crew member named Otso, who appeared quite bright, had just gone down to actually open the cabin door, to see if it was ready for the newly arrived investigators, and had discovered what Tom would now, looking at it with the freshly returned Titus from the doorway, describe internally as 'a complete shit-show'.

Papers were everywhere. Things had been pushed off shelves, or speckled in water; the answer to that lay in the fact that the porthole window, on the port side of the ship, was open. The room was freezing cold. Whatever had been in here to disturb somebody's equanimity, thought Tom, was likely long gone, floating out that window to be dispersed among put-upon colonies of seals.

This wasn't, Tom surmised quickly, an attempt to disarrange, destroy or show anger; it was a purposeful search for something specific, made to look chaotic as a cover.

'A very performative ransack,' said Titus, clearly of the same thought. They both knew, from long and exhausting experience, that there were distinct patterns of difference between a real, furious room destruction and a covert search; for one, the truly irate wrecked anything within reach, up to and including innocent furnishings. (A disgruntled ex-employee at a scene Tom had once attended had somehow pulled the filling out of several expensive sofas and rained it down everywhere like asbestos.) People combing the joint, though, looked first and wrecked afterwards, often in little pockets like mushrooms. Whoever had been in here was also trying to stay quiet – the chair, which would have come apart nicely with one giant smack, remained intact.

'And now,' said Tom with a heavy sigh, 'we'd better do fingerprinting and the rest of it. And a cabin search, just in case Sixgill's things didn't end up tossed into the wide blue yonder.' He looked at the Captain, who was goggling at the mess on his very nice ship with perhaps more distaste than he'd given to the scene on the ice. The dead man was, after all, some kind of lurid misadventure, and therefore basically not real; this catastrophic untidiness, however, was his domain, and it had Gone Wrong, and he was clearly rather put out about it. 'I'm sorry to trouble you about the ship being searched, but it can't be helped. Whose prints will we find in here, do you think? Sixgill's, and the cleaning staff? Any love affair?'

'Oh, no,' said the Captain instinctively, then clearly thought better of it. 'I wouldn't know, of course,' he said more stiffly, 'but there certainly wasn't any outward sign. My fingerprints will be in here, as will those of a few of the crew – we came looking for him when the Man Overboard sounded, and I came down with the purser after the death was observed to see – well—'

'If there was a suicide note. Very sensible of you. And you found nothing?'

'Regrettably, nothing at all. If I may say so, the man was slovenly in his habits, but I was led to believe notes are generally prominently displayed, and there was no visible sign.'

He could be lying, but Tom believed not. This, he thought, really did press the Captain's buttons; if there had been a note it could have been written off as a dramatic episode of unhinged scientific persons who spent too much time alone thinking about obscure Arctic weeds, and so decided to end it all by – flying to the ice cap and shoving a harpoon in themselves? If this was a suicide, it was an unusual one. Given certain facts – the lack of note, the raid on Sixgill's rooms – Tom's instincts were beginning to lean away from suicide and into something else.

'I would say,' said Titus in his inexpressive voice, 'that the person involved in this wore gloves and cleaned up after themselves, sir.'

And that was likely true; the visible bits of surface between the piles of detritus were eerily clear-surfaced. Somebody with a cloth and a quickness. A good biography title for a cleaner, thought Tom with some annoyance, and then said, 'Right, let's dive in.'

Titus had been, as Titus usually was, correct. They stood over the collection of scientific papers, notes, letters and journals without much to show for it: a partial print here, a smudge there.

'There is,' said Titus, picking up a journal in his own gloved hands, 'a notable absence of personal materials, sir.'

'No laptop, no diary, no phone,' said Tom. 'If they've been hidden somewhere on the ship we'll have to find them, though we can't move on that until we have permission for searches. Scientific equipment of all kinds, that doesn't appear to have been the worry for our Mysterious Bump In The Night.' He poked at a radio transmitter, which smelled of salt and looked decidedly broken. It had been split in the centre in an apparent desultory attempt to replace its battery pack. Sixgill had certainly been on his way up; a great number of the articles strewn about the desk were his, published in journals even Tom had heard of. There was also, he noted, no wallet or ID; passports were kept with the Captain in the safe, which was standard procedure on these elaborate cruises, but nothing else. If he'd been on his way out of the world he'd certainly erased all sense of himself on the journey.

'If they were all thrown overboard,' said Titus, 'we do have an advantage, sir. There is, the Captain tells me, a submersible.'

'That bubble-looking spaceship? Absolutely not. No.'

'It would,' continued Titus, unperturbed, 'allow us to pursue a thorough underwater search with a trained operative. It would be preferable to attempting to drag the bottom, for environmental reasons, and would stand in admirably for a police diver, who could not operate in this location.'

'You can do it,' said Tom hotly. 'You can go down into the freezing depths in something that looks like it belongs in a toddler's tub. I wish you luck with it.'

'Oh,' said a small voice by the door. They both looked up. The staggeringly beautiful Blanchard twin was standing there looking a bit lost. Tom opened his mouth, made a face, and shut it. It was difficult enough dealing with a bizarre case of a flying corpse without rampantly pretty men running around, he thought, indignantly.

'Yes?' said Titus, seamlessly fitting in where his superior should have said something.

'The *Mouette*'s very good, you know,' said Finn, very fast. 'I was coming down to tell you – if you wanted it – I can drive it. Rose is brilliant but she's taught me a lot. If you don't want to, though, you can just tell us what to look for – we thought it might be helpful.' He looked anxiously around the cabin. 'Did something explode?'

'No, nothing exploded. Your offer is very kind,' said Titus.

'I know it seems like a bath toy, but it really isn't,' said Finn pleadingly to Tom, who felt grumpy. He always felt grumpy when excessively attractive people were nice to him. It seemed unfair.

'I'll think about it,' he said shortly, and turned his back to bend over the pile of scientific nonsense again.

'Thank you, Dr Blanchard,' said Titus, who was apparently functioning as his social secretary today. 'We will discuss the matter more fully with you later.'

'Yes,' said Finn, with an uncertain glance at Tom's back, and left.

'You are being most impolite,' said Titus reprovingly to Tom, who made an upset noise at the floor. 'Dr Blanchard was being very nice. And besides—'

'He and his sister have an alibi?'

'Precisely, sir.'

'Stop making me friends and keep making that inventory,' said Tom, hotly. Titus smiled, and busied himself putting the radio transmitter in an evidence bag.

'Did you ask?' said Rose, when her brother resurfaced onto the deck with his curls bouncing on his head.

She welcomed the distraction. She'd been trying to get the entire situation straight in her head, and had even started making a mental spreadsheet of timelines, but it hadn't done much good. She was conscious of a grim relief that she and Finn had been safely on the *Mouette* while the chaos unfolded above them; otherwise, after the nose-splintering incident, they'd be first on the list of suspects for putting a harpoon through him. Why, she wondered, had it happened *then*, of all times? Science rarely permitted accident or coincidence, but it was still a factor one had to consider (Grapefruit, of course, created accidents like some people made cups of tea). Were the twins being protected, in some obscure way? Or was it simply the most convenient time – when everybody was watching them descend to poke around for some thoroughly innocent sharks?

'The Detective Inspector doesn't like deep water, I think,' said Finn a bit unhappily. 'He called the *Mouette* a bath toy and then wouldn't talk to me.'

'He is just doing his job,' said Rose.

'And it does look a bit like a bath toy,' added Boo Moreland in a helpful tone. He'd been poking at Rose for an hour with a paper plane he'd made, largely to try and make her stop worrying over the Sixgill situation. He poked her again in the stomach and she swatted at him.

A thought struck Rose. There hadn't been much to do on the helicopter ride back except to observe the new arrivals, one of whom seemed quite intent on not looking at Finn at all.

'Did he turn away and look a bit red when you went downstairs?' she asked, innocently.

'Yes. I know he was very busy, but I did just want to help.'

'He seems very busy. And very strong,' said Rose with

an air of irrelevance. 'He looks like he could pick up the *Mouette* and throw it, if it came to that.'

'Er . . . yes.' Finn went a very delicate shade of pink and looked a bit like a Meissen shepherdess. 'The other one seemed keen on the idea of going down in the submersible, though I don't know what they'd be looking for.'

'Well, one of us will just have to escort them. We'd better check over all the seals again in case they want to do it quick smart.'

'Ooh, and I can see if anybody's taken a bite of the camera-fish yet! There's nothing on the feed, but it could have drifted over behind . . .' Finn bustled away looking much more pleased.

Boo kicked Rose in the shin. 'What are you up to now?'

'Ouch, you moronic mutt. Finn deserves something nice now and then.'

'That,' said Boo loftily, 'would compromise the investigation,' and dodged expertly as Rose went for him with the discarded paper plane.

14

Tom and Titus, in their serene forest-scented separate stateroom, operated much as they would in a British police station, though with far more expensive pens. The stationery granted to them by the Captain was all thick and embossed with the *Dauphin*'s monogram, a dolphin soaring through a crown in a blur of expensive branding. The pens had a weight to them that indicated they had possible platinum cores, or were habitually used to scribble little notes that earned thousands on the stock market when translated by brokers. Titus had been persuaded to keep his shoes on with some difficulty, and still eyed the gloriously polished boards and months-of-rent plush carpet with concern. Tom, who had grown up on a single teacher's salary in Sheffield, eyed it uneasily too, concerned it might bite him.

They had a small and unspoken argument about Titus's pile of shivs. It seemed that he had brought several of the finest Svalbard examples aboard, out of what Tom could only imagine was a kind of officiousness bordering on nesting behaviour. Tom eyed them, eyed Titus, and demanded silently that they be put somewhere entirely out of sight where he wouldn't accidentally sit on them. Titus unabashedly complied, and Tom fervently hoped that would be the end of it.

Now they assembled their list. There was, for every

investigation, a beginning list, essentially an exercise in hope for simplicity. Said hope was inevitably dashed as the list expanded capaciously in all directions, like Biscuit settling his body on a flat surface. At the moment, the list stood nice and stark on their portable whiteboard: Sixgill Personal & Bank Accounts; Fingerprints; Passports; Interviews (Crew & Passengers); Post-mortem; Cabin Search Permissions (Warrants). From there, it would branch into a bizarre tree of unknown genus and uncertain fruit.

And in Titus's private notebook, the old M/M/O graph, as yet unpeopled by anything: means, motive, opportunity. Time of death was at least a narrow window: the Captain had managed to gather together brief written observations from the medical staff, an onboard nurse and somebody called Dr Klaus Eder. They all stated Sixgill had still been warm and the blood freely pooling when they arrived, which indicated that he was discovered soon after being struck. The cold complicated things slightly, but the window was perhaps thirty minutes – not, he thought, more. The post-mortem might give more detail. That would have to be on the ship; they'd have to call a police doctor in. They'd already asked the Captain for the cabin search warrants.

So: a shout, a splash – and then, remarkably, death.

The shape of life on the ship was sketched out using a passenger manifest. On the stateroom level, all the suites were occupied: the Captain held the one closest to the prow (Stateroom 1). From there, front to back, the labels read: Singh & Grey (Stateroom 2); Moreland & Moreland (Stateroom 3); Moreland (Stateroom 4); Highcastle &

Highcastle (Stateroom 5); and the last, Scott & Berg (Stateroom 6). Below decks, the cabins were occupied by E. Lindgren, Drs F & R Blanchard, Dr Eder, Dr Palgrave and Dr Sixgill – though no longer. There were laboratories, an infirmary and a crew mess, and, on the level below that, the crew sleeping quarters and storage. Tom, looking at this list, paused to appreciate this stage of investigation: a blankness, in which nothing yet attached to these names, no flesh or stories or inferences. It was the quiet point before the plunge. He took a deep breath.

Without any personal effects, a picture of Sixgill on an intimate level was difficult. His papers and resumé revealed him as an up-and-coming biologist from the American South with a good academic pedigree: post-docs, assistant professorships, various awards. His family was solidly middle-class. He appeared to specialise in, of all things, Arctic rabbits – or hares. Tom hadn't learned the distinction, was sure Titus knew, and was also sure that was sufficient to be getting on with. Accordingly Sixgill seemed to bounce around the world in a leporine fashion; there were mentions of fellowships in Canada and the Netherlands, conference papers in Norway, and something about tracking invasive rabbit numbers on a small island off Greenland. The picture on his university page showed a red-headed man with a wide, slightly sly smile, squinting into the light. He had no discernible relationships or children, and an infrequently updated, boastful social media page which largely showed him in sunglasses doing field work in various locales with hashtags like #blessed, all of which

Titus noted scrupulously. His nose, before being broken, had been small and delicate.

The substance of the investigation, therefore, was the same as on land: look for an overall picture, find inconsistencies. Personal interviews with the crew, all of whom were fully alibied, only revealed that they were exceptionally well-paid, thought the Captain was the sun rising out of the east, and some were frankly upset they couldn't use their overboard-passenger training and earn prestige and a hefty bonus. Nobody knew anything about any smuggling, no matter how subtly it was introduced into the conversation, though a person called Niilo confessed he was keeping some cigars in his cabin that were not strictly permitted onboard, which Tom graciously agreed to ignore. The person who had discovered the body, one Linnea Eklund, had some distinct Thoughts about the recklessness of a passenger on *her* ship getting themselves murdered, which Tom wrote down carefully to soothe her feelings.

All their stories were consistent: no crew member had been out of place, and none of them had seen any of the dinghies unmoored at any point between the end of the brunch and their launching to look for the phantom floating body of Sixgill. The life buoy on the rear had also been in situ when last inspected that morning, but it was designed to be easily removed and thrown at any time.

They moved on to look at the passports, which yielded nothing of interest beyond an instructive impression of the ways in which the itinerant rich spent their time. Aabria Scott, as far as Tom and Titus could tell, barely stayed in her university town in the US for a month at most before she was off again. She was, Tom recalled from an old *Paris Review* interview, the widow of a famously eccentric financier. Her leather passport folder was also crowded with luggage labels, old plane tickets, and one vaguely startling photograph of her in the middle of a cruise ship's shuffleboard court, surrounded by smiling naval officers in various states of shirtlessness, with the line '*Winner of Onboard Tournament – The Princess '14'* scrawled underneath.

Alicia Grey was, he noted with interest, born in an obscure bit of northern Scotland that even his own Highlander great-aunt had referred to as 'just stones and sheep farts'. Grey and Sunila Singh hopped around every winter: the Maldives, Switzerland, Mauritius! If you were born into sheep farts, it doubtless made sense to follow the sun. Meanwhile the scientist Dr Palgrave's passport, for instance, was barely six months old and bore only the marks of a few trips between the US and Canada. Dr Klaus Eder was at least representing the side; the man's German-issued passport was thick with three- or four-day trips to obscure universities, the mark of a man who sustained himself on conferences and lucrative guest-speaker positions. Tom made a pointed effort not to look at Dr Finn Blanchard's extremely charming passport photo (with his hair pushed back out of his face so that he looked a bit like a startled Botticelli angel) for more than two seconds. He put the pile aside, stretched, and looked at Titus.

'*Now* we get into the real fleshy game and tuberous veg-etables,' he said.

143

'The meat and potatoes? Yes, sir,' said Titus. The two of them took a refined sort of specialist's delight in interviews; Tom had a veritable Swiss army knife's worth of approaches, while Titus remained an extremely observant non-entity until anybody required a quiet reminder of the necessity for manners.

First there was Dr Klaus Eder: eminent, they both judged, and rather full of his own eminence. Heissen summed him up rapidly as the real deal: he'd done some quiet googling and Dr Eder's face and voice showed up as identical in TED talks and speeches, pompous and slightly affectedly low-pitched. He struck a pose in his waistcoat that was meant to radiate professional decorum. Tom supposed privately that if you spent your time pottering around in slime at the edges of rocks, it was worth assuming as much dignity as possible.

He'd been helping to man the submersible radio when the scream and the alarm went up, he said sniffily, giving the distinct air that he'd been doing all the real work. Somebody named Boo Moreland – Tom boggled at him slightly – was with him, as was Patrick Moreland, and Sandy Highcastle was making himself a nuisance on deck as usual. Aabria Scott and her nurse person were making polite conversation with Gladys Moreland somewhere or other. (Boo, then, must be the other male Moreland with the faintly insouciant expression in his passport photo). No, he hadn't seen Sixgill since the brunch, and he hadn't seen anybody dive into the water.

Titus noted all the names carefully; it would, Tom thought heavily, be much easier when they could match them to real faces rather than washed-out, bland passport photographs. 'Why did you go out on the ice to view the body?' he asked conversationally. It had struck him as unusual in the notes. People with no reason to go poking at bodies usually didn't, often out of understandable disgust.

'I have some medical training,' the doctor said, a little stiffly. That wasn't on his resumé, but Heissen made a private guess – dropped out of medical school young and switched to algae – and filed it away, just in case. 'And—' Eder bent forward a little hurriedly, squishing the buttons of his waistcoat. 'It seemed unwise for one person to go unsupervised by anybody but the crew.'

'You wanted to keep an eye on the nurse Kate Berg and the doctor? Very sensible of you. And you were curious, I suppose.' Berg herself, her passport noted, had clearly made a good deal: born in a bad suburb of Birmingham, years of nothing much, and then what Heissen assumed was a switch to private nursing, which coincided with the pages suddenly flowering with elegant watering-destination stamps across Europe. Tom felt obscurely proud of her leap up in the world, in a conceptual working-class sort of way.

'It wouldn't have been beyond him,' muttered the superior Eder, 'to cover himself in tomato sauce and then leap up and terrify us.'

Tom let this pass. *Doesn't like Sixgill*, he noted, and had no idea how many times he would write that particular phrase. 'Did you break his nose?' he added conversationally.

'Of *course* not.' Dr Eder shored himself up with indignation and left the room like an affronted ocean liner. Much to their mild surprise, Tom and Titus both noted that he made no remark as to who *had* broken said nose; it seemed clear from Dr Eder's reaction that it was, indeed, a person, and not a stray encounter with a porthole window.

'This nose,' said Tom quietly to Titus after Dr Eder had left, 'may be a problem.'

'Protecting somebody who had already committed violence against Sixgill, sir?'

'Possibly. We'll have to tread carefully. I do hate when people take up a code of *omertà* about things. Never helps.'

Sunila Singh answered questions clearly and without any noticeable reticence, as did Patrick Moreland, who bore the loose, charmingly baffled expression of a truly clever person clearly unburdened by the urge to show it off in company. Both were steady and intelligent observers. Singh was real wealth – Titus privately estimated to him afterwards that her earrings alone must be in the low six figures – all, notably, self-made. She'd left the civil service to become a tech entrepreneur, and Tom, observing her sharp eyes, couldn't blame her; she was clearly a person of rapid decisions, which wasn't the sort of thing British civil servants liked very much. She was assessing them as much as they were assessing her. She also made a light remark at one point – 'McCarthy is still head of the CID, isn't he?' – that, while delivered with absolute pleasantness, made it perfectly clear that she was connected, and that any perceived mishandling would be communicated immediately to illustrious friends. Tom had, frankly, expected more of this sort of thing, and met it with his normal tactic, which

146

was disarming pleasure that they had a person in common and complete refusal to acknowledge any hint of a threat. Sunila Singh appeared to find this approach respectable, and even faintly amusing. *Entirely too much personality for Whitehall*, Tom wrote. She hadn't been in view of the shenanigans; she and her wife had been on the top deck, and had only been called down by the ruckus. Tom made a note to check this – that deck was in full view of the bridge, so perhaps somebody on the skeleton crew besides the wife could corroborate it.

Neither she nor Moreland showed any particular grief over Sixgill, and Patrick Moreland, likeable and bending his tall head forward, had given a strict summary of the various remarks Sixgill had passed about Finn on the night before his death. 'Unpleasant,' he said drily, 'and looking for a reaction.' He did not, Tom noted, share what the reaction was. He stoppered a bubbling feeling that hoped it had been very disagreeable for Sixgill.

'Is that,' he asked politely, 'when he sustained the broken nose?'

'That isn't my story to tell,' said Patrick Moreland, with the kind of coolness one would expect him to use against an undergraduate angling for a slightly disreputable grade revamp. If Moreland had spectacles, thought Tom wryly, he'd be peering over them disapprovingly. That *omertà* again. Moreland certified that Dr Eder and Boo (the nickname remained unexplained) had been with him, and that Sandy Highcastle had hung off the rail 'making silly remarks'. Scott, Patrick's wife and the nurse Kate Berg were around somewhere too, but he'd been too fascinated with the radio to note where they were all the time. Highcastle's wife, he noted drily, had a powerful set of lungs on her.

A picture of Sixgill was building, and it was not a charming one. Eder clearly viewed him as professionally inferior and therefore slightly below notice, though there was a note in his voice – contempt? frustration? – that didn't quite line up with his attempt at detached egotism. *Sixgill got his goat somehow*, Heissen judged. Sunila Singh clearly found Sixgill's attitude mildly perplexing, but was not attempting to explain it; *that* would be your job, her clear gaze seemed to challenge them. And Patrick Moreland, as befitting a tutor in law, was mostly concerned with the precision of details in their correct order, and disappointingly free of imaginative speculation, which was the fun bit.

Gladys Moreland they both greeted with mild surprise; they knew her by sight from a murder case several years earlier, where she'd been prosecuting for the Crown. Her archness and deep knowledge of arcane parts of the law were legendary; she'd done years in the International Criminal Court before descending to the domestic level to take silk, and Tom knew that men in legal chambers across the country made soft curses when her name was mentioned. The case hadn't gone well, the defence had succeeded in an act of eel-like wriggliness, and she looked at them ruefully. 'Well, friends, let's hope this one goes better,' she said, in place of a greeting.

Sixgill, she said with a prosecutor's directness, was possessed of the absolute conviction that he was allowed to

148

bully anybody in sight, but that wasn't what interested her. 'I've known people on the make,' she said. 'He was on the make. I don't know how, but he was of that ambitious sort. Passing upsetting remarks was possibly his way of keeping people off-balance so that he could use them to advantage. This is, of course, all theory.' That amount of vaulting ambition seemed faintly out of place in a scientist, Tom thought, then reminded himself of stories of competition for tenure and funding from an ex-academic mate at the pub that had, horrifyingly, all the stakes and gore of gladiator matches. No, bloodthirstiness would seem to be an asset for Sixgill.

She was clear about her own movements – on and around the open deck, occasionally going in to the dining room to get a cup of tea 'and escape the absolute nonsense of Sandy Highcastle', she said freely. 'Talking about his spirit animal being a walrus. Honestly. I chatted with Aabria Scott and her nurse in passing. Have you met Aabria yet? You're in for a treat. Runs that nurse half demented, I suspect, but she's a character, and not in the way that old people are called "characters" as code for "belligerent and offensive".'

'She is quite an *elderly* lady,' said Tom, with a faint question in his voice.

'Not muddled or senile in the slightest,' said Gladys, promptly. 'Has all her wits, and a complement of other people's wits into the bargain. You wait.'

And, happily, as Tom had slyly hoped, Gladys was the one to break the *omertà*. 'Of course the men would be honourable and stupid about that,' she said briskly. 'Dr Rose Blanchard did it. A direct hit, and a deserved one. He was saying some absolutely repulsive things about her brother in public company, purely to cause offence – no idea why. Boo threw one at the same time and cracked himself quite hard on the arm. He's always had a good sense of honour, bless him.'

'Would you have been less forward about this if the Blanchards weren't underwater for the entire time this rigmarole was apparently playing out?' Tom asked, with a sense of being immensely brave before one's head teacher. Gladys grinned.

'I don't hold with secrets. I'm prosecution, not defence. But wait 'til you talk to the Blanchards. You'll see why other people were being protective, I expect.' She added drily that she'd had to shake Bloom Highcastle quite hard to get her to stop her hysterics when they'd spotted the floating shoe. 'In the old days,' she said, 'dapper old gentlemen of the court would say her *nerves weren't strong*, and hand her handkerchiefs on the witness stand.'

'And this wasn't on deck?'

'No, not where I found her. She was making a weird low moaning noise on the staircase between the upper and lower decks.'

'What was she doing there?'

'You'd have to get that out of her.' She looked at them both. 'I'm not going to ask what you two were doing running around Svalbard. I know you can't tell me. But I will say I'm grateful – that it's you.'

'*Is* she grateful?' said Titus quietly, after the most formidable silk in England had left the room.

'I wonder,' said Tom.

Bloom Highcastle was not going to let it, whatever *it* was, out of her particularly easily. She was a familiar sort, Tom thought: not stupid, but so worked up about a problem likely of her own making that they'd have to coax her out by essentially leading her by the nostrils, like a frantic *eau-de-parfum*-scented calf. They tried all variants of attack – soothing, Titus being strict and Tom being relenting, letting her sob in the hope she'd surface and say something sensible – but she wouldn't be drawn. Tom was of the opinion that her hysterics were partly based on the idea that she'd done something wrong and was absolutely terrified to reveal it. Perhaps, he thought with surreal frustration, she'd been trying to steal some of the ship furnishings, and comforted himself with the thought of Mrs Aldous, a Chanel-wearing old hand who was perpetually being called up for acts of kleptomania at Claridge's. Unfortunately, he remembered, the stairs didn't have anything ornate for her to steal – just a thick bannister and a white, moulded wall sculpture that looked like somebody had had a tantrum with some icing.

'I think,' he said eventually, 'that will be enough, Mrs Highcastle, but if you do remember why you were on those stairs, please slip us a note, will you?'

The hint of head teacher disapproval finally did it. 'I don't mean to be a *problem*,' gasped Bloom with a wide-open mouth. She had that particular coruscating thinness of women who subsisted mostly on acai smoothies and the chanting of their yoga instructors, thought Tom. 'It's just – it's all very terrible. I was meant to be going up to see

Sunila and Alicia – from the deck, you know, they were on the top level playing cards and invited me, and I said I'd go see them – so I was on the stairs walking up, you see.' She stared at them haplessly mid-breath, as if she'd wandered into a hole and got stuck. There was something odd in her expression – a kind of question.

'Yes,' said Tom, encouragingly, 'you were going up?'

The reassurance of the direction seemed to spur her. She gave a great breath. 'And there was this appalling noise. Just an outstanding scream. Really a scream. And it seemed to come from right beside me. I thought – honestly I thought it was a spirit. I've always been very connected to the spiritual realm,' and she tried to summon what Tom knew was meant to be a moony smile, though it mostly hovered around her face without quite landing. 'But it wasn't. It was – something else. I don't know what happened. It sounded like nothing on earth.'

'That,' said Tom gravely, 'is very interesting. I am grateful to you, Mrs Highcastle.' *Now take a note back to your teacher to excuse you from PE*, he avoided saying aloud. 'Did you like Dr Sixgill?' he added, as Bloom got up to leave the room.

She looked at him with a slight recovery of her usual manner, which was to say that she appeared faintly huffy. 'Well, *I* didn't ever really talk to him.' She made a shrugging motion. 'I mean – he was a *scientist*,' she added, as if this explained everything, and departed. And for Bloom Highcastle, Tom thought, it probably did.

Sandy Highcastle he and Titus knew all over. Blowsy market traders, men who made too many flutters and came a cropper, restaurant owners with their shirts open too far – they'd met many Sandy Highcastles, and were fully prepared for him to come in and make aggravated complaints that they'd upset his wife, which is what he did.

'You are making yourself unpleasant,' said Titus severely. 'It would behove you to sit down, sir.'

Thus flattened, Highcastle sat. 'This Sixgill business has upset everything,' he said, wiping a large hand across his seamed forehead. He went through the movements of the afternoon and discovery fairly pat, in agreement with everybody else, though Tom thought he harped on too much about how he'd been the first to yell 'Man overboard'. Then he asked, point-blank, 'Why did he do it?'

'What?' said Tom, surprised.

'Why'd he off himself?' He looked quite keen on this point, Tom noted; the face under that tan was pale and intent. 'Was he in debt or something?'

'We do not know,' said Tom quietly, 'that he did die by suicide, Mr Highcastle. He has left no signs to that effect.'

'But that's——' Highcastle gaped at them.

'Did he mention being in debt, Mr Highcastle?'

Here Sandy Highcastle floundered a bit, said the word 'chaps' too much, and left. Titus looked after him when he left. 'That,' he said, 'is a man who is very interested in money.'

'Sixgill didn't have that much money, did he? Scientists of his age don't earn much, and he doesn't come from anything spectacular.' Dr Eder had looked comfortably prosperous, but Sixgill was decades off that kind of refinement.

'We shall look into his banking details in the US. It will likely,' said Titus crisply, 'take some time.' Tom added this as a bullet point to the list, which would, he recognised heavily, likely never have a clear and simple shape again. Would somebody have killed Sixgill in that spectacular manner for some hypothetical cash? Or was it more likely – which, frankly, was beginning to be Tom's bet – that he'd got somebody's nose tremendously out of joint? Secret stabbings, hidden poisonings – those tended to be money murders. This was more florid, more outrageous, and he wanted to know *why*.

'Why would it be to Sandy Highcastle's benefit if he did die by suicide?' Tom thought of the possibility that Sandy would think he was subtly planting the idea in their minds, and dismissed it; the Highcastles of the world were not psychological operators. No, it was the first thing that had occurred to Sandy, and why remained to be seen.

Dr Salome Palgrave was at present indisposed, which nobody appeared to believe was unusual (the distinct sense of Eccentric Person floated around mentions of her, which Tom found innately suspicious and planned to investigate), so they moved onto Alicia Grey, Sunila Singh's wife. Titus and Tom both noted the auburn hair in silence. She answered questions readily – born to a good family up in Scotland (no mention, Tom thought, of the rather obscure area where this took place – perhaps keen on escaping it), orphaned young, went to London, now ran a line of prosperous rural B&Bs. But she was looking in the meantime all over their faces, and, much to Tom's astonishment, also everywhere in the room: up, down, at closets, under the bed, at places where things might be concealed. It was the act of somebody who was in fear of something. Her voice had the wisp of heartiness in it, but Alicia Grey was not feeling hearty. She confirmed that she had been on the top deck with Sunila, and fell silent.

'You asked for the ship to be searched,' said Tom, recalling something Gladys Moreland had said in her interview. 'That was very sensible of you, thank you.'

'I just felt – I *don't like death*.' And this, Tom thought, was quite true. Alicia Grey did not like death. Perhaps she'd seen something – something in that strange, bleak corner of Scotland. 'Sixgill was an ass, but nobody deserves that. It was him, wasn't it?'

'I *beg* your pardon?'

'I suppose it was – I'm expressing myself badly. It was meant to be him, wasn't it? Not – not anybody else. It couldn't have been a mistake. Could it?'

Tom, grasping her point very rapidly, said, 'Does anybody else on the ship wear that white jacket and trousers?'

'No. No, they don't; only he had one. It was for disguising himself for work, he said.' This seemed to calm her; she took several deep breaths. Then she looked at them. The hazel eyes moved into the semblance of a smile. 'I suppose I am being silly. But Sunila is really very rich, you know.'

But Alicia Grey, Tom and Titus both thought, was not petrified to the bones about the death of Sunila.

15

The non-spearfishing chef, Elisabeth Lindgren, made her entrance with no fanfare, but her remarkable face meant nobody spoke for a good ten seconds. Titus was of the opinion, when Tom expressed mild humiliation about this later, that Lindgren appeared totally used to causing consternation; she must have lived with her own face for a very long time. She had been in the kitchen doing food preparation without any of her workers to help when the Man Overboard had sounded, and as the kitchen was quite insulated from the remainder of the ship, hadn't heard it; this was why the Captain had to come fetch her. She looked faintly apologetic about this fact. Another fan of the Captain, noted Tom, and a mark in the Captain's favour at that.

The spear-fishing harpoon had, she said, been news to her. 'Those are not allowed on board,' she said with a small amount of distaste. 'Concealment must have been difficult.' She had no idea about the whereabouts of the tranquillising gun, or what anybody might have been doing with it.

Tranquillising Sixgill before stabbing him? Possible, thought Tom; the on-board post-mortem would reveal as much. There was no tranquilliser dart visible, though, so it was doubtful. It was a shame they couldn't transport the body elsewhere to do it, but the *Undine* helicopter, he had noted, didn't have the space to transport a corpse anywhere unless they hung it from the bottom on a gurney, which felt a little cruel to the nice people on Svalbard. And the longer they fussed around transporting it, the less chance they had of preserving small clues, however minuscule. Titus had, he noted, made a miniature check mark beside the Post-mortem item on the list; at some point he'd emailed the Svalbard police to organise a visitation by a police doctor.

Lindgren's life, as it was summarised in her curriculum vitae, was horribly impressive. Fortunately, Tom thought, she was possessed of such an intimidating face that you accepted her gifts as a given. People who looked like that, he'd found, either accumulated honours and glory with astonishing speed or remained in their home village running the local shop. Those were the only two options. She was unmarried, lived alone in a chi-chi part of Amsterdam, and travelled through much of the year on the *Dauphin*. There was a father living back in Scandinavia with a record for, and Tom had checked this twice in the European newspaper archives online, walking on the street behind politicians embroiled in scandals and informing them politely that they were betraying their flock. A background in restrained religious fervour had, it seemed, left Elisabeth untouched, except perhaps for a vague residual sense of impersonal distance from the masses, and – Tom knew it was there, running down her backbone – a will of total iron.

'Did you like Sixgill?' he asked directly, folding his hands across the magnificent glass stateroom desk, which made him feel uncomfortably like a company director.

'Oh, no, I did not like him,' said Elisabeth Lindgren, unexpectedly.

Tom did his best not to make a small astonished noise. How on earth had Sixgill managed to upset *everybody* within range? Lindgren's voice was deep and even, but there was something vivid in it now, a timbre he couldn't quite read.

'He behaved — badly?' He phrased this with some delicacy.

'He made a pass at me.' The face blinked slowly at him. 'Not now, around four years ago.'

'You knew Sixgill before?' Titus was, behind her, writing things down rapidly in his impeccable shorthand, a habit he had picked up from an obscure police academy booklet of the 1950s during training, and retained despite the outright puzzlement of virtually all his superiors save Tom. He raised his head very slightly at Tom's tone.

'I doubt he recognised me.' Her face was unflappable. 'He was working in the Netherlands at the time. He attempted seduction, poorly, after a restaurant dinner with his faculty. I was not pleased and he backed off.' The timbre in the voice had lightened, but Tom thought he recognised it now. A professional woman, challenged in her work environment. Yes, that would mark Sixgill for her for life.

'You don't know if he recognised you now? You are, forgive me, quite distinct-looking.'

'You think so? Perhaps. He was snide and awful to me, but I gather that he was snide and awful to everybody.' She shook her head. 'I am sorry, Detective Inspector, but I have the impression that for people like this Ben Sixgill, there were so many people in the past who had been offended, or wounded, or betrayed in some capacity, that he could not possibly remember them all.' Again there was the slight thickening, the shiver of it in that odd low-pitched voice.

'Do you have any insight as to why that might be?'

'Who am I to speculate? I had one encounter, and it was not pleasant. That is not enough to make suppositions. Perhaps he had been badly hurt in his life and felt the need to hurt others. Perhaps it was a performance. I do not know.' *And thus the oracle pronounces*, thought Tom, eccentrically.

'Can anybody verify this incident?' he asked.

'Certainly. I discussed it afterwards with the management of the restaurant at the time. I was newly head chef there. Everybody has moved on, but I can put you in contact with people who will remember.' She paused. 'I do not wish to make it sound dramatic. It was, unfortunately, not isolated. Many men in the restaurant industry do much the same thing, often with a great deal more aggression.'

'Is that why you became head chef on the *Dauphin*?'

'I am, to a certain extent, protected,' said Elisabeth Lindgren drily. 'I trust the Captain absolutely. But there is a sense of entitlement among guests in all areas of high-end cheffing, particularly if the chefs are women.'

'Sixgill was, in other words, far from the worst of it?'

'Very far from it.'

And that, thought Tom, was probably true, though it didn't make Sixgill look any better. Was Elisabeth Lindgren likely to try and kill somebody for an incident four years ago? Not really, unless he had tried it again, which nobody appeared to have noticed — and, he thought, Lindgren would have told the Captain rapidly if so. And even if it was old revenge — why bring it up?

'Do you know how he broke his nose?' he asked.

'I know it happened at some point on the journey,' said Elisabeth without curiosity, 'but I did not witness it. Perhaps an accident?'

Tom did not enlighten her that it was not, in fact, an accident.

Aabria Scott, resplendent in about fourteen layers of fluffy something-or-other, and her attendant Kate Berg both agreed on all the major points: the bellow, the splash, the shoe, and then the sudden appearance of Sixgill, dead on the ice. They had been, Scott said briskly, 'milling about', sometimes with Gladys Moreland, sometimes as a duo. Scott and Berg, it turned out, were making a game of looking at all the luxurious chairs and fittings on deck and comparing them to *other* cruises they'd done. Scott, who was interviewed first, said, 'Listen, would you mind reassuring Kate? She seems intent on the idea that somebody's after my money.'

'Why would they be after your money, Ms Scott?'

'I have rather a lot of it. Not that I carry it around on the ship. It's all bound up in a will, and no, I haven't made a new one at sea or anything. But Kate's not been mixed up in this sort of thing before, and I think it's slightly put the wind up her.'

'Do you travel with jewels? Diamonds?' Titus looked up very slightly. But Aabria shook her head.

'All costume,' she said. She showed them the pearls at her wrists, which were enormously glossy. 'They're very *good* fakes, not cheap,' she said with some complacency, 'but fakes nonetheless; can you imagine if I dropped something actually valuable in a lifeboat? My insurance company wouldn't cover a cent of it, the weasels. No, that's all in a safety deposit box in Chicago, thank you very much.'

'You travel a lot, I see from your passport.'

'Sixteen cruises since my husband died. He came from a railroad fortune, you see,' Scott said brightly. 'Generations of them, building trains all over the States! Said he'd heard every possible thing there was to know about human transportation by the time he was ten, and that home was good enough for any creature except migrating birds. Never went *anywhere*, poor pet.' She added, 'I did make sure his ashes were stuffed in his favourite chair, but after that I could do as I liked, couldn't I?'

'Of course,' said Tom seriously. 'Does anybody on board stand to benefit by your demise?'

'Kate does, but not to the tune of very much,' said Aabria, promptly. 'She's paid much more per month while I'm alive than she'd get in death. I'm not stupid, Detective Inspector. People who handle morphine around old ladies shouldn't be given huge bequests.' She said this with ruthless logic that somehow still managed to be very affectionate. Tom was, once again, reminded strongly of Mrs Aldous, who sent him elegant cards every Christmas, always with an addendum of affection for Biscuit. He

161

was pretty sure she swiped them annually from Harrods, though they'd never been able to prove it.

'I quite agree with you. So why would you be the target of murder?'

'It's always the rich old ladies, isn't it?' Aabria folded her hands and looked at him with the air of all-knowing his Aunt Sheila would bestow when she knew perfectly well who had taken all her best caramels. 'It would fit. Except it doesn't, in this case, because nobody on this ship would inherit anything worth a damn, as I don't know any of them from Adam, save Kate. If Sixgill had been intelligent he'd have tried to butter me up and become a new husband, but he was more set on going around getting people's backs up. Poisonous little particle.'

And that, thought Tom, rather settled Sixgill.

Kate Berg was indeed rattled, though she was trying very hard not to show it. She'd gone into private nursing after the NHS became a pressure cooker, she explained. She was not particularly good with stress. Blood and guts, yes, but strain . . . Her plain face carried a load of worry around in it like a pile of pudding in a bowl. Competent and shrewd, Tom thought, and likely the kind who'd work herself into the ground without some restraint. Private nursing was a good fit for this sort of person – a softer pace, with more people-managing than hard shifts. 'I know it's probably not anything to do with her, but I do like Ms Scott,' she said. 'And she's elderly, and wealthy—'

'Yes. But it does not, on the surface, appear to have been designed to be Ms Scott's demise on the table,' said Tom, gently. 'If anything I think the excitement has given her some verve.'

'That,' said Kate, regaining some composure, 'is always her reaction when things go haywire. Police raided our boat once in Cairo looking for contraband, and she flirted outrageously with half the officers and wouldn't stop talking for three days.'

'The amount of people who believe they were meant to be killed instead of Dr Sixgill is quite remarkable,' noted Titus in his soft voice after Nurse Berg had left.

'They are all very rich,' replied Tom, considering. 'Rich people always do think they're about to be murdered. Or the sensible ones do, anyway.'

The Blanchards and Boo Moreland came last. Tom realised he had heard vaguely of Gladys's brother-in-law, who showed up occasionally in society pages looking cheerily unashamed of himself, and had to grant that the person who arrived didn't look nearly as much of an ass as he'd assumed. There was an airiness to Boo that seemed untrustworthy, but Tom knew that sort of casual facade was often a blind. The sort, perhaps, to rely on pat and humorous answers while he held all his own cards very close to his chest. Eyebrows straight out of the early Clark Gable years too. Very dashing in his sling.

Boo Moreland had escorted Rose into the stateroom, and Tom thought he had quite a good view of what was happening there. Would Boo perform acts of violence to keep the affections of an intense-looking marine biologist who was currently telling him off for a bad pun? Sometimes these boyish types had uncertain, darker currents.

He asked for Boo Moreland to stay for a bit, partly to see whether the female Dr Blanchard's presence would make the man more serious or more erratic, then endeavoured to obtain more precise timings. Boo had kept a log of how long the *Mouette* was underwater, and it corresponded nicely with the readings from the vessel itself, helpfully folded under a weighty teacup by the Captain. There was, Tom noted with the usual disappointment of an idea gone south, no time or possibility for the submarine-thing to surface, somebody to pop out and stab or shoot Sixgill, then for it to go under again. It wasn't an idea he'd really countenanced, but he checked it off his internal list none-theless. He then added, 'How far does a speargun harpoon go, Dr Blanchard? You're the only one on board who seems to know much about them.'

'In the air?' Rose looked a bit taken aback, but considered the question gamely. 'I don't know, likely quite far, but you'd definitely know about it.'

'Why?'

'The recoil of the gun would be stupendous. It's designed to be fired underwater against water resistance. If you tried to let one off above water you'd end up with a kickback that'd break your arm. Also, they're attached, those harpoons; they're supposed to have little chains on them so you can haul fish back to you.'

'So somebody brought along a harpoon and somehow shoved it into Sixgill. In person or from a distance?'

'I've no idea, but if it was a speargun and they were firing it in person, you could just look at the person with the lame arm.'

Titus and Tom both glanced, without thinking, at Boo and his sling. He looked back at them, then made a face of realisation. So did Rose.

'He,' she indicated Boo, 'has a boxer's fracture, not a speargun whiplash break.'

'From what?' asked Tom, with his best air of politeness.

'Punching Sixgill in the nose the night before he died after he said some truly repulsive things about Dr Blanchard's brother,' said Boo, clearly.

'Indeed,' said Tom. Here, at last, was an immediate clarity about the situation. What a shit Sixgill sounded, he thought to himself, angrily. But there was something in Boo's manner – the forthrightness was slightly exaggerated. It led him to push, just a little. 'And that was how that injury was sustained?'

Boo looked suspiciously noble but said nothing.

'You are an idiot,' said Rose crossly to Boo. 'I punched him too, at the same time. He was being extremely awful and nobody blamed either of us. Don't be protective and secretive, you'll just make yourself look suspicious.' And Tom recognised with certainty that if anything could have endeared Boo to Rose, it was punching a bigot full in the face.

'I wasn't, really.' Boo looked shamefaced. 'Your knuckles would have shown you up even if we'd not talked about it.'

'Oh, yes,' she said awkwardly. They all looked at Rose's knuckles, which were still a light shade of purple.

'So your opinion of Sixgill was . . .' said Tom.

'He was odd,' said Rose, slowly. 'He just seemed to go out of his way to be as horrible as he possibly could. None of us could figure out why. He upset basically everybody.'

'Scientifically he seemed sound,' offered Boo. 'I read some of his papers before we came aboard. Beyond that, he had the personality of a particularly antisocial electric eel.'

'That's very interesting, Mr Moreland. Will you wait outside, please.' Boo bowed in a very good imitation of somebody in a police investigation, and left.

Rose Blanchard was, as Tom and Titus had briefly assessed her to be, a highly competent witness, with times, dates and a deeply detailed memory. More's the pity that she wasn't on the ship to see all the commotion, thought Tom with regret, with the added notion that the Blanchards' removal might have been precisely the idea.

'There's something else,' she said at the tail of her neat recitation of events, and told them briefly of the conversation she'd been informed about by Sunila. 'I have no further context than that,' she ended. 'You'd have to ask Sandy about it.'

'Exhalation?' Tom was bewildered.

Rose said, 'I know. I feel like – there's something. But I don't have anything else.'

'Did you know the Morelands before you came onto the ship?'

'No, I didn't,' said Rose, smiling and folding one leg underneath herself; her deep tan at the face, arms and feet was already starting to fade back to a more natural paleness.

Long hours in the sun recently, Tom judged, and only just beginning to adjust to the cold. 'But we get on pretty well now. Boo wasn't meant to be on the ship, you know. The Morelands booked the berth for their daughter but she got a job at short notice, so thence came Boo. If he asks stupid questions ignore him. He's sharp as a tack, that one, and pricks himself.'

'Indeed.' Detective Inspector Heissen could well believe it. 'If anything else strikes you as unusual—'

'There's something wrong with Alicia Grey,' she said promptly. 'I don't mean she's going around looking guilty or anything. She's started taking all her meals in her room, and Sunila keeps taking her teas and trying to get her to leave, but she won't. She's afraid. I don't know why.' Her blue eyes crinkled at them anxiously.

'Yes,' said Titus, unexpectedly. 'The lady is very afraid. She will not, alas, share this fear with us. But with a fellow member of the ship, she might.'

'You want me to go snooping?' Rose Blanchard grinned. 'All right.'

'That,' said Tom with mild reproval, 'is not official advice, and you are not to take it as such. There's someone dangerous on this ship, Dr Blanchard, and you and your brother must remember that before you go off being the Famous Five, please.'

'I will merely strike up sympathetic conversation.' She added, solidly, 'I do look after Finn. I know he looks like a porcelain figure, but we have survived lots of things.'

'Yes.' Tom caught too late that this sounded like he was

agreeing to her assessment of her brother's looks, but couldn't alter it in time. 'Could you send your brother in after Boo Moreland?'

To his credit, Moreland dropped his air of irrepressible mischief the second he came in. 'I suspect you'd rather call me Alexander than Boo,' he said. 'Government name and all that.' Moreland was charming where his brother was considered, witty where his sister-in-law was clever, but Tom detected a strong will and a marked curiosity. He recounted the story of how he'd been given this berth not a week before the ship sailed.

'So you weren't meant to be here at all,' said Tom slowly, making a note. Did somebody get a fright from the fact that there was the wrong type of third Moreland aboard? Was there some kind of disarranged plan?

'No. Why, has Frog got something to do with this?' Boo looked startled and suddenly worried.

'Frog?' said Tom, for a brief moment wondering if he'd sustained some kind of helicopter-related deafness.

'Fiona Moreland. Pat and Gladdy's eldest. Frog. She didn't know anybody else on the ship either, as far as I know. I'll ask.'

'It looks unlikely, but we have to check all the elements,' said Tom mildly, without remarking on the amphibian aspect. 'Do you know anything about Sandy Highcastle?'

'Charlatan,' said Boo with promptness. 'Makes exceedingly good money from peddling bad science and pure snake oil to the masses. A plague to good scientific education. Whether he genuinely believes it is anybody's guess.

168

He brought a load of his horrible candles aboard and keeps trying to sell them to people.'

'Bought one?'

'No.'

'Buy one.'

'What!'

'I'm curious,' said Heissen, innocently.

'*You* buy one. I'm not spending three hundred of any-thing at all on a candle, even marbles. Requisition it for police use. Say you need the energy of the room cleansed.' Boo grinned.

'I might. That will be all, Mr Moreland, but please warn Dr Rose that she isn't to go off sleuthing.'

'If you think anybody can warn Rose off anything, you're a far worse detective than you look,' said Boo with spirit, and went outside, jerking his head for Finn.

Finn floated in, did his interview, and floated out without, Tom thought, being at all rude, short, negative, or indeed possessing any sharp edges at all. He couldn't believe *anybody* on the ship could have been murderous; they all seemed lovely to him, or at least had some redeem-ing features. Dr Eder was 'so generous with his time', the Highcastles were 'really devoted to their work', the Captain had been 'so *lovely*', and mention of his sister brought forth a spurt of adoring hand-waving that Tom correctly deduced meant eternal devotion on both sides.

On the topic of Sixgill, where Tom would have permit-ted an understandable strength of feeling, Finn Blanchard simply folded all his extraneous edges into himself and looked miserable. 'He wasn't very nice,' Finn allowed, which was likely the worst censure in his arsenal, 'but he didn't deserve *that*. It all feels like some sort of trick, somehow. Like it's not real.'

Heissen had to assure him that it was, in fact, real, and felt mildly crestfallen for having done so, even though Finn nodded in a sort of morose acceptance. 'I know,' he said. 'Sometimes the facts of things are – hard to admit. But,' he added brightly, with a sudden surge of belief all over his thin face, 'I'm sure you'll solve it! May I have a cracker?' And he took said cracker and ate it absently with both hands, snapping it into smaller and smaller pieces, without somehow ever dropping a crumb on the carpet. Tom, who had never managed to eat anything crumbly without causing a small blizzard and giving Biscuit the cat a field day, was fascinated.

Titus, he noticed with some aggravation, was also watching Tom throughout this performance, with a penetrating gaze – the kind that said 'I have to keep a dustpan in your *desk*, sir; observe how *civilised people eat*'. Not for the first time, Tom wished he was less capable of reading Titus Williams' expressions.

Finn, he reflected, was like a large sort of gentle amphibious creature that everybody wanted to protect. A manatee. A manatee who was also intent on one or both of the officers experiencing the submersible, because it would be so useful, it was incredibly safe, there hadn't been any incidents *really* (Titus caught that 'really' and underlined a note), they could look all around the bottom of the ship and everywhere, and if anything had been dropped they really would see it, the lights on the front were so many watts and there were grabbing arms—

Tom agreed, finally, to go in the *Mouette*, because nobody on Earth had yet developed the ability to say no to Finn after an extensive barrage, and managed to ask semi-professionally what the Blanchards were actually using the submersible for. There was an explosively enthusiastic explanation about a rare shark; a great deal of shark facts ensued, plus a lot of hand-flapping, and Finn had a PowerPoint presentation if they were at all interested? Tom heard himself saying that he would indeed like to see the PowerPoint presentation and could he bring it along this evening, and Finn looked so delighted that even Titus's small cough of laughter was lost in a vague rushing in the Detective Inspector's ears.

'I would like to know what the "no incidents, *really*" meant,' said Titus at a suitable interval, once Finn had departed and his air of bonhomie had leaked out of the cabin.

'Rose Blanchard might give us an overview, and I insist on one before either of us set foot in it.' Tom sat up. 'And if I have to sit through something on Greenland sharks,' he added, attempting to regain his composure, 'so do you.'

'I have a remarkably good knowledge of Greenland sharks, thank you, sir,' said Titus, politely. 'I read an engaging book on them, quite recently.'

'Titus.'

'You enjoy yourself, sir.'

16

Rose and Finn were eating their breakfast in the crew mess the next morning when a very tall head shoved its way in through the door.

'I am co-opting your lab to do tests on Sixgill's fluids,' the head said shortly, 'and I am also co-opting both of you Blanchards.'

Said Blanchards blinked at the head, which resolved as belonging to Alva, the ship's doctor. 'What?' said Rose, eventually, with gentle politeness.

'You both have biology training, the crew do not,' Alva said with some impatience, 'and it is swifter than flying this sample away somewhere. Stop gawking and come help. The police person is going to supervise,' she added, jerking a thumb behind her, and indeed Rose could see the hovering face of one of the men – Titus, that was it – looking blandly as if he were standing in line at a café, not discussing the use of biological samples on an Arctic ship. Alva was a tall and commanding presence; Rose looked at Finn, and they both rose at the same time, with sad thoughts for their uneaten porridge and blueberries.

She and Finn had, of course, done time in laboratories with delicate biological samples – often under much cruder circumstances, in Rose's case. Grapefruit's various samples were stored in a mini-freezer kept under a card table, and hooked up to a generator so they wouldn't get overheated during power outages; the front of the fridge was covered in stickers from actual grapefruit. But this was another sort of scenario altogether, as befitted the *Dauphin*. The test tubes she and Finn fetched and carried, and the microscopes Alva fussed over, were all impeccably expensive. Alva even had her own fluid suspension collection, for testing for everything from barbiturates to opiates, which she showed off with great pride; Rose guessed she probably didn't have a lot to do with it day to day, aside from occasionally probing the blood alcohol levels of rowdy guests.

Titus Williams hovered in the background, making no interference. This, Rose believed, was only fair; they may have been underwater at the time, but she had still punched Sixgill in the nose.

She eyed the samples a little uneasily. Blood was innocent; the flesh of the person was not the person, not the living thing. But there was the oddity of the fact that it came from that extraordinary tableau – a man's blood cooling on the ice, while the crack and shiver of glaciers passed by, and the mute grey water.

Finn, she was pleased to note, appeared to have separated the personality of Sixgill entirely out in his mind from the little coagulated bits of haemoglobin and saliva in tubes and on microscope slides, and was making a delighted Alva explain everything she was doing in profuse detail. She would have to tell Boo all about this later—

Boo Moreland, hitting her with a paper airplane. Boo with his sling.

Something struck her, and began resounding like a gong. Could the light and airy Boo Moreland carry around something darker, harder? Could that expressive face, that gesturing body, conceal something bound in ice? She thought of him, of the eyebrows that flicked up and down rapidly. Of his sidelong smile. She knew so little – about anybody other than Finn.

She looked at Titus Williams, out of a reflexive movement to find something, anything else – and saw with interest that he was watching her. He nodded, but unlike a conventional person, who would at least pretend to glance away, he continued to gaze until she turned to fetch another test tube. And even then she felt it – the light grey eyes, watching.

'The fluid reports are in, sir,' said Titus to Tom, popping his head back into their stateroom late in the morning. 'The *Undine* helicopter with the police doctor will also be here shortly for the post-mortem.' It was mid-morning, and Tom Heissen was still covered in croissant crumbs, which he guiltily now swept onto the floor. Titus, he noted, still couldn't be trained to use official acronyms for anything; he'd no sooner say 'PM' for 'post-mortem' than tap-dance with one of the highly audible neighbourhood walruses.

Tom arched his back. He rarely slept well mid-investigation, even on beds that felt disturbingly as if they contained the plumage of four thousand ducks. 'How was the testing?' Titus had spent the morning supervising site samples in the ship laboratory, and Tom prepared himself for a litany of polite yet firm complaints about the limitations of police work while afloat.

Titus surprised him. 'Frankly more efficient than they do at Branch, sir. And we got some good results from what we had.'

Tom had been slightly shocked that Titus had managed to salvage enough blood and saliva from that ridiculous frozen scene to do any checks at all. And Alva's report was indeed helpfully succinct: Sixgill's fluids bore no traces of narcotics, stimulants, or indeed of the whacking great animal tranquilliser habitually found in the *Dauphin*'s guns. As Tom was pondering this, the whir of helicopter blades broke across the Arctic morning, and Tom roused himself, slightly unwillingly, to leave the cabin and plunge into the cold. Needs must.

The police doctor who'd been ferried in was short, voluble, and clearly not particularly pleased at being pulled from their normal round of warm houses to dance attendance upon spear-fished corpses off ice caps. Their name was Áillun, and they kept up a constant stream of sullen remarks as they attended the body of Sixgill, most of which were in what the Captain would later tell them was Northern Sámi, and none of which sounded particularly flattering about Sixgill or his environs.

The English assessment, when it came, was definitive. Death was absolutely from the spear-fishing harpoon. It had pierced a lung and nicked the bottom of the heart, and he'd bled out internally with a swiftness.

The harpoon itself had now been angled out of the chest,

and Titus and Tom could look at it at their leisure. It was a nasty steel thing with a savage prong that had wedged into the wound, making it very difficult for unlucky fishes or biologists to pull it out.

The man looked solidly healthy, said the doctor, except for an inconvenient hole in his chest, and a more complete autopsy *not* conducted in an adapted ship's storeroom would likely bear that out. It appeared from the wound as if the harpoon had been driven in with great force. Shot? Stabbed?

'It is at around a 90-degree angle to the body, almost perfectly perpendicular, but I cannot speculate on how it got there,' Áillun had said, then shut their mouth with an audible snap, something Tom had only ever seen in films. Only Elisabeth Lindgren's buckthorn and mallow flower tea, served incredibly strong and hot out of the kitchens, made them show the faintest vestiges of any good humour, and even that, the Captain translated, was an expression of surprise that not everything on the ship was terrible. They were, the Captain added with an air of explaining everything, a Marxist.

Tom liked Dr Áillun a great deal and quite wanted to keep them around to see what they made of the Highcastles, but Captain Johannsson handed them back into the helicopter, meeting their continued muttering with gentle muttering in the same cadence, so that they sounded like two sophisticated wind instruments operating in duet. The Norwegian police required an update and some explanations as to why they were sending their best local doctor to visit an ice cap, though Tom rather wished he had more news to send back with the helicopter – like a suspect, for instance, or the faintest hint of a theory.

'The 90-degree angle may indicate that it was wielded by a person of Sixgill's own height,' said Titus, looking at the harpoon on its metallic platter.

'Or that it was fired at a distance, by somebody who'd wedged it in a gun,' said Tom. 'Stabbings so rarely hit precisely 90 degrees. Nobody heard a great thunking gun go off, though.'

'Look at the surface, sir.' Titus traced it with his fingers. There were thin grooves down the sides of the harpoon, all fresh, as if it had run very swiftly against sharp edges. They looked similar to the markings a gun barrel might make on a bullet.

'Somebody did some work to fit this inside something it wasn't made to fit,' said Tom, contemplatively. 'Oh, for the days of sword-canes.'

'It is too small to fit inside a tranquilliser gun barrel, sir. The ones on this ship are very large, and it would not fire correctly. It could, conceivably, have been fired using some other ballistic measure.'

'Hm. Aabria Scott doesn't carry a walking stick, does she?'

'I think she'd scorn the principle, sir.'

'Probably.' They both briefly cherished the idea of Scott whipping out a harpoon from inside a stick and throwing it with full force at Sixgill, then let the image slip away from them formlessly.

'We have a mess on our hands,' said Tom blithely. 'Everybody here seems to think Sixgill was an ass, which it sounds like he was. Whom did he annoy enough to get himself skewered?'

'Is it possible that he was having an affair with Mr Highcastle, then called it off, sir?' said Titus. 'Bearing in mind what Ms Singh heard on the stairs. That would give either Highcastle or his wife sufficient motive.' *I said it was off, so it's off*, thought Tom.

'Heartbroken on the ice? Not impossible. The how remains very sticky, though. What with him yelling about overboard people and her wailing in the stairwell.'

'Either could be a blind, sir.'

'Quite. We're overflowing with possibilities, you know. Elisabeth Lindgren had a bad taste in her mouth from Sixgill in the past; the twins had a bad taste from him right now; the estimable Captain might be running something illicit on his nice ship; something has made Alicia Grey fear for her life; Dr Eder would, I think, protect his reputation with great force; the Morelands might take justice into their own hands, though I doubt it; and Aabria Scott is wealthy, but she'd more than likely deputise that loyal follower Berg to do any dirty work for her. And Berg would do it, no doubt. We're on a hiding to something somewhere, Titus, but I'm damned if I can see my way through the thicket at this point. And if there's any clear link to our smugglers, it's all in the dark.'

Titus was busily scribbling in the 'motive' column in his little book. He looked up. 'Insofar as opportunity, sir: the twin Blanchards were in the submersible, which, given the timings, rules them out, unless the death was somehow planned to occur unsupervised. Dr Eder, Patrick Moreland and Alexander 'Boo' Moreland alibi one another on the deck, though three persons to one radio may have given one a chance to slip away. Aabria Scott was accompanied by her nurse, Sunila Singh and Alicia Grey by each other; those alibis are thus insubstantial. Bloom Highcastle is very determined to communicate that she was on the stairs. Gladys Moreland was visible at some points and not others. The Captain was sparsely attended on the bridge, as was the chef in the kitchen. Dr Palgrave was allegedly asleep in her quarters. There are *distinct* possibilities, sir.' His pencil worked fluidly. Tom regarded it in silent satisfaction.

'I wonder if that Dr Palgrave is ready to be seen yet. I don't trust anybody who's too eccentric to be interviewed by the police,' he said darkly. 'Maybe she was after Sixgill's research and she's playing possum post shooting him.' A young scientist on the rise might be a temptation to an older colleague whose own work didn't look nearly as glittering. There had been a case – years ago now – where an elderly Italian professor had taken a postdoc under his wing, summarily stolen all their work, and then acted surprised when the person turned up at a conference and threw eggs at his head. Tom had had great fun learning new Italian curses from the egg-thrower as they talked to their lawyer in the city cells. And then the professor had tried to sue the police force, for daring to mention that he was a plagiarist during the court case! Astonishing, the entire thing. He'd quite wanted to take an egg to the man's head himself by the end of it.

It seemed that Dr Palgrave had been suffering from a fit of vomiting that had come on before the Blanchards even departed. Tom was naturally very suspicious of this, but Kate Berg, Alva the ship doctor, and even the angry Svalbard doctor had seen her, and all testified to the fact that she was genuinely ill. 'We've given her antiemetics and rehydration tablets,' Berg had told them, 'and we're hoping it's food poisoning, or a twenty-four-hour bug that'll end without much fanfare. Wouldn't be very fun if we all came down with it as well. If she's faking, it's the most realistically visceral faking I've ever seen.' And she'd made an expressive face that left Tom and Titus in no doubt about Dr Palgrave's apparent digestive carnage.

The Captain appeared in the doorway at that point. 'You will be pleased to know,' he said, 'that our parent company's legal department has given you leave to search the cabins.' He pointedly refused, Tom saw, to look anywhere near the harpoon on the platter.

'Right,' said Tom, with a vague sense of weariness. Getting a warrant for a British vessel in Arctic waters had been hard enough; avoiding a lawsuit for improper search and seizure by a bunch of furious international millionaires had, somehow, been stickier. By this point Sixgill's laptop and phone, and whatever had shot that harpoon, assuming it had been shot, could have been swallowed by an orca. (Tom remained a little hazy on the precise details of Arctic oceanic fauna.) 'Arm up, Titus.' Titus, taking this for its correct meaning, printed out every legal document explaining their permissions he could find, and they set off.

Tom, when conducting any search, always took note both of items uncovered and how persons reacted to the search itself. Sandy Highcastle was blustery, and his store of cashmere scarves was revealed to be a handy dozen, with silken monograms; Sunila Singh was frosty about the legal necessity of the endeavour, and her bedside table carried an entire series of paperback historical romances in Korean. The Morelands, who behaved with exactly the socially acceptable amount of grace, had well-worn cashmeres in subtle colours, photographs of various relatives with the gaunt lines of greyhounds, and a silver hairbrush that, Titus quietly noted to Tom, seemed to have originated in the court of Henry VII.

Alas, beyond these titbits there was nothing of interest in any category. And, unfortunately, there was neither hide nor hair of laptop, phone or anything of Sixgill's anywhere they could discover on the ship.

The crew and scientific areas were no more helpful. Elisabeth Lindgren was blank-eyed as Tom and Titus fished through her meticulously arranged pantries. Her kitchen contained items of culinary miscellany that Tom approached with the care one might assign to questionably tempered zoo animals: a jar of truffle the size of a man's head, enough threads of saffron to weave Sandy Highcastle another scarf, and a book that, when opened, revealed (of course) sheets made entirely of gold leaf. Dr Eder made the entire process an excuse to talk loudly about how *generous* and *unbothered* he was, leaving the distinct impression that he was neither, and insisted on trying to show them dried algae from 1957. The twins apologised nineteen to the dozen about their messy cabin – which was, of course, far cleaner than Eder's. Tom boggled at a framed Photoshopped picture of a large pink manta ray and a gigantic shark looking lovingly at each other, and prudishly made Titus search all the Blanchards' clothing and underwear drawers himself.

They also made a dispiriting trip to the hold, which was meticulously inventoried, packed like a champion Tetris player's dream, and showed not a single sign of disturbance, or indeed any place to shove an errant tranquilliser gun. Noses of snowmobiles and boxes of tent pegs gleamed disapprovingly under netting.

The last stop was Aabria Scott's stateroom, which had been delayed because Kate Berg made absolutely furious noises about interrupting her charge's nap schedule. Tom tossed aside the provocative photograph of Scott placed on her pillow – if that *was* her forty years ago, her husband was either to be congratulated or pitied – and made an exhausted noise.

'No secret troves of diamonds, no gun, none of Sixgill's effects, no nothing,' he said aloud. 'All guest laptops present and accounted for.' (Bloom Highcastle's had featured a frankly strange screen background of a naked, floating woman surrounded by glowing crystals, which on closer examination was revealed to be a painted version of Bloom herself. The artist had been, perhaps, excessively flattering.)

Titus came in from Kate Berg's attached bedroom and made an assenting noise. It would, Tom thought, have been too easy.

They went for a leisurely stroll around the deck, because it was a crisp and glorious day, the sea was so green as to be almost black against the ice, and this particular deck was custom-made for leisurely strolling, with a robust handrail if required. Everything smelt of wood polish and salt and good leather. Nobody had been told about the raiding of Sixgill's quarters, once they'd got the crew members to stop shouting about it; whoever had done that must have thought they'd gotten away with it, or at the very least hadn't attempted to return.

'How,' asked Titus innocently after a gentle silence, 'was the PowerPoint lecture, sir?'

Tom Heissen, thanks to German heritage and a healthy circulatory system, was capable of turning a shade of red that shouldn't have been possible in human faces. He circumvented tomato and went straight into beetroot. A passing crew member looked at him with concern and privately noted that the police officers must be warned about polar sunburn.

'It was fine,' he said in a determined voice.

It had been, in a word, charming. He had sat and been shown Greenland sharks in every kind of pose, along with instructive side panels and little superimposed images of hats and bow ties on the shark photographs, and on one slide (about the sharks' advanced ages) a little birthday hat with a candle. Finn had talked and talked and talked, and Tom had attempted to ask sensible questions, and had even had some of them answered; and then they had talked about Finn becoming a marine biologist and why Tom was a police officer, and compared where they'd first learned to swim (unheated council pools) and childhood pets (exotic but delicate fish for Finn, a legacy of badly behaved cats for Tom), and then it had been two in the morning and Tom had, for some absolutely absurd reason, actually bowed when he opened the door for Finn to exit. Then he'd sat down on the floor with some very cold water in a glass for a long time and looked at his own feet in their thick aunt-knitted socks.

'I'm glad,' said Titus primly. 'I spent the evening discussing the case with the crew, given, sir, that we feel they appear not to have been involved. There was some ill-feeling about Sixgill because of a bet he had posed before they left shore.'

'He was a betting sort?' This was interesting.

'He bet them that he could freeze a normal glass of water with a single fingertip, and then did a parlour trick where he used nearly freezing water and touched a sliver of ice to the top, which, of course, resulted in a chain reaction to freeze the whole thing. A simple matter of physics. I saw it done,' said Titus without inflection, 'at a magician's show once.'

Tom, suppressing any reaction to the idea of Titus on a night off amusing himself with illusionists, said, 'Ah. A bet he had rigged to win. That sounds much more probable.'

'Yes, sir. Some of them protested, but the betting was not, as I understand, an expensive matter, more something of pride.'

'Did any of them have any knives?' asked Tom with interest.

'None, save for the usual Swiss Army sort for work. They wished they knew about the harpoon, but could offer nothing of use.' Titus nodded up at the bridge, which was decadent in its crystalline shimmer in the polar light, like a lantern. 'They did mention that the Captain was known, in his long-ago naval training days, as an exceptional hand-to-hand combatant.'

'Really?'

'Yes. His accuracy was such that his nickname, they said, was *Stingrocka*. Stingray.'

Rose Blanchard stood watching in the sun as Detective Inspector Heissen eyed the submersible with a slightly uneasy eye. She hoped dearly that *he* wasn't going to start making silly remarks about seagulls – but the expression on his face did not look like it bore the properties of mirth.

'What happened on the *Mouette*?' he asked her directly. 'There was an incident, your brother said.'

She blinked at him, vaguely startled. Where had he pulled that one from? So much had occurred over the past twenty-four hours that she'd pushed the entire issue entirely out of her mind.

'There was,' she said with the most anodyne face she could manage, 'a warning alarm. There was something in one of the seals, but it wasn't visible on the scans until we were at depth.'

'And you don't believe that was a fatal flaw in the *Mouette*'s design?' said Heissen with what appeared to be horrified surprise. Like so many people who lived all their lives on land, Rose thought, the Detective Inspector seemed ready to believe that all things underwater, natural or otherwise, were ready to explode, bite you, or collapse and take you into Davy Jones's locker at any time. Rose, who had survived a tropical hurricane and once fell off a kayak onto the back of a surprised hammerhead, nevertheless thought this was very silly.

'No,' she said flatly. 'It was sabotage.' Finn, she knew, would still like to think it was a stray piece of detritus they hadn't caught in time, but Rose knew how well they'd done their checks. Her memory clarified the idea around her, until it felt immutable, set in glass.

'Sixgill?' asked Heissen, interested.

'I have no proof, understand. But he was denied access to the *Mouette* on the first day, and was hanging around the seals when we went down. He could have done enough to trigger the warning without ever leaving us in actual danger. Something very small in the fastening.'

'Why?'

'Revenge for not getting his way? Scaring me off the submersible so he could have it for himself?' Rose shrugged. 'It didn't work. He didn't know me very well.'

'Clearly not.'

Alicia Grey passed them then, looking less ashen than

before and slightly more engaged with the world, with a headscarf wrapped around her hair; Rose flashed the Detective Inspector a brilliant smile and went off to be strategically nice. A police officer might get Alicia Grey's back up, but a nice comforting scientist armed with innocent bonhomie was surely more inoffensive.

She managed to persuade Alicia into a deckchair and ply her with Elisabeth's odd-smelling tea. The search of all the cabins, it seemed, had reassured Alicia greatly, and she talked with more vigour than she had for ages. Mostly, she wanted to tell stories she'd heard about stowaways, criminals lying in wait on expensive holidays to lay waste to people's wealth. A friend of hers and Sunila's, it seemed, had been robbed on safari.

'That's terrible,' said Rose, feeling sure that her own tale of nearly being mugged in London and getting away by hitting the assailant hard in the gut with her umbrella-handle would not be welcomed.

Sunila joined them and sat sipping on blackberry tea while blinking into the sunlight behind large designer sunglasses that made her look like a very glamorous newt. Alicia wouldn't let go of the safari story. 'They came from the *slums*, the police told us,' she said sadly. 'So grim. But it was still – one can't help but feel—'

'My wife doesn't know much about slums,' Sunila said gently, as if trying to make Rose complicit in her attempts at education, which Rose doubted had gone very far. 'She spent an entire holiday in Leeds convinced we were going to get attacked by thugs.'

'Oh, but we had a *lovely* time, you know,' said Alicia, flailing at something she may have seen on Rose's face. 'Really it was so good. So many interesting little pubs.'

This, as far as it went, was not particularly enlightening. There was, however, a hint of something – not necessarily plainly secretive, but odd. They were watching her, as if to see that she believed them, that she accepted what they were saying; and there was a sense of the submerged in Alicia's face, of some emotion being rigidly and cohesively repressed. Was it fear? Or something else?

Rose, without much difficulty, managed to lead the conversation towards the discovery of the body. 'I couldn't help at all,' she said unhappily. 'I didn't see anything. You were up on the top deck – what did you see?'

And there was the briefest flicker – the two women looked at each other, then away. Then Sunila said, 'Oh, we were being very bad at gin rummy, weren't we?'

'Sunila refuses to learn the rules,' said Alicia, a touch over-loud.

'The rules,' said Sunila, 'seem pointless and strange.' Alicia laughed. Rose wondered.

'You're sure it's safe.' Tom was hovering beside the *Mouette* feeling a bit like a chicken being told all the scientific values of the farmer's knife.

Finn flapped at him. 'Oh yes. We're checking everything all over. And we'd better get it done today, you know – the sun will go in about an hour, and we don't know what the weather conditions will be tomorrow. It's important that there be minimal surface water movement, and there's very little wave action today, and no wind. And then you can get things done so much faster!' He beamed. Tom wondered, not for the first time, why nobody in the Foreign Office had commandeered Finn Blanchard as weaponry.

'Obviously currents and things may have caused some shifting, but the glacier's position means current activity isn't high,' said Rose, who had returned from importuning Alicia. 'If anything has been dropped off the side, and it's relatively heavy, it shouldn't have moved around much. And there's only silt, not reefs or corals or anything.'

Tom sat his sturdy self in the *Bathysphere*-looking thing and refused to look at Titus, who was standing by with one hand over his eyebrows to block out the glare, having pointedly refused to go in the *Mouette* at all. 'You are senior investigator, sir,' he'd said. 'Dr Blanchard appears wholly capable. I will remain on board and take notes.' Tom had tried and failed to escape the feeling that there was a conspiracy against him.

Rose Blanchard talked him through the entire process – what noises meant, what happened when – with commendable precision, and a clear understanding that the sudden appearance of bubbles or loud alarms would probably scare the hell out of him. He had the radio clutched between his fingers like a small child given a single toy for Christmas.

'Finn knows what he's doing,' she finished. 'You just focus on investigating and telling him what to point the lights at. And we're all up here on the other end of the radio.'

'Thank you, Dr Blanchard,' said Tom thickly, deciding he couldn't put off his fate any longer. He hoped they wrote a nice eulogy in the police newsletter. 'We can proceed.'

The top closed on them and the seals moved into place, and as the *Mouette* was set adrift and slowly sank, the entire thing became filled with the sound of his breath, Finn's breath, and the washing sea. Finn kept up a reassuring commentary on how many times the *Dauphin* had used the *Mouette*, how many radio transmitters there were around here – really a lot, for quite a remote area! – and how every time the logs reported it all going without a hitch—

'Is that a shark?' asked Tom in a mildly panicked voice as a dark shape swum around below them.

'Ooh! No, it's a cod. Oh dear,' said Finn, sadly. 'I could have shown you its gills. Oh – you probably don't care very much. I'm sorry I bored you so much last night, I just get very excited—' He looked morose.

'No!' Tom felt panicky, and not just because the entire thing was sinking rapidly towards the sea floor and doom. 'It was interesting! I didn't know anything lived for 500 years! And – and the hats on all their heads were very nice.'

'You liked the hats?'

'I *loved* the hats,' said Tom gravely, and Finn looked absurdly happy again. It was, Tom thought, probably an accident of the *Mouette*'s underwater lighting that his neck appeared to have gone bright pink.

The water below the ship was thick and still. It had been a mooring-point for the *Dauphin* and for other luxury cruises for some years, so the silt at the bottom was littered with various bits of detritus: part of an anchor, scattered ropes, a thing that resolved itself in the glare of the *Mouette*'s lights into one of the *Dauphin*'s beautifully branded teacups. Tom made a note, without much hope.

'Look,' said Finn.

There was a glaring white rectangle. The *Mouette*'s arms picked it up with some delicacy – Tom was amazed at how dextrous Finn managed to be with the arms of this thing – and it resolved itself into something with straps. 'A backpack,' said Finn, wonderingly. The whiteness floated in the icy water. If there had been any biological traces on it, thought Tom grimly, they'd be long gone. Maybe some fingerprints if they were lucky.

'What's that?' He pointed to something nearby.

'A fish corpse? No – hold on.' Finn shifted the backpack to be held by one of the submersible's arms, and manoeuvred the *Mouette* closer. It was small and dark and slightly rounded. 'What—' He had levered underneath it with the other arm, and they both sat blinking at it.

It was clearly, frozen and swollen though it was, another identical shoe.

'The mystery of the third shoe,' said Tom, without thinking.

Finn gaped at him, then picked up the shoe with the second arm, with the pincer movement of a woman taking a canapé off a plate without ruining her nails. 'That backpack's heavy,' he said with mild concern, and Tom's heart leapt – heavy meant Possibilities, it meant A Laptop, it meant Clues. Or, depending on how confounding Sixgill had felt, it may also mean A Collection Of Bricks And Nothing Of Use At All.

'Can you get them both to the surface?' he asked.

'Yes, but it would be better for balance if we picked up something for the other arm, not just the shoe.' Finn was clearly concentrating very hard. 'Look for anything we can use. Hold on – I see something.'

He navigated a little further away, some distance from both the shoe and the backpack, and poked at something that looked for all the world like a spur of wood. 'This might be reasonable ballast—' Then he stopped. The silt picked up, and the lights of the *Mouette* shone on the object in full. It was long, and metal, and comprised of several parts obscured in the Arctic gloom, but the shape of it was unmistakable.

Tom swore aloud. It was the missing tranquilliser gun.

17

There was no party when the *Mouette* docked again, no streamers flapping or ticker tape, but Tom felt slightly more cheerful than when he'd gone down. He hadn't died in an elaborately appointed floating sardine can, he had some things that might be a lead, and Finn's hair looked very attractive streaming in the wind when they poked their heads out of the submersible's hatch.

Tom eyed Titus and they made the kind of simultaneous, silent decision one can make with spouses or long-term work partners, the telepathy of deep acquaintance: that their finds would not be hidden from the crowd of onlookers. Most people on the ship, even if they were attempting to look diffident about their curiosity, were there to watch; Dr Eder busying himself around the docking parts, the Highcastles, Aabria Scott as ever leaning on Kate Berg's arm. Tom made a careful examination of faces. Nobody looked shocked or anxious or even upset that the backpack was hauled into the light; the gun, however, made several people cry out, and Bloom Highcastle made an almost angry terror-noise and dived into her husband's arms. Sandy jutted his chin out in the sprinkle of water that came with the *Mouette*'s hatch-opening, and must, thought Tom, have at one time been at least a bit handsome, in a bluff sort of way.

'I do not know,' said the Captain, assisting Tom officiously out of the deep *Mouette* seat, 'that this is very wise. Surely—'

'I'm afraid the time for decorum is over, and the time for *shocks most lurid* is now,' said Tom seriously, in a low voice. 'We operate with a purpose. Do trust us.'

Captain Johannsson acquiesced, but with the first show of hesitation in his ready grace. Tom regarded him thoughtfully. *Stingrocka*.

They did stop short of emptying the backpack on the deck, though not out of consideration for the Captain's feelings; evidence required order and method, and also no chance of an errant seagull filching something. (Tom hadn't seen any seagulls, but refused to trust the Arctic sky not to deliver some.) The sun was also beginning to descend, and he didn't want to risk losing anything in long polar shadows.

In the safety of the stateroom, they made some observations. The backpack itself was a fancy make without external markings, but several highly decorative emblems indicative of boggling expense. Tom and Titus fished out the contents and laid them out in rigidly precise patterns (Titus liked everything symmetrical) on several of the *Dauphin*'s beautiful thick dark towels. The salt hadn't done the interior much good. A set of papers came out in Tom's gloved hands as one block, with the title and a crisp series of diagrams of hares all clearly visible, but fell apart almost immediately.

The rest of the backpack was, in some ways, an eminently well-prepared collection. Survival gear, water, heat packs, dried food, a little pup tent. Portable chargers. And a little pouch containing – for reasons neither Tom nor Titus could explain – a variety of very fancy masks.

Tom leaned back on his haunches. 'Here's the laptop and a phone, which might function with a lot of work at a lab somewhere, but good luck to us extracting anything from them right now. I think, you know, he really was planning to manifest an unauthorised fracture for it.'

'To make a break for it? Yes, sir. Though he wouldn't survive very long on the ice, even with all this,' said Titus, picking up the edge of one of the ration packs in a scrupulously gloved hand and dropping it. 'A slow suicide, maybe? Shades of Ernest Shackleton, sir. But there's no note.'

They stood looking at the detritus. It brought a slightly unreal edge to the stateroom, as if something weird and abyssal had crawled in there to eat its lunch and left bits everywhere in charmingly neat lines.

'That pack looks very expensive,' said Tom.

'I recognise the make, sir.'

'How much would one cost, new?'

Titus did a quick internet search and named a sum that made Tom cough with astonishment. 'It's a high-end laptop and phone too, sir.'

'We need those bank accounts, Titus. We need them pretty immediately. Dr Sixgill was definitely not just surviving on stipends.' The list on the whiteboard looked taunting. A curse, Tom thought, on the morbid slowness of American authorities.

'A rich benefactor, sir? Aabria Scott?'

'*Titus.*' Tom rolled his eyes.

'No, I know, sir. I was not convinced of the idea either. But the alternatives are – confounding. Perhaps it isn't relevant, after all.'

Tom pondered for a minute, then asked, 'How far away is the shack from here?'

They pulled out a map. It would, at best estimate, be a full day away on foot; Ben Sixgill would have spent an uncomfortable night, but then—

'If he were headed for the shack,' said Tom, reflectively, 'he must have expected something there. Supplies, at the least. Shelter. And then transport onward. To do what, and for whom?'

'He was a scientist, sir,' said Titus. 'Do you suppose he might have made life too uncomfortable for himself on this ship and decided to strike out on his own? He was, per the witness statements, inclined to ruffle feathers,' he added, with some understatement. 'This rendezvous may have been with another scientific vessel or research group.'

Tom made a frustrated noise. 'If so, why did he take that collection of masks with him?' They were the one very eccentric note in an otherwise fairly standard travel pack. Not only the porcelain Venetian carnival mask, quite torn in the lining but none the worse for having waited out on the ice under a tarp for many hours, but the sodden, thawing remnants of several others, including one in velvet, one blue one with spangles, and one a strident hunter-green tweed. 'What in the wide world was this unpleasant gentleman doing to get himself made into a kebab on the ice as he scarpered? Having a masquerade?'

'I had hoped,' said Titus without answering, because there was no available answer, 'that we might find the remains of some conveyance, sir.'

'A bit of raft or a sunken coracle or something? Yes, me too. Even a paddle. But nothing. It's still as the grave down there, Titus, so it wouldn't have gone anywhere. He grew wings on his feet and flew, it seems.'

This line of thought being both unproductive and depressing, Tom stuffed several of the excellent aniseed biscuits from Elisabeth's kitchen in his mouth and they turned their attention to the tranquilliser gun, which was thawing itself on a towel like a particularly unpleasant breed of fish.

'Look at this,' said Titus, angling the interior of the barrel. Tranquilliser darts, they both knew, were wider in circumference than the thin metal of the harpoon. This gun had scrapes all around the inside of the barrel, glittering in the light.

'Hm. Something shoved in, perhaps to make the harpoon fit, then possibly pulled out again after firing. Or it came out with the shot. It was crude, whatever it was, but it worked.' The gun was a pressurised one, Tom noted, meaning that it would fire almost silently – and it wouldn't have the horrible kickback of an underwater weapon. No lame arms.

'We assume, then, that the harpoon was fired, and not stabbed at close range, sir,' said Titus.

'This gun has a long range in the air,' said Tom with faint disgust. 'It could have been fired from the ship. It may have been a difficult shot, but—'

'If they leaned out the starboard side of the ship and

fired, with all the fuss on the stern about the overboard man, they would have a clear line of sight, sir.' Titus started drawing a small map of the ship with his precise hand. 'I really *must* get schematics; I'm sorry, sir, I have been remiss on those. Sixgill was definitely shot where he stood; he could not have carried that wound any distance at all, and there were no blood marks.'

Tom made a forgiving noise. The lapse wasn't quite like Titus, but between post-mortems, supervising chemical testing and poking around the crew for gossip, his second-in-command had hardly had an easy schedule. 'So anybody on deck – or in sight of a right-hand window. Sixgill, Dr Eder and the twins have rooms on the right side on the scientific level. All the staterooms on the floor above have a right-facing window, but they're also positioned back off the deck, so it would be a harder shot from inside – more likely to be from the deck itself. Yes, all right, I know it's starboard and not right, stop looking at me like that, Titus. We should do a run-through and see how quickly the whole thing might be done. The Captain may be out, as he was surrounded by a skeleton crew on the bridge who all watch him devotedly.'

'He went to get Elisabeth Lindgren,' Titus reminded him. 'That likely bought a few minutes, sir.'

'You'd need nerves of steel.'

'Stingray nerves, sir.'

Tom breathed out through his nose, considering. 'Elisabeth was in the kitchens; those have no windows at all. It would be very tricky for her. We must get onto that restaurant source of hers about what really happened with Sixgill. All right.'

They continued in this way for some time without much progress. Given a bit of imagination – one of the three men around the radio slipping away, Gladys Moreland in one of her unseen periods, Scott and Berg or Singh and Grey in their carefully alibied pairs, either Highcastle, Lindgren or the Captain in a mad dash – anybody, with the exception of the Blanchards, might feasibly have been able to dash to the starboard side somewhere and fire off a shot. Though how they hadn't been seen remained a mystery. 'Or maybe they were,' said Tom softly, 'and we're the last to know.'

'Alicia Grey, sir?'

'Or something. Boo Moreland being right-handed means he couldn't shoot very easily with that banged-up arm, and he was on the radio to the *Mouette* multiple times, but perhaps—'

They were interrupted by Rose Blanchard knocking on the window. She looked shrewdly interested, but had the manners to apologise.

'I'm sorry to interrupt the sleuthing, but I popped along with a good excuse to get back the radio for the *Mouette*; you took it off with you when you got out, Detective Inspector.' She stretched out a wiry hand. Tom looked at his pocket, sighed, and handed it to her.

'You said excuse?'

'I don't know what this means, but listen.' She told them of the faint strangeness between Sunila and Alicia when they were talking earlier. 'They didn't seem afraid or upset, or anything. It was just – it was odd,' she finished, uncomfortably. And quite probably it was just odd, and that was the end of it, thought Tom irritably, and wished everybody would stop being so bloody mysterious when they'd probably just had a tiff about gin rummy. Still, he thought, Rose was a person who saw both the real and the emotional worlds with a distinct and curious clarity. It was an interesting gift – and a reliable one.

'Thank you,' he said. 'We'll add that to the notes.'

Rose caught sight of the pile of detritus from the backpack. 'Hello, you found the masks!' she said.

'The masks?'

'We had a masquerade. A bunch of them went missing after. It was a bit chaotic. It was the night I punched—' she coughed. 'This was Bloom Highcastle's, this was Alicia Grey's. And Dr Eder's. That thick white one with the torn felt on the inside is Aabria Scott's.' She pointed them all out. 'Did he nick them? What a little slug.' Titus made careful notes of all the owners.

'We're due to see Dr Palgrave this afternoon,' Tom said, 'if she's well enough.'

'Dr Palgrave's been vomiting so colossally in the shared scientists' bathroom that we've all been given access to a crew bathroom instead,' said Rose promptly, catching the note of scepticism in his voice. 'If she's given herself something to stave off talking to you, she's *really* overdone it.' *Chalk one up to Rose's suspicious mind*, thought Tom, pleased.

'Is she that type, Dr Blanchard?' asked Titus, in his quiet voice.

Rose considered. 'No,' she said, 'I'd have to say not. At least – she's perfectly likely to have picked up somebody else's sandwich and eaten it, and made herself sick that way. An allergy or something. But deliberate self-poisoning wouldn't feel in character. And she's had enough of a difficult journey – oh.' She looked at them suddenly with clear eyes. 'Did Dr Eder explain the hares to you?'

'The what?' First frogs and then hares. Tom battled a mild feeling of hysteria and put another biscuit in his mouth to relieve it.

'There was some mystery with Sixgill and the hares,' Rose said. She explained the incident with the talk, Palgrave's leaving, and Dr Eder stalking off to talk to Sixgill about it, without any explanation.

'There were,' said Titus, 'notes about hares in Dr Sixgill's cabin, but they weren't his own. They were typed-up notes by somebody else. I believe they were only initialled. I shall find them.' He beetled off fastidiously to a box in the corner.

'Finn very much enjoyed being a part of the investigation,' Rose informed Tom brightly. 'He can't stop talking about how excellent an assistant navigator you are. And how receptive you were to his talk about sharks.' She blinked at him innocently.

'It was a very good talk, yes,' said Tom, again feeling the incoming sensation of becoming a beetroot. 'Very informative. Williams, do you have it?'

'Yes, sir,' said Titus. 'Here it is.' He brought it out with two fingers and spread it on the desk. The paper looked quite old and had certainly been crumpled many times, but the initials were on the corner of each page. *S.P.*

They were all three staring at this with various degrees of puzzlement or theorising on their faces (theorising on the part of Tom, puzzlement for Rose, and a careful blankness that clearly hid whirring gears for Titus) when the door opened.

'Hello,' said Dr Palgrave. She was extremely pale but clung onto the doorway with an intense strength. Rose, Tom saw, instinctively moved forward to hold her up. 'I would like to tell you that I have committed a murder.'

18

'Please repeat that, Dr Palgrave?' Tom felt suddenly as if he were back in the *Mouette* and everything was sinking very fast.

'I killed Dr Sixgill,' said Dr Palgrave, quite clearly.

'I would like you to sit down, please,' said Tom, slowly, without any physical reaction, 'and tell us what you know. Thank you, Dr Blanchard,' he added to Rose, who left with an extremely shocked and puzzled look on her face. Whatever theory she might have had, Tom noted to himself, Palgrave as murderer hadn't featured high on it. Titus caught her at the door, doubtless to impress on her that she had to keep schtum on sudden and unexpected confessions, while Tom regarded the woman who sat down in the stateroom chair.

She was blank-faced and black under the eyes. Tom wondered whether she'd been sleeping well, and briefly canvassed that she might have a drug problem, but dismissed it. She had deep furrows across the forehead, a slightly flat skull, undyed light hair, multiple piercings but only one on each ear used. Long fingers with short nails, with none of the burns or cuts or sun damage of a practising chemist or field biologist. Theoretical only, then, or at least had somebody else doing the nasty stuff for her. She was short-sighted, but the glasses, of an old and not particularly expensive make, weren't very powerful. Good teeth and a high clear forehead, sunken cheeks. She was also, from the look of the skin, once quite a lot fatter, and had lost the weight rapidly – stress, thought Tom, not a health scare or a diet kick.

Titus, he knew, would have other more precise notes. Titus was an observer of the trees while Tom looked for the woods; their combination tended to be quite powerful. A case had once turned on Titus's observation of the main suspect's toenails.

Dr Salome Palgrave, as was her full name on the documents before Tom, looked between them. Rather than terrified, her gaze was petrifyingly intent. It was also identical to the expression in her passport.

'He stole my work, you see. So I killed him.'

'Your work on Arctic hares, yes?'

'Yes. He displayed it for the guests. It was my research. He had come across it in some underhand way and was planning to submit it to *Science*. He had already put it through early peer review.' The *S.P.* on the documents, now explained. 'Dr Eder, with whom I have corresponded occasionally, tried to persuade him otherwise. Dr Eder is a very boring but fundamentally upright man,' she added, firmly.

'Did you attempt to persuade him too? Were there threats?'

'We had one conversation. He had leverage,' said Salome crisply. 'I do not wish to discuss this further.'

'And so you killed him.'

'Of course I killed him.'

'How?'

'I've no idea.'

Tom looked at Titus. Titus examined the back of Salome Palgrave's head with deep interest. She did not appear to be masking or baulking or lying; Tom was very good at telling liars, and so was Titus, and neither of them – it was clear from their shared glance – had detected a single flicker.

'I have,' said Dr Palgrave with the same complete concentration, 'done some background reading into criminal psychology in the past few days, while dealing with a severe case of vomiting. Apparently it is quite common for perpetrators to black out and have situational amnesia until well after the criminal act has in fact been committed. I believe this must have happened in my case.'

'You have a gap in your memory starting – when?'

'Shortly after the lunch on the day of the murder. I remember feeling strange and going to lie down. I suspect this was my homicidal urge developing. Then I remember nothing else until at least six hours later. It is a complete blank and I have no history of blanks or of any other kind of amnesiac tendency. I can have my family doctor testify to the fact.'

Tom made a note. Titus looked at him.

'Are you a good shot, Dr Palgrave?' Tom asked, conversationally.

'As far as I know, I've never handled a firearm in my life,' said Dr Palgrave. 'I say as far as I know because—'

'Because of the amnesia.'

'Yes, precisely.' He felt the beam of approval Salome

205

Palgrave must grant to her most attentive students. She was, he decided, eminently and provably sane, which would make the defence very unhappy.

'In your supposition, then, you were taken over by a kind of rage – or an emotion we don't at this point understand,' said Heissen, seriously. 'You threw the life buoy overboard, or perhaps somebody else did that, and then you saw Dr Sixgill standing on the ice, found a gun with a spear-fishing harpoon in it, and shot at him with high accuracy. You then returned to your cabin to sleep.'

'I could have shot him from the window of my cabin,' said Dr Palgrave. 'At least – oh, no, I couldn't have, could I. The positioning would be quite wrong.'

'I'm afraid that is the case,' said Tom sadly. Dr Palgrave's room was one of three on the lower scientific level on the port side of the ship, not the starboard. 'Do you have any memory of being shown a tranquilliser gun?'

'Yes. It was in those cases on the deck. They weren't locked. I must have extracted one during my – my towering rage. I suspect,' she added conversationally, 'that this vomiting afterwards was a psychosomatic symbol of guilt.'

'Do you take any medications or have any substances in your cabin that might have caused you to black out? Could a tranquilliser gun itself have had that effect?'

'No, I don't carry any such things. And if I had somehow pricked myself on a tranquilliser gun intended for a large mammal, it would nonetheless only have knocked me out for a good hour or two, not the six hours or so I appear to have – well, lost. Those guns, you know, only carry enough to tranquillise bears and the like for a very brief amount of time.'

Tom looked at Salome Palgrave. A great mind, he knew, reading between the lines of the professional resumé and various interviews he'd collected in preparation for this dialogue; one with a host of field-shaping ideas, but who hadn't produced something seminal in a few years. This hare-camouflage theory, he thought astutely, would likely have meant a great revival in her career. Whatever Sixgill had on her, it must have been formidable. She was a woman entirely of the mind, and wouldn't give up her work for lighter forms of blackmail.

'And you felt antipathy for Sixgill?'

'Sixgill was,' Palgrave said, in a slightly bored tone, 'a bad person. I mean morally. Scientifically he was a brilliant if lazy thinker. But he did not behave with any integrity and I have no regrets whatsoever that he is dead, as can be imagined, since I—'

'Since you killed him. Yes.' Tom looked at her with a level stare. If she was covering for somebody it was an extraordinary piece of acting. Could she do it? Disappointingly, he rather doubted it. 'I think that will be all for the present. If you regain any memory of what might have transpired, please produce it.'

'Aren't you going to arrest me?' asked Salome, with professional interest.

'Innocent until proven guilty,' explained Titus, clearing his throat mildly, 'can also apply in circumstances where the pronouncement of guilt comes from the suspected person.

You have provided, in other words, a legal supposition we must endeavour to prove.'

This seemed to satisfy her. 'What if I kill again?' she said, with the tone one might use to ask about the correct procedure for renewing a licence plate at the DVLA.

'Do you feel violent antipathy towards any other person?' asked Titus.

'No. I do not, you know, tend to feel intense emotions of any kind. They all seem so petty. But I did sincerely hate Ben Sixgill. I have only felt that sort of emotion . . . once before. It did not, however, result in murder, I assure you.'

'If you begin to feel any,' Tom said politely, 'it would be in your interests to tell us immediately, so that we can take steps to ensure everyone's safety. In the meantime I feel you have helped us a great deal. I would ask you not to mention this to any other person on board, as they may—' He thought of Alicia Grey. 'They may make complaints,' he ended, weakly.

Dr Palgrave, however, saw nothing apparently wrong in this, nodded, and said, 'I shall keep to my room, nominally to recover from my illness. Once you have discovered how I committed this crime, I would like very much to hear it.' And she left.

'It is possible,' said Titus to the suddenly empty room, 'that this previous strong emotion may be related to Sixgill and his blackmail, sir.'

'I've seen the amnesia story run three times in court, twice clearly by shysters and once by a person who ended up displaying a truly impressive skull fracture,' said Tom thoughtfully. 'The first two went away for good long stretches, the third ended up with a reduced sentence after an MRI found the skull fracture had been there for weeks, bleeding into the brain. The husband she'd killed had gone after her with a baseball bat a month before, and the ER doctors had tried to keep her in to treat her, without success. Salome Palgrave's skull looks eminently intact, but I suppose—'

'She would have mentioned if she'd had a contributing head injury,' said Titus. 'She's that type. Very thorough.'

'I'm afraid she is,' said Tom, with vague disgust. 'So now where are we?'

'Further on from where we began, sir,' said Titus, beginning to put everything from the backpack into labelled evidence bags that would be filed according to his astonishingly precise system, ready to be recovered at the touch of an obscenely organised finger. The whole thing seemed almost dreamlike or fractal to Tom; the remnants of this person's apparent bid for freedom or desperate dash across the ice, lying on the floor in the sunlight, glittering . . .

Glittering.

'Here, Titus.'

Titus looked up at his superior immediately. Tom was looking at the arrangement of the belongings with a fixed expression. 'Yes, sir?'

'Do you still have that jeweller's loupe I made you pack?' They'd both taken a course on how to recognise and grade diamonds, largely out of Tom's own stubbornness and his suspicion that Interpol wouldn't lend them any of their gem experts in a month of Mondays. Another person in the class had, inevitably, attempted to get Titus interested in a 'gem-based business opportunity', and they'd had to politely extricate themselves.

'Yes, sir.' Titus's hand went to his jacket. Of course, thought Tom; he carried everything around on him like a fisherman with his favourite fishing-flies.

'Do me a favour. Look at the things on that crumpled little blue mask.'

'On a costume mask with *hot glue*? Surely not, sir.' Titus granted him the rare distinction of a disbelieving look, but hooked out the loupe, selected one of the gems – all, Tom had noted, still in formation, without a single one apparently missing – and then, after some time, lowered the loupe from his eye. 'The Highcastles,' he said, in stunned wonder. 'The Highcastles?'

Tom looked at the light that gathered on what were, indisputably, diamonds. 'Murder has been done, Titus,' he said grimly, 'for much, much less.'

19

The occupants of the *Dauphin* were beginning to feel jumpy, Rose could sense it. It was a full day after the discovery of the ex-Crimson Horror and they still hadn't steamed silently away from its location on the ice. People were inclined to avoid the prow of the ship, even though a *Dauphin* cleaning crew had now been given police clearance to wash away all that bear-tempting blood. It was as if there was still an after-memory of gore in every mind, as lurid as a backdrop in some deeply amateurish production of the Scottish play. Even the sight of some walruses off the port side, rolling their bulk through passing fragments of broken ice shelf and occasionally hauling themselves on top of one to gaze around imperiously, couldn't alleviate the sense of oppression for long. Rose leaned over the railing and watched them swim effortlessly around segments of ice bigger than a car, and dwarf them.

Finn, standing beside her, was quiet, and she was grateful. Rose was refusing to tell anybody about what Dr Palgrave had said, for the very good reason that she didn't believe it. Sixgill may have nicked her work – Rose had come to her own conclusions about that *S.P.*-initialled document, yellowed with the age of several years, and had decided that two plus two equalled Sixgill stealing Palgrave's ideas – but whatever was wrong on the *Dauphin*, it didn't seem to radiate from her. No. She'd also seen Dr Palgrave go back into her cabin and lock the door, which seemed *very* unlikely if Detective Inspector Heissen and his frighteningly colourless partner thought she'd been going around murdering people.

But it was odd and hard keeping things from Finn. They sat next to one another in the softening light, which frittered through mackerel clouds, and looked out onto the ice. The reflected sunlight still hurt her eyes. She remembered Dr Eder telling her about the best glasses for work on snow: white ones made of bone, carved to fit close to the face, with just two thin slits over the eyes. He intimated to Aabria Scott that he'd been given the secret by an Inuit scientist. Sixgill, Rose remembered, had said Eder had probably just seen the snow glasses in a museum, and laughed.

She wished she could put her face in some snow glasses, shut the slits, and sit in darkness.

She roused herself. Finn was deeply quiet. 'Maybe we'll move soon,' she offered aloud. She had always been the pragmatist to his dreaminess. Even in extreme situations, jetlagged or miserable or frustrated, she could do *that*. 'Then we could get in another camera drop. What do you think?'

'Hm? I was thinking of Martin,' said Finn. His face was flushed, not just from the scour of the wind.

'Why?' Rose restrained herself from asking whether he'd been cherishing secret visions of Martin with a harpoon in him; she knew perfectly well that Finn hadn't. She was the vengeful, angry one; she worked to preserve Finn's innocence as much as she could.

'You were very angry at him,' said Finn, as if he could read her mind. Which, she thought, they sometimes could; not with supernatural ease, but with the sort of connectedness that one never really gets away from. They'd text each other the same joke at the same time, even when separated by oceans.

'Yes,' she said.

'I wish you hadn't been. It just——' Finn waved his big hands, with their tapering fingers. 'It seems like you have to carry all the weight, of being mad at people about me. And look where anger got somebody.' He gestured at the ice at the front of the prow, and they both knew what he meant.

'I know,' said Rose, quietly. 'Listen. Anger's not frightening, not really. You're not a hothead like me, so you fear it, but it can be powerful. And it's——' She struggled to explain what she was thinking. 'What did *this* wasn't brief, hot fury. That's what got him punched in the nose. And he ended with a punched nose, and I ended with a bruised hand, and that was the end of it. This was something colder. Suppressed, I think, and hard, and sad.'

Finn shivered, and they huddled together in the wind.

'I hate that you have to keep fighting things for me,' he said in a small voice.

'I never have to,' Rose corrected. 'I want to. I can do it better than you can, anyway.'

'I could protect myself. Sometimes.' He sounded slightly hesitant, which Rose knew would mean, in any other person, a full-blown sulk. She thrust away a sudden feeling

213

of irritation – didn't Finn realise protection was *her* job? – and smiled.

'You want me to teach you how to throw a punch?'

'Better you than Boo,' said Finn, reflexively, and then went, 'Oh dear.'

'He would have landed that punch without much injury if we hadn't been aiming at the same time,' said Rose, laughing.

'Still. I think – I think it's a lot for you. I do want to be strong and do things myself.' He sounded determined, and, she thought, quite adult. People often thought they were siblings, not twins – that Rose was older. Usually she was proud of this fact. Right now, however, it filled her with an obscure feeling of shame.

'All right.' She tried to grin easily. 'If there's ever a next time you can tell them what you think of them, very firmly. We can be a team. And then maybe, with your permission, I'll kick them.'

'Whoever you're kicking, I pity them intensely,' said Boo Moreland, plonking down beside them. He was very warm against Rose's side.

'How's your arm?' asked Finn.

'Bearing up,' said Boo gaily, and they chatted. Rose was silent. She was remembering her terrible moment in the laboratory. Boo with his splinted arm – who couldn't have shot a damn thing, as he was lamed – but the reality of the suspicion, the fact that it had come to her at all, was still distressing. As if a low long eel were lying in the shadows of a reef.

'I'm going for a walk.' She tried hard to keep her voice casual. Neither of them, she felt, truly bought it – Finn made a small mouth movement, and Boo turned his head to look at her more fully – but they let her go. She stomped up the deck, getting more blood back into her feet, and went to look at the *Mouette*. She endeavoured to move her thoughts back into the clear waters of professional discovery. The Greenland shark drifting under the ice, with its slow-moving blood, its centuries-old skeleton and eyes. She began, soothingly, to mentally list all the research outcomes they'd highlighted in the application . . .

The *Mouette* gleamed in the light like a bald, elderly scholar. Somehow science was not the refuge it normally was. Things felt sour, and even the idea of a Greenland shark emerging at that moment and staring cavernously at her from the dark water didn't give her any charge of excitement.

All those people, milling on the deck, or in various rooms, while she and Finn were under the waves. These faces she knew only as surface, or as passed remarks, or small judgements – somebody among them had taken a spear-fishing harpoon and put it deep into Ben Sixgill's lung. She felt a convulsive horror, and put one hand onto the *Mouette* to steady herself.

Rose Blanchard was not a person easily surprised by the hidden parts of others – her vocation guarding her brother meant she'd seen some soft, charming people reveal horrific prejudices and blank cruelty. But the complexities of the problem here felt overwhelming. One needed data – not emotions – and there seemed too much of both.

'It gets into your head, doesn't it?' Gladys Moreland had come around the back of the ship, in full *Dauphin*-orange with a giant bobble hat on her head.

'What does?' Rose reflected that Gladys's very direct stare must be highly discomforting for people on the witness stand. It was, at the moment, a kindly stare. The pompom helped to ease it, though not as much as you'd expect.

'Suspicion. It makes you question – oh, all the things.' She waved one hand. 'That, you see, is why justice is so important. Real justice. Not punishment, you know, that's something for the law and the state, and long arguments after the fact – but *knowing what really happened*. You see?'

'Yes.' Rose did see. 'Knowledge. I'm feeling the want of it, at the moment – or at least an organising principle.'

'You like things to be orderly. I know.'

'And people and crimes aren't.'

'Oh, you'd be surprised.' Gladys Moreland's intelligent face wore its expression lightly, but her eyes were intense. 'When you place things in the right light, they can seem remarkably simple.' A woman supremely confident in her ability to understand complex patterns, Rose thought.

'Do you have a theory?' she asked, interested, and then slightly cringed at herself for how ridiculous it sounded.

'I'm not going to go around hinting to people that I know all,' said Gladys Moreland, twinkling. 'I can assure you that's hardly a safe procedure. Anyway, in my experience, people who know important things often don't realise it.'

'Something they saw or heard, and haven't put in the proper context?'

'Precisely. People don't, you know, pay attention to their surroundings consciously all the time. I was barely paying attention to the world at all when that ridiculous young man was killed. I was trying to avoid Sandy Highcastle – and thinking of my daughter, Frog – and of Boo.' She sighed, in a kind of self-recriminating way, and did not explain what she'd been thinking about Boo.

A system appeared to Rose suddenly – of collecting what people observed, rather than what they *thought* they'd seen, and so making some real conclusions. It was an organising principle. It was *good* science. She breathed into the wind, and felt better.

Gladys paused, then hooked her arm into Rose's. 'Tea, now. That's my professional judicial opinion.' And they passed indoors.

Tom Heissen knew who he was looking for in the dining hall, and wended his way over to the table with quiet directness.

'Hello, Highcastles,' he said genially. 'I have a present for you.' He gave them back the mask. 'I'm afraid the hot-glue-gunned stones and spangles have mostly been washed off or been nicked by fashionable fish, but—'

In fact Titus had been at it with a precision glue-removal system involving tweezers and a hot lamp. The glue involved, he said, had been remarkably strong; a kind of setting cement. The diamonds themselves, once removed, had been confirmed to be very small – the largest wouldn't even be a quarter of a carat – but were, in their mass, worth, to the best of Titus's limited knowledge, tens of thousands. 'That's if they're without inclusions or only have very slight ones,' he said professionally, placing the last of them into a black velvet tray. 'We'll have to find a real jeweller, sir.'

'Oh, you found it! Oh, it's all yucky.' Bloom's happiness turned to slight disgust as she handled the blue silk, which had, Tom admitted, taken a beating, particularly since they'd run it under the sink after the diamonds had come off, to give it a more successfully undersea-damaged look.

'That's very nice for you, dear,' said Sandy Highcastle, soothingly. 'Thank you, officers. I suppose it was off the side of the ship with the rest of the bundle?' His eyes, under the creases of the sun-beaten brow, were only mildly curious.

'Yes, sir,' said Tom, and left it at that. If he and Titus were trying to locate the source of the diamonds, it was best not to yell about their suspicions in a public place and risk rumbling everything.

Titus, who was standing beside Tom and did not appear to be looking at anything in particular, supported his observations afterwards: Sandy Highcastle didn't look miserable or surprised at the reappearance of the mask with very few diamonds on it. Neither did Bloom, who was merely revolted. Either they were unaware that it had been carrying real diamonds instead of crystals, or they were involved in the diamond cartel and had been expecting that it would be picked clean – by Sixgill, or by somebody else. What somebody else? How much did the Highcastles know about their very expensive, soggy accessory?

It was conceivable that they'd been tricked into hot-gluing gems instead of crystals. People could be astonishingly incapable of looking past their own expectations. Gems had been smuggled using that principle before now; Tom remembered a case involving a whopping emerald in a child's plastic princess tiara.

And what was the victim doing with the mask in the first place? Had Sixgill somehow discovered that the mask was covered in diamonds, and fled with what he hoped were a lifetime's worth of riches? He'd have been disappointed; the handful was worth a lot, yes, but not enough to mean he'd never work again. Had he uncovered something desperate, taken the mask as proof, and attempted to go for help – and ended up like the intern? Why take all the masks at the same time? There were a lot of empty spaces in Tom and Titus's theories, too many to support any weight yet.

Their next port of call was Dr Eder, who was drinking strong coffee and received his mask – not spangled with anything, and not carrying any hidden gems, thanks to Titus's very careful investigations with a thin incising needle – with no great grace. 'This,' he said, 'will not be of any use to me. You may keep it as a souvenir of the investigation.' He acted as if he'd just given a boon. Definitely, thought Tom, a remnant of the nineteenth-century era of naturalists, where men of wealth pottered around with servants discovering fossils and spending fortunes on menageries, and made obsequious gifts to kings. Dr Eder was designed to be depicted in a portrait with a peacock on one shoulder and a specimen of a rare fish in amber by his weighty hand.

He appeared to feel that the divide between scientists and paying guests upon the ship was an unnecessary indignity, and was perhaps subconsciously sitting on a rampantly expensive chair in the guest area with an air of complete belonging.

The doctor received the enquiry about Sixgill stealing Palgrave's research with some surprise. 'Oh, yes, it's quite true,' he said. 'I knew of Dr Palgrave's research into hares; I'd read the preliminary notes of her work, and was astonished when Dr Blanchard mentioned it to me as being Sixgill's. I did my best to explain to him the code of ethics of our profession. He laughed at me.'

'That must not have been very nice for you.' Tom was grave-faced.

'No.' Dr Eder puffed up slightly like an incensed frog.

'Why did you not mention this to us before?'

'Dr Palgrave asked me to keep it a secret, when it happened,' said Dr Eder, with a show of embarrassment. 'I am pleased that she told you. Having one's work stolen, and paraded as the thief's own, is deeply unpleasant – and I understand he must have had some great hold over her to permit it.' He knew nothing of the hold itself. 'That,' he said with offended dignity, 'is *not* something you ask a fellow scientist,' and Tom assessed that he'd probably probed, likely with an offer to throw around his heft to help, and been rebuffed with some vigour.

'We will keep the mask,' said Titus, filing it away in a small plastic bag.

'Do you think he was playing a joke?' demanded Dr Eder.

'A crew member told me on enquiry that he'd gathered up the masks that were laid aside and put them in a pile, including mine – *most* distinctive, he said, he remembered it immediately. What reason could the boy have for taking a bunch of masks and dumping them into the sea?'

Niilo, who'd been working at the ball, confirmed this. He had seen several of the masks around the place throughout the evening, and had placed them on a side table for safe-keeping, so that the guests could retrieve them at their convenience. This was quite common for the crew to do after the masquerade on the *Dauphin*. Yes, Alicia Grey's green mask and Dr Eder's black velvet – 'most enthusiastic, that gentleman, to tell me how expensive and well-made his was,' he said, without the faintest hint of a smile, but nonetheless implying it strongly – and the porcelain mask of Aabria Scott. No, the spangled silk of Bloom Highcastle had not been among them. No, he would have remembered, as it looked delicate and he would have folded it in a napkin to preserve it.

Tom went out, looked at the encroaching darkness as the sun set heavily over the ice, and sighed. He was feeling weary. The source from Elisabeth's restaurant past had come up dry that afternoon. He was Dutch and very well-spoken. There had been, he said over the telephone, many incidents with her as a nascent chef – a restaurant critic who would remain nameless had been truly unspeakable – but yes, there was something with a young academic, an American. It had, he added, not been very explosive, particularly considering the rest of her experiences in the industry. (The stories! Tom received many bits of gossip, and got the distinct sense that this manager had seen entrenched sexism for the first time with Elisabeth, some of it very shocking, and it had flavoured the rest of his life.) Sixgill had made 'an unbecoming request', she had rebuffed him firmly in front of the kitchen staff, and he had appeared chastened. That was all. The university was not informed, he had not been banned. Nothing, in other words, to influence revenge on her part or anger on his, four years into the future. Just a further piece in the mosaic of Sixgill, who had been, it appeared, a disreputable nuisance for years.

Titus joined him. 'So Sixgill gathered the masks, put together all his gear, somehow got to the ice, and put on a performance of sudden violent invisibility,' Tom said softly.

'A disappearing act? Yes, sir. To tell the police what he'd found? A smuggler who'd gone straight and was trying to escape? To disappear into the sunset with a sprinkling of diamonds? Or – what, sir?' Titus's breath rose warmly from his nose.

'Unclear. If he *were* going for help, he may have chosen not to warn the authorities beforehand, just in case the message was intercepted. It would fit. It might. An aggravating little monstrosity grows a conscience. And yet, somehow, Titus, I'm not quite satisfied . . .'

He and Titus walked in silence. Just when the mists began to clear a little, Tom thought, more wind blew in.

The gloaming of the Arctic crept into the stateroom where Kate Berg stood fluffing pillows and rearranging sheets. This wasn't technically her job – the personnel of the *Dauphin* were more than capable – but years on a ward meant she got itchy when she wasn't doing something. And Aabria Scott was, in her old age, particular about her arrangements in bed, complete with a specific Royal Copenhagen cup for cocoa every night.

Kate Berg was not in fact as young as she looked; her age showed in her arms and hands, in the pink thickness born of long hours of scrubbing and cleaning agents, of the sanitised interiors of hospital gloves. Even expensive hand creams on her nice salary from Mrs Scott could only do so much. She was, she reflected, exhausted. She had picked a superlatively tiring line of work; but there was satisfaction in it, in its precision, in the achievement of all goals.

There was a knock on the stateroom door and, to her minor surprise, the tall blonde head of Sandy Highcastle stepped in.

Hypertension, not enough exercise, too much rich food, a lifetime without proper sun care: Kate knew all the things that were wrong with Sandy Highcastle just by looking at him. Now, however, something was eluding her. He kept shifting from foot to foot, staring. 'I'm afraid Aabria is out on a constitutional,' she said, in a friendly way. If he was after jewels, she thought coldly, he'd have a fun time of it; Aabria very rarely brought anything that wasn't costume. She was no fool.

'No, no,' said Sandy in a high, artificially friendly way. 'It was you I was looking for.'

'What can I do for you.' Kate folded her hands professionally.

'It's – well.' Sandy dropped his voice. 'It's my wife. She's having – last night was very bad. She's having real trouble sleeping. Nightmares. Real thrashing night terrors.'

This, thought Kate Berg, would be entirely in keeping with her assessment of Bloom Highcastle, who was faintly malnourished, definitely deficient in several vitamins, and likely thought she had many sensitivities she didn't actually possess. *Not*, she thought in her very private self, the kind of person who coped well in a crisis.

'That's very unfortunate,' she said politely.

'I was wondering – do you have anything? A night draught, or? My grandmother used to give us warm milk, but of course it's all considered old hat nowadays.' Sandy smiled foolishly, the foolish smile of a worried husband.

Kate looked at him for some moments in silence. He blinked at her.

'If she is concerned about her sleep, she should see Alva,' she said seriously.

'No. No, I meant – I only wanted to enquire, you see. She used to take melatonin—' He launched into a long litany of the sleep aids his wife had tried, some, Kate noted, with genuine scientific efficacy, others embroidered out of the mind of some Instagram herbalist. The list was extensive.

'It sounds as if she has run the gamut,' she said, adopting a cheery but strictly professional tone. 'I can't prescribe, you see – I'm a nurse, not a consulting doctor – so I would recommend no caffeine in the afternoon, staying away from sugar, not eating too late, and some ear plugs, perhaps. And a discussion with Alva, who is very competent. I'm sure she'll be right as rain when this is all over.'

This, she saw, was entirely unsatisfactory to the insistent Highcastle, but in the face of her outright refusal – in which, he clearly saw, there was no wiggle room – he had no choice but to retreat. He was effusive in his praise of her kindness, which slightly put Kate's back up.

Once he'd left she stared at the door for some moments. Aabria Scott came through it, puffing. She'd done several laps of the deck in the lights of the ship and was clearly tired out. 'What,' she said quietly, submitting to being lowered into her chair by a clucking Kate, 'was he doing in here?'

'Behaving like a husband in a second-rate melodrama,' Kate said crisply, and explained what he'd wanted. 'He's a fool. No chance in hell of it and he must have known it. Maybe he was scoping out the room and wanted an excuse.'

'Men like that,' said Aabria, 'fall apart so easily.' Kate waited, but there was no elaboration. She snorted aloud.

'Going after sleeping drugs! You'll have to warn that wife of his that he means to bump her off.'

She said it to be shocking, but her charge was rarely shocked. 'Oh, but that never works.' Aabria blinked up at her. 'You know that. She wouldn't believe a word of it, and he'd get angry.'

'I sometimes get the sense,' said Kate with a sigh, plumping the pillows, 'that you have seen almost everything there is to see of humans.'

'No, I haven't, but I extrapolate well. I was born very

poor, you know that. Poverty gives you an insight into character in a way very little else does.' She settled back in her chair. 'So cold out there, but such a lovely evening. I'd like some peppermint tea, thank you.'

'Did they give you the mask back? The detectives. I saw they were handing them out in the lounge.' Kate put the nice hefty *Dauphin* kettle on. So nice, to have a little kitchenette in the room, she thought absently. They'd been on so many boats that were ramshackle, or well-appointed but not clean; this one had everything, in spades.

'No,' said Aabria, without much interest. 'They won't give that back. And it's covered in blood anyway. Not very nice.'

This time Kate looked up at her. 'Why won't they give it back?'

'Because it's useful,' said the elderly woman, closing her eyes. 'I know. You do too; just think about it a little. Or go and ask them. They could tell you what to do about Sandy Highcastle and his wife. I think I shall have a little nap, Kate.'

But Kate Berg did not go and ask the police.

Alicia Grey was huddled on her bed when Sunila Singh came into their room. It was remarkable that for such a long-limbed woman – at full height she slightly resembled an auburn greyhound, with tapering ankles and wrists – she could curl up to such a small size. The vast shell of the *Dauphin* bed dwarfed her; she looked like a tooth in a very large mouth.

Sunila shut the door carefully and immediately came to

her, reaching to touch her shoulder, to enfold her.

'Don't,' said Alicia, her voice thick.

'Another one?' Sunila went to the bureau and examined the flattened white paper, which had been found shoved under the door and was presently lying half-opened.

She read it, and made an inarticulate noise of fury. Then she took the paper and folded it up into a drawer, on top of two more virtually identical papers. All had been delivered since the murder, after the cabins were searched, and all bore much the same message.

'I can't go on like this.' Alicia's voice, stripped of its glowing heartiness and also of decades of upper-crust English pronunciation, was deep, throaty, and slightly rolled at the consonants. It was not, at its heart, a British voice, and it was not one she exposed to anybody, not anymore. 'You know I can't, Sun.'

'I know.'

'I haven't said a thing. The police ask so many questions, and I have been silent – and still they come, these missives.'

'I haven't said anything either.'

The deep, dark eyes of Alicia Grey looked suspicious for a minute, then relaxed. The eyelids closed, thin and purple-veined, with long pale eyelashes. Sunila sat on the edge of the bed helplessly.

'What do we do?' Alicia sounded desperate. 'I don't know what we can *do*.'

'We keep our heads,' said Sunila, crisply. She had always been the one capable of an even keel in substantial upheaval. It was one of her great strengths. She looked at her wife,

227

her passionate and sensitive wife, with intense, almost fero-cious love. She had been in charge of her in one capacity or another for much of her life, and she knew, as always, what to do. 'We do as we're told. We uphold our end of the bargain. And *you* need to shower. You've been eating toast in the bed again.'

Alicia sighed and smiled. She straightened her long back. 'You always take care of me, Sun.'

'Old habits,' said Sunila smartly. And the two of them laughed.

20

Titus Williams was not visibly a particularly fast man, but he carried in his short pale limbs the legacy of a lineage of messenger-boys, many of them risen to eminence in their Welsh city during the industrial era for their fleet-footedness, as well as their ability to dodge obstacles and their preternatural memories for who'd paid their bill to the couriers that week. (Many was the business owner or householder who cursed the Williams name as the small person winked out of sight or reach, having left bills, unwanted *billets-doux* and angry court summons smartly on their doorstep.) So it was Titus who looked to Tom now with his arms held in a racing start position. They were on the stern of the ship, right near the *Mouette*. The night had fully drawn in; the golden lamps of the deck glistened, and salt was brushed over the polished wood to stop ice forming overnight.

'Go,' said Tom, starting a stopwatch.

Titus bolted. He threw the nearest life buoy overboard, and any passengers eating inside the lounge who heard the splash jumped; but there was no yell, no warning noise. Niilo, Linnea and Juhani, with some other crew members, were watching with interest, and possibly to see that the ominously terrifying young policeman didn't come a cropper over the side. He ran to the starboard deck, pulled

229

out a nicely readied tranquilliser gun, and pretended to fire it over the side at the ice. He dropped it, not over the side but on the ground, and ran back around.

'Eleven seconds,' said Tom, clicking the watch. 'Swift, but leaves questions. You're a dab hand with that gun.'

'It is,' said Titus, breathing strenuously, 'not the kind of thing one absolutely likes to use, sir, but I am glad to know I would be reasonably able against marauding wildlife. We assume, of course, that it was pre-loaded with the harpoon.'

'So. It could, conceivably, happen. They could have been on deck, or somewhere else, thrown a life buoy, and then made it to the side and back while the *Mouette* was still well underwater and the alarm was going up. It doesn't explain how on earth Sixgill got out there without anybody noticing, which was presumably the intention. But it could be done. I don't suppose Sixgill could have swung over the side and hung there in hiding?'

They both looked over the side of the *Dauphin*'s hull. Smooth, almost unweathered from the harshness of the Arctic tides. Nowhere for him to catch hold. Tom made a gesture of disgust.

'We have to factor in the angle of attack from the deck too,' he said aloud. 'Remember that harpoon was stuck in him at a right angle. Perhaps they ran down the stairs or something and shot out of the cabin portholes on the right – sorry, starboard side? They'd be level with him then. In which case somebody with a cabin on the lower levels might have seen them. But from up here – it *could* be done.'

'We're assuming that the personage who threw the life

buoy was also the one who shot him, sir,' said Titus. 'When in fact the incidents could be entirely separate.'

Tom sighed in annoyance.

'What is happening?' The Captain appeared beside them, looking with concern over the side. 'Is there something on the ship that is worrying?'

'No, no.' Tom explained what they'd been doing. The cooperative crew were now hauling back the life buoy, which had been hooked, as ever, with a rope.

'But such a risk!' The Captain looked horrified. 'And surely – to fire from this level – it would be an enormous gamble.' They walked around to look at the expanse of open deck to starboard. Inside the lounge the lights glittered, people moved and shadows shifted; there was a quiet air of elegance, a radiant lantern spilling outward into the ink of night. If anybody had noticed Titus running in the dark, they hadn't moved to watch. Yes – shooting from this level was a hell of a risk. But this person, whoever they were, seemed prepared to do almost anything. And they were clever. A life buoy, a scream, a bobbing shoe – what a perfect distraction for sea-faring wealthy neurotics.

'I fear,' Tom said conversationally, 'that we are disrupting your ship most intensely, and I am very sorry for it.'

'Not at all.' The Captain smoothed his hands over the air as if parting the hair of a small child. In fact he'd been dealing with several enquiries about moving forward, from the *Dauphin*'s owners, the ever-irritating Sandy Highcastle, and even Elisabeth Lindgren (he wondered whether there wasn't a person waiting for her back in home port; she'd been a little distracted on the past few trips). He had dealt with each of these in a fitting way. The investigation had to reach conclusions; the remains of the itinerary would have to wait, and yes, refunds would have to be given if appropriate, and there was nothing he could do about this, what a shame, yes.

'You cope with all of this very well,' Tom noted, astutely.

The Captain lowered his eyelids. 'It is part of my training, Detective Inspector.'

'Yes, I'm sure.'

'There are,' the Captain continued, 'other ways to leave the ship besides the dinghies, of course. The snowmobiles, for instance, which are transported to solid land in their own carriers. Tomorrow we were due to take them out for a drive, as it happens. The activity is designed for a more scenic stop—' He gestured out to the barren view of the ice cap, disturbed in the distance only by some rising patches of snow. 'Nonetheless it will be amusing, and relieve the monotony.'

'You have snowmobiles!' said Titus. Tom shot him a look. Titus had few weaknesses, but this was one of them. They had worked on a complex ring of motorcycle spark-plug thefts together early in their partnership, and Tom was a dab hand at wiring them into basically anything, but Titus had apparently taken that incentive as a chance to learn about the workings of anything fast-moving, motorised, and prone to making a gigantic racket. He'd once spent an entire plane journey scrutinising the manual for a helicopter engine, which seemed to hurt the plane pilot's feelings.

'Yes,' said the Captain, 'but rest assured, we have checked

and all of their gear remains firmly in place.' Possibly seeing the look on Titus's face, he launched into a clearly well-known spiel about the safety of the top-of-the-line *Dauphin* vehicles with which people could skid through the snow at sixty miles an hour. They could, he explained, be taken out of the ship onto the ice using a sort of inflatable, like a pool lounger. Tom resolved to double-check the Captain's search, in case the errant scientist had somehow nicked an inflatable without drawing any attention when they'd searched the hold – and then caused it to disappear into thin air. Anything, he thought with some indignation, was possible with this case. Scarpering scientists laden down with glued-on diamonds, which they may or may not have been trying to steal or get to the police, which may or may not have been related to a smuggling ring, and which may or may not have caused said scientist to get skewered!

He looked over the side while Titus and the Captain discussed horse-power, and retreated to his usual place for grumpy days, which was an imaginary pub he fantasised about running in the future, called the Aran Knit. He had detailed this pub very lovingly in his head over many years, and on this occasion stared down at the dimness of the ice cap, almost invisible off the prow in the dark, while mentally scrubbing the tables and lighting the lamps. It was a mindful practice, in its own way.

Somebody running across the deck, firing a gun. Or perhaps not running – walking idly, as if basking, to the side of the ship, or to a porthole – and firing, precisely and accurately, at Sixgill's chest. Whose face? What steady and quiet hand held that gun? Somebody had seen or knew *something*.

He watched his breath float in the dark air.

'It has been a long day for you,' said the Captain sympathetically. Of course, Tom thought, mildly startled; the man must have an internal encyclopaedia of knowledge about sighs and their corresponding emotions. What a legacy from years of passive-aggressive guests! 'Should I send some sandwiches? Or would you like to join us this evening in the dining room? I have suggested that we dine en masse, as—' he paused, with a diplomat's delicacy, 'community is paramount at present.' And more eyes on everybody at the same time, thought Tom.

'Do we have to dress for dinner?' enquired Titus politely. Tom felt a panic rising – he'd not worn a bow tie since his sister's wedding, and had found it so difficult to untie that he'd finally, shamefully severed it with nail scissors and hidden it in the waste basket.

'If we insisted on that,' said the Captain drily, 'we would never see a single scientist. Except, perhaps, for Dr Eder.'

'Except for him,' agreed Tom. 'We'll come. Please ask the kitchen to provide coffee. Lots of coffee.'

Bloom Highcastle disliked unpleasant scenes. She'd married Sandy Highcastle in part because he was already quite rich, and in part because he was clearly devoted to her and she thought he was sweet, but also because they had gelled quickly into an ability to deal with one another without anger or loud words. She could sulk, and he could pout, but they did not yell; they did not smash anything; they went into their meditation rooms, and took deep breaths, and lit candles, and then came together and talked it out while their maid made them extremely smelly teas from Nepal.

The marriage was, on the whole, a successful one. Why had they come on this cruise? She was fretful. They were fighting constantly. What was the matter with Sandy? He had said this would be a great treat, told her all the fun they'd have – and even before the murder he had been jumpy and sad. Everybody else on this ship was frighteningly unenlightened – those Morelands! Really, from such supposedly keen minds she'd expected better – and she didn't even have the comfort of his belief echoing hers.

'I just want you to tell me what's going on,' she said now, despairingly, as she sat on their bed. She knew how to get him to tell her things – she wasn't so young anymore, but she knew he loathed her sadness, that he'd come to give her anything if she would stop being miserable. But this time he wouldn't, and she didn't understand why.

'My lovely one,' he moaned. 'I can't. I'm sorry. It's – it's nothing.' Then he started walking around the stateroom – really pretty it was; she'd put up a few hangings and laid out a few crystals to cleanse its energy a bit, it was very peaceful – in his cashmere jumper, and talking wildly. About what it might mean to be poor, or unlucky – and how she would still love him, wouldn't she, if it came to that. About how true she was.

'We aren't poor,' she said, in surprise. The business was flourishing; she'd seen the accounts. She was surprisingly business-minded. People thought she was fluffy, and it was often useful to develop that impression, but there had been a strong flow of investment, and the markets appeared to be growing. Her father had been a grocery-shop owner, and she'd known double-column accounting before she was ten.

'No. No, my lovely. I just – I promise you, you'll be safe. Everything will be fine.' He sat and kissed her fingers then.

'Is there – another woman?' she asked, out of pure confusion, and he looked at her as if she was speaking another language. Which was very comforting, because she knew, in her bones, that Sandy was not a loyal type for life; he was besotted with her now, but perhaps not forever. But it seemed that was not the problem.

Eventually he left, and she gave up on further direct attacks for the present. Bloom was a woman who knew her powers, and her last card to play was pretended indifference, a casual near-cruelty. In the face of *that*, Sandy's most intractable moods often became worry, demands for reassurance, and eventual capitulation to whatever Bloom wanted. And, she thought a little crossly, this was an expensive holiday, despite its lack of penguins, so she wanted to enjoy it. Like many wealthy people, Bloom viewed value for money as sacred, and she required her £24,000 worth of happiness, whether Sandy participated or not. She made up her small, rather hard mouth with exquisitely heavy lipstick, and left the stateroom.

As the Captain entered the formal dining room that evening, Rose was catching a quick breath to herself. The evening of the second day PCH felt almost surreally glamorous. (PCH

236

meant Post-Crimson Horror, as Boo was now calling it. He planned all their meetings in that manner: 'We'll gather at 1400 hours, day two PCH.' To her annoyance it had stuck in her mind.) In obedience to the Captain's gentle prodding, the ship occupants had started gathering in the dining room around cocktail hour, and now, post-dinner, things were swimming along in an atmosphere of almost chaotic gaiety; it was as if there was a determination to have fun, despite the miasma hanging in the Arctic air.

The two married Morelands, Aabria and Sandy Highcastle were playing a card game, badly, all in a very good temper; Sandy was even laughing, while Aabria flirted so intently with Patrick Moreland that he'd gone a springtime shade of pink. He kept appealing to Gladys to rescue him, and she kept refusing to do anything of the sort, and grinning. Everybody had temporarily forgiven everybody else for the sins of believing in the power of crystals or having a birth certificate with eight middle names or being entirely too incisive in polite conversation; the situation had made them all, briefly, democratic.

Dr Eder was telling Kate Berg and Finn a series of outlandish stories about his old mentor, Dr Fothergill, which had the unfortunate side effect of making Dr Eder himself look very staid by comparison, but his audience were absorbing the tales of a young marine biologist fleeing the French Legion in the 1950s with absolute attention – and fair enough too, Rose thought. Kate, with the skill of somebody used to listening to elderly people tell interminable stories, was clearly poised to look interested and ask intelligent questions while thinking about something else, but Dr Fothergill's career was sufficiently absorbing that this muscle didn't need to be used.

Dr Eder, she noticed, was slightly vague when it came to his own meeting with Fothergill, and Rose got the impression that it wasn't quite the mythic meeting of minds it sounded. Perhaps young Eder hadn't been greatly impressive to the formidable Fothergill, at first.

Boo had been attempting, with some apologies, to teach Rose the foxtrot; 'the most important thing you learn at a prep school', he'd told her, and romped her through it until they were both bruised and almost sore at the sides from laughing so much. He'd made references to the future, to where they might go in London and in Paris, which she knew well, and she hadn't demurred. Now he was whirling an ecstatic-looking Bloom Highcastle around the room in a dance that *looked* like a waltz, and Bloom was alternating between giggling and yelling at him for stomping on her. Sandy Highcastle, Rose noted, was looking at this performance with what appeared to be sincere cheeriness. He really *does* want that woman to be happy, she thought.

Alicia and Sunila hadn't appeared for dinner. Kate Berg, slightly flushed, had suggested going to find them, but Dr Eder had advised against it. 'They deserve their quietness,' he said. 'There was a woman of my acquaintance—' And a complicated story followed of some woman related to the Greek royals and her nervous condition, about which she'd told him a great deal; though Rose strongly suspected that Eder had only met this esteemed personage once in passing, or caught sight of her at a reception. But the two women did turn up afterwards, along with Tom and Titus, whom she noted entering with only a slight turn of the head; if she just let them drift across her sight, she could pretend they were merely other party guests, that this was all normal and fine. She could forget the crew member stationed casually outside the door of Dr Palgrave's room. She could forget the blood on the ice.

She realised, almost in the same thought, that this was impossible; that her mind had clasped its jaws around the problem and was refusing to let it go. It was a vaguely despairing feeling and an exhilarating one.

'It is nice,' said a voice beside her. Elisabeth Lindgren had come out of the kitchens and was standing in her starched whites, watching them. 'It was time for you all to cut loose.'

'Yes,' said Rose. 'I think it was needed.'

'He seems good,' said Elisabeth. She nodded in the direction of Boo, dancing with Bloom. 'The boy. His name? Boo-boo?'

'Boo,' said Rose, and suddenly understood the phrase 'covered in confusion'. She felt as if it had descended over her like a huge set of wet jungle leaves. 'Yes. I mean – yes, he is.'

'I am happy for you.' The chef sounded serious. This was not, reflected Rose in the depths of her discomfort, a woman with a twinkle of meaning in her voice at any time. She said what she said, and you mined in it for meaning as you chose.

'It's not like that, really,' she said, in a low voice. 'I travel a lot and – we've only really known each other a few days.

It seems – all very intense. That's all.' She felt the heat of the dancing slowly leaving her face. 'And he's such an *idiot* at times.'

'Ah, but when you love, you forgive them – anything.' And here there was a sudden shift in Elisabeth's face, if not her voice; light seemed to stream out of her, the planes of it glowed; she was for a moment softened. It was extraordinary. *What*, thought Rose in a flabbergasted way, *must it be like to have that face look at you with that love? Some people might drown.*

She tried to follow Elisabeth's gaze out onto the floor – perhaps it was directed at somebody. At the Captain? His long face was vivid in the luxurious glimmer of the dining hall. She knew the Captain had his own stateroom, and Elisabeth was rarely in her own little cabin on the lower floor with the scientists; but she also knew Elisabeth often slept in the kitchens, there was a little berth for her there; it was common knowledge among the crew, who laughed about it in the mess. Perhaps it was somebody else, or somebody who had never been here on this ship at all.

'Sometimes,' she said slowly in the silence, thinking of Martin, 'it's not wise to forgive. Sometimes things are too much to bear. They shouldn't be borne.'

'Yes.' The light went out of the face, and Rose felt an inexplicable pang of grief; she knew, somehow, that it was an expression she would never see again. The serenity returned. Perhaps in it there was a hint of sadness, but Rose might be imagining that. 'That is so. You understand. You will be wise, I think, about this man.'

Rose wanted to ask – there was so much here, so much love that wasn't explained, an entire story under the surface of this remarkable woman – but couldn't bring herself to do it.

'I'll try,' she said. Elisabeth nodded to her and went back into the kitchens.

'What was that about?' It was the strapping young Detective Inspector, sidling up sideways, which was an improbable thing for him to do considering his size.

'We were just talking about love,' said Rose frankly, and was pleased to see Tom Heissen colour at the cheeks. Finn didn't give a private viewing of that PowerPoint to just anybody. She detailed the conversation a bit more fully.

'Do you think she was talking about somebody in the room?' said Heissen.

'I don't know,' said Rose, considering. 'It felt – more like a memory. Like something had gone wrong, with some-body she loved very much.' She was, she thought, enjoying the feeling of conspiratorial data collection a bit too much, and diverted accordingly. 'She also called Boo Moreland Boo-Boo, which I may institute as his new name.'

'We shall tell him immediately,' said Detective Inspector Heissen in his most serious voice, and before Rose could stop him said, 'Moreland!'

'Yes?' Boo and Bloom stopped beside them mid-whirl. Bloom looked so happy she was faintly overwhelmed and drooping.

'Your new name in police files is Boo-Boo.' Heissen gave him a strict nod.

'Rose, what on earth have you been *doing*,' said Boo despairingly. 'Bloom, I think we need a glass of water before I rescue my impugned reputation.'

'I'll just go to the bathroom to freshen up a bit – my *hair*,' said Bloom, in a voice that, Rose thought, sounded suddenly very East London. She rearranged her necklace, a beautiful long loop of gold that went to nearly her waist, and busied herself out of the room. Rose, laughing, went over to join the Moreland couple, who were now cajoling Alicia and Sunila to join their card game with Aabria. Tom and Boo came behind them, discussing whether Boo-Boo Bear was in fact an accessory to the thieving of picnic baskets.

'We can consult your sister-in-law,' said Tom. 'She'll know the jurisprudence of smarter-than-your-average ursines.'

'Good idea. Hi! Gladdy!'

'Shut up, Boo,' said Gladdy cheerily, 'I'm trying to get these two to play.'

Patrick, free of Aabria's attention for about a minute and looking extremely grateful for it, was shuffling cards. 'Yes, do. You two look all in. Poker?'

'Let's make bets!' said Aabria, gaily.

'Let's absolutely not,' said Kate Berg, and Aabria stuck her tongue out at her. Kate stuck hers out back.

'What about gin rummy?'

'Of course,' said Alicia, leaning forward easily out of her chair to pick up a drink, 'but I don't know how.'

Rose blinked at her. 'But you said you were teaching Sunila. That day up on the deck.' She had spoken aloud before she'd realised; in the beat of silence that followed she cursed herself. But she was too far gone now, and she was a stubborn woman. 'You remember, you told me Sunila refused to learn the rules.'

Detective Inspector Heissen was there, at her shoulder. She knew he was there.

The two women didn't say anything. They looked at each other. Alicia then looked at the cards in Patrick's hand, almost fixedly. Sunila continued staring at her wife, a strange stare, one Rose couldn't quite read. It wasn't fear – or anger. It was something else. A sort of blush had come over her; her mouth was hanging slightly open.

'What were you doing up on the deck, if you weren't playing rummy?' asked Heissen, genially. It was a very gentle question, without a hint of suspicion in it, but the delicate atmosphere all of a sudden went to pieces.

Alicia burst out, 'Oh, God,' in a shout of embarrassment. Sunila went incredibly red and started to laugh.

'What?' said Finn, worriedly. He'd appeared at Rose's side, feeling that there was a ripple of trouble in the room, and gravitating to her immediately.

Rose suddenly started to laugh as well. She knew, somehow. She didn't know how, but she did. 'On the *deck*?!' she said, gasping. Alicia covered her face with her hands. Tom Heissen, Rose saw, suddenly bit his lips to keep a straight face.

'We didn't get a proper honeymoon, you see, and it was twenty years this year, and—' Sunila was now sitting back holding her sides, trying hard to talk without, it seemed,

243

nearly wetting herself. 'And I thought it would be romantic – to do it at least once—'

'You were *having sex*,' said Boo Moreland disbelievingly. 'You were! In broad daylight just underneath the bridge!'

'Bravo!' said Aabria Scott in high delight.

'I *told* you it was a bad idea,' said Alicia's voice from between her hands. 'I *told you* somebody might see us, even if all the staff were distracted or in a meeting.' Kate Berg leaned forward over a chair and began to cackle. Everybody had to take at least a minute to calm down.

'*That*'s why Bloom was stranded on the stairs,' said Rose, trying hard to get air. 'She came up and saw you, and just ran out like a jackrabbit. And then somebody started screaming in her face. Oh, my God, you've got to apologise to her.'

'We *couldn't*,' moaned Alicia.

At this point, with the cinematic timing of an excellent comedian, Bloom re-entered the room. She saw Alicia, and Sunila, and everybody staring at her, and then she collapsed on herself in a whoop of what was a mix of horror, hysteria and wheezing laughter.

'I'm *so sorry*,' said Sunila, coming over and taking her hands with an effort.

'I was just *mortified*,' Bloom said in her high voice, which she was trying to steady. 'And I didn't want to tell the police because it's not their *business*, but I didn't know what to do, so I just ran and cowered in the stairwell—'

'And then the alarm began just outside the stairwell window and you went up in smoke,' said Sandy Highcastle. 'Oh, my love. That's *ridiculous*.'

Aabria Scott handed her a champagne glass, which she downed with alacrity.

'This will have to go in the police files,' said Titus, to which Alicia Grey said, 'Oh *no*,' in a hapless voice, and Sunila nearly started off again and had to be told to breathe. The chaotic joy of the room seemed to wash over them all.

'Hold on, though,' said Rose suddenly. A possibility had appeared in her head – suddenly soared upward in the air, as mobula rays do when they perform for their mates. Jumps of six, eight feet out of the water, into the sun. She looked at Gladys Moreland. 'You found Bloom on the back stairway?'

'Whimpering under that bizarre artwork,' said Gladys, without judgement. She looked at Bloom with a small smile. 'I thought she was on her way somewhere else.'

'But, Bloom – you'd been there the whole time,' Rose continued, eagerly. 'When the giant splash happened and the life buoy went off, and all that. And there's a *large window on those stairs.*'

'So Mrs Highcastle could have seen something, through the window?' said Tom Heissen, quickly. 'Somebody who threw the things – or pulled on a rope, or something of the kind – just at the *Mouette* dock?' He looked at Bloom Highcastle.

'But I didn't see anything,' said Bloom, confused, staring between the two of them. 'I promise I – *nothing*. Nothing at all!'

And that, for most of the guests, was perfectly acceptable. Dr Eder said, 'No wonder, dear lady,' and began another story of a high-born person of his acquaintance who had lost his prized sausage dog in a palace once, because of the distraction of a daily four-cannon salute outside. Rose wondered if he was attempting to help a lady in distress, or simply being morbidly egocentric again. Gladys Moreland merely shrugged her shoulders and started adjudicating the dispute about bears and picnic baskets, which took a reasonably long time and ended in a ruling that would have got Boo-Boo community service for acting as an accessory to petty larceny. Alicia and Sunila talked to Titus quietly, giving him, Rose was sure, the actual details of what they'd been doing, while Titus took scrupulous notes. They were holding hands.

But Bloom, thought Rose, looked more confused than ever; she sat alone with her husband, who was plying her with treats and blankets as usual, and when Rose looked back about ten minutes later, she was gone.

The evening tapered off at what must have been two or so in the morning. Boo had danced with virtually everybody, including a spirited folk-inspired kicking number with a few crew members and a surprisingly nimble Sandy Highcastle. The lights in the dining hall were being turned out when they finally all went out onto the deck. Tom Heissen and Finn, Rose noted with a deep haze of tired pleasure, were in intense discussions about the best types of knitwear; Finn plumped for Aran knit, while Heissen was arguing strenuously for Fair Isle. Given that Rose had observed Tom wearing an Aran knit at least once, she strongly suspected he was being contrary for the sake of flirtation. Both Titus and Tom, she'd noted, had circled the hall perpetually throughout, as if taking constant notes, and talked to one another frequently. They were, she supposed, on a job. However, so was she.

'Hello,' said Boo Moreland, appearing as ever beside her. 'I have a request.'

'Yes,' said Rose, squaring herself to think as clearly as she could.

'It is a very nice night, despite it being four below freezing, and you look very pretty in your orange parka. And I would like to kiss you. Is this acceptable,' said Boo, very distinctly.

Rose considered.

'I think it is acceptable,' she said.

The interlude of the next ten minutes was interrupted by nothing except the occasional huff of the *Dauphin*'s engines at rest, and the distant sound of movement as the lounge was set up for breakfast.

'I wonder,' said Rose eventually, 'if Finn and the nice Detective Inspector are doing something similar somewhere.'

'I think,' said Boo Moreland in a slightly shell-shocked voice, 'that there cannot possibly be enough good luck on this ship for this to be happening to more than one person at once.' Rose grinned at him. 'And,' he added more steadily, 'the Detective Inspector seems very professional. He likely can't kiss anybody until he finishes the job, no matter how nice they look in orange.'

'I knew it was the parka,' said Rose, mournfully. 'I'll go

back to wearing tropical wetsuits and you'll lose interest entirely.'

'Yes. A skin-tight outfit that gets wet. How very uninterested I will be.' Rose kicked him.

Then there was a sound. An odd sound, that neither of them recognised at first – but it repeated, again and again. It echoed off the hull of the ship, off the railings, off the soft furnishings in the lounges and staterooms. It was screaming.

A member of the crew named Astrid was standing in the stairwell, leading onto the upper deck. It was her screaming. On the landing, between the two decks, lay Bloom Highcastle; and around her neck, wound four times and pulled to incredible tightness, was her rope of gold.

21

The Arctic night seemed infinitely long; the sun had set so long ago that, though it was around 6 a.m., it now felt as if it might never rise again. Tom Heissen stretched his back and heard the crack of several relieved spinal vertebrae, which had suffered nobly through all the minute aspects of investigation – crawling, fingerprinting, jumping, pacing – around Bloom Highcastle's body for hours. He wished acutely for coffee, for biscuits, for Biscuit the cat, for a hot bath, but this was a flicker of temptation for lesser persons, and he moved his head back down to his work.

Bloom – originally Bernice – Highcastle had been killed with her own necklace; it likely hadn't taken the culprit more than a few minutes. The necklace bore no discernible prints. Stranglings were, in many ways, the most repulsive of murders, because they destroyed identity so profoundly; Titus had matched the fingerprints carefully to make sure that it was in fact Bloom, because the vestiges of her ravaged prettiness had long ago disappeared. Tom thanked heaven for the fact that they'd managed to get everybody's fingerprints during the interviews. It had felt like a fool's errand given the total lack of useful prints on Sixgill's room or body, but this, at least, proved its use.

He and Titus had compared their own perspectives minutely and could not identify with firmness anybody who had been present absolutely all the time after Bloom Highcastle was seen to leave. The exception was, of course, Dr Palgrave – herself guarded all through the night, with a locked porthole. So whatever she'd done to Sixgill, or hadn't, this wasn't her work. He comforted himself briefly with the idea of her somehow jimmying a porthole and climbing up like Errol Flynn, but, he reflected, she had no reason to.

Nobody else had a solid alibi. And he had let this woman, this silly bronzed blonde person, be killed, as he talked to a handsome young man in the dining hall below.

The guests, exhausted and terrified, were waiting in the dining hall for statements to be taken – but also, frankly, so they couldn't wander off and throw anything incriminating over the side. The strong arms of Linnea and Niilo, Tom knew, were barring the doors.

Tom sat back on his haunches. The sweep of the stairwell from the top deck to the middle was operatic, with ocean-blue carpeting, and the shift of the sea visible through an array of windows. Above the stairwell a set of elaborate white mouldings stood in abstract, three-dimensional shapes, vaguely suggesting sea waves. Below, the dim head of the *Mouette* glittered in the ship lights, like a bald man adrift.

'She must have been attempting to reconstruct the moment of the splash, sir,' said Titus, carefully. He likely recognised that Tom was awash with guilt, and was being as assiduously tactful and helpful as possible.

'Well, whatever she saw, somebody was intent on her not

revealing it,' said Tom. He passed a hand over his forehead. 'What a waste.' Bloom Highcastle's body was now covered in a thick, expensive sheet with a thread count somewhere in the region of the population of France.

There was a voice behind them. 'You will excuse me, sirs.' It was the Captain, moving over the makeshift cordon they'd constructed out of plush gold rope usually used to delineate spaces on the ship (not barred to guests, no, never, only perhaps *temporarily unavailable* while a floor was cleaned or a ball arranged).

'What's the news?'

'The authorities on Svalbard have asked us not to move for the time being, so that a police doctor might again be sent via helicopter. At this point I may give them a berth on the ship.' The Captain's long and ascetic face looked dismal. A lack of sleep was no knock to somebody who regularly piloted ships around terrain filled with dozens of tons of ice, but the deaths were hitting him hard, in a place where no amount of soothing or generosity could help.

'You won't need to,' said Tom grimly. 'We'll get them.'

The Captain looked at him for a long moment, then placed a hand unexpectedly on the Detective Inspector's shoulder. 'It isn't your fault, Heissen.'

Tom made a surprised and upset noise.

'No,' continued the Captain, 'I am aware of that look. You did not neglect your duty. You could not be in fifteen places at once. It is not possible.'

If he turned out to be the murderer himself, thought Tom, this would be the most presumptuous conversation in history. 'I know,' he said, with as much charm reflected back at the Captain as possible, 'and I thank you.'

'I bear the responsibility,' said the Captain, soberly. 'But naval law recognises – a certain limit. You can run when the bell comes that a person is overboard, you can do all that you can to save them, but nature and the sea have their own rules. There are things beyond our power.' He paused, then began to depart, and nodded to Titus. 'There will be a coffee maker on the side in the lounge when you require it.' Tom noted that this would likely be one of the first times in the *Dauphin*'s history that guests would make coffee for themselves, and praised the Captain for thinking of it; nobody would take something made by others, even from the kitchen, in the present climate.

'I believe, sir,' said Titus softly as the Captain left them alone, 'that we must operate on the assumption that Bloom Highcastle and Sixgill were murdered by the same person, or associates.'

'Or her husband or a girlfriend of his decided to take advantage of the charming atmosphere,' said Tom in a flat tone. 'I need fifteen more officers. I need round-the-clock teams. I need interviews with everybody, again, all over from the start.'

'Have a biscuit, sir,' said Titus, having apparently listened to Tom's unspoken fourth need for something, *anything* reasonable. It was, Tom saw, a digestive, likely from the bottom of Titus's pack, and slightly smushed. It didn't have aniseed or fifteen types of grain or a miasma of gold leaf. It was perfect.

'God, that's good. So: statements. The husband last. Financials, whatever we can glean. And anybody – Sunila, the Morelands, anybody – who might have caught a flicker, *anything*, of what Bloom might have seen through these windows.' He went up to them, their plexiglass several inches and layers thick to keep out the cold, and sighed. 'Are there any prints on this?'

'They're cleaned every day, sir,' said Titus, with the sound of genuine regret in his voice. 'They're very diligent.'

'Of course,' said Tom Heissen, and sighed. He shut his eyes and gently headbutted the window. *Bof*. The window took the hit very well.

There was a slipping noise of metal against plastic. Something above them, something small, skittered, whistled, and fell onto the carpet beside Bloom Highcastle.

There was a loud scream.

The guests in the dining room, many of whom were now sleeping in chairs or on piles of pillows arranged by staff – Aabria Scott had sunk into one and looked like the head of a harem – collectively felt that their extraordinary night was getting, gradually, less real. Time suddenly seemed to collapse, everybody sat horribly upright, as the noise – a horribly familiar noise – broke in. That scream, the scream of Sixgill going overboard, had a horrid clarity: the same notes, the same tailing off into a screech, and then silence. Nobody moved. There was no splash of a life buoy.

Titus, still gloved, leant forward onto the carpet and turned off the voice recorder. He looked up at Tom, and whistled.

'What's going on?'

It was Rose Blanchard, standing by Niilo's protesting face at the door of the dining room. Tom had half-expected it to be the bluster of Sandy Highcastle, occupying once again his space as breezy and bluff and demanding – but the man was white-faced, sitting in the corner of the dining hall, folded in on himself. Finn was beside him, because, Tom thought to himself, Finn would comfort a cannibal on Death Row, but everybody else was avoiding him assiduously. The ship, it seemed, had taken a silent vote, and Sandy Highcastle was to be hanged, drawn and quartered. Though not quite unanimously: Tom saw Gladys Moreland was with Sandy as well, leaning out of the shadows to give him water. Her face, he saw, was filled not with the milk of human kindness but with the professional calm one applies to a defendant in shock. If she ever switched to the defence side of things, he thought, the Crown would be cooked.

'It was a recording,' Tom said shortly. He knew Rose Blanchard had a good head on her shoulders, but he wasn't about to reveal that a giant clue had dropped beside a body because Tom had decided to headbutt something in frustration. It wasn't, somehow, the impression he'd like to give. She raised an eyebrow at him and said nothing. 'There was,' he addressed the room at large, 'a replaying of the original scene. We apologise for the disturbance.' He gave no further explanation.

'When will we be allowed to go to *bed*?' demanded Sunila Singh, who was enveloped in about five parkas on the floor and looked like a small irate tangerine. Alicia Grey was actually asleep nearby. The tall woman was, Tom thought, absolutely exhausted; even asleep her face carried marks of deep and ravaging strain.

'Once we've taken all your statements, you can proceed to your cabins,' said Tom, formally. 'After that, if you can be of assistance to the investigation, please call Stateroom Four and we or the personnel of the *Dauphin* will assist you.' Juhani had leapt at the opportunity to be useful, and promised to man their phone while they were out for any reason; Titus had locked away all of their investigatory materials, because they weren't stupid, but also out of consideration for for the young man, who clearly had never seen death before, in any capacity.

'Where is Palgrave?' Dr Eder looked ashen. His waistcoat was in disarray and his beard was coming out of its established waxen shape. 'We're all meant to be *here*. Is she all right? Have you conducted a search?'

'Dr Palgrave is in her cabin where she has been all evening, and is being guarded in safety,' said Titus briefly. They had, in fact, checked this; Dr Palgrave had been sitting doing something complicated with numerical modelling, and had registered the check-in by requesting some tea, calling the person Nancy (the name of her assistant back in Chicago), and absent-mindedly shutting the door in their face.

'Why does she get a guard all night and we had to be *here*?' Sunila sounded very annoyed. The tangerine rustled with indignation.

'Dr Palgrave has not been well. Now, if you'll allow, we'll take some brief statements.'

The statements, which were held in the small serving room just off the dining room because it was too darn cold on deck, were all much the same, not that Tom had expected anything different. It was an evening of mirth, of glamour and distraction; nobody could define *exactly* where other people had been all night, though Sunila and Alicia vouched for each other's continual presence. Kate Berg accompanied Aabria Scott, who was clearly battling her own tiredness by sheer force of will. Even Rose and Finn Blanchard had lost sight of each other at various points. Rose, Tom noted, looked haggard.

The Captain broke in to have a murmured conversation with Titus, who was, by this point, looking so pale with exhaustion that he resembled a parsnip. 'We should have guards,' the Captain said. There was a glimmer, in the shape of his mouth, of naval training, of a dormant strategic dynamism appearing on his surface. 'We can't leave them in the dining room all night, but—'

'At this point,' said Tom in a low voice, 'I think it's not the worst plan. Keep a log of who's assigned where, at least; if one of the crew is in on it – which I doubt,' he added, as the Captain's pale eyebrows rose formidably towards the ceiling, 'we need to track that. But on balance it's a good idea.' Titus nodded.

The Captain's entrance into the dining room was a bit like watching a farmer walk into a field of entirely wilted cabbages. His voice travelled even further than normal, Tom thought. 'We thank you for your kind assistance. Please lock your doors; there will be a crew member stationed outside each of them overnight. They will escort you back personally.'

He gestured, and people began to neatly file past him with their escorts; it was almost like watching a procession into a dance. But there was no music, not now.

Kate Berg came past Tom and murmured almost too low for him to hear, 'Listen. Didn't want to talk about it in front of Aabria. Highcastle asked me for sleeping stuff for his wife. Earlier today. I'll send details later by phone,' and went out. Titus's eyebrows rose.

Tom made a note. He and Titus likely thought the same thing: if he had wanted to bump her off with sleeping stuff, it was odd that he'd go for swift violence instead. Unless – unless there was suddenly something pertinent, something pressing . . .

'Now, then,' he said, and went towards Sandy Highcastle, who had remained seated, without being asked.

The interview was perfunctory. Highcastle looked as if he'd been hit around the head multiple times with a lead pipe. Not, Tom thought with well-honed judgement, a man who was faking his shock; but there was such blankness there that little could currently be gleaned. Bloom's will stated that much of her property went to him, with around a quarter to her sister, who lived in New Mexico. They had no children. She hadn't a lot of liquid assets, most of it was tied up in the business, but there would likely be some savings. She was half owner of their house and cars; her life was insured, though not for a large amount; she wasn't carrying much real jewellery except for her wedding and engagement rings; she preferred their crystals. The gold chain itself was probably worth a little. He answered without pausing or looking up. He did not appear to be collecting or assessing himself in any way – simply pouring out information dispassionately, like a tap.

As for his movements, he said Bloom had simply mumbled something and slipped out, and he'd assumed that she'd gone to bed while he caroused. This, thought Tom with annoyance, was perfectly plausible.

'That'll do for now,' he said, closing his notebook.

Sandy Highcastle looked up at them and said, bewildered, 'Why would anybody hurt *Bloomie?*' It was the confused cry of a child.

And that, thought Tom with some discomfort, was the question. He felt the sound recorder in his pocket, and imagined the absolute chaos surrounding Bloom Highcastle, embarrassed on the staircase, suddenly engulfed in unexpected sound that seemed, as she said, 'as if it came from right beside her'. Things were feeling murkier than ever. If the scream wasn't real, as it now seemed it wasn't, how much of the rest was a stage set – and where was the action happening while the audience were being misdirected?

Sometimes, Rose reflected as she bolted down the deck after Aabria Scott's retreating back, it would be sensible to keep her mouth shut.

It had started simply: she, Aabria and Boo Moreland had

kept in a clump as they walked down to the staterooms, with the novelist's hand firmly around her wrist. Elderly people, she'd noticed, had extraordinary grip, or otherwise they had the grip of younger people but refused absolutely to temper it anymore. There was no removing herself; but she didn't entirely mind, as she, Boo, Aabria and their three designated guards, Linnea, Otso and Niilo, walked slowly through the blackness, breathing deeply. They were all very tired, but Aabria herself seemed sparkier. 'I don't sleep very much these days,' she said cheerily to Boo. 'I need far less, you know. Up at four, put the radio on, then Kate starts bustling around at about seven.'

Rose, at that point, was battling with a dark sensation in her head, something that felt distressingly sharp-edged. She had figured something out, she had said it to Bloom, Bloom had sworn she'd seen nothing – and now Bloom was dead. Was it related?

Knowledge, in Rose's field, normally did not have these kinds of costs. It was an untempered good. There was no question of ethics in the *revealing*, only in the procedures: whether to interfere with Grapefruit's illnesses using medication, for instance. But this was now a different proposition. She was revisited by the sensation of the reef, its flickering and fluctuating light, and of a profound disorientation.

Aabria had requested a further constitutional around the deck – one lap, she'd pleaded with her guard Linnea, and could they keep all together, so everybody felt safe? The three had acquiesced, with the long habit of agreeing to the whims of guests but also, Rose suspected, the knowledge that they could keep watch if anybody did something truly threatening. One of them went ahead, the others followed behind.

'It's like being the President,' said Boo Moreland, wonderingly. 'I keep expecting people to put on those little earphone microphones they always wear in the movies.' He hadn't moved towards Rose, hadn't touched her; they had kept entirely distant since the screaming. She wondered if they'd ever touch again.

'You're keeping on the inside,' said Aabria with a shrewd smile. 'Protecting us against the doorways and windows. Very gallant of you.'

Boo bowed genteelly, but made no dissent. 'If anybody tries anything they'll be diving into a thicket of witnesses,' he said lightly, 'so I don't expect much, but Gladdy would have my head if I didn't anticipate an ambush like a sensible human. All the time I've spent listening to her cases.'

They proceeded around the deck as if they were in a cotillion, thought Rose, rather than on a deck in minus six, with sunlight hours off, the North Pole closer than the nearest supermarket, and two corpses lying around the place like dropped pencils. She made a savage noise through her nostrils.

'I do hope,' Aabria Scott was saying in her slow way, 'that Dr Palgrave is well. I know she was very ill, for a while – but it does seem odd that they would coop her up in her cabin so much, without any warning of contagion or anything of that sort. They're all behaving as if she's done something wrong, and yet, you know, it seems quite ridiculous . . .'

'It does, doesn't it?' said Boo reflectively.

Rose didn't say anything.

'Dr Blanchard,' said Aabria, turning to look at her, 'you're keeping very quiet.'

'Yes,' said Rose. 'I'm – I'm very tired.'

'You're a terrible liar,' said Aabria. 'It'll do you good in life, though not, if I might say, in marriage.' Boo, she could sense, coloured intensely at that, but she was trying very hard to look at Aabria's mound of parka and not at her face. 'What is wrong with Dr Palgrave?'

'Nothing, you know, except – oh, I think she might be mad,' said Rose miserably. 'She honestly seemed to think – she wandered into the stateroom with the police and told them, without any preamble – you know how she talks – she wandered in as if she'd just bumbled past on the way from a lecture, and confessed to the murder.'

'What!'

And Aabria Scott was off – with surprising speed and vigour considering her age – sprinting towards the stateroom with Tom and Titus in it, saying, 'I must speak to the police – at once! At once!' with Boo and Rose pelting after her, and the guards in hot pursuit too. Boo managed to nudge Rose mid-sprint and make an expressive face that said 'this is pure chaos we're in, isn't it'. It made her feel unexpectedly and swiftly better.

Tom had settled in to make a range of very boring calls to various solicitors in London about Bloom Highcastle's earthly affairs, and those of the crystal business, when he heard the running down the corridor, and immediately went for his sidearm. Titus dived behind the sofa into a defensive crouch.

Juhani poked his head in. 'Sir, it's a collective of passengers, sir,' he said, looking as surprised as he was mildly chilled. And Aabria Scott, Rose Blanchard and Boo Moreland reared up like the Three Magi, with their three escorts puffing behind them. (Good work to Niilo, Linnea and Otso, he thought; these three were like molecules bouncing around a gas cloud.)

'What's this nonsense about Salome Palgrave killing people?' Aabria Scott looked incredibly indignant.

Titus came out elegantly from behind the sofa, shut the door, and made her sit down, with the silent but somehow emphatically expressed requirement that she be quiet.

'Dr Palgrave states,' said Tom, with as careful a tone as possible, 'that she blacked out and murdered Ben Sixgill while in a state of pure fury, one she can no longer recall.'

Scott looked at him very hard. He was, he thought, beginning to develop a catalogue of strong glares from women on this ship. Then she started to laugh. 'She doesn't. She does! Oh my word. Salome *is* an idiot.'

'What,' said Tom Heissen with interest, 'do you know about Salome Palgrave?'

'Her name is *Salome*?' asked Boo Moreland in delight. 'Why change that to Sally? It's a glorious name.'

'Women in science find it hard enough to be taken seriously,' said Rose, with asperity. 'I once had a lab boss address me every morning with songs about roses, and then tell me I'd never find a husband if I kept going on remote fieldwork expeditions.'

'I hope *he* gets murdered,' said Boo remorselessly.

'Shut up,' said Tom politely.

'Thank you, Detective Inspector,' said Rose.

'Quite,' said Aabria Scott. 'Salome Palgrave is brilliant, you know. She worked at the same university as I did, for quite some time. Came from a family of academics, all of them geniuses but quite batty. The usual things – trailing around in pyjamas, putting toast in pockets, missing her own highly crucial keynotes because she'd had a good idea. Not anything unusual in that context. But Palgrave, you see, isn't—' She paused.

Titus made a small noise. Aabria Scott looked at him and said, 'Yes. I know.' Tom was mildly astonished that she'd read Titus's meaning so clearly, which was that now was *definitely* the time to tell tales out of school.

'She isn't, you see, taken in by hard luck stories, or by lavishings of praise. But she is completely and rigidly moral, particularly about science and its uses, and that has got her into trouble.' She sighed. 'It was such a long time ago. She was very young. I fancy I'm one of the only people who actually knows about it – and that was only because the university vice-chancellor was extremely worried about the whole affair, and his wife, before she died, was one of my best friends. Small, very secretive communities tend to grow in academic places,' Aabria added. 'It's one of those things about isolating yourself from the world. Anyway, Angela – the wife – told me that young postgrad Palgrave, as she was then, was working under a marine biologist who was developing something quite significant on – I believe undersea surveying technology, or something. And it was kept very secret, because of the national security implications; the military were involved in the funding, and all that sort of thing. But,' and Aabria made a face, 'somebody got to her.'

'Got to her?' said Rose.

'Found her in a pub, or something, and pumped her for information about the lab, and talked to her quite seriously about how it was a crime that this sort of scientific advancement be confined to national borders, and what it could do for undersea exploration all over the world. I imagine they were very persuasive. And Palgrave – Sally – who has a very strong internal sense of justice, decided they were quite right, and handed them all the plans.'

'Oh my God,' said Boo.

'They were, of course, agents for some foreign power, no idea where, who were luckily under quite close watch and got as far as the door of the pub before they were nabbed,' said Aabria cheerfully. 'But our idiotic Salome very nearly ended up in military court on charges of high treason. She was only twenty-one. I have no idea what happened, but I imagine it was terrifying – though Angela said Palgrave's only real emotion was fury when she realised the agents hadn't been advocates for international scientific cooperation after all.'

Had *only felt strongly once before* – yes, Tom thought, that would fit. 'How on earth did she not go to jail?'

'You'd have to ask her that, but I rather fancy the agents poking around in campus pubs in peacetime were higher on the CIA's priority list. Still, it mustn't have been fun for her. I suspect she's been on a watchlist for her whole career. You can, of course, look into that. But getting herself a passport and a visa for this must have been an ordeal, even some thirty years later; she's lost a lot of weight since I last saw her. I fancy she was only allowed to come because it was all seen as a bit innocent and innocuous – a little scientific cruise on a ship filled with wealthy people!' She folded her ancient hands. 'She must have *really* believed in this new theory of hers, to wrangle herself a berth here for fieldwork. Likely to try and finally snag herself tenure somewhere. Poor thing.'

The passport, fresh and new in his hands, with only stamps between the USA and Canada. Young Salome Palgrave, looking over her spectacles at the military police with utter pious conviction, which rapidly turned to fury. Yes.

'Sixgill must have found out,' said Rose, rapidly. Tom could see her brain working; when she was on a particularly strong line she put her hands in her hair and scrunched it aggressively, so that it became a shrubbery of dense curls. 'That's why he could steal her research with such impunity. And he taunted her with it! How the hell did he find out?'

'There were always rumours, you see, that she was on endless parole or something, or had a phobia,' Aabria said. 'People do notice when a big-time marine biologist doesn't travel and outsources all her hands-on research to others.

But the vice-chancellor did retire many years ago, and men, when they get old, do like to *talk*, I find.'

'If all this came out,' said Rose, 'she'd be sunk. She's got at least a decade 'til retirement, and nobody would want to employ her. Or at the very least she'd become a controversial figure, and people don't usually want to employ or pay appearance fees for controversial figures in the sciences.'

'Particularly not female ones,' said Aabria Scott, and twinkled.

'What you've told us is very interesting.' Tom kept his voice bland. 'It will certainly factor into our investigation.' He was aware, beside him, of Titus's swift pen working in the Motive column.

'I'm sure it will,' said Aabria Scott. 'Now, we should all get back into our beds, shouldn't we? You young people are probably frozen to death. And Kate will have my head. She's probably upended half the ship looking for me.'

The three of them departed, but Aabria looked at Tom very hard on the way out. 'I *know* Salome Palgrave,' she said. 'And people like that don't go around harpooning strange men on ice caps.'

And Tom knew in his bones that she was probably right.

22

Aabria Scott did indeed find Kate Berg, furious, at the door of their suite, fully prepared to call out a search party, the crew, the Norwegian police, the Mounties, and anybody else who might be available or unavailable as the case may be. Kate channelled her evident, now-receding fear into insisting on checking Aabria's blood pressure with the portable pump, poking her tongue for signs of a cold, and looking at her toes for frostbite. Aabria submitted to this show of angry professional zeal with a good grace; it was, she knew, a mark of affection, much preferable to Kate leaving her employ or sulking passive-aggressively, and it was always good to know whether one had frostbite (one hadn't).

Aabria had had several nurse attendants over the years. She wasn't an ill woman necessarily, but a broken hip in her early seventies meant a companion for globe-trotting was useful, and women her own age tended to drive her gently but swiftly up the wall. Finding a good private nurse was laborious and annoying. One absolutely infuriating early specimen, Nurse Hominy Graves, had responded to any of Aabria's shows of vigour or personality by adopting a saintly air and then clashing all the dishes together in the sink. Out she went, along with Nurse Buttel – not at all a battleaxe, in fact a small whimpering person who made up outrageous stories of Aabria's injustices for her fellow nurses (luckily

267

one of them worked for a friend, who passed it on, pretty certain Aabria *hadn't* gone after Buttel with a poker) – and Nurse Patchet, who stole. She'd been tempted to keep her on in any case, as Patchet had a lovely florid face and an entertaining series of war stories from terrible boyfriends, but stealing the Scott emeralds for the latest of the terrible boyfriends was a bit *too* much.

Kate, by comparison, was ideal. She was practical, refused to be smug when she was correct, and treated Aabria like a delightful but occasionally aggravating great-aunt. She'd taken to the round the world's cruises with aplomb, and could probably now find a ship's medical supplies without even being pointed to the doctor. And, vitally, she was flawed; Aabria was highly suspicious of perfection in paid companions, and liked the fact that Kate both actively and openly despaired of her, and had no imagination to save her life. She enjoyed provoking her to use her brains.

Now, for instance, she told Kate in great detail about Salome Palgrave, and watched her consider it and fit it into her filing system of thought, while mostly making astonished noises and poking Aabria's toes.

'That,' said Kate after the story had ended and she'd evidently satisfied herself that Aabria wasn't about to die of being a nuisance, 'is absolutely nutty.'

'The Sixgill boy was what in my day we'd call a rotter,' said Aabria with satisfaction. 'Blackmail! Of all the idiotic crimes.'

'Why is it idiotic?' Kate looked interested, despite herself. It had probably never occurred to her to blackmail

268

anybody; and nurses really did know a great deal about their patients, Aabria thought.

'Because it never ends.' Aabria sat back and drank the fresh mug of tea before her with satisfaction. 'The blackmailed person never stops being threatened – and so they never stop hating, absolutely hating, the blackmailer. And so the blackmailer is always in horrible danger, and must never stop being on their guard.'

'So you *do* think Palgrave did it?' Kate looked puzzled.

'No,' said Aabria, crisply, 'I do not. She would just carry around the hatred, and pull it out and look at it as an oddity every so often. But Sixgill was, I think, a very silly young man.'

'Good luck to him if he'd ever tried to blackmail *you*,' said Kate. 'He'd have gone away with an entire flea circus in his ear.'

'He didn't try, which is well and good, because I haven't got very many secrets and if he found one I'd be interested to know it,' said Aabria with spirit. 'People *have* tried, you know.'

'To blackmail you?'

'Oh yes. One woman – after Albert died, you know – came in with a whole story about how she'd had his child and all this and that. I said all right, we'll have a paternity test and then we'll go forward, but she just wanted to be nasty and said she'd go to the papers. I told her to tell them everything if she liked, but nobody would be all that interested to hear about the mole on Albert's buttocks. He was dead!'

'Was it his child? Oh, I'm sorry—' Kate looked suddenly ashamed of herself.

'Not a bit of it,' said Aabria and laughed. 'He couldn't have any! Shot blanks all his life, thank heavens. Only a few people knew that; they always assumed the problem was me. Usually people do, with women,' she added, without rancour.

She looked at Kate Berg, who was thinking this over in her usual quiet way. Sensible, fussy Kate. She'd never mentioned her own family. Nurses, the most professional ones, didn't.

'Can people really have sudden attacks of amnesia?' Aabria asked, suddenly.

Kate Berg considered. 'I mean. Yes – if there's a head injury, usually. Temporary coma – or migraine can do it.' She got up and started putting away all of the paraphernalia into her medical bag. Heart pump nestled beside stethoscope, bandages, morphine, burn cream, everything all in its place.

Aabria watched her do it and sipped her tea, thinking.

Then she said, 'Kate.'

'Yes?'

'You do promise to protect me, don't you. Bloom Highcastle – I'm not young anymore. I couldn't fight if somebody did that to me. Will you try?'

Kate lifted her head and shook it briskly, as if to return to the room. 'Whether you like it or not,' she said grimly, and came to stand by the side of her chair, as if she were a knight beside her queen, mercilessly against the world.

Boo Moreland walked Rose back down to her cabin. They were both slightly shocked by Salome Palgrave, and by Bloom Highcastle, and sleeplessness, and the fading effects of champagne in the Arctic early morning, and the fact that several hours ago they'd had an exceptional, crystalline moment while the waves lapped below. Rose recognised that, without her conscious awareness, her brain was working away furiously; it did this sometimes when she was exceptionally tired. She'd once come out of a jetlagged haze in the Azores and sketched out a ready-made engineering solution to a problem with the manta ray tags. In the moment, however, she felt keenly that they were walking in exhausted silence.

'Do you have a mysterious past?' she asked, if only to say something.

'My first wife left me because I wasn't serious enough,' said Boo Moreland politely. 'Is that what you mean?'

'Oh. I'm sorry.'

'Don't be. I did love her, honestly, but I spent a lot of my twenties trying to be very grown-up and sensible for the sake of her family, who were very strict and had lots of ideals for everybody, which they wielded like – what are the things you use to cut open champagne bottles?'

'Sabres.'

'Thank you. And then she decided I wasn't steady enough, even when I was trying very hard, so she's married to a merchant banker now and only smiles on Sundays, and I am blissfully unserious about most things, and much happier for it.'

'You're very good at it. Only – be careful.' Rose pushed her hair back from her forehead and scrunched her face.

'Why?'

'I just have that horrible feeling about court jesters, you know. Who say so much nonsense but are actually so penetrating. This is a dangerous situation to have that power,' said Rose, quietly.

'If I'm an idiot who hits on the right thing I'll end up a dead idiot? I know. I am trying very hard to look as utterly ornamental and useless as possible. Up until I'm not.' And he looked hard and serious, then, and she wanted to hug him, but they settled for a gentle touch on each other's hands before she said goodnight, and he went, carefully escorted by Otso, who had tailed them the whole way, back to his cabin.

Tom hadn't slept, and was actively protesting against Titus's attempts to make him. 'It's still a fresh crime scene,' he said. 'I can be doing – I can be doing something.'

'It is currently 7 a.m.,' said Titus firmly. 'I will leave you to sleep until 10 a.m., while I circulate amongst the crew, make enquiries about those schematics, and maintain an obvious police presence on the ship. Then I will sleep later. This is not an argument; if you refuse I will make Juhani sit on you.' Juhani, outside the door, made a protesting noise. Titus turned the full force of his strange malevolence on Tom, who gave up and bundled himself into a blanket like an upset sausage roll.

'Well done, sir,' said Titus, and left, giving Juhani

instructions that Tom gathered through the muffling of the door involved threatening Tom with real bodily harm if he attempted to stop napping. Juhani made some weak argument, but eventually acquiesced. Titus then trotted off, like a well-mannered beetle in search of some nice dung to roll.

Tom grumbled to himself about how he was absolutely going to be unable to sleep, then immediately fell into deep slumber. The blankets on the *Dauphin* were astonishingly comfortable.

He had a strange and not particularly soothing dream. The body on the ice was surrounded by rose petals instead of blood, and Gladys Moreland was standing over it saying, 'Well, of course it was for *love*,' hoisting her own tranquilliser gun over her back. He was trying to get closer, to pick up some of the petals – this seemed necessary, *crucial* – but he was being borne backward, the tide was pulling him away from the ice cap, he was adrift, like a walrus on his own little broken bit of ice, and Bloom Highcastle was sitting beside him happily counting all the wildlife as they did after all drift into a walrus colony, there were thousands of them, roaring and fat and tusked and violent, and Bloom turned to him and said, 'Well, it's easy for a walrus to hide among other walruses, isn't it?' And then he woke up.

Titus was standing over him with a cup of tea.

'Sir,' he said with a minor sense of reproof in his voice, 'it is 10 a.m., and you were shouting.'

'Was I?' Tom struggled upward and had to sit cross-legged to take the tea; he was unable to free his legs from the knot he'd made of the blankets.

'You were telling a walrus to leave you alone,' said Titus. 'Does this bear relevance to the case?'

'I'm not——' There was something. Tom tried to grasp it. He described his dream as best he could. Titus nodded and, unbelievably, took notes. 'I'm very tired,' he said. 'God, this tea's good.'

'Dr Blanchard came asking if you were all right,' said Juhani helpfully from the doorway. 'The boy one. He didn't want to disturb you, so I sent him away.'

Tom disliked this piece of information intensely for many reasons he didn't wish to interrogate, but thanked Juhani for his tireless vigilance and asked Titus if he'd found anything out.

Titus produced a list. He had finally been given ship schematics, on the express understanding from an officious-sounding person on the bridge that the *Dauphin*'s engines were patent protected and therefore needed to be concealed from competitors (Tom made a snorting noise). Examination of the plans hadn't revealed any previously unknown nooks or crannies where mysterious assassins could be hiding. The mouldings where the recorder had been wedged weren't regularly cleaned, except before and after voyages. No cleaner had noticed anything stuck in there at any point. It was, Titus had found, possible to reach the top moulding by leaning out very far from the top of the stairs. The recorder itself was a Bluetooth model that could record and store audio and could be triggered from around 100 feet, rather like a car key fob. It was of a brand that was not immediately obvious on Google. It had no further recordings on it save for the scream, which was definitely a male voice, thought it was uncertain whether it was Sixgill's. He could have recorded it before he left the ship, or somebody else might have played it as a distraction while they killed Sixgill.

'So a man is definitely involved in this somehow,' said Tom. 'Right.' He looked at the recorder itself, which was about the size of a small TV remote, and white. Against the cream of the moulding it wouldn't be visible at all.

It was, continued Titus, unclear to whom the recorder belonged, as nobody had filed any lost property for it. Guests were still waking. Sandy Highcastle had been watched all night, and had not done anything of interest except express grief and go to sleep in all his clothes.

'Titus,' said Tom, gently.

'There are plans today to mount the snowmobiles, but there is some disagreement on the bridge as to whether this would be disrespectful—' Titus's briefing was ploughing forward.

'Titus.'

'Yes?' The Detective Sergeant looked as perturbed as he ever would be, which meant that an eyebrow very slightly rose.

'I think this is Dr Eder's recorder,' said Tom.

'Why, sir?'

Tom's hand moved, and he showed what he'd briefly brushed over with a thumb, and read rapidly with touch: some very small, likely highly expensive initialling along the base of the thing. *DRKE*. 'Doktor Klaus Eder,' said Tom.

'I thought that was the brand,' said Titus with some disgust.

'The doctor,' Tom said comfortingly, 'is *exactly* the sort of person who would get a small white electronic device engraved with initials that nobody would ever be able to notice.'

Klaus Eder did not appear to have slept well.

'Yes, that's my recorder,' he said with a trace of his usual charm, but his eyes were faintly bloodshot and the neat, waxed line of his beard had run amuck. 'It was very kind of you to find it, particularly under such trying circumstances. I fancied I had left it at home.'

'You missed it soon after arriving on board?' Tom was not handing back the recorder, which Dr Eder appeared to think was a sign of deep rudeness.

'Within the first day,' he said with some huffiness. 'I use it for dictating to myself, for book chapters, and for recording of lectures. You can trigger it from a distance using a laptop or a phone – very helpful! I looked through my suitcase for it, under the impression I had packed it, but on not finding it I concluded I had left it on my desk, which I am wont to do. I have been making notes by hand for the trip instead. It is an expensive piece of machinery,' he added, with a distinctly persuasive strain to his voice, but Tom smiled blandly and continued not to give it back.

'Did you have anything recorded on it?'

'Haven't you listened to it?' Dr Eder looked put out. 'It must have hours of my talks on there.' Was it possible, he appeared to be asking himself, that this pillock of a police officer didn't recognise the voice of Dr Klaus Eder when it was presented to him?

'I am afraid,' said Tom, mildly, 'that they had all been erased before it was found.'

'What!' This time Dr Eder really made a grab for the recorder, and Tom let him have it. Luckily, they had turned down the volume since they'd found it, so that when Dr Eder pressed play only he, Tom and Titus heard the replaying of the now soft, wild scream. Dr Eder pressed back and forward frantically. 'But this is barbaric! I had hours! Half of my new book!'

'It will have backed up to your cloud,' said Titus. 'I looked up the manual.' He had located the correct model, not, after all, called DRKE, on the website of an obscenely expensive technology company. 'Things deleted on the device itself will not affect the recordings saved to your storage.'

Dr Eder virtually deflated with relief. 'Young man, you have saved science four years,' he said, and clearly meant it. 'But what has replaced it? This scream? Somebody recorded the person screaming at the back of the ship? Whatever for? I think,' he added with vigour, 'that we are surrounded by the mad.'

'You may be entirely right,' said Tom. 'Would you be so kind as to allow us to continue to borrow the recorder? Titus can show you how to access your files, and I will of course give you a receipt.'

Dr Eder was so evidently delighted that he hadn't lost the spoken-word version of his new tome – Titus pulled it up on his laptop within three minutes – that he waved them off with it. 'Don't go recording anything unsavoury,' he added with a kind of dark gentleman's laugh.

'Of course not,' said Tom, and before his attitude of deference broke up entirely under extreme strain, he exited the dining hall. He made an expressive face at Titus. 'Doesn't look to know much about it. Or he was acting up a storm.'

'We are, perhaps, making progress, sir,' said Titus. They'd tested the recorder for fingerprints and discovered none, but neither of them had expected any.

'Yes – as to that. The scream wasn't Sixgill going overboard – it was played as a distraction. For Sixgill to get away and warn police of the diamond smuggling ring? For Sixgill to be safely murdered? Is the voice another person on the *Dauphin*? It seems likely. Someone strong – and very precise with a tranquilliser gun and a harpoon. Somebody who could get down to the bottom levels, shoot, and re-emerge without drawing attention. Sandy Highcastle, Dr Eder, Scott and Berg, and the Morelands were all on the deck. The Captain, Bloom, Alicia and Sunila were nominally high up; they could dash down, but it might be trickier. All those stairs. Dr Palgrave was AWOL but plausibly asleep, Elisabeth Lindgren was in that windowless kitchen, the Blanchards were safely out of the way hunting happy sharks, and Sixgill was – somewhere.'

'If Bloom Highcastle observed, or didn't observe, her husband doing something, he took a great risk by killing her on the stairs by the recorder rather than somewhere more private, sir,' Titus noted. 'He could have simply waited. Or maybe he panicked.'

'Bloom Highcastle heard that scream, perhaps, and realised it was too close to her, that it couldn't be quite real. So whatever happened at the back of the ship is the issue – perhaps she saw someone press a button that meant the scream began, and push something, or somebody, over the side? It was telling enough that she needed to die.' He and Titus were striding now. Their voices were very low, almost whispers.

The Captain's fine head suddenly loomed out of the grey morning and greeted them. 'Gentlemen,' he said in a voice so distinctly enunciated it virtually boomed, 'would you like to see our snowmobiles?'

The snowmobiles were, to Tom, what all snowmobiles looked like: long things with snouts and little skis that went unwisely fast over snow. They were stored in the nose of the ship, and could be taken up in bits and assembled on the ice. Titus was, of course, fascinated, not least by the fact that they were broken apart for transport like so much Lego, and was discussing this at high speed with a very tolerant crew member who was adjusting the pieces to be hauled out. The inflatable floats for the snowmobiles really were, alas, all accounted for, much to Tom's chagrin. Where Sixgill would have put a floatation device designed to cart around large lumps of metal was anybody's guess, but it did work better as a theory than his apparating around in the blink of an eye.

This storage area, Tom thought dispassionately, looking around under the strip lights, was astonishingly well-organised; everything was slotted into place, labelled in both English and Norwegian (and, in some handwritten rebellious places, Swedish, though Tom didn't know that), and filled to the brim. Medical supplies, long-life milk, flares, drums, skis, binoculars, the ubiquitous orange parkas, something resembling a folded-up bucket that turned out to be a portable open-air jacuzzi; the detritus of the luxury life was all here, catalogued and fastened and strapped, so that nothing could surprise anybody. They'd done a search here for the laptop and gun earlier, but deeper examination revealed just how much *stuff* there really was.

There was, however, one thing that appeared unusually dumped: a cube-shaped wooden box, pushed to one side in the very limited floor space. Tom wandered over to it and poked a finger inside. Cream and gold appeared, swathed in plastic, and a smell of sandalwood and something redolent of a fir forest floated upward.

'Sandy Highcastle's candles,' said the Captain, looking over his shoulder and making a wry face. 'He insisted, you see, that he bring extras. For the guests to purchase. We thought perhaps six or seven, but no, he brings a pallet! And then we must fit them somewhere. First we tried the food storeroom, but Elisabeth rightly made a fuss; she has a system. So they ended up down here. They are nice-smelling things; I understand perhaps why people would pay so much for them.'

'Mmm.' Tom had leaned forward to pick something up

between two fingers. On the very top of the pallet, caught between two ribbons strapping the candles in place, was a flaming red hair.

'So Sixgill was hanging around with Highcastle's candles,' Tom said in a low voice. They were coming back up to the deck from the storage area, going past the lower kitchens and the staterooms.

'A strange thing for a scientist to be doing, sir,' said Titus. 'Perhaps when he was purloining Bloom's mask? Doing some sleuthing of his own before he ran?'

'If he thought he was unsafe onboard, he couldn't easily notify Svalbard police,' Tom said, then paused. 'Wait a bit. Hand me the schematics.'

He'd seen something on the folded ship plan before, and noted it with interest: in this corridor, just past all the staterooms and near a door to the open deck, there was a small, almost-invisible dotted blue square. It was not signified in the schematic's key. Now, he calculated, they must be just about where it was located.

'What are we looking for, sir?' Titus followed Tom's finger on the plans.

'Not sure, Titus.' Tom looked up, and then down. The flooring looked like the perfectly normal matting and steel of the *Dauphin*'s cushioned internal corridors.

'Curious,' said Titus. 'Something in the walls?'

'Hmm. Look.' Tom moved one foot. There was a neatly hidden metal ring, visible clearly to anybody who was looking for it, flush against the floor. It was so matte that it was unlikely to catch any light. Titus hooked it with one finger and hauled it upward. A small hatch clicked open, and a miniature set of footholds descended down the wall to a well-lit corridor on the bottom deck.

'Yes, you have found part of our service hatches,' said the Captain, coming around the corner from the stairs. 'Is there a problem?'

'This forms a passage between the middle and lower decks without needing to go down the stairs?' said Tom.

'Yes; it is usually used by the crew to get to places quickly if required, but it isn't usually opened. It is only really an additional exit, you know, and not as safe as the stairs for evacuations.' The Captain regarded them both. 'There is a point here I feel I am missing, gentlemen.'

They all went down the ladder, and found themselves in a small room with a door. It opened into the corridor of the lower decks, leading onto the cabin bedrooms on either side, with the crew mess at one end.

Tom and Titus exchanged glances.

This meant that anybody – anybody at all – could have slipped down unseen to a starboard window, fired a shot, and been up on the deck again without, perhaps, anybody noticing.

23

The midday sun, when it eventually showed itself in the small arc of the horizon, showed a striated sky, covered in lines of cloud as if slashed apart into ribbons. The light wavered and slipped around. There were shadows everywhere.

Sandy Highcastle, in his assiduously guarded cabin, rolled over onto his front and wept again into his pillow.

The crew members began, in the frittering light, loading and crafting the two snowmobiles on the ice. People gathered to watch in silence; it must have been the first time, Rose thought, looking down on the construction of the large orange-liveried beasts, that they weren't greeted with squeals and masculine huffs of appreciation. The atmosphere was not carnivalesque; it was surreal.

'I hate it,' said Sunila, in a small voice beside her. 'I don't think we should be doing it. Not with – not with all this death.' The silent, reserved mirth had gone out of her. The snowmobiles were being constructed a good forty feet away from the remains of the dome and the orange tarpaulins, all of which had remained untouched even now the body had been brought aboard, and had begun, in the weather, to drip and gather lances and pikes and shields of ice, covering every surface. All those pegs would, Rose knew, now be harder than ever to lever out of the ice.

'I think it's a good idea.' Alicia Grey sounded, for the first time in a while, quietly assured. Rose looked at her; the cheery back-slapping aspect was gone from her voice, for now, but there was some strength in her still. Her hair was rich and very beautifully coloured in this light. 'It's sensible. To get away from this place for a little while. We all feel – well, a bit trapped, don't we. Some adventuring – that will help.' She nudged Sunila. 'Maybe we'll see a polar bear.'

And this, thought Rose, was probably why the Captain had overseen this. The *Dauphin* was meant to be an escape into unreal climes, full of extraordinary sights and sounds most people would never see, and instead it had been a journey into – into what? Surreal death, and violence, and suspicion. And the ship could not move. No, she thought, the Captain was being shrewd. And, indeed, as the snow-mobiles were put together more fully people began to talk more, to share ideas of what they might see; Aabria Scott was being persuaded most ardently by Kate Berg that she wasn't allowed to go, and wasn't countenancing any of it.

There was a small surprised noise from Dr Eder, who rushed away from the edge of the ship. Dr Palgrave was emerging from the stairway, flanked by a patient crew member named Kalle. They all had their attendant guards, who were doing their best to remain inconspicuous and retain the sensation of being luxury servants devoted to fulfilling every need, rather than a protective detail. It was, for the most part, working; this was an environment where you were meant to be waited on hand and foot, where spaces were designed to be filled at all times by busying bodies cleaning and fixing and smoothing.

'My dear Palgrave,' he said, and leaned forward to help her up over the last step. Dr Eder, Rose thought, was the kind to extend courtesy to a few different categories of people: those he could condescend to, those whose rank and titles were impressive (he was an inveterate snob), and those whom he professionally respected. Dr Palgrave was clearly in the latter category. He'd tried, hadn't he, to talk to Sixgill about the hares.

'I heard there was something happening,' said Salome Palgrave, in her clipped voice. 'I have never been on a mounted snow-traversing vehicle. I once rode a motorcycle, in California. Do you believe it might be the same sort of thing?' She had managed to come up onto deck in -4°C without gloves, and immediately two crew members were upon her pushing them up onto her wrists while she looked at them in passive wonder.

'If she's driving,' said Boo Moreland to Rose, 'we're going to end up in Greenland. Or Cuba.'

'I'm glad she's out,' said Rose in a low voice. 'They must know she couldn't have done anything to Bloom.'

'I wonder if they've told her. They must have.'

And, indeed, there had been a short interview last night to make sure that Palgrave was alive, well, and hadn't somehow monkeyed her way out onto the stairwell to kill Bloom Highcastle, not that Tom had seriously considered it. 'Dead? Oh,' she'd said, as if she'd been informed that a particular menu item she didn't much care about was no longer available. 'What a shame,' which was, Tom noted, likely the thing she'd registered that one said about deaths.

'I had no amnesiac attack, so I didn't do it. Do you suppose I could have some more tea?'

'I'm glad she didn't go to federal prison for selling secrets,' said Boo very low in Rose's ear, as they watched Palgrave talk about motorcycles and how they had scared off populations of Californian eared seals from the rocks while Dr Eder made polite noises. 'It would seem deeply cruel, somehow.'

Rose nodded. Some people were simply too unreal; they were so vulnerable. She wondered, suddenly, about Aabria Scott looking at Elisabeth Lindgren. *Intense and sheltered.* Is that what she'd said?

'If you two decide to have a *new* honeymoon somewhere near a polar bear colony,' Boo Moreland said to Sunila and Alicia, 'I'm leaving you behind, I warn you now. I mean it. They can eat you.' They both turned hot shades of pink and started to laugh, again. Boo, Rose reflected, had a talent of creating smoothness and light in dark places. Like Finn, whose sweetness made heavy things feel easy.

Finn himself had emerged and was looking over the side. 'Are they for the police?' he asked. 'Are they going somewhere?'

'No,' said Rose innocently, 'Detective Inspector Tom will be staying on board. You can continue to tell him all your theories about Fair Isle knits being inferior.' Finn coloured and made a very sweet embarrassed face.

'Aran is just so *obviously* the best,' he said, without much conviction that this point was indeed the reason he'd spent hours talking to Tom Heissen.

'Is it,' said Rose, and poked him hard in the ribs.

'Just like the foxtrot is the best dance,' said Finn, and poked her back.

In their stateroom, Tom looked up from the computer and said, 'Titus.'

'Yes, sir?'

'I've got something.'

'Yes?'

'Sixgill's accounts have just come through.' The US were notoriously sluggish about producing banking information, even when it belonged to persons skewered in very suspicious circumstances on ice floes. The various bureaucratic machineries of the British embassy had, however, now done their work. Savings, checking, a host of accounts across multiple banks. Titus and Tom leaned over the opened PDFs and both made the same faintly stunned noise at the totals.

'Christ, the man was *loaded*,' said Tom, unprofessionally.

'Inherited money?' Titus began to look at the statements more forensically. 'An investment that went well, sir? That rich benefactor theory – perhaps a woman—' Tom thought of Dr Palgrave – but surely not; he was blackmailing her for research, not money – and yet she had been asleep throughout the entire thing. Drugged? He made a note to discuss this with Titus.

'No, look; the payments are regular. Month on month. Money streaming in.' And the locations, they saw, were immediately waving flags of vibrant scarlet. The Cayman Islands, Switzerland, the Netherlands, the Cook Islands.

Whoever had arranged it had been very careful not to signal money laundering to the US banks, because these were typically not places commended for their financial transparency.

'I begin to think, Titus,' said Tom slowly, 'that Ben Sixgill was *not* fleeing overland with evidence of a diamond-smuggling ring on a mask in order to go to the authorities about it.' And wasn't earning his money through the penury of academic appointments either, he thought, unnecessarily.

'No, sir.' Titus fiddled, searched. 'The tracks are impeccably covered. Getting the sources of this money would take – years, I would project, conservatively, and many of the ends would come up dead because of banking protections in the countries themselves.'

Tom got up and began to pace. 'A scientist. A *scientist smuggler*? How on earth did he manage that kind of double life?'

'He did specialise in Arctic work, sir,' said Titus. 'His passport recorded many trips to and from the Arctic Circle in the past few years. And, remember, all his papers were destroyed – or something was, in any case. No visible partner or family, and no real connections except to research institutions. It does fit.'

'And the research institutions were unwittingly paying him to go off and smuggle diamonds. They'll be *very* pleased.' Tom made a wry face. 'So he was killed – what? Because he decided to go straight?'

'It is,' said Titus, 'a rather *melodramatic* way to go straight, sir.'

'A case of causing conflagrations on all the water crossings?'

'Burning all one's bridges? Yes, sir. Surely he was more likely to have safer escape options somewhere, well, populated, rather than running off a ship onto a glacier.'

'Let's label that one improbable. All right. Because he knew too much? Which implies there's somebody else on this ship who knows about it too.'

'I would not be greatly surprised, sir.'

'Which implies a schism – or a problem in their machinery. Which we could exploit. But murders are messy; they attract attention. If it were to protect the organisation, he must have been a serious threat. I doubt very much the ring *wanted* us showing up and ruining their fun. Entirely too much heat in a cold place.'

Titus made a face of disapproval at this temperature-based pun. Tom ignored it and continued, pacing the stateroom. 'Or he was killed for something entirely unrelated, because he was an unlucky sod.'

'Also on the probable list, sir.'

'He had it all planned out and then somebody sniped at him with a harpoon for being an ass. Certainly not out of the realms of possibility.'

'Perhaps Bloom Highcastle killed him, sir,' said Titus in a helpful voice. 'She glued the diamonds to her own mask, then he ran off with them, so she shot him.'

'But then,' Tom said, pacing faster, 'who on earth killed *her*, and why? Are Sandy Highcastle's accounts in?'

'Yes, sir. They look, if you'll excuse me, sturdy. The

overheads of the business are heavy, as might be expected in luxury retail,' said Titus with the air, Tom thought, of somebody who had owned a cashmere-selling company for twenty years, 'but they had significant investment. One investor in particular has been keeping them in the black for some years now.'

'Where from?'

'No idea, sir. An LLC with an innocuous name.' Tom thought hopefully for a second of Aabria Scott, but the idea of her funding a candle company was as likely as Rose Blanchard declaring she believed in poltergeists. 'We will, of course, hunt it down, as it's likely a shell company for somebody.'

'No inflow from the Cook Islands?' asked Tom hopefully.

'Alas,' said Titus, with the mildest hint of sadness, 'no.'

'And he wouldn't benefit in the slightest financially from his wife dying, despite what Kate Berg says about trying to get her sleeping drugs.' The practical nurse had indeed put in her call to them about her conversation with Highcastle, and they had added it to the large and suspicious pile. She had also asked for Aabria's mask back, to placate her employer, and Tom had refused politely; that mask had been beside the body for a reason and he was damned if he wouldn't figure it out.

Tom sat down, took off his socks, and looked at his own toes moodily. '*Now* what do we do,' he said, with some annoyance.

'We keep digging, sir,' said Titus. 'We continue ever downwards.'

'Into the belly of the beast,' said Tom heavily.

Boo, Gladys and Patrick Moreland were taking tea in the latter's stateroom. Rose had, slightly guiltily, acquiesced to join; she felt as if she should be doing her scientific work, plotting new places for cameras, observing the feed, corresponding with other scientists about likely Greenland shark behaviour. But the lure of the warm cabin and the Morelands' gentle familial calm, particularly against the horrifying unreality of the past few days, was intense, and she surrendered to it.

'It feels a bit unfair to Frog,' said Gladys, leaning forward to pour, 'going on the snowmobiles and having a feast on the ice. That was what she was looking forward to most.'

Rose smiled. 'Why Frog?'

'Why not Frog?' Boo contrived to look affronted, but conceded when Rose levelled a stare at him. 'She was capable of opening her mouth extraordinarily wide when she was very small, to hoover up cake. It was a remarkable performance. She looked like a tiny frog. And it stuck.'

Intensely posh people, thought Rose with a faint sense of exhaustion, appeared to have an utter immunity to the surreal. Though she supposed endless legacies of privilege protected you against the indignities of having a nickname like Frog.

'It was the night ride she most wanted,' said Patrick Moreland, affectionately. 'There's one in the programme, you see. To go out in the snowmobiles onto the tundra and see the constellations without any light pollution. She said she was most interested in seeing her zodiac sign, if the Northern Lights didn't get in the way.'

'I have tried to explain to Frog,' Boo said to Rose with some exaggerated sadness, 'that astronomy is infinitely more interesting than astrology, but there are some things you can't teach. Somehow for her the glamour of Galileo and the possibility of water on Mars garner less enthusiasm than rising moon signs and tropical equinoxes hiding all your socks when they go in the wash.'

'I had a roommate at university who was very interested in that sort of thing,' said Rose, amused. 'She plotted everybody's star sign. Made charts and predictions, about solstices and things, and—'

She stopped.

Something – something which had been buried now floated to the surface.

'You look like you've seen a ghost,' said Patrick Moreland.

'No – she's just had an idea,' said Gladys, shrewdly. 'You need to go to the police now, don't you? Take a crew member with you. No, Boo, you sit down.' Boo had stood up and resettled with a bad grace. 'Be safe, and don't talk to anybody on the way there,' Gladys Moreland said, and waved her out of the room.

Sandy Highcastle was sitting on his bed when Rose Blanchard, Titus Williams, Tom Heissen and the Captain entered. He had the small blue silk mask between his hands. He didn't attempt to get up when they came in.

'Exaltation – I've remembered what it means,' said

Rose, rapidly. 'When you were talking to Sixgill on the first night, and he got angry, you said *exaltation*, not exhalation. Somebody heard you. Sorry,' she added, and Tom recognised the guilt of a minor sin (eavesdropping) temporarily eclipsing a major one (murder). He reflected admiringly on the Blanchards' moral fibre.

Sandy looked at her as if she was speaking Esperanto. The Captain, who had been fetched from the bridge with little explanation, also looked uncomprehending. Tom, who had only been given Rose's quick-fire explanation of her idea in the police cabin ten minutes before, sympathised. He still felt the concept was an eel-like thing – just about to slip from his grip. His large hands tightened, as if grabbing hold.

'It's about the phases of the zodiac, isn't it, Mr Highcastle?' said Rose. 'It's when a planet is particularly well-placed towards the Earth. You have Exaltation Candles, don't you?'

There was a long pause.

'What exactly is in those candles, Mr Highcastle?' asked Titus, quietly. There was a silence.

'Crystals, aren't they?' supplied Tom, gently. 'Except I imagine, for a precious few, they weren't crystals. The ones carried in cases for special customers, on cruises. The jewels in those were *real*.'

Rose Blanchard, who had not been told anything about any diamonds of any kind, maintained an admirably straight face considering this revelation. Tom, swiftly glancing sideways, saw one of her hands go into her hair and start slowly forming a thoughtful fist.

Highcastle made a weak noise. 'It was for Bloom. She didn't know anything about it — she wanted it to be a success so badly.'

'Do you mean to tell me that those candles I put in the cold store have *actual jewels* in them?' said the Captain with astonished aggravation. 'That were sat under ham and quail for days?' The disruption of his routine for the sake of ridiculous trinkets had, perhaps, been justified as part of the eccentricities of passengers; the fact that he had been disturbed, and had his chef in an uproar, for the sake of *illegal items of great expense* clearly affronted him on a very deep personal level.

'Some of them, sir, almost definitely,' said Titus, in a soothing voice.

'I'm sure the police will look through them *thoroughly*,' added Rose Blanchard, 'won't you?' Tom nodded enthusiastically, as the Captain's Easter Island-esque face now appeared to be quivering on the verge of apoplexy.

'We know that at least one had the diamonds from Bloom's masquerade mask within it,' he supplied, in an attempt to sound helpful.

'I separated them out myself,' said Sandy miserably. 'The hot glue gun had some setting cement in it. It was strong stuff. I suppose he levered them all out.'

Tom and Titus exchanged a quiet look over Highcastle's bowed head; Rose, who had seen that the mask fished out of the depths had all its diamonds solidly intact, intercepted that look, read it correctly, and kept entirely quiet.

Tom had been putting together some aspects in his mind since Rose came knocking. The red hair on the candles – the anonymous LLC. A flow of Exaltation candles filled with crystals to locations all over the world. And behind it a shell company, and another shell company, and behind that—

Sixgill! Sixgill, from the beginning. *I said it was off, so it's off.* Not *investigating* the candles – at all.

'Your investor – it was Sixgill, wasn't it?' he burst out. 'This was one of the smuggling ring's ways of getting things around the world.'

Sandy laid down the silk mask reverently and sat looking at it. His voice, when it came, was slow and lax, as if his tongue was dry. 'I didn't like it. But the business was failing without cash injections – and he came to see me, and said it was so simple, just a few here and there. No harm to anybody, no violence. The process was no different from suspending the crystals. He had a great cover, he really was a scientist; I checked his profiles and his university contacts, I'm not a fool. And it kept things going, remarkably well, for a while. I'd make them, and they'd go on cruises all over the place, though I was never told where. But the bills kept coming – and Sixgill started to get distant, not answer calls. I was desperate. I convinced him to let us come on this cruise ourselves, to show that I was reliable, he could count on me. Then after we'd paid all this money, he said—'

'He didn't want to do it anymore,' said Rose. She had guessed this part. The argument on the stairs, observed by Sunila and reported scrupulously to the Blanchards. Not a lovers' quarrel, but a statement from Sixgill that the business arrangement was over.

'Did he explain why?' Tom asked. 'Probably not.'

Sandy shook his head. Tom wondered. Was the candle situation too perilous? Or were the ring notified they were being watched? Two English police officers dispatched up to Svalbard. Was Sixgill instructed to cut and run? Sandy Highcastle was, Tom reflected, incredibly lucky that he himself wasn't yet dead.

'He backed out, and I – I was alone. I kept hoping he'd change his mind. I'd brought along the candles anyway, you see, even after he'd said not to.' The Captain made a furious noise. 'And then he was killed, and Bloom kept asking questions, and I was just terrified. I destroyed all our notes, all the business records in his cabin – and then little Bloomie was dead, somebody killed her, and it was all because of me, because I got her wrapped up in this terrible mess, and I caused her death just as surely as I put a stake in her. But I don't see why – why she had to die.'

He was a vast, pathetic, sobbing mountain. Rose flinched, clearly wanting to give him a hug, but Tom carefully nudged her, and she stayed still.

'You didn't want the sleeping drugs from Kate Berg for *her*,' said Tom, suddenly, with a small expression of realisation. Rose blinked at him.

'No.' Highcastle didn't look surprised that they knew this. Kate Berg would, of course, have talked; he must have realised that. 'I thought – ending it all – the shame – but I was too cowardly to press the issue.'

'Why do you think Sixgill was murdered, Sandy?' asked Tom.

'I didn't do it,' said Highcastle, almost shrilly. 'I still hoped that he'd see the error. That he'd help us again. I told Bloom to make the mask, hoping that he'd pay just for those ones, the diamonds, even if he didn't want the rest in the pallet of candles. And then he took it and ran! I don't know. I wish he weren't dead. What will I do now?'

'You thought he had killed himself initially,' said Titus. 'Why was that, sir?'

'I figured there was some trouble coming. That maybe he'd been taking an illicit cut or something. He seemed horribly agitated. He'd riled everybody on the ship. He was always very charming to me, all the times I'd met him – and then to cancel things so suddenly, to be so *awful* – something seemed very wrong. So I thought he'd taken that way out.' Highcastle shrugged.

'Sandy,' said Tom, evenly. 'You need to be very frank with us now. Anything you have on the smuggling ring, or on Sixgill – any evidence at all – you need to hand over. You may have extremely valuable information. We can, of course, offer protections against the cartel – who will, I'd say, be watching you very closely indeed right now.'

'I don't know very much at all,' said Highcastle, looking entirely unmoved. The loss of his wife had kicked the guts out of him. *He'll go to jail and he won't fight it at all*, thought Tom dispassionately, *if he survives that long*. 'That was deliberate. Sixgill was my only contact; for all I knew he was the whole operation. It was all very legal on paper, just a private investor, done with my lawyers. I supplied the candles to a shipping warehouse at the same dock where the *Dauphin* leaves from; some small brown-haired intern always took them in. I don't know his name. Marcus or something. You can have the diamonds. The business will fold; that's all right.'

The intern, of course, was dead, but it didn't look as if Highcastle had any idea of that, and Titus and Tom exchanged a look which meant that neither of them was going to talk.

The Captain said, when they left Highcastle alone, 'Well?'

'Double the guards on the room,' said Tom softly. 'Let people think we believe he killed Bloom and Sixgill.'

'Because then . . .' The Captain was following the logic slowly. Rose was gripping her own elbows very hard.

'Because then,' and Tom's voice was very dark, despite it being softer than the wind, 'they may not realise we're hunting them.'

24

It is more difficult than it seems to imply that a person of interest is definitely the murderer without saying so, more so when you don't in fact believe they murdered anybody. Tom and Titus endeavoured through sleight of hand to convey as much of Sandy Highcastle's apparent guilt as possible; they put a highly visible guard on his room (Linnea Eklund's file had indicated she knew judo), and told the Captain to allow the snowmobile trip onto the ice to proceed without their protest. They would not, however, go so far as to let people roam around without crew members. 'There's putting on a show and then there's being fools,' said Tom. Titus made a minute movement that could be interpreted as a nod.

Gladys Moreland, Tom thought privately, was not particularly convinced by this pageantry of imprisonment – she gave the array of guards a very incisive look that if rendered as a kitchen knife could have produced a finely wrought sashimi – but had the good manners, or the practised legal sense, not to question anything. Nobody else raised a murmur; Aabria Scott was too busy distracting Kate Berg with her insistence on snowmobiling with her arms twined around the waist of the most stalwart crew member she could find. Several crew members were auditioned for 'stalwartness' (size of biceps and abdonimal muscles being the primary criteria), until Kate threw down the gauntlet, insisted she be put in the competition, and then threatened to haul Aabria bodily into port wrapped head to toe in compression bandages if she went off on this high-speed vehicular deathtrap without her. Nonplussed but, Tom thought, also deeply charmed, Aabria raised her nurse's arm in triumph.

'Some of the crew,' observed Titus, 'look quite upset about not winning this competition, sir.' And indeed the Nordic best and brightest filed away looking, in some quarters, a little hangdog.

'Well, you can supervise Ms Scott and Ms Berg to make sure they don't pilot one of those pocket rockets into a snowbank,' said Tom.

'Sir?' A rare flare of hope went up on Titus's face.

'Oh, yes, you're going on the ice. I'll be here looking casually relieved at solving the mystery, and meanwhile doing a little sleuthing.'

'Are you sure that's wise, sir?'

'Frankly, no, but I refuse to let that lot go out without some police presence, and they'll be suspicious if we leave Highcastle entirely unattended on the ship. And,' he added truthfully, 'motorised blunderbusses on skis sound like my idea of hell.'

'It will, of course,' said Titus, controlling his enthusiasm with a noble effort, 'be a very good opportunity to look around unhindered, sir.'

The Captain, clearly feeling at least mildly personally thwarted by his inability to Clean Up This Mess alone, had elected to focus his powers where they could be of use, and expedited some charm on their behalf overnight. And lo: a second search warrant post-Bloom's death, and a personal letter from the *Dauphin* parent company's board of directors which, between the lines, begged Tom to do something, *anything* to pause this nightmare of public relations, up to and including doing a jig naked on the helipad. Tom hoped dearly that it wouldn't come to that.

The collective personnel of the *Dauphin*, scientists and all, were on their way to make merry on the ice en masse. Elisabeth Lindgren, it was rapidly spread across the ship, would be providing her world-famous rotisserie goose, and indeed a glance inside the kitchens revealed that formidable woman meticulously basting a collection of ex-waterfowl on a series of compact spits that had been assembled from a box of horribly sharp and pointy objects. The smell was outrageous; if, Tom thought, there were vegetarian wildlife nearby, they would be called upon to convert.

There had apparently been a silent and firm agreement that the dome would not be reconstructed; people were perfectly willing to enjoy their platters of goose in the Arctic wind if it meant not going near the site of recent and vicious death. The half-geodesic construct remained, still hunkering in the sun, its pegs still wedged deep in the ice, its deconstructed parts weighed down against the wind. Indeed, Tom observed from the prow, everybody on the ice – from the collection of guests to Elisabeth's kitchen skivvies – was unconsciously turning their backs on it.

He contrived to look airy and relaxed. Alicia Grey, he noted, was clearly taken in by the idea of Sandy Highcastle's guilt in the eyes of the police; she looked almost parodically relieved. Her buoyancy and verve were faintly unnerving, even from a distance, and that loud cheery voice floated back to the ship. Which was why Tom, ambling away as the first roars of the snowmobiles came to fruition, planned his afternoon around a visit to the Singh and Grey stateroom. He didn't like that anonymous LLC behind the cartel one bit, and he remembered those six-figure earrings of Sunila's thoughtfully.

This was, of course, not a thing to be done lightly. He did what could casually be interpreted as a stroll, but what Titus would immediately recognise as a sweep; was everybody save Highcastle, the Captain and a suitable amount of crew indeed off the ship? Had all and sundry taken advantage of the brisk Arctic air? He ambled high and low, hands in mittens in his *Dauphin*-orange pockets (the Captain had, at last, convinced the police contingent into the deeply warm signature wear), and ascertained a few things. One was that everybody was indeed off the ship; another was that Titus better save him some goose, because the scent was floating back onto the deck from the open camp after the snow-mobiles had departed, and it was driving him mildly crazy. Then he dipped below deck.

Alicia and Sunila's room was scrupulously clean, with the wide sweeping windows of all the staterooms, and a thankful lack of booby-traps. (Titus, he knew, had never forgotten or forgiven the thugs who'd put a bucket of dog excrement above their door to dissuade coppers from coming inside; he'd arrested them regardless and maintained an extraordinary calmness when recounting the incident at the trial, but

Tom knew never to joke with him about offensive smells of any kind, given that the stench took several days and multiple scouring showers to remove.)

Tom was a very old hand at sweeping a room, and took frank pride in the fact that he could do it without leaving a trace. Footprints swept from the grain of the carpet, everything noted just so to be replaced in exact positions; people didn't remember things explicitly, he'd found, but they did know, unerringly, if an item was out of position, even if they couldn't identify what it was, let alone where it had been before. This particularly mattered in hotel rooms and other suites of temporary occupancy, in which personal effects showed up bright against a bland background, like spotlit actors on a blank stage. A glove in the wrong position struck a note so loud and angry that people would be unnerved without knowing why.

He worked with finesse, slowly, and met with very little of anything for the most part. Novels in various languages. Highly expensive clothing and shoes, all in impeccable repair and folded with sweet-smelling pouches between them, even in the suitcase, razor-sharp edges to starched shirts, even the toothbrushes aligned in parallel. Two very organised people who had, he thought, found the zenith of their skill in one another, forming some kind of megasystem like a giant piece of origami.

The organisation spread to the best items of interest, which were the letters – folded up in the drawer of the bureau. All three still bore some messiness, likely, Tom thought correctly, from being shoved under or into something, that made them stand out. He read their contents thoughtfully. All carried much the same message, on *Dauphin* notepaper, in strong printed capitals.

IT IS BEST TO STAY SILENT, IF YOU KNOW
WHAT'S GOOD FOR YOU. FROM THE ONE
WHO KNOWS WHAT YOU ARE.

So. A nice little series, requiring silence under the threat of exposure of some identity. Whose? Sunila's or Alicia's? He could make an educated guess.

'There are entirely too many mysteries on this ship,' he said reproachfully to the stateroom, which responded with heavy, citrus-scented silence that somehow felt unutterably smug. He refolded the letters to be just so – to catch in the same way as the bureau drawer opened.

Rose and Finn had been persuaded onto the snowmobiles with some difficulty.

'Maybe we shouldn't come off the ship,' said Rose, thinking guiltily of all of the data she could be collating, and also of Sandy Highcastle, grieving in his big room. She wondered, with a more powerful worry, about the candles in the hold, with diamonds and God knows what else held in their waxen stillness. Perhaps the Captain had moved them somewhere more useful. (In fact they were now in the stateroom of Tom and Titus, who could at least corroborate Elisabeth's statement that they were horribly inconvenient and kept getting in the way.)

'How can science stand in the face of the arguments of roast beast and fast cars?' said Boo dramatically, throwing his arms around like a herald in a bad interpretation of a medieval court. 'Cars that go on ice. Ice-cars.'

'Snowmobiles, in fact,' supplied Gladys, drily. 'And you'd better come; I think it's best to leave the Detective Inspector to get some peace and quiet. It's been an eventful couple of days.'

So here they were, watching Kate Berg be given a lesson in steering while gripping the handles of a vast sleek orange machine in two very white hands, bearing a gigantic pearlescent helmet upon her head while Aabria Scott sat behind her in triumphant glee. Aabria was, Rose noted with a smile, wearing an Hermès scarf with patterns of polar bears on it.

Rose insisted on driving, first with Finn on the back (gripping very hard, as was his wont, because he was so gangly that otherwise his arms flew everywhere and made aerodynamics difficult – they knew this from sharing bicycles late at night going home from college parties) and then with Boo. Boo was respectful with his hands, but at one point turned his head to look at what might have been an Arctic bird and turned it back at such a speed that their helmets collided. 'You idiots,' said Gladys, who for some absurd reason had hung onto Patrick with both arms while riding side-saddle (this was, she would confess later, how she had been taught to ride horses from her grandmother and she never learned another way), and looked completely at home being roared around the Arctic tundra at dozens of miles an hour.

The lines of light were growing ever thinner; it would, Rose thought, be dusk by the time they got back onto the *Dauphin*. She felt a grief for the way things could have been, without the Crimson Horror, without poor Bloom Highcastle; a beautiful, strange journey, with seals and dolphins and cameras in the deep, and good food and pale pink skies, and her and Finn laughing in their cabin late at night. They hadn't paid for their berths, but it still felt as if something had been stolen from them.

When they came back for their goose dinner she leant her head against Finn's shoulder and they watched Titus Williams assist Sunila and Alicia off their snowmobile, for all the world like a liveried footman. Alicia, unsurprisingly, had been driving. Sunila was keeping up a long monologue about how unwisely fast it had been and how much ice she'd got in her gloves, which, Rose reflected, was probably her way of showing that she'd enjoyed herself despite being terrified. Kate Berg appeared to be regathering her sense of equilibrium by wandering off to one side, looking at the remains of the dome and its assorted detritus gleaming in the low light as bits of ice floated past, and taking deep, huffy breaths with her hands on her hips.

It was lovely, Rose thought, to be out there on the ice at dusk – without that daytime glare boring a hole into her head. Maybe she'd have to fashion herself a pair of Dr Eder's Inuit glasses, with the thick white exterior and the slits, to look out at the glacier the next day—

And she realised, suddenly, *why* Sixgill had stolen Aabria Scott's mask. Sixgill with his smashed sunglasses; Sixgill an old hand on the ice, knowing he'd be blinded without something to cover his eyes. Of *course*.

There was a sudden odd sound on the wind, over the snow – not from the *Dauphin*, or from the strange vocalisations of the ice, which made itself known in the night like a living thing, but from somewhere else. It was hot and full and angry.

'Walrus,' said Elisabeth Lindgren, raising her remarkable head over the spit. The light from the fire made it primeval and haunting. 'They are far away. It is just the wind. Who would like brioche buns, please, and who would like sourdough.'

There was a clamour of guests returning. Tom, having searched all the other staterooms again with no more fresh discoveries, decided to go down that evacuation hatch at the end of the corridor to hunt around the bottom level. For what he wasn't sure – but he felt disinclined to sit in his own stateroom and make angry faces at a whiteboard and try not to think about Finn Blanchard. He swung it open by its neat little ring, and stood for a minute, leaning over it.

Then there was a heavy shove in the centre of his back—

And he fell straight downwards into the hatch.

25

Darkness.

A wild beating sound. Heart.

There was a dim sound of shouting. Tom recognised, through the haze of adrenaline, that the whole front of his body was smarting. Why was it smarting? Why was his elbow hurting? Ah, he was hanging by his whole weight on one arm – and his body had slammed, yes, against the wall of the ship, as he'd caught himself on the way down—

'What in high heaven—'

With some difficulty Tom leaned his head backward. A face was leaning through the hole above him, staring. After some seconds of blinking it rearranged itself into the very red visage of Kate Berg.

'Are you all right?' she shouted.

Tom considered a wide range of factors. 'No,' he said.

Kate Berg swore. It was, somehow, comforting. 'Right, I'm yelling for help. Can you hold on?'

'Yes,' said Tom, with substantially more authority than he felt.

Berg did indeed yell, with a blast of volume that seemed unlikely, then manoeuvred herself so that her arms were through the hatch. 'Can you lift your other arm up to me? No? Can you wiggle your right toes? Good. Put that foot into a foothold. Does that hurt? No. Excellent. Put some

weight on it. A few more breaths now, somebody's coming.'
And, indeed, blissfully strong arms were opening the door
behind him, hoisting him from below, and laying him flat
on the corridor floor. Berg, he could see, climbed down
through the hatch after him, and started administering to
him with efficient hands, poking all the bits that hurt. 'You
idiot, what are you going around falling through floors for.'

'I didn't fall,' said Tom, with a faintly upset sense of
dignity. 'Where did you come from?'

'We all got back about five minutes ago,' said the nurse,
palpitating his legs and arms busily. 'You made an awful
racket. Fell like a bag of saucepans. That shoulder's bruised
but no bones broken.'

And, indeed, there was now a crowd of faces around the
hatch, staring at him and making noises, like a very luxe
and well-rugged-up collection of angels come to announce
something from heaven. 'He's fine,' Kate Berg called up to
them, and relieved noises floated down.

'Sir!' Titus had emerged from among them and was
putting himself down the ladder at a rate of knots unwise
anywhere except perhaps down a fireman's pole. Kate Berg
told him so.

'I will not have more than one policeman crashing down
a hole on the same afternoon,' she said with spirit.

Tom was going to make another attempt to salvage his
reputation but stopped himself. 'I lost my footing,' he said
instead.

'I'll go for Alva,' said another crew member.

'Listen,' said Tom to Titus, 'if you start apologising for

going onto the ice I will throw myself down another hatch just to show you.'

'You'll do nothing of the sort,' said Kate Berg ferociously, 'and if you try I'll have Elisabeth bind you to one of those sharp rotisseries of hers and rotate you over a nice fire. Here, flex that foot. Can you stand?'

Tom could, and felt himself all over; he'd be bruised, particularly on the stomach where he'd slammed most of his weight after he'd caught himself, but he was in no particular danger.

'You could have broken your spine,' said Alva, who had done a swift assessment of everything after appearing with amazing speed. 'Please do not do this.'

'I have no intention of doing this,' said Tom with great seriousness. This gratified Alva, who was now palpitating his leg. Titus offered Tom a goose sandwich out of one pocket, which Tom accepted as an impeccable apology for not being present when his superior was being shoved down holes, and began to eat for the sake of its medicinal value.

'Somebody get Aabria away from that hole,' Kate Berg yelled overhead. 'I know she's there.'

'I'm just *looking*,' came the familiar voice.

'Nobody on this ship cares for their health at *all*,' said Kate with exasperation, and climbed back up to the hatch again, presumably to argue with Aabria about not putting her aged head into open holes in the deck.

'Sir,' said Titus furtively.

'Yes,' said Tom. 'Back in the stateroom. God, this goose

is heavenly. If Elisabeth Lindgren wants a beard I'll marry her.'

'We shall ask, sir.' Titus's face was impassive as a rock.

'Definitely pushed, Titus.' It was half an hour or so later, and the bruises had truly set in. Tom felt a bit like he sometimes did after a Friday night game of rugby.

'It could have been anybody, sir; we all streamed onto the ship at the one time. You were on the level with the staterooms, so any person could have stepped around the corner from the stairs, seen you, and taken their chance, then fled. There is no window on that part of the corridor.' Titus was feeding him paracetamol and biscuits, and had placed a picture of Biscuit the cat in easy viewing distance without comment.

'And then they could innocently reappear on the scene when it was time to fish me out. Ouch.'

'Precisely, sir. I heard a crash, but as it was beside the kitchens, I simply thought—'

'That it was a bunch of saucepans? Yes, Kate Berg said something like that.'

'There was a decent interval between your fall and her shout for help, sir. At least thirty seconds. Plenty of time for anybody to slip away.'

'Unfortunately, yes.' Tom poked his own stomach reflectively. 'That could have been nasty, you know. Somebody very much isn't fooled by the idea that we're taking Sandy Highcastle as the culprit.'

'This may,' said Titus, slowly, 'be too much for the two

of us, sir. If there are more people involved – we may be outnumbered.'

'Yes. I know. They were trying to scare us off.'

'Perhaps we would be sensible to be scared, sir.'

'A scientist being skewered on the ice is one thing, but a conspiracy to protect a smuggling ring is another, is that it?'

'Yes, sir. Clearly they are highly motivated and take enormous risks. Bloom Highcastle's murder and this attempt – they were opportunistic, brutal, and *we didn't catch them*. We can stay together at all times to reduce risk, and there are the crew, of course, but – we cannot be everywhere at once, sir. It's not possible.'

'I hate feeling outmanoeuvred, Titus.'

'I know, sir.' Titus was smoothing Tom's blankets automatically with his long pale hands.

'I keep wondering *why* Sixgill was killed. If he was just meant to get off the ship with the diamonds, and fake his own disappearance to the bottom of the sea, they'd surely have let him run. There'd be some headline somewhere – 'promising scientist dies in accident in Arctic' – and that would be it. Something went badly awry, and brought the ship the wrong kind of attention, and now I'm being pushed down hatches and you'll likely soon be party to an exploding snowmobile.'

Titus looked horrified at this imprecation of his new most dearly beloved of vehicles. '*Sir*,' he said insistently, into the silence.

Tom sighed and made a face, which was recognisable as his I-know-you're-being-reasonable-and-I-hate-it face.

'All right. We'll tell the Captain to move on tomorrow. Svalbard, the Norwegian police, the whole lot. I refuse to be murdered on a ship that costs more than my entire childhood neighbourhood.'

'Thank you, sir.' They then fell to discussing Alicia Grey, and who on earth she might have been to prompt somebody – Sixgill? – sending her upsetting messages under the door that scared her half to kingdom come. Titus agreed that Alicia's terror made her a more likely subject for the letters. 'Though she may simply be scared for her wife, sir. Or it could be a blind.'

Rose Blanchard stopped by, with the inevitable and limpet-like Boo Moreland, to see how Tom was, and to share her thoughts on Sixgill's purloining of the porcelain mask. Titus helpfully found some pictures online, and they gazed at the Inuit snow glasses with a collective sense of wonder.

'That would fit, Dr Blanchard,' said Tom, with a sense of gratification. 'If his sunglasses had been smashed and he needed to be on the ice for a good while, he'd need the protection. White for sun reflection, and the little eyeholes to allow him to see. That's why the inside felt had been ripped up, I suppose – to make them into slits.'

'That's right,' said Rose, with a satisfied sort of sigh. 'He took this mask because it would help him on the ice. And I guess he took the Highcastles' mask because it was worth so much.' Boo Moreland looked mildly baffled at that, but wisely kept his mouth shut.

'Likely,' said Tom, shortly. He didn't want Rose

Blanchard to know any more about Sixgill's involvement with diamonds, masks and candles than she had to – she already knew far more than a civilian should, and Boo was an added complication. 'He probably gathered the entire crop of masks to conceal his interest in those two.'

'Very scientific of him,' said Boo Moreland. 'Take the entire data set, not just the points of interest.'

'It may have been the only good science he ever did by himself.' Rose sounded scornful.

Titus, perhaps feeling that they were ill equipped to comment on Sixgill's scientific prowess, explained that they'd decided they'd be moving on shortly, and Rose looked thankful. 'I don't like that you fell down that hatch,' she said, drawing her fair hair out of her face. 'It's like the whole ship is cursed.'

Tom and Titus didn't look at one another; Tom felt oddly like a straight man in an old comedy trio.

Rose Blanchard made a face and looked between the two of them. Then she spoke, quietly.

'Listen. I come from a family that specialises in pregnant pauses. I know what they mean. You *didn't* fall down the hatch, did you.'

'I did not,' said Tom seriously. 'Please don't tell Finn,' he added, with an air of irrationality. Boo swore with deep violence, and, Tom noticed, moved unconsciously closer to Rose, as if to protect her from any persons attempting to throw her through vacant spaces in the nearby floor.

'For *God's sake*,' said Rose savagely, and clutched at her hair. 'Next we'll find Titus shut in the larder with a kettle

on his head. You really do have to call in reinforcements –
there's only two of you!'

'As Titus keeps reminding me.' Tom made a wry face.
'And we can't be in two places at the one time.' He stopped,
and looked thoughtful.

Rose continued. It was noticeable that every so often
her foot brushed against Boo Moreland's. 'It feels as if poor
Bloom had to die – because she saw something. Not the
murder – something else, something she wasn't supposed
to see. Or hear?'

'No. No, that's not right.' Detective Inspector Heissen
got up suddenly, ignoring the bruises that were forming on
his skin in various places into a giant and elaborate world
map. 'I don't think—'

'Sir?' Titus was looking at him with great alertness.

'I don't think,' said Tom, pacing, the machinery in his
brain working at enormous speed, 'that Bloom Highcastle
saw anything.'

'She didn't – she didn't *see anything*.' Rose, whose brain
clearly worked at around the same speed as Tom's, got up
abruptly. 'Because. There was nothing to see.'

'*That* was why she was killed,' said Tom triumphantly.
'You *can't be in two places at once*. All this time we've been
hunting for somebody who could have taken their chance
to run to the back of the ship, throw things off, make a
ruckus, then go round the other side and shoot Sixgill
while everybody was preoccupied.'

'But what if there wasn't anything to see?'

'But there was,' said Boo, looking between the two of

them in utter confusion. 'There must have been. We all heard it.'

'Yes, but you didn't *see* it,' said Tom, gaining speed. He and Rose were onto something and he was pretty sure he knew the scent of accuracy when he smelt it. 'You *heard* a splash and the sound of the life buoy and a scream. But actually nobody saw anybody. Because there was *nobody there*.'

'It's like the bloop,' said Rose very fast. Facing a sea of absolute incomprehension, she said, in a slightly less accelerated voice, 'It was an underwater noise that everybody picked up in 1997 in the South Pacific, and nobody knew what it was. It was *extremely* loud. People decided it was a sea creature unknown to science, and kept sending out expeditions to look for it. It took decades for scientists to discover it wasn't an animal at all – it was a part of the Antarctic ice sheet breaking off, thousands of miles away. The noise misdirected us all. The bloop!'

'It *is* like the bloop,' said Tom with some relief that this extremely competent investigator wasn't having some sort of episode. 'Listen, you two get into a stateroom and stay there. No, Dr Blanchard, this one really has to be police, and you're both too valuable to be thrown down any holes. Titus.'

He and Titus went out onto the deck and quickly gathered some crew members.

Now that they knew what they were looking for, they found it in about twenty minutes. Suspended on the ledge of the deck jutting out above the *Mouette*'s docking area, where the life buoy usually was, were some ropes that, Otso, Niilo and Linnea said in chorus, were not in their regulation places. Titus, who was excellent with ropes, made a gentle estimate. 'Could have held something weighty, a brick or a rock.'

'And a life buoy?'

'Definitely a life buoy. Did you see anything heavy when you were down on the bottom, sir?'

'I wasn't looking for anything of the kind, but – there was part of an anchor, I believe. That would make a bit of a hefty splash, surely. Or it could have been something that floated away before we ever saw it.'

Somebody, they thought, looking at the arrangement of knots in the dusk, had hooked up these things to fall – had pulled a rope, possibly from a lower window or just off the side of the deck – and everything had tumbled down, and a recording of screaming had sounded, and everybody had run to the back of the ship. And Sixgill, meanwhile, was attempting to flee with the diamonds, and being killed.

And Tom would lay a hundred to one that the same somebody had shoved him, very hard, in the small of his back that afternoon, and hoped he'd break his neck.

Elisabeth Lindgren was alone in the kitchen, laying the rotisserie segments, long and gleaming, back in their box. They were very beautiful, she thought, insofar as she noticed the beauty of anything, which these days was rare. There had been a time – but no, not anymore.

She had had hopes, yes. She was not a woman who

317

dwelled on lost possibilities – they lifted away from her like so much ash in the wind, as soon as it became clear they would not come to pass, and she moved forward. It was, in part, what made her a courageous and experimental chef: that refusal to ruminate on failure, merely to push on to the next thing, the next mouthful.

But this failure was sour. It burned deep in her, far worse than anything visible on her skin – more painful than oil burns, fat burns, burns from oven doors. She wondered if she could recover, or if she would perpetually be feeling the loss of it as she did right now. The future she thought she would have. The way she might have lived in it – so happily.

Her eyes were very dark in her skull.

Somebody came in out of the dark doorway and began talking, very low and very fast.

Elisabeth paid attention. At the end she paused, and nodded her head slightly. The person disappeared, and Elisabeth Lindgren was once again alone. She placed the box away, put down her gloves, and closed her eyes for one second, two. Then she opened them and moved away.

26

The next morning, Tom Heissen was feeling bruised in more ways than one. They'd be handing the operation over to the Nordic authorities tomorrow, and essentially admitting defeat. But, he thought, they had at least gathered a collection of good and solid evidence, to give them some gristle to chew on: how Sixgill had managed to misdirect everybody to get off the ship, the weapon used to kill him, the diamonds he was carrying, why Bloom Highcastle was likely killed. Alas for the smuggling investigation – that was where the diamond ring began and ended, as far as this story went. Perhaps it would be determined by the snobs at Interpol that he was working on his own . . .

That, thought Tom, was about as likely as the *Mouette* sprouting albatross wings and doing four rings around the *Dauphin*'s decks, but what did he know. If Tom could just get to that odd hut, could find some evidence that Sixgill really *had* been the mule – but there was not much point now.

It bore the mark of a dedicated and elaborate mind. Sixgill's? Somebody else's? Pulling the life buoy down, triggering the shout, then somehow getting him across to the ice with only one shoe – and killing him before he could escape and begin, perhaps, another stage in his life. If the jig was up and he had decided to flee – abandoning, perhaps, his entire scientific career, and being certified as disappeared off the back of a ship – there must have been something substantial waiting for him, something big. People in rings like this, Tom knew, changed people's identities all the time, gave them new passports, new homes. Sixgill was ambitious; what would he have been willing to sacrifice for such rewards?

And why, in the end, was it decided that he was to die – not out in the tundra somewhere, not at that mysterious cabin, not in a hotel room somewhere in the rest of the world, but by the *Dauphin*, skewered straight through the lung like Saint Sebastian?

He shook himself. Even with Titus's assiduous assistance, it was hard trying to package up a murder investigation to hand it to some nice Nordic police without too much of a 'here, *you* deal with it' expression. And – here he felt a surge of deep annoyance – there was so much here he could almost solve, that he knew was just within reach.

He stood up. 'Titus.'

'Sir?'

'I begin to feel the value of a frontal assault.'

'Sir?' Titus had, apparently, taken the thought of a person hitting Tom in the back and sending him down a hole as a personal, bone-deep offence, and had been interrupting their packing to check on Juhani at the stateroom door at improbable five-minute intervals. Now those grey eyes blinked at him, lucid and calm as ever, if slightly questioning at the eyebrows.

'There are too many *things* on this ship, Titus, and I'll be damned if I let them all get away from me.' Tom savagely threw on his *Dauphin*-orange parka over his jumper and pulled on his boots.

'We are to take a surprise approach, sir? While the Captain is speaking to them en masse about the end of the cruise?'

'Nothing else to lose at this point. Make sure this door's guarded, Juhani,' said Tom, and charged onto the deck and into the polar daylight.

The mood in the dining hall was constrained. People were looking at one another – sidelong and polite. Even under the lustrous lights of the *Dauphin*'s oyster-nacre walls, faces were tightened, and shadowed.

The Captain was finishing a speech to the assembled passengers as the two policemen arrived.

'—will be coming into Svalbard tomorrow. You will, of course, all be due refunds for the journey's curtailed nature, and I do encourage you to consult with your insurance providers for appropriate recompense.'

'And then?' It was, as ever, the insistent Dr Eder. 'We will be allowed to leave, yes? Highcastle – a maniac. A maniac!'

'When it is judged that you have offered all you can to the investigation, you will be permitted to leave, yes. I am sure the police on land will allow this quickly; you have all been most gracious.' Somehow, even after this collection of catastrophes, the Captain's ability to smooth ruffled waters remained unimpeachable. Tom was beginning to think he was a miracle of nature.

Patrick Moreland spotted the two men coming into the

dining hall and saluted them gently with his glass of tonic. 'So you're letting us go into other hands? Very sensible,' he said, in a low voice.

'You're not quite out of my hands yet,' said Tom. Boo and Rose were there, as was Finn – good. Sandy Highcastle was, of course, locked up, and Palgrave was, as usual, nowhere to be seen – still requesting that the eternally long-suffering Otso make her tea as he guarded her room, Tom guessed, accurately. The rest of the company simply stared at him. He raised his voice. 'As the Captain has explained, we will be handing off the investigative materials to another force tomorrow. They have substantially more resources than can be available to two men. However.' He suddenly felt immensely tired – almost grey. He thought determinedly of Biscuit, and carried on. 'There are some matters that remain unexplained, and that perhaps are – too *personal* to be put into international police files.' This was, of course, nonsense – but he was trying to dislodge *something*, something worthwhile.

There was a small noise. Tom looked at Titus – but it was simply the door to the kitchen, slightly opening. Elisabeth Lindgren, he thought, wondering if this was any of her culinary beeswax.

He kept pushing. He had a hunch on this one. Embarrassment was a much more powerful motivator to a certain class of people than virtually anything else.

'For instance.' He had an excellently resonant voice. The room virtually rang with it. 'Numerous incidents of threatening letters – to Alicia Grey, we believe. Saying they would reveal her identity if she spoke out. If anybody would like to explain those?'

There was a protracted silence. Alicia herself looked faintly white at the lips, but refused, it seemed, to crumble. Then—

'I believe I know.'

It was Gladys Moreland. Much to everybody's absolute astonishment, she unfolded herself from her seat and stood, and the room was reminded, intensely, of the fact that this was a woman who stood regularly before the highest bar, who wore the law as lightly as a coat.

This did not seem to come as a surprise to Alicia Grey. 'Yes,' she said. 'Yes, I thought it was you.' Her accent was no longer distinctly upper-class London, or Scots; it was something deeper, with long rolled R's.

'You were very young,' said Gladys. 'I did wonder if you'd remember.'

'I remember,' said Alicia Grey. And there was a strange look on her face, one that Rose Blanchard would never be able to locate again. It was the look, she would realise many years later, of a child, resettling on an adult's face, with a child's memory and perspective; an intelligent child who was trying very hard to pay attention, to understand.

'It was the ICC, wasn't it. The International Criminal Court,' Moreland said, to the rest of the company. 'I was a lawyer for the prosecution. Mikhail Kapetanović, the warlord, was on trial for acts of despotism and genocide, in the wars of his region. It was a long case, decades ago, and we didn't allow televising. He went away, in the end, one of the rare successes of my career in that court. He died in prison some years after the verdict.'

'I was made to come every day,' said Alicia. 'My nannies dressed me and placed me to watch him, in the dock. I assume they thought it might sway sympathy. I spoke little English then, or French, and they didn't give me a translation headset out of respect for my age, but I saw all the photographs. The terrible photographs.'

'You were Kapetanović's daughter,' said Tom, wonderingly.

'So. My birth name is long lost, but you can find it, if you like. I was his sole child, and my mother died before the coup. I was kept beside him in the palaces for many years, with a huge security detail, and I was brought along when we fled to France, then to Spain, or wherever he was arrested.'

'Portugal,' said Gladys Moreland.

'Yes. It was Portugal. By the time the trial ended—'

'You must have been eighteen, at that time, or nineteen. It took so many years,' said Moreland. The two women looked at one another, Moreland with acute sympathy. Rose looked for hatred in Alicia's eyes, but saw something else – an old suffering.

'It was not safe for me in my homeland; it never would be again, not with my real name. And people knew my face. There was an offer. To live unknown, to make another person of myself. The government in question was very kind. One of my father's old handlers arranged it all, secretly.' She breathed. The auburn hair moved brightly around her head. 'I was given my wish: a new life. Sunila, who is exactly what she says she is, if not infinitely more, was only twenty-one then. She was my government liaison, and my first friend.'

Sunila smiled.

'We really are married, you know,' she added conversationally. 'Alicia is a great woman.'

'I am very sorry, Alicia,' said Gladys Moreland, who looked very distinguished and, while standing with her fingertips on the dining table, enormously powerful.

'My father was an evil man,' said Alicia. 'I watched you every day tell him of his evils, and I learned of them too. It was a great thing you did.' She looked at the room. 'I apologise for any confusion this may have caused. But I do not think Dr Sixgill knew who I was, you know.'

'Somebody else did, though,' said Boo. 'Somebody tried to blackmail you.'

'No,' said Sunila. 'I don't think it was blackmail. It was an attempt to ask that we stay silent – because Alicia recognised them too, you see.'

'Whom?'

'Dr Eder,' said Alicia simply.

'Yes,' said Dr Eder. 'Myself.'

It took some time before Dr Eder was encouraged enough to explain. Titus's threatening aura took on a new force before the great academic sat on the edge of his chair and attempted to clear his throat, with a little of his old pomp, though his nerve clearly failed him at the last moment and it gurgled away.

'Before I became a PhD, you see, I was an MD. Yes. I do not put it by my name now, but it was so, then.' The medical school drop-out, Tom thought – but not quite. 'I was the personal physician to Alicia's father, to the Great Leader as he was then. I was a very young man, and was very well paid. I saw such things – and was terrified by them. But that is no excuse. I went with them in his entourage, with his little daughter, to France, to Portugal. When the arrests came I – slipped away. I too changed my name, though without any exterior help. I had been hiding in that Basque fishing village for a year and a half, observing the algae, when I first met Dr Fothergill, and formulated theories with him.'

'We tried to find you, the young doctor who went everywhere with the leader,' said Moreland, with disgust. 'We thought perhaps he'd had you killed, for knowing too much. Because you did know a great deal, didn't you.'

'He went away without my help, madam,' said Dr Eder, but looked horribly grey. 'You were capable. And I, I lived with my cowardice.'

Alicia said something that was clearly extremely intense and insulting in her own language. Dr Eder gathered his face as if he had been slashed across it with a knife. He bowed, and left.

27

An hour later, Tom was alone in the stateroom with a pile of papers, a collection of evidence, and a sense of self-satisfaction. Eder! Eder with his medical training, looking at Sixgill on the ice. He imagined Eder fitting a tranquilliser gun with a harpoon; people had done such things for the sake of reputation in Tom's experience. If Sixgill had somehow uncovered Eder's true identity, the scientist would possess a strong motive for murder. But, he thought heavily, the real target would then have been Alicia Grey – and Eder had contented himself with little threatening notes. A coward, then. Not a person who wished to get his very bloodied hands dirty ever again.

Titus's little squares of means, motive and opportunity, now scribbled over in every direction, were burned into the backs of his eyes. Sixgill getting off the ship somehow, with thousands of pounds worth of diamonds, a protective eye mask, and a journey ahead of him. An intricate distraction so he could do it in peace. And, for some reason still obscure to them, his body on the ice.

Tom travelled back to the day of the murder itself, meticulously constructing it in his head as if with small paper figures on a model of a theatrical stage. The actors in this vision all had their motives attached, on small neatly written tags. Sandy Highcastle, with his little empire crumbling, standing on the deck talking about walruses; Salome Palgrave, black-mailed, asleep in her bunk; Boo Moreland, protective of his prospective lover's brother, standing by the radio. Singh and Grey, with their ancient secret, fooling around on the upper deck; Dr Eder, whose lies were intertwined with theirs, staring at the *Mouette* as it descended; Elisabeth Lindgren, furious about candles or years-old wounds, in the kitchens. Scott and Berg, a woman who could pay anybody to do anything and her guardian, perambulating; Gladys Moreland, perhaps intent on meting out her own sort of justice, drifting around the open deck; Husband Patrick, a man of intellect and scrupulous loyalty, at the rail; the Captain, imperious and possibly powerless against a cartel that ruled his ship, on the bridge. And Bloom Highcastle — seeing nothing, understanding nothing, and screaming . . .

There were so many gaps, still. How Sixgill got onto the ice; who had rigged the elaborate escape mechanism for him to vanish from the world. Who had recorded that scream. Who had, when the time came, leaned out of a window and made that perfect shot. Who had, after Bloom's revelation, returned to the scene and perhaps asked to rearrange her necklace for her, and drawn it tighter, tighter . . .

Tom had quiet ideas. But he had no proof.

Titus, in the absence of anything further to file, had begun to spend his time huffing around the deck. He was not usually the patrolling type. Now he stuck his head round the door.

'Nothing to report,' he said officiously, then disappeared again.

Tom went over to shut the door behind him, turned around and whacked his shin on the slab of Highcastle's candles.

He landed hard on his front, which made the bruises that had been kindly quiet for the last few hours wake up and start squawking at him like a nest of particularly voracious parrots. Tom rolled onto his back, looked at the *Dauphin* stateroom's beautiful moulded ceiling, and swore with such extensive and linguistic complexity that he felt a dim sense of pride in himself. (Juhani, who was as ever manning the door, would later report to Titus that Tom seemed to be doing some elaborate and bumpy exercises, perhaps burpees?)

Then he sat up and looked at the crate. Tom Heissen was blessed with a mind disinclined to revenge, a gift to any investigative officer; a man might swing a punch at him and he'd still strenuously embrace the puncher's innocence until proven guilty. So it was with the candles. Tom's annoyance dissipated, and he was seized by a promise Rose Blanchard had made him make in front of the Captain, back when they were confronting Sandy Highcastle. *The police will search the candles most thoroughly.* And — they hadn't.

Rose Blanchard's instincts hadn't led them wrong yet. Though he was so *very* sick of candles.

Tom sighed, got up and prepared to dismantle the entire thing, lock, stock and crystalline barrels. The job felt unnecessary, perhaps even finicky — but if he didn't, he'd always feel an irritation at the bottom of his stomach at a job *not fully done*. The irritation would, he knew, pursue him off this ship, through the case handover to the Nordic police, back to Blighty, and probably interrupt his life at inopportune times, like Biscuit suddenly appearing at 2 a.m. to stand on his face.

He got his gloves and his evidence bags regardless, spread out a towel, and brought one of Titus's shivs up to the netting.

The top layer of candles shifted apart, and the rich forest smell rose into the room like so much incense. He remembered Sixgill's hair, floating among them. Sixgill being faced with the candles, Sixgill shoving them to one side in disgust when Highcastle presented them hopefully.

Much to Tom's absolute astonishment, something moved under the second level of candles – something with a metallic gleam, loosed from its position by the relaxation of the weights around it. Tom reached down carefully, took hold and pulled.

It was a small round cylinder made of metal – steel, he thought, at a guess. A mechanism for levering the diamonds inside the candles somehow? But it didn't look like any candle-making equipment he'd ever seen. It smelt of something odd – fat, or grease, and smoke. He took a small torch and peered inside.

A long series of scratches greeted him, all tracing right down the inner surface in parallel lines. As if something very narrow had been placed inside, and then shot out at great force.

At the moment Tom was making this discovery, Finn was making one of his own.

'Oh,' he said in a very quiet voice to his laptop.

'Oh?' said Rose's voice, muffled inside a camera casing on the table in their cabin. She pulled her head out and looked at him enquiringly.

'Martin and his husband have adopted another child,' said Finn, still in a barely audible voice.

'Well, that's——' Rose paused in what was going to be a furious diatribe of pity about the future of this child and the other children raised by a complete pillock, and stopped. 'Finn, how do you know?'

There was a deep and painful silence.

'Finn. *How do you know.*'

'I emailed him,' said Finn, in a voice that nearly wasn't a voice at all, more of a whisper. 'When the trip started. Just to tell him that it was going well and that we were going to set the cameras as planned, and——' He faltered under his sister's disbelieving stare. 'I wanted to see if he was sorry,' he added, desperately. 'And he said he was. And that, you know.'

'No, I don't,' said Rose, as gently as she possibly could, which was not very, because she could feel rage swelling in her from the stomach up, rising through her abdomen over her heart, her lungs, up to her eyes.

'That he still loved me, and that – we were going to meet up when we got back, and I thought . . . he was going to leave.' Finn's lashes were pricked with moisture. 'His husband. For me. He really seemed like—— But he just emailed. Her name is Ricarda.' He turned the screen towards Rose so that she could see the round, innocent face of a bald infant, gazing up at the camera.

'Finn.'

'I know,' said Finn, to his hands. 'I'm such an idiot.'

'You are,' said Rose, without thinking. 'You ARE.'

'I *know*.' Tears were running down Finn's nose now, the thin fine nose they had in common.

'After everything! And how you cried, and how he hurt you, and how he hurt *me* – what he stole, all the lies he told – you were going to go back?' Her eyes were burning now too. She felt dry-throated.

'He said he still loved me,' said Finn. 'I was going to forgive him—'

'*You* get to forgive him,' said Rose. Hot and hard and furious now. 'And I, what, sit and look pleased for the rest of our lives, when he treats you like hell again and again and again? Because he doesn't give a shit about you, and you know that, and he knows that, and *everybody knows that*, and you somehow want to pretend it's not the case?'

Finn said nothing.

'This entire time,' and Rose's voice was accelerating away from her, she could see it, white-burning with rage, 'you've been talking to the man who betrayed you in the deepest way possible, and *keeping it from me*, and meanwhile you've been carrying on with that really lovely police person who genuinely likes you, and doing what with him, exactly? Using him to bolster your self-esteem so you can run back to Martin and have it destroyed again?'

'That's not fair.' Finn's nostrils had gone a bit white. He was looking despairing.

'Which bit?'

'Tom didn't have anything to do with any of it.'

'I'm sure that will be a huge comfort to him,' said Rose with real acid in her voice. 'Am I meant to be shocked that Martin did something unbelievably shitty, and pick up all your pieces? I've already done that once.'

'I didn't ask you to,' said Finn, quietly.

'Good. Are you going to actually learn the lesson this time, or will we revisit this once every six months?'

'You're being massively horrible about this.' Finn had stood up. They were the same height. 'You're being really, deeply horrible. It's my life. It's my heart. Everybody deserves a second chance—'

'*No, they don't,*' said Rose, bitterly. 'You don't get a second chance at all those years you spent with him. And,' she added, gaining speed and misery, 'I don't get a second chance to watch you be happy. I don't get a second chance to spend time with you *without* mopping up tears and agony over a man who doesn't deserve it. I don't get that time back. And neither do you.'

'Well, you can feel completely satisfied, you were right.' Finn threw up his hands. 'He was awful all along, and you were right, and I got hurt again, and I didn't tell you because I knew you'd react *just like this.*'

'I hope you meet up and he convinces you to become *au pair* to his nice new baby,' shouted Rose.

'I hope Boo Moreland finds out just how *completely* self-righteous you are,' shouted Finn.

Rose went out and slammed the door.

Boo Moreland, coming down the corridor, said, 'Hey, what's up?' She pushed past him, unnecessarily hard, and went up onto the deck. The tears prickling out of her eyes formed into small patches on her cheeks in the sudden hit of cold.

Without any particular direction in mind, but with a clear desire not to *talk to anybody*, she headed to the prow of the ship. It was a part of the ship people were avoiding, since it looked out directly onto things that were beginning to plague their dreams: the dome, the scattered tarpaulins, the last bits of blood. They would, she thought, have to remove the dome tomorrow. That odd little half-haven loomed on the ice, gloomy and dark save for some reflected light from the *Dauphin*'s lanterns. It was now about two in the afternoon, and the light was already thinning, casting long shadows. The snowmobiles had been left too, covered in tarpaulins and netted down. If a polar bear came along to try and roll one over, she thought, they'd probably be more daunted by the weight of the thing than by a net.

It was easier to look at blood than it was to think about Finn. About how *stupid* he was – and how exhausted she felt.

There was, perhaps, a little flicker of movement against the gloom. She focussed her eyes and peered into the blue-black, but there was nothing more. A hare, perhaps, or something else, moving in the wind. Her cheeks felt unbearably hot, even in the chill of the air; there was sweat on the palms of her hands.

Underneath the prow, broken-up parts of the ice cap continued to shift and move in the current. She'd grown

334

so used to their appearance that she'd forgotten to actually look at them for some days, with their tessellated edges, some of them blackened in parts or brown from some encounter with dirt or grime. Many were small, smaller than a hand, though others were wider and thicker and could, the *Dauphin* passengers had seen, carry the weight of an entire walrus. The sound of their movements together, clicking and scraping and gently bouncing off one another at low speed, had become just background noise, but Rose found herself listening to it acutely for the first time in some time. The seascape was so filled with visuals that sometimes you forgot its sounds. Rays, clicking against danger.

There had been more bellowing from the walrus colony far off, with the wind in the right direction all afternoon. A strange, haunting sound, as males – she knew this from a long-ago biology class, somewhere in a past that barely seemed real – fought and roared amongst themselves for dominance, slamming bodies weighing several tons each against one another, drawing blood with long tusks. She watched the ice drift past the dome, in a silent parade against the hard black glaze of the water. Paving to nowhere.

Above her there was some quiet movement on the bridge, crew members talking. Somebody hauled on a rope pulley to solve some problem or other; the geometry of the ropes on the *Dauphin*, despite being extremely limited as it was engine-powered, still mystified Rose in its entirety. It was, she thought, a peaceful sort of scene, there in the dark. Her animal heart still beating away rapidly and miserably inside her.

Sixgill's death drifted loosely across her mind, like the ice floes themselves. The odd shape of it, all its mysteries – how he got into the ice in the first place. Things bumped into one another, formed connections, cracked away again. Her brain did this often with questions, without her noticing or paying much attention.

Gradually, however, much to her own surprise, a picture began to form. And one piece of ice, and another, and another, began to fuse – without anything to break them, strong and fast and hard enough to support weight. It worked. She tested it, looked at it sideways, another way. It still worked.

Tent pegs. Ropes.

But there was only one person who could have gone to the dome, who could have arranged everything—

She thought of Finn, white-faced, saying *Everybody deserves a second chance*.

Then she turned and sprinted, in a turn of speed that surprised even herself, towards Tom and Titus's stateroom.

Tom was sorting out the candles decorously while Titus carefully noted things down on a blank pad, and packed up their things.

Then an explosion rolled through the door: Juhani, who had clearly attempted to stop the movement of an unstoppable force, and the unstoppable force itself, which was revealed to be Rose Blanchard. Tom, in the midst of his astonishment, thought sympathetically about how often Juhani had been thrown through doors by various people on this case, and whether he could claim compensation. Rose had an odd look on her face, one that Tom didn't quite have the brain space at the time to decipher.

'Listen,' said Rose. 'No, *shut up. Listen.* Did Sixgill have something to do with Amsterdam? Did he live there?'

Tom obediently picked up Sixgill's accounts and looked.

Yes. There it was. A monthly payment on something in Amsterdam – he looked it up. A residential complex. Very beautiful duplexes, looking out onto the canals.

He looked up at Rose, who was breathing hard and triumphant.

'How the hell,' he asked conversationally, 'did you figure that?'

'It's – how do I explain this? It's the way she looked in the dining hall, talking about forgiveness and love,' said Rose Blanchard. Her face was narrower and sharper than he'd seen before, but she was also intent, as if on a fixed point. There would, Tom knew, be no diverting her. 'And the fact that she trailed her hand over the side when she came back from the dome, in absolutely *freezing* water. She lives in Amsterdam. And – oh, I'm jumbling it up, but it makes perfect sense. Nobody else could have done it. If Sixgill was living in Amsterdam, that clinches it. He was there *with* her. She was the one who got him off the ship. She was betrayed by *him*.'

Tom stared at her. So did Titus.

'*Elisabeth Lindgren*,' she breathed.

28

It was a beautiful theory. A very beautiful theory of a motivation for murder.

Cupid's arrow, Tom thought. Elisabeth and Sixgill – in it together, somehow. Walruses hiding among walruses. And something stirred in his head, and clicked into place without his fully realising it.

'We've got to find her,' he said shortly, rising.

'I'm coming too,' said Rose. 'She likes me. She might tell me about it.'

'And it'll give us a good opportunity to watch over you in case you come to any more daring and acerbic conclusions,' said Tom drily.

But Elisabeth Lindgren was not in the kitchens. Nor, when they went and gently knocked, then loudly pounded, was she in her bedroom. Dr Eder popped his head out of his own room with a white face, and watched them without speaking.

Tom's sense of foreboding – and, worse, of being bested, of somehow being three chess moves behind in a game he hadn't really understood until just now – worsened. He made a silent decision, and went to the bridge, Titus and Rose Blanchard hurrying behind.

The Captain eyed the three of them, nodded, and sent out the troops. The search brought back nothing. Elisabeth Lindgren was not on the ship. And – Juhani came to tell them this, white-lipped – *there were skis and a pack missing from the hold*.

The decision to leave for the hut happened extremely fast.

If Elisabeth was going anywhere on skis, Tom thought, she was going there. It was unclear how long she'd been gone; nobody appeared to have seen her since the scene with Dr Eder that morning. She could have been missing for a long time. Preparations for the dinner service, where her absence would definitely be noticed, hadn't yet begun. The crew kept searching staterooms, the hold, anywhere they could think of, but the chef had left no sign. She had taken almost nothing – her passport was still in the Captain's safe – and slipped away like a fox in camouflage against the ice. It would be a ski of five hours at least to the hut, he estimated, on strong legs.

'But how did she get to the ice? All the dinghies are still here,' said Rose hotly. The kitchen staff were all on deck looking, Tom thought, faintly distraught; there had been talk of launching a dinghy to scan the water, but news of the skis and the pack had made them settle down for now. Elisabeth was off the *Dauphin* and headed for an unknown destination, but she was, at least, alive to the best of their knowledge, and the kitchen that ran almost entirely on the strength of her personality was buoyed by that idea.

'The same way Sixgill got there in the first place.' Tom felt buoyed as well: almost balloon-like with satisfaction at how well the pieces fit. It was a kind of professional helium filling his skull. He was fastening his boots. Lindgren was

339

young, strong and on skis; if at any point he had to run her down he wanted to have grip underfoot. He gestured out the window at the ice floes, and noticed his own hand trembling with absolute triumph. 'Quiet, quick, efficient, and doesn't need a dinghy!'

'That was the one bit I couldn't figure out,' said Rose almost angrily. 'I thought some kind of temporary floatation device—'

'Sir?' said Titus, uncomprehendingly.

'Think of walruses,' Tom panted.

There was a silence. Then—

'An *ice raft*,' said Rose, with the face of a person whose theorem has suddenly and elegantly come together. 'A big piece of ice he could kneel on and pull himself along using a rope! He didn't even have to hunt – his escape was just out his window *the whole time*. He just had to crawl out and drag!'

Walruses, thought Tom with immense satisfaction.

'The tent pegs were left out on the ice deliberately.' He was talking very fast as he levered feet into shoes, arms into jacket sleeves. 'Lindgren placed them precisely, to give them something to hook a line onto. One was hammered close enough to the edge of the ice that a rope could be passed through it, and a loop fed back to the ship. I imagine that happened while the dome was being packed down.'

'Elisabeth with her hand over the side of the little dinghy,' said Rose. 'That's what I'd figured out – that she must have arranged it. That they must have been in it together. There was no reason for her to do that unless she was fixing *something* to the *Dauphin*, but I couldn't figure out what it was.'

'Yes. She was carrying the line back to the ship,' said Tom to Titus. 'She must have hooked it under the lifeboat before she went up the ladder. Her room was on the right side; it was easy to put the rope under the window, it must have just looked like another rope. It did to us, when we saw it on the seafloor. They looped it through a tent peg, tied it, and then Sixgill used it to pull himself over onto the ice shelf, hand over hand. They had to time it to happen while you were underwater, and exploring the far side. But the submersible wasn't enough to distract everybody all at once.'

'So the shout, and the shoe and life buoy, sir,' supplied Titus, grabbing radios and signal flares and God knows what else and stuffing them in his pockets.

'So the shout and the life buoy. They were in her room – of course, it's right up the front on the starboard side, closest to the ice cap – and at the signal Elisabeth triggered the recording and the falling anchor, and then the life buoy to follow. That elaborate system of pulleys somebody had rigged.'

'*That*'s why she was fiddling around the back of the ship when the *Mouette* was leaving,' Rose added.

Titus made an approving noise. 'It works, sir. She pulls a rope and clicks a switch, and everything falls, a scream echoes, everybody sensibly travels to the back of the ship—'

'And meanwhile Sixgill is crawling out of Elisabeth's porthole window and kneeling on an ice raft, pulling himself towards the ice on the circular loop of rope,' said Rose rapidly.

'He must have been extremely quick,' Tom said. 'Elisabeth must have pulled too. Dr Palgrave *might* have heard, given she was in her bunk, but her room's on the other side of the ship. And she was conveniently drugged.'

'That's why she was asleep!' asked Rose, pulling a nicely knitted hat down on each of their heads. 'The amnesia as well. Of *course* she was drugged. To protect her? That seems weirdly . . . gentlemanly of Sixgill.'

'I'm inclined to believe that was meant for the Captain, sir,' said Titus with an air of sudden inspiration, grabbing his gloves. They'd discussed the drug theory briefly before, but hadn't quite figured out what purpose it might serve. 'Of course Lindgren was best placed to drug anybody from the kitchens. And the Captain knew her well; perhaps he knew she was in a relationship, perhaps he suspected. But Dr Palgrave picked the Captain's coffee cup randomly from the table at lunch; she was always doing that. The Captain being under the weather would hamper any rescue operations quite significantly. A conscious Dr Palgrave probably wouldn't pay any attention to odd noises from Elisabeth's room – she's not the curious type. Now, sir, we *have to go*.'

Tom took Rose's hands. 'Titus has a radio on the ship's frequency,' he said. 'If you need us, or something goes wrong, we'll listen. Take care of yourself and your brother.'

'For God's sake don't do anything stupid,' blurted Rose, in a mild panic. 'I won't be able to explain it to Finn. I mean—'

'I know,' said Detective Inspector Tom Heissen, and they fled out into the dark.

—

Above Tom and Titus, with perverse timing, the Northern Lights began to flicker and flow; an aurora of glorious and upsetting beauty unfurled its ribbons and danced across the polar sky. Their helmets pressed tightly together as Titus drove in the direction of the cabin. Tom felt a brief surge of professional pleasure that they were, at last, going to this blasted cabin that had hovered on the edges of his consciousness for days.

On the snowmobile, shouting at one another in the haze of darkness as its headlights coursed before them, they hashed it out.

'Her fleeing rather clinches the theory, sir,' he yelled over his shoulder. 'Perhaps she used the skis as paddles on the ice raft.'

'I'm afraid it does.' Tom felt no particular happiness at the idea of catching Elisabeth Lindgren. She may have murdered Sixgill, and he was almost certain that she had, but he had the odd sensation of setting out to hunt a rare bird.

'Why did she kill him, do you think?' Titus's voice ricocheted between their helmets.

'I think, you know, that Elisabeth was in love with him,' said Tom slowly, to the dark. 'Remember Rose telling us about her face when she talked about forgiving a lover anything? And of course he'd been paying for that bolthole in the Netherlands. I don't know how long it had been going on. Possibly years. He must have made a hell of an apology for that horrible come-on. But he was suddenly planning to do a bunk – and she went along with it, but when it came

343

to actually letting him go, probably into an entirely new life without her, she refused.'

'A man of precious little empathy, sir,' said Titus. 'Keep a lookout for ski tracks. The cabin is a while off.'

'I think we were correct in thinking that he wanted to be certified as falling overboard, and his body lost forever.' Tom was speaking partly to himself and to the floating world above him, rotating in icy motion. 'So Sixgill gets to the ice, no doubt planning to hide in the dome 'til later – why would they look for a drowned body there? Then she'd come over to dismantle it once the fuss had died down, give him his pack, and he'd slope off as fast as he could towards the hut. Remember he was wearing white and the mask, to camouflage himself against the snow and ice and protect his eyesight. He knew about the white hares, of course.'

'I wonder about the extent to which Elisabeth was part of the smuggling ring, sir,' said Titus. 'If she shot Sixgill she was certainly not afraid to stymie its plans. Perhaps she knew nothing about it.'

'And killed him for her own reasons, and thus blew up the whole ring by accident,' said Tom, thoughtfully. 'Or believed he was faking his own death to try and break free of the relationship. I don't know, Titus. Perhaps she was helping them too – though she'd certainly started to try and throw a spanner in the works this trip. Remember she tried to get the Captain to look more closely at those candles. Perhaps she was being a bit willingly blind, until the love-mist wore off.'

'An odd choice of partner for such an extraordinary woman, sir.' Titus's voice was quietly uncomprehending, as if he were a seraphim observing the messy ways of mortals. 'Though Sandy Highcastle did say that he was usually very charming. Perhaps he was unpleasant on this trip so that people wouldn't look too closely into his supposed death.'

'A fair theory, Titus.'

'And so she shot him, sir.'

Tom said, watching his breath fog up the inside of his snowmobile helmet, 'We won't know what happened exactly, unless she chooses to tell us, but – I imagine she leaned out of the starboard porthole of her room as he landed on the ice cap, watched as he stood up, then shot him with the tranquilliser gun she'd modified. She must have formidable aim, but at that level it was a shot straight forward into his chest, which would have helped. Not nearly as risky or difficult as doing it high up on deck. And as he watched, dying, she cut the belaying rope, so it fell away helplessly into the sea – he had no way back.'

'The harpoon came on board with the knives, sir?'

'Or the rotisserie. One walrus among so many other walruses, Titus. I don't know if she planned to kill him then, or if he wanted it himself for protection. Anyway, I'll lay bets that's how it got there. The little shaft that went inside smelled of grease, or fat. I think that was kitchen paraphernalia too. Possibly the shaft off a long blowtorch or something. We'll find out.'

'Yes. I don't understand the one shoe. That seems rather pointless, sir.'

'It's possible that was an accident,' said Tom, into the wind. 'They must have planned for the shoe to fall and bob in the water – evocative, really. Because shoes do come off on drowning people – and then realised too late, getting dressed and halfway out of the porthole, that he hadn't got the spare handy. No time, he had to go. Another spare was hurriedly found and attached to the rope after him, so he could grab it and run into the dome with it, but Elisabeth cut the belay before it could arrive, and so it and the rope sank to the bottom.' He paused, and then added, 'Possibly it wasn't an accident; possibly Elisabeth did it on purpose, so that he'd have to wait and turn towards her on the ship, giving her a better chance at the shot. Even if he survived the harpoon – which was possible; it was a long way and she was aiming at him out of a porthole – he'd still have to flee, and lose the foot to frostbite.'

'She must have been very angry, sir,' said Titus. There was a reverence in his voice.

'She still will be,' said Tom. 'And she's a fine shot with a harpoon. That thing was an absolute bull's-eye. Don't take off this helmet if you can help it.'

'No, sir.' They drove onward. The rocks and mounds of the ice shelf echoed with the rotation of the engine; in the dark animals heard the rumble, rolled over in their burrows, and were still.

It took some time to find exactly what they were looking for – the confused documentary crew had only given an approximate location – but eventually the cabin loomed. It was small, squat, and lay low against the ice. There was no light inside.

There were, to Tom's annoyance but not surprise, no ski tracks outside – and it was a night of clear pristine snow with no wind, so even if Elisabeth Lindgren had attempted to conceal her tracks, they'd still see them. A five-hour ski on flat terrain – yes, they might well have overtaken her. No matter how fast she could go, she was not as fast as a snowmobile doing top – or perhaps above top – speed over a flat surface. The snowmobile had also begun to make odd noises – it had run very hot and fast for a good hour, and Titus was something of a lead foot.

The cabin was a construction possibly left over from the nineteenth century, from hunters or somebody else who'd had ambitions of doing something out here: hunting for walrus skins, perhaps, or drilling for oil. It was made of heavy wooden planking held together with nails and what looked like tar. It had no windows and carried a heavy padlock on the outside – possibly to deter rare passers-by, but also to dissuade polar bears, Tom thought, thinking of the tranquilliser guns.

They'd hidden the snowmobile out of sight. It had started making some odd noises before Titus turned off the engine to cruise in unnoticed. 'Engine overheated,' Titus said now, coming back around the cabin breathing hard. He'd insisted on pushing it himself round the rear of the shack. 'It will be fine in a few hours in this weather, sir.' Tom swore, very gently.

Titus got to work, fiddling with lockpicks through his thick gloves. Cato could learn a few tricks from his brother at the Williams family Christmas, Tom thought. There was no movement nearby. This was the only shelter for miles in any direction. The odds were strong that Elisabeth Lindgren was coming this way. Sixgill must have told her about it, as the place he was headed to begin his new life. There was no other shelter for miles, nowhere to hide.

The lock gave, with a brutal click.

The inside was freezing but surprisingly dry. Perhaps somebody else had been there recently to thaw out the surfaces. Whatever Tom was expecting, it wasn't a wood-burning stove with a printer, a portable generator and a compact combination safe laid out in one corner. It was a mystery how these things had been hauled over the ice. Never, he thought, underestimate the ingenuity of persons intent on transporting sparkly things.

'An odd set-up, sir,' said Titus Williams, very quietly.

'Let's get that safe open,' said Tom, perhaps even quieter.

They weren't safe-crackers by trade, though Titus could probably tell a few men who'd been in the dock before Gladys Moreland a thing or two about their occupation, but they both knew how tumblers worked, and this wasn't exactly a sophisticated model. (Why would it be, in the middle of nowhere? Polar bears couldn't raid safes, and if they could the smugglers would have much bigger problems.)

Many of the documents inside were in cipher, but Tom could make educated guesses as to what they were: shipping manifests, plans, placements for this or that bunch of diamonds.

'Look, sir,' said Titus, lifting one up with a still-gloved hand. It was a passport and travelling papers out of the Arctic – all bearing a name that distinctly wasn't Sixgill's, but with Sixgill's head in all the photographs. His red hair burned like flame in the dazzling light from their torches. Tom looked at him still alive, at the thin cheeks, the light and intelligent eyes, and at the start of the new life he didn't get to make. The passport was immaculate, with chip, embossing and all the trimmings; these were thorough people.

There was money: around 3,000 in euros, a few hundred kroner and a little in American dollars. There were warm clothes, and packs of the nutrition-heavy, dense rations one got in the army or the Special Forces, so useful for long treks across barren parts of the globe. There was also a velvet tray for sorting diamonds – at this moment, completely empty – and the accoutrements for assessing and grading gems of all kinds. And, Tom and Titus both noted silently, a small pistol. No passport for Elisabeth – which lent weight to the theory that this was not a long-held plan, and that she was just running blindly, out onto the ice, to a place where she knew there might be shelter and help.

'I don't understand *why* she ran,' Tom said to the freezing air in general. Titus was lighting the small wooden stove.

'People do odd things when they're frightened, sir,' Titus said, poking at the stove with the poker. Poking was actually not the right verb; he was stabbing at it in order to produce bursts of sparks and embers, rather surgically. The fire was having what could only be described as a fit of the sulks.

'She's been pushed to desperate straits,' said Tom heavily. 'It's one thing to commit a meticulous murder involving stagecraft and distractions; it's another to spontaneously strangle women and shove policemen down holes. Even her reckless acts have been neat and tidy. When she arrives

– and I don't see where else she could be going – I'll want to know what tipped her off that we were onto her. She might even tell us. Depending on her head start, we might be here for a little while.'

'We can't move for several hours, so we may as well get warm,' said Titus, and nudged the fire, which had apparently realised it was in the presence of a superior will and was begrudgingly doing what it was told.

Tom picked up the pistol from the safe. It was loaded, and he wasn't going to leave it lying around. 'I don't suppose, Titus, that you brought one of the guns those helpful persons in Svalbard gave to you?' asked Tom, without much hope.

'No, sir,' said Titus, sounding shocked. 'But,' he added contemplatively, 'I'm sure that if necessary I could fire a signal flare at her.'

'We'll try to deal with Elisabeth Lindgren *without* pyrotechnics, thank you,' said Tom.

Rose was on her bunk. Dinner had been late but reasonable; passing by the kitchens, she had been greeted by the astonishing vision of the Captain in a chef's apron, wiping his hands and looking vaguely floury of face. He had bowed to her with his usual impeccable manner and gone back to directing the small horde of kitchen workers, who appeared highly relieved to have *somebody* at their helm. It was simple – homemade pasta and sauce for the crew and scientists, large bowls of deliciously spiced vegetables and a spread of falafels for the paying guests – but, she reflected, it was a mark of his skill that he'd managed to rustle up the entire thing with a chef on the loose and her kitchen in hysterics. She supposed high-end kitchens were a little like well-funded laboratories directed towards one project: everybody had their contributing job and did it extremely well, but the process required a dominating intelligence, *somebody* making decisions, even if they themselves did little of the actual work. The service was mildly deranged – balsamic strawberries and a basil ice cream were plonked on the table as they were starting their mains – but in general it was far smoother than she'd anticipated.

The problem now was that Finn was out. And had been out for many hours. And she didn't know where he was, and she didn't want to go find him, and she had been rehearsing her apology until it grew blurred in her head and she needed to get up to stretch her legs. It was, by the mark of the clock, around 10 p.m. Tom and Titus had been gone for hours; there had been no word; so all must be fine. Mustn't it?

There was a knock at the door.

It was Kate Berg. In one hand was the pair of the radio Tom had mentioned before he and Titus left for the cabin. There's news, Rose thought, rapidly – they'd sent the small, capable nurse to relay it.

'They're in trouble,' she said very fast. 'Somebody's hurt – I've got all my supplies, but Detective Inspector Heissen asked for you. Hurry.'

Tom stretched his legs; the fire's long-life logs wouldn't last that much longer after three hours of burning. Soon, he reflected, they'd run out of heat, and have to resurrect the snowmobile and head back to the *Dauphin*. Perhaps she was watching, waiting for them to go.

There were many things that Tom was expecting from that evening. A confrontation; a quiet conversation in which Elisabeth Lindgren explained everything; stonewalling, and her magnificent face refusing all entreaties; or complete silence, and the revelation that she had gone somewhere else, that she had fled perhaps to another part of the ice cap, or that it was all a grievous misunderstanding.

What he was not expecting was the gradual flow of sound in the distance, resolving itself into a mechanical hum, then a wall-shaking purr. 'Another snowmobile,' Titus said, raising his head.

'Did you have anything on the radio from the *Dauphin*?'

Titus shook his head.

'I think, sir, that a quiet ambush might be in order,' he said. 'If someone is coming to check the cabin—'

'Snuff the fire,' said Tom. 'All lights out.' He felt a pang of regret as the little mouth of the stove went black. 'Do we have time to get outside?'

Titus listened. 'It's coming fast, sir. It's dark, but—'

'They might see us. Right. At least our vehicle is hidden. Concealment positions, Williams.'

'Yes, sir.' There were precious few places to hide in this cabin – probably, Tom thought, partly by design – so they both ended up sheltering behind the door, which would envelop them as it opened inward. Titus, with a protective air that brooked no argument, took the outer spot, further into the room.

The snowmobile came closer, drew up in a shearing of snow, turned off. There was talking – Tom recognised Rose Blanchard's voice, and was immediately comforted, though confused. 'I *think* it's all right,' he whispered to Titus, 'but stay here.' And he went round to the door, and slightly pulled it open.

Two figures were dismounting from the repulsively orange-rind carapace of the other *Dauphin* snowmobile. One of them, as he'd heard with great relief, was Rose Blanchard. She saw his face and darted forward, with a fearful and purposeful expression. 'We came to help,' she said. 'One of you is hurt? Where's Elisabeth?'

'Oh, no, we're fine,' said Tom with some confusion. 'At least—'

The other figure took off its helmet and revealed – he was startled out of his mind – a pure white face. Oh – the porcelain mask from his stateroom, the one that had been splashed with blood, though it was now scrupulously clean. What was that doing here? It was, he noticed, a surreally beautiful thing, floating as if in mid-air; the whiteness almost disappeared among the pale surfaces of ice and snow. A beautiful, inhuman protection against wind chill, against discovery, against anything.

The mask moved aside. It was the small, precise face of Kate Berg.

'Hello,' Tom said, growing more confused by the minute.

'My apologies, sir,' said Titus behind him. And there was an absolutely colossal crack across his head, and then nothingness.

353

29

Tom woke up. That was to say he became conscious; it was one of the worst wakings-up he'd ever experienced, short of the time his aunt had attempted to convince him that brandy and home-brewed thistle wine mixed perfectly at Christmas, and everybody had to stay in bed for three days afterwards, making dehydrated angry noises.

His eyes hurt. He was conscious of a supreme cold. His old bruises from the fall the day before had resurfaced with a vengeance, and were banging with blood all over his front; and he discovered, much to his annoyance, that he could not in fact move. This, it turned out, was due to a highly competent series of ropes around his torso, arms, legs and wrists, which he immediately recognised as the work of Titus Williams. Against him was something warm. Rose Blanchard – also trussed, and awake, though also looking groggy.

'Titus,' he said, in a faintly bloodied voice. He had probably chipped a tooth when he fell; there was sharpness in his mouth.

The pale head did not turn. It was, at present, taking all the other papers out of the safe and tossing them into the open door of the wood stove, which was delighting in this new fuel source. The door of the cabin stood open onto the night, which was why this exercise provided no heat whatsoever.

'Titus!'

'Yes, sir, I hear you,' said the quiet voice.

'Do you mean to explain yourself?' Tom asked, faintly petulantly.

'I don't think you require it, sir.' And Titus was quite right. Tom had the misfortune of understanding the situation perfectly. He had been had; and the criminal bent of Titus Williams, which had appeared to be diverted for so many years towards the pursuit of good and the safety of the populace, had shown itself, crooked and honed to a fine point, to be dominant after all. Elisabeth and Sixgill had made a mess, and Titus and Kate Berg were ruthlessly in charge of cleaning it up. Titus, who had been privy to the entire investigation – who had been trusted to do searches, to assemble evidence, all by himself. Little brother Cato's painted-jerky schemes, he thought dimly, eat your heart out.

'What on earth is going on here,' said Rose in a quiet voice to Tom. She appeared to be ready to be convinced that this was all a performance, that there was some greater aim afoot that could be easily explained. He shook his head at her, and her eyes widened.

'Thank you, that will be enough talking,' said Titus, and turned to face them. He was, Tom saw with astonishment, pointing the small gun from the safe directly at them. Rose sucked in a breath.

Kate Berg re-entered the cabin. Her face was perfectly calm. Tom remembered how slightly shaken she'd seemed that first interview – which she'd hid, quite convincingly, under the veneer of worrying for Aabria Scott. This was a woman who didn't like surprises. And was now in complete control of the situation.

She was carrying the radio paired to Titus's. Of course that was how they had communicated, Tom thought, probably when Titus was out moving the snowmobile. It wouldn't be on the ship's frequency at all. She didn't look at them; she simply walked up to Titus and asked a question.

'Is it all here?'

Titus nodded.

'Show me.' Kate Berg's face showed neither trust nor distrust; just a clear professionalism that demanded all i's and t's be attended to in their proper manner. Titus, one hand still pointing the gun at Rose and Tom, put a hand into his exceptionally well-pocketed jacket and gave her two bags: one Tom recognised as the evidence bag holding the mask diamonds; the other was heavier, in a kind of waterproof material that he didn't remember at all. Berg emptied them both onto the velvet tray from the safe. Yes. Diamonds. The ones in the heavier bag were substantially bigger.

'Where did those come from?' he asked, without much hope of being answered.

Titus, with the apparent remnant reflex of answering to a superior, said, 'Inside the radio transmitter, sir, from the sea floor. I purloined them from a drawer when we were searching Sixgill's room. He didn't take them with him when he left the ship.'

The split-open radio transmitter on Sixgill's desk. Of course. He'd been stupid. You don't *crack open* a radio transmitter. Not unless there's something hidden inside.

'He was just instructed to leave them and to get off the ship,' said Berg, rapidly counting and assessing. She was speaking as if by rote – reciting the rules. Good, thought Tom – she liked order, she liked things to be scrupulously neat. He could press on that, and keep her talking. 'He wasn't meant to have obvious jewels on his person, in case of capture or disaster. Of *course* he'd try to stage a giant scene to make an exit and ruin everything. Dramatic. Yes, they're all here. Good.'

'Those were the main haul,' said Tom. 'Highcastle wasn't meant to bring his load on this trip at all. The mask diamonds weren't part of the plan, so Sixgill simply took all the masks with him; who'd look for gems in that pile?'

'*The undersea radios,*' said Rose.

Of course; it was, in its own way, completely brilliant. Leaving diamonds inside armoured, heavy weights on the seafloor with radio beacons, to be picked up by the next member of the cartel going through. An easy thing for people to modify, and what reason would customs have to search something that had been sitting in brine for six months? Rose, Tom noticed, looked absolutely *furious* at this misuse of science.

'Do you mean,' she asked Tom, 'that Finn and I genuinely went down to the bottom of the sea to aid and abet in smuggling those stupid lumps of carbon?'

'Afraid so.' Tom felt vaguely giddy.

'Do shut up,' said Berg, with the mien of somebody talking to an irascible patient.

'Is Elisabeth out here too?' asked Rose, hotly.

357

'No,' said Berg. 'Go load up,' she added to Titus, who handed her the gun and exited.

'She must be hidden on the ship somewhere,' said Tom. He wondered what hidden parts he'd missed; he had, of course, trusted Titus to direct half the searching – and to fetch the ship's plans – and so many other things. Gaps, inconsistencies. The cold was already beginning to seep into him. He wondered how many hours he'd have, in the elements here. They were well rugged up, but hypothermia would get them eventually, if they were given the chance to live that long. Berg didn't answer.

Rose was talking softly and rapidly – to herself, he thought – about the nuances of the smuggling radios. The ire of it seemed to be keeping her warm. 'Radio points all over the Arctic and the northern seas – must be at least a dozen of them – Finn *said* there were rather a lot! And picked up every six months for *maintenance* – the added weight of the jewels keeping them in place so they don't move – for *God's sake*.' Her breath clouded at her face.

Finn *had* said that. Tom had heard him. He briefly cursed himself for paying too much attention to curly hair and freckled hands, and not listening, *really* listening.

A nurse companion. Tom wiggled his toes and did his best to keep his brain working and his heart rate up. It was a brilliant cover. She travelled everywhere on the sea with a wealthy woman who'd naturally have jewels as part of her luggage; what better disguise? Going on shore, getting little gifts for her employer, and in the meantime doing deals, arranging payments. What did she say to them once? Police raiding their boat in Cairo looking for contraband? A neat, cool little person. Meticulous.

He made a small gamble. 'Was Aabria Scott part of this too?'

That, as he'd suspected, got a reaction: a sharp movement of the head. That relationship was a real one. 'Absolutely not,' said Kate Berg, looking straight at him.

'That's her mask. She's probably hidden Elisabeth,' he said to Rose, conversationally, noting the faintly white tip of her small nose. 'She's sharp, that woman, for all she's over eighty. She'll be threatening Elisabeth with all sorts of horrors unless she cooperates as we speak.'

'She has nothing to do with this,' said Berg, sharply. 'It's *my* mask. I bought it for her in Venice. There seemed to be some kind of evidence on it, so I had Titus retrieve it for me. It's very good against windchill.'

'Come off it. You mean to tell me that Aabria didn't figure out Elisabeth had killed Sixgill? That seems far more her style, not yours.' He was playing for something – for time, for information, for anything. His bonds were incredibly tight. Titus did not fool around when it came to knots, regrettably.

'Damaging my ego doesn't do very much, Heissen,' said Berg, beginning to put the diamonds one by one into another pouch. 'You were a bit of a dunce on that, to be honest. You really should have seen that Elisabeth was the only one who could have brought any sharp objects on board, or arranged things on the ice. A first-rate brain – I'm glad I didn't have to kill *her*. She'll work for us quietly enough now. I didn't know Sixgill was carrying on with her, but it wasn't a far leap once the pieces were together.'

'He didn't know who you were,' said Tom.

'Of course not,' said Berg, placing things into her pack swiftly. 'People don't. This route will now be officially closed, if that's any comfort to you. Police work at its finest. It was a good thing while it lasted, but you two have brought far too much heat.' She gestured at Rose and Tom. 'That and Sixgill accidentally killing that kid in the port. Idiotic behaviour.' Her small mouth was grim.

'I did *think* the port death was clumsy.' Tom's cheeks were very, very cold. 'Far too much heat on your operation. Sixgill bungled it, I guess. Was he just meant to pay Michael Keren off?'

'Yes,' said Berg crisply. 'We are not by default murderers, Detective Inspector.'

'I believe you,' said Tom.

'Bloom Highcastle didn't have to die.' Rose Blanchard was many things – deeply intellectually offended, for one – but her primary feeling at the moment was one of moral upset. She raised her voice. 'She didn't actually *know* anything. She just saw that there wasn't anybody at the back of the ship.'

'It was judged to be the best way forward,' said Berg absently, packing away folders and parcels of money with a neat hand, 'in the grand scheme of things. The Highcastles were a liability anyway.'

'The diamond-smuggling route had been rumbled and Sixgill wasn't meant to be actually dead,' Tom explained to Rose, still conversationally. His teeth were beginning to sting at the roots from the cold. She opened her mouth and shut it. 'Whoever knew *anything* about that death would bring investigators closer to the truth. Which, in the end, is what Bloom did, despite being murdered. She didn't die for nothing.'

Rose shook her head. Tom looked at her face and saw a kind of blue-flame outrage, the sort that's too hot to approach or touch. He wondered whether it might keep her warm in the freezing air. Boo Moreland, he thought, was going to have a hard time replacing her. He didn't want to think about what Finn Blanchard would do.

Titus came back in and muttered.

'You've made sure? It absolutely won't start?'

'No. I've taken out various spark plugs and other components and put them on the ice; it could only be repaired very slowly.'

'Good. We'll ride the other one back to the *Dauphin*.'

'Are you going to kill us now?' asked Rose. She sounded, Tom thought with a streak of high admiration like a comet, completely fearless.

'We will,' said Titus, 'leave you two to die of hypothermia. It will likely be quite swift. The story as I understand it is that Tom was a confederate of Elisabeth's, punched me out, allowed Lindgren to escape, and lured Rose out here with a false distress call, in order to silence her. She, regrettably, brought Kate to help her, and so she was also attacked. We will escape the scene and get help. Is that correct?' he asked Berg, with a deference that, perversely, hurt Tom's

361

feelings to see applied to anybody other than him.

'Quite,' she said shortly. 'Corrupt cop comes to a bad end. It was,' she added, 'only meant to be you, Heissen. Rose Blanchard simply stuck her nose into the wrong place. I'm sorry, Doctor, but you were far too involved in the investigation; Williams updated me scrupulously on your knowledge. But as it stands you balance things quite well. Three innocents against one plays better than two. Speaking of which—'

She punched Titus hard, directly in the face. He took it without flinching. His nose began to stream, blood upon blood.

'I throw better punches than that,' said Tom grimly.

'With your pardon, sir, you don't.' Titus's voice was slightly muffled. He had his head down, tracking blood and footprints all over the interior of the cabin, to make it look like a grand old fight, Tom thought.

'How will you excuse not taking Rose back to the ship?' Tom demanded. 'Me, I understand. I'm dangerous, apparently, and you've clearly subdued me. But you could balance three on a snowmobile, with an effort.'

Titus answered by taking the gun out of Kate Berg's hand, and shooting Rose Blanchard in the abdomen.

She looked at him with total fury and bent over to one side. Berg made a pleased noise and went outside.

'She was,' Titus said in his colourless way, low and baritonal, 'too far gone for us to risk bringing back on a snowmobile, sir. You tied her up and shot her, you see. We will, of course, try desperately to untie her and stuff

362

the wound with gauze, to make it look as if we attempted first aid while fleeing—' He took some out of Berg's pack and placed it expertly against the wound, ignoring Dr Blanchard's spirited attempts to headbutt him. 'But it will prove futile.' Tom looked at the wound, then at Titus's face, then looked away.

'This all seems very well thought-out. I shall commend you to the Devil when I inevitably meet him.'

'Thank you, sir.'

'My brother is going to kill you,' said Rose in an eerily calm voice.

Tom made a very conscious effort not to think of Finn at all. Of his face, his hands, floating through space.

'Put them in position,' said Berg, putting her head back in. 'I want to get going back to the ship before we run into bad weather.' The bellowing of walruses against the dark sounded for all the world like the howling of terrible wolves.

Titus obediently dragged Tom away to the corner of the cabin (no picking of ropes with one another's teeth), put the small parcel of diamonds carefully in the pocket of his parka – Tom would, of course, take the fall for those diamonds, along with Sandy Highcastle – and tightened his bonds behind his back. Rose's bonds were, Tom noted, done in different knots to his; the pretence that they'd been tied up by two separate people had been well thought out.

Titus stood. Berg watched this without expression.

'I am terribly sorry, sir.'

The door clashed shut. They were left in the polar dark.

Tom, drying his lips so that the spit didn't begin to freeze, took inventory. Brutally difficult knots. No internal heating. Rose, leaning her head against the wall of the cabin, with blood pooling on the floor. 'Tom,' she said. There was a question in her voice.

'I know,' he said.

The fading memory of the pale, impeccably correct face of Titus.

And, snuck at the last minute into Tom's hand – reassuring, so weighty it almost felt like bone – a sailor-made, small, incredibly sharp shiv.

30

Kate Berg adjusted her helmet and sighed. She knew by the passage of time that they were nearly all the way back at the *Dauphin* on the remaining snowmobile. Its lights were appearing muzzily on the horizon.

Messy. She had a nurse's ingrained acceptance of a certain amount of mess; the human body accumulated it, and one simply organised the mess into recognisable patterns to fit various definitions of health. This, however, involved more moving parts than she'd desired. Still, it had ended in the correct manner, and all that remained were the final things to do. To scrub the theatre, as it were.

Titus's back before her in the dark showed no signs of strain; indeed it had barely moved from its position since she mounted behind him at the cabin. Absolutely wary as she'd been to have a corrupt police officer foisted on her – and one who couldn't even distract his superior from landing on the *Dauphin* to chase around after Sixgill's little murderer – this Titus had proved himself an extraordinary asset. Once she'd cautiously made contact, while his superior was off romancing pretty marine biologists, Titus had made regular and almost impossibly detailed reports, secreted the diamonds from the radio, and generally behaved as her arms, her legs, her eyes, and now her artillery. She had expected a vague sign of displeasure when she had to shove his superior down a hole (no broken back, worse luck), since the two of them appeared to enjoy a closeness Titus could manipulate as he chose, but he had merely accepted it as a given and moved forward.

There was something in Titus she recognised, something faint but powerful: she had decided that it was ambition, and thought in her most private of selves that it was necessary he remain stationed in the police force for as long as possible. Otherwise he'd rise above her in the smuggling ranks with the inevitable force of a glacier crushing its way across rock.

'When we get back we'll have to get Lindgren to stay in hiding,' she said. The ice beneath them was very smooth and sheer; the repeated tracks of snowmobiles had made it glassy. It reflected the sky like a dim mirror.

'What were her instructions?' he said politely, as if asking what she wanted for tea.

'To remain hidden and safe on the ship while we took Heissen and Dr Blanchard out onto the ice.'

'Was she expensive?'

'To buy? Oh, no, I knew about her killing Sixgill. I figured it out pretty quickly after she messed up his exit so spectacularly. Some people are blackmailed with barely a fight. She'll have to work for us nicely now that she's a fugitive.' Unlike Sixgill, she thought. For all his personal bitterness – which, thankfully, he hadn't directed at her, a nurse of no apparent moment – she knew he'd been enthusiastic when they'd brought him in as a young, underfunded scientific type. Those were always easy pickings; they needed money for their work, and so justified the whole enterprise with much more elegance. How could a few stones *hurt* anybody? He'd begun casually, just small packs of diamonds here and there as he hopped around Arctic ports, and then, as he proved reliable, more and more. And, she had heard, not a single drop had gone wrong. Once the route had been rumbled he'd assured the ring not to worry about his plan to get off the ship; he *had it all figured out*.

More fool them for trusting his competence! Men like that never thought more than a few steps ahead, or beyond themselves. He'd never considered what his superior herself might be risking – the price of failure. People in her position did not survive long enough, if arrested, to go to trial. The ring was very clear on this, and it was a policy with which she agreed. Power required such safeguards. With the *correct* kind of management, of course, no such sacrifice was necessary.

She snorted to herself. She'd only finagled Aabria onto the *Dauphin* to watch the proceedings from afar and make sure he didn't abscond with the goods. Had patched his nose silently while he fumed post-fight, and thought casually, *If you knew who I was, you'd start bleeding from more than just your nose out of panic.* It was a hoard of mute power, her anonymity. Aabria Scott's nurse, a *nice loyal sort of woman*, nothing else. She had been a private nurse for seven years and the lead in the ring's seafaring operations for four, and the two were driven by the same truth: that people of wealth and privilege would do anything, anything at all, to avoid looking directly at the people whose labour contributed to their comfort. Their gazes all slid off her as if she were too bright, too shameful to be viewed in full. Even Aabria herself, clear-eyed though she otherwise was, had this blind spot seared into her vision . . .

At the thought of Aabria her thinking diverged into two streams, one continuing to mull over Sixgill, Heissen and the inexhaustible propensities of men to foul things up, and the other cataloguing data on Aabria's care, when she was last given her medications, the day's pains and problems. This thinking was so ingrained as to occur simultaneously and without conscious effort; she held these two bowls easily, without spilling a droplet out of each. *A lower dosage of warfarin, perhaps, a conversation with that cardiologist Buller in the States—*

Aloud she said, 'You can go back to London and tell your chief it's handled.' With more debris than strictly necessary, but handled. And how useful, how triumphant to have a chief of police on board. She must remember to send him those ridiculous personalised golf clubs for Christmas. 'Are we going as fast as we can? We need to look as if we're in distress – that we've left them behind in duress – you know that.'

'I am afraid this is the vehicle's top speed,' said Titus, his voice dampened by the wind raking across their helmets. And it did indeed feel swift, almost careening, as if they were ice-skating. The aurora borealis insisted on making itself known in ribbony shimmerings; Kate, who had no taste whatever for beauty, wished it would go away so that they could work in less light, but this was one thing over which she had no control, so she relinquished thinking about it.

Kate felt a kind of branching serenity through her veins, the sort she had after long brutal shifts in the hospitals, when the wards quieted under waves of morphine and exhaustion and she could stand, cup of tea in hand, in the breathing silence. She could see, now emerging from the dark, the *Dauphin*, lights on and torches sweeping the ice, waiting for them as anxiously as a child awaits a parent. She readied to tell them everything, of Heissen's betrayal and Rose's dramatic injuries, to pant and cry—

There was, far beyond them, a cracking noise. The ice shelf, Kate thought; it must be beginning to carve off—

No, there was a sizzling bang, and the air above them was rent in two by a blooming flare. From the ship? No – from behind. It soared above them in beauty, the snowmobile and the floating ship, shimmering its orange across the wide waves of the aurora borealis. A star of danger; a star that all was over.

Because now, behind them, shielded for some time surely by the horrendous wind, the sound of another machine: a snowmobile, making its way through the dark.

Kate Berg knew, then. Somebody – most likely Tom Heissen – was free, and was bearing down, full to the brim with truths, likely half-wild with pain and anger, but lucid, too lucid. Rose Blanchard, like Bloom Highcastle, must now be dead. The branching paths blurred, solidified, into one path, one path alone. The knowledge settled into her as a stone falls into clear polar water, and lands, and is still.

She was a courageous woman. She knew when to let go.

———

Titus was easing off the throttle gently, to control the snowmobile's run up to the ship and avoid skidding near the ice cap's edge, when the flower of the flare appeared above them. It shimmered gently in the reflection on the mirrored carapace between his knees.

He was watching it thoughtfully, the glitter of its spreading reflection on ice and water, when he felt a sudden, decisive cold – the woman attached to his back had slipped off. He braked, hard, and turned his head.

The landscape seemed suddenly livid with many overlapping types of light: the searchlights of the *Dauphin* pooling over the ice, the dapple of the aurora, the searing, fading glint of the flare. Against all of them, Titus saw a small precise black shape that moved swiftly away from him, and dived off the edge into the dark, and was gone.

31

'I do wish you'd stop saying you're sorry,' said Tom irritably. Even with both feet in a scented bath aboard the *Dauphin*, and his fingers round a mug of obscenely thick hot chocolate, his temper still hadn't quite recovered.

'Yes, sir. Sorry, sir.' Titus was still very white. His nose was as purpled at the side as a violet.

Tom coughed. 'I am forced to think that this, Williams, was a complete gathering of obscene activity from beginning to end.'

'A clusterfuck? Yes, sir.'

A voice came from the other side of their stateroom. It was faint but steady, and it clearly had Scientific Questions that demanded solid data. It was a voice that Tom thanked numerous deities very vociferously had not been silenced forever, out on that glacier.

'You were working for them all the time, but not, then?' Dr Rose Blanchard was on a wodge of painkillers administered by Alva with a great deal of tongue-clicking, and her wounds made a giant lump of bandages under her jumper, but she was ruddy of cheek. She was not, Tom thought thankfully, the kind to let dramatic injury or contretemps in freezing cabins get in the way of curiosity.

'I was, I'm afraid, obliged to conceal the facts from the very beginning of the investigation, sir,' said Titus, with the closest thing to dejection Tom had ever seen on his placid face. 'The chief in London informed me that you were engaging in something that would be very problematic for his career if it came off, and that it would be more than worth my while to stop it. There was,' he added with some disgust, 'a substantial increase to my monthly pay, which I have put aside into an account and will be donating to a benevolent amnesty fund for the proceeds of crime.'

'You couldn't have brought me into your confidence, because I'd have made things much worse for myself by pretending not to investigate properly,' said Tom. 'I know. I'm not upset about it. You played a very good lone hand.'

'It was not pleasant,' said Titus. 'On more than one occasion I had to make choices very much against instinct. I felt, however, that because they believed they had an inside influence on the police investigation . . .'

'That they would make mistakes, and so it happened.' Tom shook his head. 'And then they decided to maroon me, and say I was the crooked one. What a nice bunch of people, I don't think.'

At this point Finn re-emerged, carrying another tray of hot drinks. His eyes were still red.

The reunion of him and his sister on the ship, when Rose had been hauled up a ladder covered in blood and it looked for all the world as if she'd been fatally wounded, was not one anybody cared to remember or repeat. Finn had made a noise that Tom, who was coming up the ladder behind, had never heard out of a human. He'd charged across the deck to get at her; Dr Eder had been fully knocked down.

'I'm all right, Finn, I'm all right; I'm here, we're together, I'm here.' Rose had said this with startling volume at first, probably to cut through Finn's horrible noises, and then low. She stood shakily, reciting it, repeatedly, into Finn's hair as he held her around the neck, making convulsive sobbing noises and cursing in language more colourful than even Rose had ever heard him use. '*We're together. I'm here.*'

'You couldn't have given us a hint?' Boo Moreland, who was taking a drink from Finn's tray, wasn't looking entirely forgiving about the near-frostbitten nature of Rose's nose. Trying to get him away from Rose's side had been the equivalent of prising a muscular limpet off a barge, and everybody had ultimately given up.

'I'm afraid I myself did not know the identity of Bloom's murderer until very late. They kept information highly compartmentalised.' Titus took a drink himself and blinked as the steam rose through his pale eyelashes. 'I was trusted, but not trusted enough for that.'

'Did *you* push Tom down a hole?' asked Rose, with interest.

'Absolutely not,' said Titus, and Tom was pleased to see he looked mildly indignant about this. 'That was Berg. As was the murder of Bloom Highcastle. She was a very efficient woman who acted alone and with swiftness. I had no foreknowledge to pause or circumvent her in either case. Sir, *please* let me get you another blanket.'

'All right.' Tom felt crotchety, but also triumphant; ninety years old, but also about nineteen.

'I can't believe you *shot* me,' said Rose, in her clear voice.

'I really thought I was dead.' Boo and Finn made identical upset noises, then looked at each other. Boo squeezed Finn's shoulder.

Tom regarded the pile of padding under Dr Blanchard's thick jumper with a distant sense of appreciation. What aim! The bullet had, after all, not gone into her stomach; it had instead wounded her arm, barely grazing the abdomen, though Titus — clever, clever Titus, thought Tom with exhaustion — had angled the shot so that it looked for all the world like he'd shot straight through the side of her stomach.

That, not the shiv, was what had clued him in. Titus, for all his antipathy towards firearms, was too good an aim to make that mistake, or not to know he was stuffing bloodied gauze onto a miniature graze.

'I am afraid,' said Titus, 'that it was necessary. Kate Berg would have gone for the head.'

'I know,' said Rose quietly. 'And then my arm started to hurt, and I realised you'd played a feint. I still tried to headbutt you very hard, though.'

'You nearly caught me a blinder, Dr Blanchard,' said Titus with politeness.

'We can have matching arm slings, my sweet,' said Boo grandly.

'Speaking of things we can't believe,' said Tom, 'I can't believe you made me replace a spark plug in a snowmobile in the middle of nowhere. Thank you for the small heat pads you put in the saddlebags, by the way; they worked wonders when we put them in our socks and mittens.

Titus bowed his head.

'I did believe, sir, that you would be able to catch us up,' he said. 'I moderated our speed as much as I could. Took a more angled route back to the ship. But there was only so much – with Berg right behind me—'

'I know,' said Tom, softly. He wished dearly for Biscuit, who liked Titus and would sit on his thin knees in an aggressively calming posture for hours on end. 'I know. I do wish she hadn't dived.'

'Me too, sir,' said Titus.

'She'd never have talked,' said Rose. 'But still—'

'Yes.' That was the look on Titus's face, as well – they were, Tom thought, of a kind, as thinkers. They desired the final piece of the evidence, the information that would seal the puzzle into place. After it had caused so much suffering. And now that had been thwarted.

Finn, who clearly recognised the frustration of his sister's expression, came over and headbutted her gently on the forehead. To Tom's mild surprise, she grinned. They looked hugely alike when they smiled.

The Captain came through the stateroom door now, and was boggled at for several seconds before he realised he was still wearing his chef's apron. It was now nearly five in the morning.

'I am afraid,' he said, stripping said garment off, 'that there is no hope for Berg.'

The collective absorbed this, and their hot teas spiked with brandy, in silence.

Kate Berg had proceeded almost all the way back to the

Dauphin in the full belief that all was well, Titus had told them, but Tom and Rose, pausing in their hot pursuit on the once-again-moving (and never really broken) snowmobile, had let off a flare in the dark. They couldn't let her get back to the ship, with all its resources and guns and places to hide. The signal had to be sent. Tom wasn't sure what it would do, but it would put somebody on the alert – and he knew the Captain, *Stingrocka*, he of the responses swift as stingrays, would see it.

And Berg had known then. She hadn't believed that Titus was involved; that, Tom thought, was why she hadn't shot him. And she had dived, with the efficiency of a person of incredible will, to her death.

Tom had hoped wildly for a prepared boat, a submarine, anything – but they had found her frozen, floating, and her revival, it now seemed, was impossible.

'What were you going to do if we couldn't get back in time?' he asked Titus.

'Involve the Captain,' said Titus, briefly. 'Whom Berg actively distrusted, and who could overpower her physically. We would have figured something out.' The Captain simply bowed as if receiving a light compliment on his ability to navigate ice shelves, and everybody in the room was struck by the enormous dynamism of the man, the charismatic force behind his correct, blank face.

'I bet the board of directors for the *Dauphin* are going to have *kittens* over this one,' said Boo, with an air of mischief that seemed slightly too tired at the edges. 'Two murders, one suicide, two attempted murders-that-weren't, and a veritable stream of illicit sparklers from God knows where.' Tom had retrieved the planted diamonds from his pocket with some disgust; the entire hoard of gems, including the previously candle-bound ones, were now in the ship safe, in a lockbox, under guard by Linnea and another stern-looking Norwegian, who happened at that moment to be intently discussing what to name the small fat kitten they were adopting when they went home on shore leave. (Forerunners included *Småkake*, i.e. cookie, in partial tribute to the serene face of Biscuit the cat, whom Juhani had repeatedly invoked as some kind of very cute justice-bent animal deity in the crew mess. Well-fed cats are good luck on ships.)

The Captain said seriously, 'It is something I had contemplated, yes. The report for their latest meeting will, I fear, involve substantially more excitement than it normally does. I will inform their staff that precautions may need to be taken for heart health, the average age being, I understand, approximately seventy-nine.'

'But they can't be mad at *you* about it,' said Rose, suddenly very seriously. 'We'll tell them. You've done everything you could.'

'Thank you, Dr Blanchard,' said Captain Johannsson gravely, with what Tom detected as a very faint note of amusement, likely at the thought of the two Blanchards, Boo, Tom and Titus all turning up en masse at the board meeting to insist on the Captain's excellence, like a gaggle of persistent and voluble birds. 'I am sure your testimonies will be very helpful. I must now go to Ms Scott and continue the search for Elisabeth,' he added, bowing once more, and left the room, once again in his beautiful captain's uniform.

Into the silence that remained behind him, Tom asked, with his usual conversational curiosity, 'Was there a plan from the first? Or were you not told what to do until the radio communications?'

'Berg informed me,' said Titus, gingerly stretching out limbs that must also have been aching, 'that Lindgren had been given instructions and would be remaining safe on the ship while we lured you and Dr Blanchard out to the cabin. She explained we had to move fast, considering the ship was leaving for Svalbard tomorrow. No loose ends.'

'Given *instructions*?' Boo sounded nonplussed.

'Of a sort. Berg's description of the process leads me to believe that she came to Aabria Scott's stateroom and was given a drink with a drug in it,' said Titus.

'Like Palgrave before her,' muttered Tom. 'Though she's not asleep in her cabin; they'll find her soon enough. You think you know where they stashed her, don't you?' Tom had missed Titus's instructions on this point, due to the annoying and time-consuming process of being declared 'not quite dead' by Alva.

'Yes, sir. I have passed on my ideas about that to the search party – Berg had a few hiding spaces she preferred, in which I concealed messages and the items she would ask for, including the mask. I trust we will hear from them soon. Elisabeth was, of course, blackmailed into doing whatever Berg said.'

'Poor woman,' said Rose.

'She killed Sixgill,' said Boo disbelievingly.

'Yes, but she seems so pitiable,' said Finn. 'To love somebody that much.'

'Are *all* the Blanchards capable of feeling sorry for completely abhorrent people?' asked Boo, with an air of utter bewilderment.

'Yes,' said Tom, authoritatively, 'and you'd better get used to it.'

'*Oh*,' Finn said suddenly. 'Look! While you were away!'

He dragged out his laptop – Tom hadn't yet told him about the gems secreted in the radio beacon, though he was prepared for a hilarious conversation in which Finn worried about what would happen if local wildlife ate escaping diamonds – and showed them the feed from the camera, far beneath the ice. And luminous in the infrared dark, slow and majestic and older than all of them put together, a vast, ugly shark's head drifted into frame, chewing contentedly on the gifted meat like a cow chewing its cud.

Rose hollered and punched Finn in the arm, then whimpered as her own wounds made an angry rejoinder at her. She sat down on Boo Moreland's lap, which he had cunningly manoeuvred to be directly beneath her, yelped, then submitted, elbowing him hard with her other arm.

Tom decorously settled for squeezing Finn's hand. 'You will,' he said to him, 'have to edit that feed to add a party hat.'

Light streamed over the *Dauphin* – moving light, light that had buoyancy and momentum from the splash and carve of shifting waves. The ship was on the move. Foam spread from it like parting hands.

Elisabeth Lindgren, after the redoubled search with Titus's inside knowledge, had been found where he'd said she'd likely be: still in Aabria Scott's cabin, in a small luggage space under the bed Kate Berg was known to stuff with medical paraphernalia. She was, to Tom's unutterable gratitude, not dead; Titus had been firm on the point that Kate Berg said she wasn't intending to kill her, but they both knew Berg always played a lone hand, even to the end. However, the chef was heavily drugged, and they were awaiting her return to consciousness. There would, he suspected, now be another *Dauphin* teacup lying on the seafloor, beside the first.

'She's breathing well,' Alva, the doctor, had told them. 'Whatever she has had, it is a high dose, but she survives. She will awaken, yes, with enough time.'

Rose was sitting with her; there was a constant vigil of multiple crew members by the bedside, and she'd joined in. She looked up as Tom and Titus came in. 'I feel all in,' she said cheerily.

'You've had a busy night being fake-murdered,' said Tom. Titus made another pained noise. It would, Tom thought, be a long time before his conscience allowed him to joke about it.

'It was a very good fake-murder,' said Rose soothingly. 'She's all right.' She indicated the sleeping woman. The crew member who had been monitoring her pulse nodded assent.

'All of this out of love for Sixgill, sir.' Titus looked unbe-
lieving. 'It seems impossible.'

'Sometimes, I think,' Rose said, screwing up her face,
'you *know* a person's bad, and you think you're the only one
in the world who'll be able to change them, to teach them
how to be good. Finn and I – knew somebody like that.'
She paused, as if considering something – re-evaluating it in
the light of new evidence. Tom eyed her but didn't ask any
further questions. Finn, he thought, did have the vague air
of a disastrous reforming angel about him.

'Finn was the one who made me think of Elisabeth,' said
Rose, quietly. She was, perhaps, no longer quite talking to
Tom. 'Of the people who give and give – and that's their
right, isn't it. They have to be allowed to do that. To trust
things, even when you think it's bound to end in tears.' She
shook her tired head, and looked up at him, and smiled. It
was a smile of slight wonder. 'I really thought when I came
back onto the ship that he was going to kill somebody. I've
never seen anything like it. The sheer strength of him.'

Dr Blanchard, Tom thought accurately, was learning that
she did not need to protect her brother from everything,
from the slings and arrows of outrageous fortune in all its
forms. He looked at her face and understood it: the face of
a person who had been vigilant, hunched over something,
for many years without entirely realising it, and was just
now releasing her muscles, standing up, looking at the
world around her.

The specifics of this terrible person who'd plagued the
Blanchards could remain vague. Finn's past, he judged,

was a matter for conversation after at least three months of dating, not a four-day courtship on a murderous cruise ship. *Court-ship*. He must, he thought, really be tired if that pun seemed funny to him.

'It must,' he said gently, 'be devastating when you realise you cannot change them.'

'Yes,' said a voice from the bed. 'Yes, it is so.'

The purple eyelids had started open, and the chef was awake, life flowing again in her calm body.

'Elisabeth Lindgren, I must warn you,' said Tom, and gave her her formal warning. 'Would you like a lawyer present?'

'I am afraid of nothing,' said Elisabeth Lindgren. Her face, as Rose had thought once before, was awe-inspiring; the light in it was the light of a candle inside a skull. 'I murdered Ben Sixgill. I have suffered enough in this life. I will plead guilty; it is the truth.' She sat up, and drank some water.

'You loved him?'

'He was all I wanted,' she said simply. Rose thought of Finn's face, watching Martin walk across a room. 'I forgave him everything. We met in Amsterdam, and he was deeply rude at first, but apologised. He said I helped him to reform his ways, and that nobody could ever love me like he did. He forced me to do – many things. To smuggle things aboard ships when I worked. Still I thought we would be happy. He promised a life together; we had bought an apartment. Then he came on this journey and told me that the smuggling route had been discovered, and that he might lose everything. He had been ordered by his employers to leave this all behind – offered a new life, a new identity – and that was the only thing I could not forgive.'

'Why did he tell you?'

'He could not do it without me,' she said, and turned her deep-set eyes on Tom. 'He trusted nobody else. He thought I would never hurt him; he promised he would come back to me in a few years, perhaps, if his job permitted it. But he had already hurt me so much—'

When Titus asked why she had brought the harpoon aboard, she lowered her eyes.

'I was afraid,' she said. 'I saw him at the port; he didn't realise that I'd seen him. He had some sort of argument with a boy – young – and punched him; the boy collapsed. It looked like an accident, but I was still afraid. And – he was not kind, when we argued in recent months. So I had the harpoon in with my knives, just in case. When we began to plan his false death I knew I must use it. The tranquilliser gun did not work at first; I had to put a pipe inside it. I suppose you know that.'

'Yes,' said Tom.

'Perhaps I had been afraid of him for a long time,' said Elisabeth Lindgren, thoughtfully. The blue shadows underneath her cheekbones were rich in the light. 'Perhaps that is why it felt like such a relief, in the moment, to kill him. Though thereafter I have had – only pain.'

The fact of it – the absolute devotion of this phenomenal person, the sheer focus in it – weighed in the room like lead. Of course Sixgill would be sure of it, of her assistance in all of his plans; you could no more believe Elisabeth Lindgren would stop loving you, once she had begun, than believe the moon would fall out of the sky. It was a natural force, like the glaciers themselves. And so she had, and would. Perhaps, Tom thought, Sixgill had been beginning to chafe under the sheer power of it. As if being in an unending light, with no shadow, no escape.

'Kate Berg is dead,' Titus said crisply.

'Yes,' said Elisabeth without any real reaction, 'I thought it would end that way. A very determined person. But she took great risks. She knew, perhaps, that they would not pay off.'

'What did she say to you?' Tom was curious about this point.

'She came to me in the kitchens and revealed herself. Ben never knew. She told me briefly that she knew I had killed Ben, and promised me what she had promised him. A new life, in service to her and her employers. She could sense, I think, that I would not take it willingly. So she brought me here to talk, and threatened that she would supply proof that I had murdered Bloom Highcastle also.' Tom wondered briefly at that – a feint by Berg, most likely, but Lindgren wouldn't know that. 'And so – I drank the tea she had given me.' She shook her head; the fair hair slid across her bones. 'I would like to go to the bathroom now, please.' The crew member helped her from bed; the staunch vigour was gone from her, and would perhaps always be.

Aabria Scott had watched this process, gently, from her chair by the window. She was as much a feature of the room as its portholes, and had also lost her nurse and spent half the night sleeping unwittingly on top of a drugged

384

murderous chef, so they hadn't felt they could refuse her request to stay.

'Poor girl,' she said again, and Rose remembered vividly her saying this, on a day that felt like a lifetime ago.

Tom heard something in her voice, and understood. He came over and took her light, much-wrinkled hands.

'You knew, didn't you? About Kate.'

'I saw that some of Kate's morphine was missing from her medicine bag,' said Aabria, softly. 'I asked her plainly what could cause amnesia, and she didn't mention drugs. That's when I suspected. I made her promise, then, not to hurt me. I don't think she realised – that when I asked her to protect me from harm, I was asking for protection from *her*. I believed her promise. She was very devoted to me, you know.'

'Yes,' said Tom. 'She treated you like family.'

'Yes, you noticed. You're a very observant young man. This is a guess, but her mother, I think, told her that my husband – Albert – was her father. It wasn't medically pos-sible, but I don't think Kate was ever told that as a child. German measles, you see, when Albert was very young. I doubt her mother knew.' Aabria sighed. 'Kate must have changed her name, of course. And then came to work for me – and that's quite natural, isn't it? When you've been told someone is your family, even if they don't acknowl-edge it. She believed I was her only link to her real father. Other than myself, she was all alone.'

'I am very sorry.'

Aabria Scott silently turned her face to the window, and tears flowed down her ancient cheeks.

385

32

The morning before the *Dauphin* docked there was something of a performance. Tom, feeling as if he was being asked to explain a conjuring trick, stood in the dining hall and told everybody, crew and all, what had happened, from Sixgill onward. Well, almost everybody — Dr Eder was, to the surprise of nobody, absent, and would not resurface for the remainder of the journey.

'But it's extraordinary,' said Dr Palgrave. 'You mean *I* didn't kill him.'

'You absolutely did not kill him,' Tom confirmed.

'Ah.' And the beluga retreated, having left that matter entirely behind. He suspected she'd never remember it again.

'My poor mask, being used to hide those faces,' said Aabria Scott, who had been tended to by Alva and was looking no more frail than before. 'I did *think* that was why it was stolen. So good against snow. The Venetian who sold it to Kate would be horrified. Or perhaps not. Some people never are.'

'It was perfect camouflage on the ice and a fantastic eye-shield,' said Tom politely. 'Nobody could have designed it better. If Sixgill had succeeded he could have evaded detection on the ice cap from everything except thermal imagery, and saved his vision into the bargain.'

'Do you mean,' demanded Gladys Moreland, 'that I have been eating the culinary creations of a murderer this entire time?' Her thin face was, to Tom's mild astonishment, rapt. 'Broder back at Chambers will *die*. It'll knock his stupid story about being at the same cocktail party as the Perthshire Strangler in 1982 into a cocked hat.'

'My wife,' said Patrick, in a dry and adoring way, 'is perhaps a *touch* competitive.' Gladys whacked him on the arm with a cushion.

Sunila Singh stood up from the sofa where she'd been sitting with Alicia, and extended one beautiful hand each to Tom and Titus. She smelled extremely expensive, though not, Tom noted with some relief, anything like candles. 'I am very pleased that you dealt with the problem regarding my wife,' she said in a low voice.

Tom took the hand graciously. 'You are most welcome,' he said, with perhaps a slight visible edge of sarcasm; most people would prioritise the capturing of murderers, but he had the faint sense of being thanked for retrieving a lost brooch. Sunila, of course, caught the visible edge without offence.

'I place my own difficulties first, as is human nature,' she said, without a trace of self-recrimination. 'And Alicia – has suffered enough.' She paused. 'Do you want to come on a cruise next year with us?' she asked Aabria Scott abruptly. 'You no longer have a nurse, but you can hire another one.'

Tom had a terrible flicker for a second that Aabria would say that she was done with cruises, that this was her last hurrah, and it was time for her to retreat into the shades and disappear. It felt like the dying of a great mammal by a watering hole.

'Ooh,' said Aabria Scott, 'that would be very nice indeed. One with extremely handsome crew members, please. The *Dauphin* sets a high standard for that at least.'

Juhani, who had been holding her arm in his own, looked mortifyingly bashful, while also trying to flex his muscles as obviously as possible.

The *Dauphin* would be pulling into Svalbard within an hour. The Sámi doctor was awaiting them, and was already making angry muttering noises in radio conversations with the Captain, who was deploying his spectacular charm to great effect once again, to settle like pollen upon all upset surfaces and turn them golden.

Tom and Finn were standing at the prow together, in a nook protected from the wind. Tom had finished Saying Some Things and was now blushing so intensely that the blood-rush was felt in the bones of his skull. He was an inarguably brave man, and had faced some difficult and dark things in his life – some of them in the past forty-eight hours – but Saying Some Things (particularly These Sorts Of Things) was a strain on even the steeliest constitution. Particularly when one was saying them to a curly-haired marine biologist who'd cocked his head to one side like a mildly baffled German Shepherd.

Tom felt as if he had been precipitated over a cliff—

Then Finn made an incoherent delighted noise, wrapped

his arms around Tom's neck, and attempted to climb him like a baby bear climbs a tree.

It was like a strange mirror image of the scene the previous evening, Tom thought, at a slightly hazy distance. Tom had come up the ladder off the dinghy behind Rose, and had pushed her, still bleeding, over the side onto the deck, then rested, breathing hard, on the rungs, resting his weary and heavy skull against the side of the *Dauphin*.

An immense racket of noise, and a voice, startlingly close – Juhani, he'd thought. 'Get Dr Blanchard to the doctor – Detective Heissen? TOM.' And underneath the clamour, a voice, drifting: Rose's. *'I'm here. We're together. I'm here.'* Tom had stayed on the ladder, contemplating a little nap—

Then several arms, including two gangly freckled ones that essentially grabbed at his collar and one of his ears, pulled him up. He'd been delivered precipitously over the side, straight into a body he'd recognised as Finn's, which had immediately cracked him a horrible headbutt in the melee. The gangly freckled arms, which were also Finn's, had then wrapped around his head, while the curled head made long snuffly relieved noises into his shoulder.

Tom, very cold and half-crazed with adrenaline, hadn't known quite what to do, so had kissed Finn on the forehead, which seemed like the natural thing to do at the time and had been accepted as such by all parties. Alva had had to poke Finn quite hard in the ribs before Tom could be released for medical examination.

Right now, there was no Alva. There was, instead, a Finn who was hugging Tom's torso and neck with all four limbs, with surprising skill and alacrity; Tom held him up under the legs with ease.

'You are,' he said with some surprise, '*very* good at climbing.'

'I do rock climbing on my days off,' said Finn's face, cheerily, right beside his left ear. 'I bet I could get up onto your shoulders if you stood still.'

'I bet you could,' said Tom, gravely.

'Tom!'

'What?'

'Nothing. Just Tom!' And Finn's face proceeded to kiss him on the ear and the cheek and half in one eye, which was undignified but which Tom couldn't pretend not to enjoy.

They had, fortunately, detached from one another by the time Boo, Rose and Titus appeared. The five of them stood, breathing in the Arctic air and listening to the slithering near-silence of the emissions-free engines.

'Now what happens?' asked Rose, turning her head into the wind. She and Boo had had their own tentative attempts at navigating some future plans – reticently practical on Rose's part, enthusiastically lavish on Boo's. It was, she reflected, one of those things that would have to be examined on steadier land, once they were away from the *Dauphin* and its aura of faint unreality.

'This'll turn into a very long and annoying ethics investigation that'll end with the chief given a golden handshake and told to go away and play with his toys,' said Tom, hotly. He'd kept the shiv as a souvenir and idly contemplated sticking it in his golf-playing treacherous superior's big toe. Having Titus turn tail and promptly turn right back again was one thing, but entrenched corruption all the way through the entire pile was another.

'No,' said Titus quietly, 'I hope not. I made the choice to record a good many conversations that the chief will, I think, find very difficult to explain. People,' he added with a sigh, 'do tend to think I have naturally criminal tendencies, and so say rather stupid things. They have all been forwarded to persons rather interested in a clean police department, some of whom own powerfully opinionated newspapers.'

'Titus,' said Tom, 'if I weren't otherwise spoken for I'd marry you.' Finn, who had put both his hands in Tom's belt loops from behind while balancing his head on one of his broad shoulders, looked immensely pleased. 'Nevertheless I think we might have some rough seas ahead of us.'

'You could, of course, retire,' suggested Boo.

'Cut and run? It's not a bad idea, Moreland.'

'Would you like to start that pub with an attached market garden you always talk about?' said Titus, with interest. 'The Aran Knit?'

'Oh!' said Finn, who had, until that moment, absolutely believed that Tom had fervent opinions on the superiority of Fair Isle and wasn't just trying to flirt with him.

'That'll be a retirement project,' said Tom, hurriedly. 'No, we're going to see this one through, Titus. I want to know how deep it goes. And,' he added with a colossal sigh of satisfaction, 'I want to see the looks on Interpol's faces when we turn up with copious evidence of a real, non-mirage smuggling ring.'

'Yes, sir.'

'I might bring along a photographer. Or a portrait painter. Just to memorialise the moment.'

'That,' said Titus, with an equal and compelling note of deep professional contentment, 'sounds like an *excellent* plan, sir.'

The *Dauphin* coasted onward. Behind it, walruses on the ice cap lifted their heads, observed the grey of the polar sky, then dived into the immense green deep.

Read on for a preview of book two in the
Blanchard twins series

DEATH ON WATER

PROLOGUE

The wind flowed in spate down the side of the mountain, scoured several snow-bound valleys as if in search of something entertaining, then contented itself with opening shutters and lifting up the hems of trees across the university town of Perėja, its lamps cooling on the squares. It was after sunset, and deep shadows were nipping at people's ankles; the mountain had swallowed the sun comprehensively, with an almost mythological satisfaction. It was the sort of landscape you still find in pockets of middle Europe, which remembers clearly how its features were once worshipped as pagan gods, and isn't about to let newfangled things like electricity or GPS interfere with its atmospherics.

The university itself was undoubtedly, dustily, angrily old. It had layers upon layers of towers and burnt-looking stone, and felt as if it had pulled itself out of the glacial loam like a mushroom. The town around it tried to be fulgently charming and simply looked overstrained.

The Cossacks had come through on their way elsewhere, as had the Huns and the swift Persians with their gorgeous horses, who had looked at the mountain and, like all intelligent animals, baulked. There had been no battles here, only indifferent people feeding their hordes, catching a few days' rest, then slipping off the map into other lives, other wars.

Small mounds held their various dead. Later, travelling monks fleeing something or other had paused in the valley out of exhaustion, and established an abbey to justify lying down for a bit. So St Ludmila had been born, and the town moulded to its whims, brewing beer for its abbots, breeding lambs for the vellum of its scriptorium. In return the abbey attracted new blood, new money: generations of raw-tonsured young men, scholars, merchants, even travelling nobility on obscure pilgrimage. By the time the abbey became a university the two entities were symbiotic, a great crusted lichen of need and supply, and could not be separated.

The mountain, meanwhile, had its own partner. Stretching down the entire length of the valley was an ancient glacial lake.

Perėja sat crankily by this lake like a parent watching their child dance with somebody gorgeous but eminently unsuitable. And the lake was beautiful: serene freshwater, reflecting the skies in still perfection. Children ran on the promenade or paddled on stony shores at its edges, but did not swim in it, or tread on its ice in winter; it was too cold, and far too deep. Tales said it reached right down to the hot heart of the earth, and certainly tourists in pleasure-boats who drifted out towards its centre would look over the side and be seized with vertigo, as miles of darkness solidified beneath them. It absorbed the darkness of the mountain smoothly every night. University researchers talked enthusiastically of its rare microclimate, its unique populations of fish, its mud filled with cold-tolerant larvae. Fishermen, in the local dialect, called it *smug*.

On this evening, two notable things occurred in the valley, neither of them widely noticed.

In one corner of the lake a small circle of ripples appeared; a thin white and blue fin, translucent and coloured like expensive painted porcelain, stood in the air. Then, as if it had been dreamt, it was gone.

At the other corner, high within the university's magnificent clock tower, Nina Hussar sighed.

Her sighing was not notable. She sighed often. This being the evening of her death, however, it took on a significance otherwise undeserved.

Time was running on. And a decision had to be made—

In previous centuries Nina Hussar would have been seen as a middle-aged spinster with Good Brains, the sort who became a lady's companion, or perhaps ran some scion of nobility's country house for them. Women more strident became Scout instructors or rode to hounds or chaperoned for wilting young women at dances; women more coddled were allowed to sit by fires and be quietly ignored until they exhausted their allotment of intelligence on complex knitting-patterns and crosswords, and finally, smothered, died. Hussar was not among either store. She was something else, something specific: the unattached woman with a completely precise mind.

She was, of course, *fussy* – but people like Nina Hussar are fussy by right, because their intelligence allows a constant view of life's machinery in all its detail. Rather than tell people their office supplies were crooked or their paperwork out of date, she simply corrected these elements herself, and proceeded about her business with glossy grey hair and soft little shoes, totally impervious to allegations of being interfering.

She had held an indistinct office at the University of St Ludmila (USL) since she was twenty-three, after taking a first-class degree in the philosophy of logic: something middle-ranking in the administrative department that was paid the same as a very junior civil servant. Over decades, from this quiet anonymity, she had succeeded gradually, in the manner of an artisan carving an intransigent block of stone, in transforming USL's system into a replica of her own efficient mind.

Men had occasionally expressed interest – competence had a stunning kind of allure, like a beautiful steam engine – but she, recognising quite clearly that they wanted her to organise *them* and would not, after all, really enjoy the experience, had remained unimpressed.

Now, at the end of the day, she took what she regarded as her one softness. She paused at the top of the steps in the high tower beneath the university carillon, and listened to it play.

The carillon was a stupendous instrument. Forty-seven bells, with a range of six octaves, rang the hour in various complex configurations. Once were the days – before Nina Hussar's time, and indeed before *anybody*'s time, no matter how much Lubenov hinted darkly at being over a hundred to impress undergraduates – that there had been a player, a *carillonneur*, who had depressed with a gentle fist the individual rounded peg-keys tied to each bell, and so produced music. That occupation had gone the way of medical leech-sellers and trepannists, and now the carillon was automatic – and, to Nina Hussar's mind, no less impressive for it. The bell-wires were now connected to a vast internal clockwork mechanism that marked the hours with gentle refrains, and could be customised to bellow, tinkle mournfully, or intimidate visiting donors as required.

Every evening at six o'clock – in winter far beyond the time of sunset, in summer while the sun still stood high above the lake – it was programmed to ring a curfew song, an anthem to Saint Ludmila. The air had been composed by a long-ago student who'd looked back on their university years shivering in drippy student rooms with the silvery, forgiving nostalgia you get when you move to a much nicer country and make some money. It was lilting, minor in key, and Hussar had long ago determined the precise point at the top of the stairs that was best for hearing it; the stone was slightly dipped at this point, under the long wear of feet, including her own. Below her were five storeys of narrow tower steps, rotating around a central axis, rarely used. The carillon song fell over her at this point like water.

It was late winter now, the term had ended, and the students were absent; the long library that issued onto this tower was empty all day, save for a few hard-worn assistant researchers doomed to look up references. The library was at least warm – she'd seen to that – but the tower itself was freezing; nothing could induce the thick and ancient stone to take on any kind of heat, even though radiators blared at each landing. She knew this cold. She was its friend. She stood and waited for the carillon, and let her worries quiet. Some murmured louder than others.

Time pressed – she *hated* time pressing – and a choice must be made soon, and things set in motion. She already sensed which way her decision would lie, and how disappointing that would prove for others, but it was the correct choice. Nina Hussar, once convinced of a course, was no more vulnerable to the judgements of others than the mountain itself.

But for the anthem, there was time. And then she would proceed.

She stood and listened. The bells began, filling and overlapping the dark tower space.

Did she, in the midst of the song, hear a faint difference – some percussion that was not recognised, a beat out of time?

A swift movement, in the darkness. As if an owl had swooped. Or as if a part of the song had come loose, and was lost—

Nina Hussar did not cry out when the impact came; not when her hands flew forward in the darkness to grip at nothing, not when the first tower step met her skull, or the next ones her hip, her ankles, her spine. It was, perhaps, too inefficient a use of her voice.

1

It was three months after Nina's death, and everything was apparently once again as it always was.

Spring had crept into the valley, performing its annual trick and surprising everybody. Nina's quiet grave in the small St Ludmila cemetery was beginning, unnoticed, to sprout crocuses through its grass and mosses. The mountain slopes were covered in meltwater streams and snowdrops, though the peak was still resolutely wearing its hat of snow, like an ancient person who won't doff their battered cap for anything short of cataclysm. The university sulkily let some sunlight play in its courtyards, and its old towers looked prickly against the fresh sky. New undergraduates were dared by older students to dip their bare toes in the sun-beaming lake, and lived to regret it.

There were the facts of spring at the University of St Ludmila: squealing young people, a certain misty light in the evenings, and rampant mud along the mountain road.

Navigating said road was, of course, difficult regardless of season. A Roman general, passing through on his way to deal with angrier people in sunnier places, had ordered his legionaries to build a winding path through the mountain pass. This was still used, less because ancient ingenuity was unimprovable, and more because (as the general's infuriated diaries attested) the mountain resisted human incursions. People on the daily bus from the city still faced the same obstacles as the poor legionaries: snow slides, rockfalls, bears sitting across both lanes and cleaning between their toes. In spring, the drivers also threaded softened mires of yellow mud, and swore more intently as a consequence.

Dr Finn Blanchard, currently on said local bus atop said local mud, was ignorant of all of this. This was not because he was one of those people who insisted on going into foreign places blind and wandering its streets, insistent that it give up all of its pleasures entirely without context. Indeed, he had a remarkably thick guide book, the only one he could find on the internet with a segment on Perėja. The segment was barely three pages and mostly talked about the university archive's collection of 'unicorn' horns, all of them nicked from hapless narwhals.

He'd read this, and the small list of recommended restaurants specialising in venison and plum sauce, and the one pub doubtfully mentioned for its 'historic appeal', which in practice meant an arch reluctance to serve anybody with more than two teeth. He'd even put in little neon Post-its. He was, however, preoccupied with another problem, which was that there were bits of fish viscera loose in his backpack.

Dr Blanchard was a marine biologist, and a good one – one of a collective of rising stars in the European firmament of sea sciences. Anybody watching him, as the bus went down the thick ravine on a tender strip of road as naked-looking as a vein, would see a tall, curly-haired, gangly sort of man with the kind of fluidly expressive hands that always seemed to be wandering off on their own, acting as a kind of unconscious extension of his feelings. He was gathering the spilled bits – samples from a breed of eel only lately found in England, preserved as a kind of hostess gift in a little Tupperware container more commonly used for cheese sandwiches – with faint flutters of dismay. The container's seals had broken under the weight of several heavy books, so the efforts were not hugely effective.

'Bother, bother, bother, bother.'

It would not have occurred to Finn to swear. It very rarely occurred to Finn to do anything that was even faintly uncouth, or disruptive to other people, or in the vague category of behaviour known as 'negative'. People tended to come away from interactions with him bathed in goodwill and an odd sense that people were somehow more inherently good than they'd seemed at breakfast that morning. His twin, Rose, called this The Finn Effect, and (also being a scientist) had only faintly humorously started collecting data on it. Thus far her notes included such things as 'Subjects convinced to stop having road rage: 3', 'Subjects charmed into giving Finn very unwise discounts: 7', and 'Subjects who went and sat in the sun post-conversation with an oddly serene expression: 16'.

This aura of softness was, perhaps, what was preventing other bus passengers from making more volubly angry noises about the fact that the bus was rapidly beginning to smell of eel. Finn flapped his hands and looked unhappily around. His curls bounced.

'Here,' said an efficient voice. A hand appeared over the back of the seat, held up a napkin, placed all the visible parts of eel (now piled into the Tupperware on the seat) into it, twirled the ends as if creating a parcel at a very expensive sandwich shop or a sweets packet at a department store, deposited it inside an empty sandwich bag, sealed that, and handed it to Finn. The entire performance took around ten seconds, but to Finn's dazzled eyes it looked like a magician's trick. 'Thank you,' he gasped.

The owner of the hand retracted it and regarded him impassively. It belonged to a compact sort of person with an intense brow-bone and a pushed-forward cleft chin. They'd inherited an undiluted Cossack face, coming down the bloodline from some militant ancestor who'd plunged his sword into the land by the lake and stayed. The voice, when it came, was deep and quite gentle. 'You're welcome. You are coming for the university?'

'Yes.'

'I work in the art history department. Eirene.' The hand was extended again. Finn reached to shake it, then wiped the eel slime off himself tentatively, and shook it with a little more confidence. 'Fish people come down on the bus from the city all the time.'

This was, of course, true; specialists in all manner of freshwater wonders came to interrogate the lake's depths and ask it questions. Finn accepted being called a 'fish person' without question. It was why he was here. He was buoyed again, moving lightly past the eel disaster, by his sense of purpose.

A whole semester here with Dr Martine! Martine Saluto, the great mentor of the freshwater dynasties in biology, discoverer of the world's rarest lake-bound sharks, author of towering treatises, brief but generous in emails. In photographs at conferences she gathered all the light and shadow around her without perhaps intending it, casting other attendees into greyness.

The university had invited – and he had come! Finn had recently published a groundbreaking monograph on Greenland sharks, which float around at the top of the world doing extremely little for centuries. It had been a sensation, and to his surprise, he had found that eminent biologists and editors at places like *Nature* suddenly wanted to talk to him earnestly at parties. He could afford to be picky about postdoctoral jobs this season (Harvard and a researcher in Hawaii had both made fawning noises over email), but this was an enormous opportunity.

He explained this at great speed to Eirene, whose own face was gently unreadable, though perhaps there was a slight glimmer in the dark eyes. Even the most tectonically stony people tended to find Finn disarming.

The town came fully into view then, and the lake, and Finn left off describing enthusiastically the wonder he was feeling at meeting Dr Saluto, and how far he'd come to see her. 'What a *place*,' he said, astonished, as the afternoon sun made the entire body of water a sheet of shifting light. Then: 'What's that?'

For it was six o'clock, and out of the centre of the university came the sound – rising and striking against the mountain rock – of bells.

'The carillon,' said Eirene, shortly. 'A machine with lots of bells. Like a church tower, but not an organ. It is very old.'

'Oh yes,' said Finn. 'The guidebooks do say – but it's another thing to be here, isn't it, to actually *hear* it.' He looked more intently out the window, shading his eyes enthusiastically. 'It looks like the sort of place where nothing really changes, doesn't it? Where things are just as they were centuries ago.'

It was perhaps his rapture in the lake's charms, his relief at being so close to the source of his adoration, that meant he didn't catch the pause in Eirene's quiet voice before they said, 'Yes. Just as they have always been.'

The lake dazzled, the fish inside it sank grumpily lower to avoid the last rays of sun, and the bus descended into the valley.

2

The light outside her office in the university quadrangle had thoroughly faded. Dr Martine Saluto sat back in her chair. Journals called her *esteemed* or *a figure of note*. Postgrads, in private, called her *absolutely terrifying*. A particularly uninspired rival at another university called her *Baba Yaga*, a reference to the fact that her hair hadn't been cut since she was young and now swept at the back of her legs. She knew about this nickname, and as with most things that were meant to be insulting to her, usually thought it was funny.

At this moment, however, she rather wanted a nice house with chicken legs. Maybe it could walk her away, somewhere calm and warm. Instead there was just this office, and the lake out the window with its encroaching darkness, which always managed, even to the flattest of minds, to look menacing. She wished, as she often did, that the place didn't have such an abundance of atmosphere that it absolutely didn't deserve.

Dr Saluto was in her seventies. She looked younger, because she came from a lineage of women who simply looked more direct and black-eyed as they aged, and lost weight around their mouths and shoulders.

She was also, she reflected, exhausted, and it took a lot to make her exhausted. It was not a physical exhaustion – this was a woman who had once stayed awake for thirty-six hours chasing down a shark who'd swallowed an expensive camera lens – but a mental one. Demands on her dragged her body downward, like fishing-weights attached to a net: on her loyalty, her skills of negotiation, her devotion to her friends. When one was cut loose, another was added. The edges of her brain felt burned.

As she did in her most private moments, she drew the thick curtain of her hair around both sides of her like a caul, around her shoulders and down across her face. She'd done it since she was small. If anybody came upon her now, they would see what looked, sitting behind a beautiful modernist desk, like a very large, silvery gourd, possibly related to a pumpkin. Mendes had observed this once, simply walked out, and never commented on it.

At the thought of Mendes, of that supercilious face that always seemed to find its object beneath contempt, Martine simply drew the cape of hair more thickly.

Saluto was a woman of considerable intelligence, but that was not special; in places like Perēja smart people lay thick on the ground, like cabbages. Her distinction in her field was toughness. She regarded herself as like a vessel of heavy bronze, like those things from ancient Greece that carried around the blood of sacrificial oxen (what were they called? Eirene would know): strong, hard, insensible of any blow. She didn't like feeling that resilience challenged. She didn't like feeling that the vessel was filled with somebody else's blood—

There was a knock at the door.

—

Finn had come straight off the Perėja bus to Dr Martine's office, with the single-minded focus of a spaniel intent on a toy. His eyes had reflected but not truly seen the great, dusky university walls, the courtyards now holding bowlfuls of lantern-light, the undergraduates smoking behind anything wind-sheltered. He climbed multiple stairs hoisting his suitcase and the eel container and beaming beatifically at the people who offered to help him. (Several of these people felt a little flame begin burning under their lungs then, one that wouldn't ever really go out. But that was Finn's tragedy: he bestowed this sort of thing so generously that he was like a god of harvest, throwing out flowers and seeds in great arcs.)

The office door opened.

Finn, entering gently with his hands paired together around the eel-packet, did in fact think the thing in the chair was not a person but something else entirely. His brain went for 'extremely hairy and faceless dog'.

As he wasn't the type of person to judge an animal for not having a visible face, he simply said, 'I'm sorry, I thought perhaps – the secretary said Dr Saluto would be in – I'll come back later,' and then reflected that he probably shouldn't trust a dog to take messages. Then he castigated himself for believing that this large and motionless creature would *not* be intelligent enough to communicate things, wondered whether it was a Saluki, and backed out.

Dr Martine heard the footsteps die away and the door swing shut, gave herself one more second to overcome her sense of complete astonishment, then opened the sheet of her hair like stage curtains and barked, '*Come back here!*'

Finn, who had been preparing to ask the nice secretary (who was already clearly upset about the suitcase sitting in his office) about Dr Saluto's elegant dog, made a surprised noise. Then he opened the door again and put his head through, hesitantly.

The two scientists stared at one another.

It was the sort of moment that bears the risk of cataclysm: Finn realised that the elegant dog was in fact his most cherished academic hero, Dr Saluto realised that this Botticelli-angel-looking person had seen her in her moment of vulnerability, and they both realised that the other person felt humiliated.

Finn, taking a deep breath, rescued everything.

'I'm Dr Finn Blanchard, and I brought you a specimen of a slender snipe eel, *Nemichthys scolopaceus*,' he said in a determined, rapid voice, 'the deep sea duck, as it's called – found, if you can believe it, actually in an *inland river* on the Norfolk Fens, twenty or so miles from the sea. Incredibly unusual behaviour from a deep-sea species, you'll agree – though the preservation isn't quite what I'd like.'

Dr Saluto had felt her normal reaction to extreme embarrassment descending: a kind of rage that turned her into volcanic rock, and would have doomed Finn to a semester of rejection and blank surliness. Instead the deft manoeuvre did what it was meant to do: it distracted her so entirely that the rage wandered off disappointed.

'What – *inland*?' she said, reaching for the eel. 'But they normally live hundreds of metres down. A storm? Some kind of tidal event?'

'I did wonder!' said Finn happily, watching as her scientifically precise hands picked up the creature's long tail, and then the elegant, duck-like lines of its head. 'It was actually found alive, which is remarkable, though I suppose they do travel up from the depths at night to feed. The fisherman handed it into a university immediately – though I suspect he showed it around the local pub first.'

'Yes – see how the anus is actually *inside* the throat – a remarkable thing.' Dr Saluto felt the lightness in her palm of this improbable creature, which never saw the sun. She was not in the habit of allowing *disjecta membra* onto her gorgeous desk, but the slender snipe eel, diplomatic envoy that it was, had done its job.

'Angus Calderhead has a paper forthcoming on it, but said I could take the evidence to you now that he's done with it, and sends his best,' added Finn.

'How *is* Angus?' This was more of Finn's intelligence at work: Dr Calderhead was a Scottish deep-sea expert and one of Saluto's most successful ex-students, and had recommended Finn for the St Ludmila post. He was an enormous, quiet man who cheerily constructed cameras that could withstand the pressures of oceanic trenches.

'He's on sabbatical, so he's off in Brussels arguing for total bans on deep-sea trawling in EU waters,' said Finn, brightly.

'That's my boy.' Critics were prone to remark that Dr Saluto's protégés got themselves into more hot water than other marine biologists, pun intended. More than one had disrupted illegal shark-fin fishing boats, or chained themselves to railings at environmental conferences. Nobody would have dared say this to Dr Saluto's face, of course.

'Well. This is a rare treat. And you're Dr Blanchard.' Dr Saluto looked up from the vanishingly rare specimen to its bearer and made a swift assessment of him. Young, but not scatty-looking; optimistic face; prone to excessive gesturing, but good manners. 'That work on Greenland sharks really was remarkable.' She was not exaggerating. It had been sent to her by about five colleagues, and she'd watched videos of colossal sharks complacently ruminating in front of Finn's perfectly placed Arctic cameras with a sense of deep intellectual pleasure.

'Thank you,' said Finn, and looked as uncomplicatedly happy as if somebody had given him a biscuit. He was, Dr Saluto noted, neither a self-effacing sort nor particularly egomaniacal. Good. Those things annoyed her in brilliant young men. 'Your work on freshwater shark metabolism was enormously helpful.'

'Yes,' said Dr Saluto simply, 'I know.' She received the praise with the grace it was given, and both of them felt soothed. 'And now you want to help me with my last gasp at prising the Delft shark out of hiding.'

The young scientist made an enthusiastic face. The Delft shark was a lake species described in a handful of local sources going back to the twelfth century, but not sighted in perhaps two hundred years. It was an animal in which Saluto believed so fervently that her dreams were blue and white, full of the flash of fins. Even if she sometimes felt a doubt in her craw, a miserable feeling that she was tilting at windmills, and that her later career was staked on the existence of a myth . . .

She put the weight of her hair over her shoulders and stood. 'Well, we can start – oh. You need to be shown to your quarters and things, don't you?'

'The head of housing,' said a quiet voice from the door, 'will be arriving shortly.' It was the secretary, whose name was Damyan and who was already viewing the eel parts with a long-suffering expression. As with most academic secretaries, he was used to being a tether to reality, though guts on desks were hardly his worst foe in this job.

'Sorry.' Dr Saluto gestured at Finn and looked briefly lost. 'Everything has been a bit at sixes and sevens since – well. Since the winter.'

A silence elapsed in which something unknown to Finn fell into the space of the office, a piece of unspoken history. He sensed it pass, and wondered at it, but also trusted that – as people often did – they'd tell him all about it when it was the right time.

Damyan cleared his throat. 'Shall I fetch a plastic box – for the – research materials?' He gestured, with perfect restraint, to the desk.

'Yes, Damyan, thank you. I'll label them and send them to the lab for long-term preservation. Angus will have my head otherwise.' She looked over at Finn. 'Well, Dr Blanchard. A pleasure to have you. We'll postpone research chat 'til another time.'

This was clearly a mark of dismissal, and Finn took it

without offence. On his way out he looked at a picture mounted on the wall, smiled sunnily to himself, and then departed, shutting the door behind him.

The piece, which Martine had ordered to be mounted in a weighty walnut frame, was an artist's interpretation in inks of the Delft shark. It was the only drawing of its kind, done by a St Ludmila-based illustrator in the eighteenth century, and even in the darkening office it was a shimmering thing: a beautiful flattened head, broad at the snout, and a tapered body leading to elegant fins like a dog shark, though with more fan-like, elaborate edging. And the entire specimen covered in sharp, delicate spikes and whorls, with royal blue across spectral white scales. The artist noted on the back that the Perêja locals called it *ghost fish*. Believers in its existence, inspired by the ragingly popular Dutch porcelain of the time, had since named it the Delft shark.

Dr Martine looked at it, half-drowned in the darkness, the lines of it almost vanishing. She closed her eyes. Then she opened them again and turned back to her desk, to the beautiful unworldly eel, its slender head poised as if watching her.

The head of housing turned out to be a very brusque person with about fifteen other apparent jobs, who deposited Finn in an upper corridor of a building at the east side of one of the university's courtyards, told him which door was his, handed him a key, and then left. Finn had the feeling that USL was a place running constantly to catch up with itself, and not in the usual half-brained chaos of an old university;

there was a strain about it. (In this, as it happened, his theory was right, though he wasn't yet to know why.)

Finn sighed, wriggled his shoulders, and moved to unlock his rooms, but was arrested by a new noise behind him: a door rapidly opening, hitting something hard, and a loud 'OW.'

He turned, and discovered that a head had popped out at him from the quarters directly opposite. It was a long head that would have delighted Giacometti: the cheeks sloped to a point underneath the lips, and the brown hair clung irresolutely to a slender skull. The eyes were slightly over-large and well-lashed, and the mouth, if left unattended, tended to droop a bit. The rest of the man, from what Finn could gather, was about the same: lean, stooped, prone to looking ashamed of itself. It wasn't a handsome head, but it had an appeal to it, and was looking at him with interest.

'New neighbour moving in,' said Finn, in his brightest voice. 'Finn Blanchard. Visiting fellow in marine biology.'

'Oh – lovely to meet you,' said the head happily, then added, in a distracted voice, 'Hold on.' It withdrew. There were some bangs that sounded like large quantities of books being balanced on each other, followed by a thump that indicated the balancing act hadn't worked, and a minor epithet. The head's voice, Finn noted, was softly English. Now the head reappeared, extricating itself from what was, Finn was gathering, a labyrinth of obstacles near the door; the man had to lift his second foot like a dog attending to a fire hydrant to get it out safely.

'Stephen Huskins. Assistant prof in literature.' The hand

415

the man thrust out was pocked with bits of ink Finn recognised as the product of cheap ballpoint pens. 'So you're one
of the visiting lot! 104? They're good sets of rooms up here
– lots of hot water, and the bed's comfortable.' He paused
in this rapid, rather staccato recital. 'Sorry, I'm talking like
my aunt.'

Without explaining this phrase, he encouraged Finn to
unlock the door, and helped to haul the suitcase into 104.

Stephen was right – they were nice rooms, well-
painted and, to Finn's surprise, replete with hot radiators
and plenty of electrical sockets exactly where they were
needed. Visiting-postgraduate rooms tending to be con-
verted student cells, with pasteboard beds and desks that
collapsed when you put a cup of tea on one corner, he was
pleasantly surprised.

'See? It's good. Good bones. You look out on the courtyard – quiet at night – it's a better vista than the other side,
to be honest.'

Finn was filling the room's kettle and putting it on the
ring. 'Do you have those rooms?'

'Me? No. I live in town. Little tumble-down house, but
I don't need much room.' Like many very tall people, Finn
intuited, Stephen Huskins tended to curl up in balls when-
ever at rest, like a greyhound. 'Bit of a garden. I try for
vegetables every year, but nothing grows in this blessed soil
except turnips and potatoes; it seems to think everybody's
a fourteenth-century peasant. Loamy and sandy, all of it.'

'Would you like some tea?' Finn had no idea whether
one should be sympathetic or enthusiastic at the prospect

of loamy earth, but he did keep tea – good Darjeeling, and a herbal minty blend, in silken pyramid tea bags – at the top of his suitcase for precisely this sort of encounter. Making friends at new universities was so easily lubricated by hot beverages. 'Is the other suite of rooms your office, then?'

'What? Yes, tea. Lovely. No, I'm clearing out my aunt's possessions. It was her place,' he added, a bit sadly. 'I should have had it done over the winter, but lesson planning and marking, and making reading lists – *you* know.' He was rubbing the material of his jacket between thumb and forefinger.

'I'm sorry,' said Finn genuinely, guessing from the phrasing that the aunt was no longer with us. The kettle on the hob stirred and began to make a squeaking noise as the water heated. 'What was her name?'

'Nina Hussar. She passed away in the winter,' said Stephen Huskins. The words came out in a rush. 'She was *somebody* here, you know? She practically ran the place. They're barely getting on without her, but nobody will say so. As if people don't exist if they don't have PhDs. Oh, sorry—' He looked momentarily horrified.

'Universities can be like that,' said Finn hastily, to smooth the moment over. 'I only handed my PhD in on time because somebody in the printing room kept it open especially. I had to reprint twenty-eight shark skeleton charts; for some reason my computer spell-checked all the Latin species names into Spanish.'

This, as it happened, was quite true. Finn, being Finn, was innocent of the fact that his imploring face at the administrator's desk at five minutes to six was as impossible to deny as a child in a Victorian novel. If he knew that staffers actually competed to share Finn Blanchard Stories, and that the IT chief at his last university was currently winning with her tale of rescuing Finn's shark monograph from oblivion (a cat called Biscuit had chewed a crucial flash drive), he'd be beyond astonished. 'Nothing happens without administrators,' he said simply, now.

'You *understand*,' said Stephen with an enormous burst of friendliness, and Finn received the impression that Stephen Huskins hadn't had many people to talk to about his aunt, or gardening, or really anything at all. 'Do come and take your tea in with me.'

Finn, who was as incapable of refusing a summons from a lonely human as an iron filing of resisting magnetic force, went, holding two cups of Darjeeling delicately.

The rooms of Stephen Huskins' aunt at 106 were along the same lines as 104's, but larger, and clearly well lived-in. A full wall had a built-in bookshelf, the kitchen area was filled with neat objects of use, and the whole bore the impression of an apartment of gentle long residence. Or it would have, if it didn't appear to have been ransacked by a collective of white-handed gibbons. (This was not a random metaphor; Finn had seen this once while visiting his sister on the coast of Sumatra, when a local troupe had broken into the research station via a badly fastened window.) Books, pictures, cushions and small whatnots were stacked or strewn everywhere, in and out of boxes.

'Aunt Nina lived up here for ages – decades and decades.

She called it her eyrie. Could have lived off-campus, most
of the staff do, but she always said she wanted to be on
hand if there was a *crisis*. Sense of duty.' Stephen drank his
Darjeeling a bit like a child, holding both big hands gently
around the cup. The windows, Finn noted, did indeed
look outward over the university roofs, and beyond that
to the circle of the lake; it must have felt, to the late Nina
Hussar, as if she perched on high and observed all. 'I don't
know what I'm doing,' Stephen added, morosely, almost
to himself.

'She left it all to you?'

'In her will – yes.' From Stephen's expression, Finn
judged that this hadn't been a windfall – had, instead, meant
responsibility, an added burden of care. Stephen gestured
around him, a little hopelessly. 'I feel like I should devise
some sort of system – but there's so much. She'd know how
to do it best, but of course she's not *here* . . .' He seemed
frankly overwhelmed. 'I can't even find her diary.'

Finn did understand. 'Can I help?' He lifted a few books
– a selection of local histories, and some poetry, and a
much-thumbed copy of the Old Testament with a ribbon
in it. Finn flipped it open to see it was marking Proverbs.

'Oh – no, thank you. Sorry, I shouldn't be dragging you
in.' Stephen looked abashed, took the books off Finn, stood
a bit helplessly and then put them down on top of the neat
little blue sofa.

'It must have been sudden.'

'Stupid accident. She fell down some stairs.' Stephen put
a painting down on another book with an explosive noise,

then jumped when the frame fell off. 'Pointless bloody waste.' He didn't elaborate.

Nothing more suspicious than a fall down some stairs, said a familiar voice in Finn's mind, pulled quietly from memory. Soft, sweet with tiredness. An afternoon on the couch, months ago. *Professionally speaking. Up there with accidental food poisoning. Or an oligarch mysteriously falling from a window . . .*

Be quiet, Finn said back to the voice, and to his traitor memory that had brought it out of darkness. Like many gentle people, he was far more ferocious to himself than to anybody else.

Aloud he said, into a silence that had stretched and expanded as Stephen looked around sadly, 'I'll leave you to it, then.' The lights of the university at the windows were golden streams, and beyond he could see that a yellow slice of moon was beginning to rise.

Huskins roused himself. 'Oh – yes. Very good of you. Thank you for the tea. I'll be in and out of here for the next few weeks, I expect. Or however long it takes. Still! It's a thing I can do for her. That's good, isn't it?'

'Very,' said Finn, and gathered the extra teacup from the man's absent hands before quietly vaulting over the pile of books. Stephen bent enthusiastically to his task again.

Finn retreated to his own rooms, brewed another pot of tea, and unpacked. There was a lovely view over the courtyard, with the lanterns playing over the ivy and the grass square – and soon he'd go for dinner, though it was always a risk with these university kitchens. Sometimes it was rich food for gouty stomachs, or all puff pastry and no substance, and sometimes it was institutional canteen food in great grey squares of potato and fat, like the kind Tom used to tell him about from school—

Tom.

Finn said, 'Bother.' He had managed not to think of Tom for nearly an entire day. It was a good record. But the thoughts would keep bobbing up, like ice, inexorably buoyant on the surface of deep water. That ridiculous memory – Tom casually expounding on suspicious death scenarios while bandaging Finn's knee, because Finn had failed to notice a stray shoelace and gone headlong off the front steps into a rosebush.

He allowed himself a medicinal tincture of Tom thoughts – just a few moments. Tom at home after a long day, now, with his giant cat Biscuit kneading his knees. Tom making his own tea, resolutely un-fancy black tea with so much milk it could be poured over cereal without anybody noticing a discrepancy, and dipping two Hobnobs at once into his wide mug. Tom in his socks, putting on the TV, and lying and resting his wide head, his rumpled reddish hair, on the side of the sofa where Finn had sat, where his lap normally would be . . .

That, Finn thought, was quite enough.

His pattern of unpacking was perhaps a little more unnecessarily aggressive after that point, and involved too many systems of organisation. If it kept Unhelpful Thoughts out of his head, he'd learn to think in ancient Greek.

He also sent a brief mental apology to Stephen Huskins' aunt for that thoroughly irrelevant memory he'd had in her rooms. Poor woman. 'Suspicious deaths' indeed.